7/23

D1137676

HIS LIFE WAS A LIE

Jonathan S. Harvey

Book Guild Publishing
Sussex, England

First published in Great Britain in 2014 by
The Book Guild Ltd
The Werks
45 Church Road
Hove, BN3 2BE

Typesetting in Sabon by
Keyboard Services, Luton, Bedfordshire

Printed and bound in Great Britain by
CPI Group (UK) Ltd, Croydon, CR0 4YY

A catalogue record for this book is available from
The British Library.

ISBN 978 1 909984 33 2

1

The shadow pressed further back into the trunk of the old and gnarled oak tree, trying to escape the incessant drops of rain that filtered through the growing leaves above. He would have been barely visible to any passer-by but at 11.30 on a rainy March evening there were none anyway. The dog walkers had cut short their pets' walks because of the rain and in any event the three walkers he had seen in the two hours he had been in this place only looked at where their feet were treading. This man wore a black nylon jacket and black jeans with his black balaclava rolled up on to his head. He kept his hands stuffed into his jacket pockets. He remained still, his head moving slowly from side to side as he watched the road that ran along in front of him at the edge of the park. His position also gave him a view of a road junction almost opposite him. That road he knew contained expensive five-bedroom and larger houses in their own large grounds and it was owing to persons living in these houses that he had taken up this position.

This park was towards the edge of the city, an area that he didn't know well, and this was the first time he had come there with the intention of committing a crime. His usual area was Brighton seafront and the pub and club area near West Street and The Lanes. That area he knew like the back of his hand, the old fishermen's area of the original hamlet of Brighthelmstone; he knew every alleyway, every twitten and every cul-de-sac, even the believed escape route of King Charles II, along Black Lion Lane, though of course he was totally unaware of any historical relevance. That was the area that over the years he had used to follow then attack unguarded and invariably drunk people as they made their way home. He had a very simple MO or modus operandi, as the police formally say – to stalk the proposed victim before running up to them quickly from behind and pushing them on to the pavement then grabbing their handbag or wallet and running off. This he had done many times over the years, taking whatever was of value then discarding the wallet or handbag. He used the money to score drugs. He did not consider himself an addict – they were fools – but he certainly liked the buzz he received from doing some lines.

He had been arrested by the police and after several cautions he had appeared at the local magistrates' court. It was only on the sixth occasion that he had been sent to prison where he had learned that because he always committed the same style of crime in the same area it didn't need the best detective in the world to know who had been responsible for a mugging. Still, that was in the past and now he was watching this new area for possible targets, and to throw the clever detectives off his scent he was also going to wear the balaclava to hide his distinctive long red hair. He had planned it all by himself earlier that evening; he never worked with anyone else anyway. He didn't need very much cash, enough for a few lines at a mate's place later and then he would see what tomorrow brought when it arrived. He was determined, though, that he was from now on going to be smart, more professional and clever in keeping with the new area and style. That was why he was wearing the balaclava as well as his new black jacket; he had thought of everything.

The only thing, though, was that during the two hours he had been there he had been unable to light a cigarette, as the glow would have been seen. That was a hardship but being strong enough to resist the urge also proved to him that he was being much smarter now and more like the few clever inmates he'd met in prison. Sharing a cell with someone meant that you had to listen to them and when they were experienced criminals you listened to them carefully. He had paid attention to their stories, of how they had outwitted the police and been taken to court for only a small fraction of the crimes they had committed. He had heard about how they had enjoyed the thrill of the crime and their strength of mind when interviewed by the 'filth', denying the facts that were laid before them, no matter how overwhelming they appeared. Their capture was usually a case of bad luck, because of a 'grass' or the police getting lucky. Never was it mentioned that the police used skills to gather the evidence and make the arrest, nor that their capture had frequently been due to their own stupidity. He had listened for hours about how precautions could be taken against being identified, how it was clever to change your style of crime and to use new areas. He also learned not to talk after the crime, as there was a new breed of people who, because of the financial rewards, would happily inform to the police. 'They'd shop their own mother' was how it was put to him. He knew this was true, as the detectives had always asked him after he had been charged with an offence whether he could tell them something about a friend of his. If the info was good, he was promised it would help him when he was sentenced later. He knew this was true and so the rest of what he was told must also be true.

He watched the road and glanced from time to time behind him towards the empty park. There were a few streetlights along the main road in front of him but even fewer on the road that had the big houses.

He felt a trickle of water run down his neck under the turned-up collar of his jacket and he silently cursed. To be clever he had to stay there. He needed to be patient.

2

Sir Roger Knight kept the umbrella steady over his wife who held his arm as they carefully sidestepped the puddles on the pavement. The streetlights were bright so their passage was made easier, but they took care that their shoes and outer coats were not going to get wetter than needed on the fifty-yard walk from their car to their destination. The walk along Old Bond Street south towards New Bond Street in the exclusive Mayfair district of London would only take three minutes, but after the rain of the past few hours they also had to be aware of passing cars throwing up spray from the road. He was still powerfully built, over six feet tall, with only a little stooping of the shoulders, belying his eighty-four years. Beneath the black hat was a full head of silver hair. He wore a long dark-blue cashmere overcoat with a thin suede collar and brown leather gloves. His wife, some twenty-six years younger, was wearing three-inch heels that helped bring her close to his height, but her build was slight and, while her figure was still shapely, that could not be seen beneath her full-length coat. As they neared their destination, Sir Roger lifted his head to see the entrance to the building which was brightly lit from the inside; music could be heard spilling on to the street. They were met at the door by a man in his thirties who under his open overcoat wore a dinner suit. He greeted them with a polite 'Good evening' and stood to one side to allow Sir Roger and his wife access while in one smooth movement taking the umbrella from Sir Roger. As the doorman gently shook the water from the umbrella, he pointed towards a portable rack of coats.

'If you'd like to leave your coats there, I will put your umbrella with them and...'

'Mummy, Daddy!' Sir Roger was starting to help his wife from her coat when their daughter Josephine arrived and ignoring their wet clothing went to her mother and gave her a strong hug. Josephine was beaming as she left her mother and turned to her father who had at least managed to unbutton his coat before his daughter put her arms around him and kissed him on his cheek. 'Thanks for coming. It's really great you could manage it. I was worried the weather might put you off.'

Gently extricating himself from his daughter's hug and finishing the task of getting out of the overcoat, Sir Roger looked at her and said, 'You are joking. Nothing could have stopped your mother and me from coming tonight. By the way you look absolutely stunning, yes, really stunning. So', he continued, 'this is the new place in town is it, or is it called the *in* place?' he chuckled.

'Well, it is the newest and it will be the best small gallery in London. I'll show you around. I'm just so thrilled about it. I never thought it would actually happen ... my own art gallery.'

Josephine took her mother's arm and smiling at everyone she gently escorted her mother towards the centre of the room, only pausing for her mother to collect a glass of champagne offered by a dinner-suited waiter. Sir Roger followed his wife and daughter and looked over their heads at the walls on which hung paintings that appeared to him to be hung according to subject rather than by painter. He declined the champagne but asked for glass of water or fruit juice as he was driving. The room was just about full to bursting of persons in various styles of cocktail dress and dinner suit; everyone wanted to be seen at the opening of this new gallery, it seemed. Sir Roger noticed people on the stairs at the back of the room looking at paintings that were hung on the wall leading to the first floor. From the chattering he thought that the upstairs room must be crowded as well. He was very proud of what his daughter had achieved and was also pleased to see some faces that he recognised as being Josephine's friends from years back. Of course, their names were pretty much forgotten but he prided himself on never forgetting a face.

He caught up with his wife and Josephine just as a waiter offered Sir Roger his orange juice. 'Thank you,' smiled Sir Roger, who then turned his attention to what his daughter was telling her mother.

'... Everything just fell into place in the last couple of days, the food and drinks, staffing, everything. I had nightmares that we would be standing here with only a dozen paintings on the walls and nothing to eat or drink...'

Sir Roger continued to look at the various paintings, trying to look interested even in those that he considered to be too modern for his taste. He was a traditionalist and liked his paintings to tell a story, to recount something in history or to show a beautiful scene. In truth, he knew very little about paintings as such, only that he either liked the picture or didn't. He had never painted and had often wondered where Josephine had got her love of painting.

Sir Roger recognized a face from Josephine's past, a young man in his mid-twenties who stood out from the crowd not only because he wasn't wearing a formal or dinner suit but because of his long black hair which flowed down his back. In fact, from the back with the hair covering a light-blue silk shirt Sir Roger had initially assumed the person to be female. Sir Roger cast his mind back and remembered that the man had visited their home on a couple of occasions back when Josephine lived there and that this man was in the art world. He thought back and could see his daughter holding his hand and leading him up the stairs to her private kingdom that was her room. Sir Roger's recollection became sharper in that instant and he almost felt himself blush as he remembered the events of that day – what, eight or ten years ago? He had waited until the boy, as he was then, had left the house before approaching his daughter and expressing his disapproval at her taking men to her room. It had led to a row between him and her, one of the few in her growing-up years when she had developed from a girl to a young independently minded woman. The row had ended when, having let her father vent his moralistic concerns, she had announced that Paul was gay, yes, gay.

Sir Roger brought himself back to the present and listened to his daughter as she talked about the layout of the gallery and the backgrounds of the many artists whose work was displayed there. Many, it seemed, were unknowns who had been discovered by her network of friends at art classes throughout the country. This exhibition was in part a showcase for them as well as being an example of how Josephine could be bold and brave in selecting and recognising new talent.

For the next twenty minutes Josephine escorted her parents around the gallery stopping every minute or so to introduce them to a guest, many of whom were the artists whose work filled the gallery.

After Josephine had given a short speech to thank all the contributors and helpers, Sir Roger and his wife edged towards their coats to leave. Their trip home to Brighton on the south coast, some forty miles away, would take over an hour so they said their goodbyes to Josephine and walked back to their car, this time without the umbrella as the rain had stopped leaving only the road and pavements wet.

Sir Roger always drove carefully and at a steady speed, enjoying the luxury of the Rolls-Royce Camargue and allowing other drivers to race ahead. He was content to allow the engine purr gently through the automatic gears as he listened to his favourite radio station playing the classical music that he and Mary enjoyed, occasionally humming along with the orchestra. His wife listened only absently – her mind was elsewhere, thinking of how Josephine had grown up and the friends she had at the gallery that evening. There was something troubling her, but she couldn't quite put a finger on the source of her worry. It was just a nagging something that wouldn't come to the fore, but it was there. She watched the houses thin out as they approached the start of the M23 motorway that would take them to their home in Brighton. As she thought back over the evening, she closed her eyes knowing that her husband would be driving along the motorway at exactly seventy miles an hour in the middle lane until they reached the dual carriageway when he would reduce the speed to sixty. He always did; it was his way and he always did what he wanted.

She realised that she had fallen asleep when she awoke as they approached the twin concrete pylons that marked the northern boundary of the city. She recalled learning about the pylons at a local history meeting. Now what did they signify? She thought back; it was the sort of question that would appear on a television quiz show, when the answer would be a million-pound prize. She smiled to herself as she thought of the answer she would give: 'They were built to mark the boundary of Greater Brighton, and the foundation stones were laid by the Duke and Duchess of York on the 30 May 1928. Various items were buried at that time, two newspapers, the *Sussex Daily News* and the *Brighton and Hove Daily Record*. Also a book showing the laying of the stones and, yes, some coins.' The denomination of the coins she couldn't recall, and had she been watching herself she would have been amused at the frown on her forehead. 'Anything else about the pylons you can tell us?' she could hear the quizmaster ask.

'Ah yes, the inscription,' she would say. ' "Hail guest, we ask not what thou art. If friend, we greet thee hand and heart. If stranger, no longer be. If foe, our love shall conquer thee." '

She laughed to herself then self-consciously glanced at her husband to see whether he had noticed, but he hadn't; he was still looking at the road ahead with his mind lost in his music. A few minutes later they entered Dyke Road, the long road that dropped from the Downs to the north of the city, almost straight towards the town centre by the sea. On both sides of the road were large, individually designed houses set in their own grounds and with electrically operated front gates.

As Sir Roger slowed the car on the approach to their house, Mary pulled her handbag from the floor on to her lap and began to search for the house keys. The car slowed again as they approached the twin stone pillars that marked the driveway, and Sir Roger reached for the remote control attached to the sun visor. He pushed the green button and slowly the twin gates began to open.

The house appeared large from the outside, though it was not as grand as some of his neighbours. It had been their home for over twenty years and it was now just as they liked it.

'Ah, it's been a lovely night and thank you for a lovely drive home as well,' said Mary as she watched Sir Roger slow the car to a halt. As the car stopped, Mary opened her door and began to walk across the newly laid brick-effect driveway to the front door. She didn't stop or look around as she put the key into the lock and turned it. She kept on walking into the hallway, aware of the bleeping noise now being given by the alarm system whose controls were situated in the cupboard under the stairs. She put her head into the cupboard and pressed the four digits to stop the bleeps and had just turned around when she became aware of a lot of noise from the front door. She expected to see Sir Roger there – perhaps he would have been carrying his overcoat, or maybe closing the front door – but her mouth opened and she stood stock still as she saw her husband falling forward towards her while framed in the doorway was a man wearing a black balaclava. He appeared to be wet, very wet and his mere appearance shocked her so much that she was unable to understand what this person was saying.

She didn't move, just stared as if in a trance, her mouth open and her eyes bulging as the shock hit her. She didn't see or hear Sir Roger land on the thick pile rug that covered part of the wooden floor. She didn't look at her husband, just stood and watched as this man closed the front door.

The man was moving towards her and still she remained as if she had turned to stone. The man took her arm and was saying something else to her. He was very close to her and she could feel his wet hand and clothes against her hands. She stared into the eyes inside the balaclava; they looked unreal to her, threatening and forceful while at the same time almost frightened and panicky. Everything passed in slow motion for her, as her arm was pulled and then her chest pushed, and all the time this man was shouting at her. He pointed to the floor and as her eyes followed his arm she became aware of her husband lying there. The shock brought her back to real time as she started to bend towards her husband who she could see had a cut on his forehead from which a small amount of blood was trickling on to the edge of the rug. She was abruptly pulled back up and she registered what the man was saying: 'Safe, where is the fucking safe?'

She pointed upstairs. 'Up there,' she said. She felt a sudden push into the small of her back, making her stumble towards the bottom of the stairs.

She heard him saying, 'Get up there. Go on!' as she received further pushes. Her arm was still being held but somehow she found the energy and started to run up the stairs. She just wanted this man to go and leave them alone. At the top of the stairs she rushed into the first bedroom on the left, which overlooked the front of the house and served as their marital bedroom. The curtains were drawn and a sidelight

10

at either side of the bed lit the room. She moved to the glass-fronted built-in wardrobe and slid the door back. She moved back and pointed to a metal box on the floor on which were stacked various shoeboxes. As she held her trembling hand towards the box she said in a small voice, 'There, that's the safe. Just help yourself and go, please, just go.'

The man pushed her to one side and looked down at the box before facing her and in a fury shouted at her 'Open it!' He moved behind her and pushed her head down causing her to stumble forward into the clothes rail above the shoeboxes. She half fell into the clothes then collapsed on to the carpet in front of the safe. She felt tears welling. Her mind was racing and unable to comprehend what was happening. She tried to focus, to slow down and think of what she had to do. A further hard push in her back then a smack to the back of her head made her thoughts more difficult to organise. She bent towards the keypad at the front of the safe and reached forwards, but the tears had now formed and her eyes became so misty she was unable to see the numbers properly. She was sobbing as she slowly keyed in the four numbers, pushing a key then moving by touch to the next until she heard, to her relief, the click of the lock being released.

The man also heard the sound and reached down over her as he pulled the safe door open. She fell on to the shoeboxes aware that the man was now almost lying on top of her as he searched in the safe. It was only a few seconds before she felt the pressure release from her. She felt unable to look at the man, frightened in case her actions were interpreted as a threat. She felt him pull at her necklace; it was her favourite string of pearls that her grandmother had given her on her twenty-first birthday. Her hand reacted before she could think and grabbed the front of the necklace as he tore at the back. The resulting sudden release and cascading of loose pearls around her told her that the necklace was broken, but in an instant his hand had moved from the necklace to her hand.

As he tried to hold her hand steady, his other hand moved towards her rings.

'No!' she shouted. 'You have got everything else; you're not having these!'

Her anger and fury now took over as she pulled her hand back and lashed out with both feet towards his legs. She couldn't register where she was kicking him; she just wanted to hurt him, punish him. As she fell back further into the wardrobe she found herself clutching a shoe, which she now tried to hit the man's legs with. She was beside herself and was screaming at her attacker, using words that she had rarely if ever used before. How many times she called him a 'bastard' and told him to 'fuck off' she didn't know. How long her fury lasted she couldn't have said, nor the number of thuds she felt against her legs. Suddenly she felt drained, her breath loud and rasping, her shoulders heaving with the effort of her trying to get air into her lungs. She was physically spent and fell on to her front among the shoes, not caring what happened next.

Such was her condition that she was unaware that the man had left her.

His legs hurt and there was a tear in his jeans where that bitch had caught him with the heel of a shoe. A small amount of blood showed at the tear but that didn't hurt as much as his groin where she had landed the first and most painful kick. He had looked at her as she lay on the floor among the debris of what had been a carefully arranged wardrobe, among shoes, boxes and loose pearls. He hadn't wanted to hurt her and doubted that he had, but he was aware that she was in no state to cause him any further problems. Her breathing was so laboured it would take her minutes to recover.

The man ran down the stairs looking into the hallway where he saw the old man slowly getting to his feet. Their eyes met and the old man said something, slowly and with a slur. He moved towards the old man and noticed the blood from his forehead had trickled down into his left eye, then on to his cheek towards the white shirt collar. Again, the old man tried to say something

'What?' shouted the attacker.

'Safe in there ... Just leave us alone.'

The attacker looked at where the old man was pointing and saw towards the back of the house a closed wooden door.

'What?'

'There, in there, safe, cash ... Just leave us alone, take it and go. Don't hurt us please.'

The attacker looked at the old man. Was this a trick of some sort? he thought. A delaying tactic? Was he trying to lure him into a room for some reason? His instinct was to run as fast and far from the house as possible. But what was it the old man had said? Cash? He stopped in his tracks – cash. There hadn't been any in the upstairs safe so perhaps there was another safe downstairs?

'Show me!' he shouted directly in the old man's face. 'Come on, get up!'

He reached for the old man's arm and helped him to his feet. The old man was taller by a few inches than he and would certainly weigh more, but the attacker felt confident that if needed he could win any fight and beat any resistance. In the event, there was no fight or resistance; the old man just moved unsteadily towards the door. He turned the door handle and pushed the door open with his right hand and then started to move his left arm, which the attacker still held, towards the wall-mounted light switch. The attacker saw the switch and he let the arm go. The room became bright. The attacker saw a large desk at the far end of the room with two hard-backed chairs facing it. There were piles of paperwork, some in brown slide-in folders, others in box files on the floor leaning against the walls.

The old man moved forward towards the desk and leaning

on it he moved to the side and reached to slide open the top drawer. The attacker had watched the old man move and it wasn't until he saw the drawer open that he realised there could be a weapon in there. Frozen to the spot he could only keep his eyes fixed on the old man's coat sleeve as the hand disappeared into the drawer. Slowly and only a second or two later the arm was moving back. The attacker was suddenly confused – there wasn't a gun, or even a knife; instead it was a key. His whole body suddenly relaxed. His breathing restarted. The old man said something to him that he missed. The old man then smiled at the attacker. 'Here it is – the key to the money.'

He continued to smile as he kept his eyes on the attacker but walked towards a seascape painting on the wall opposite the door through which they had entered. He reached the edge of the painting, a picture of a wild night with sea waves crashing on to the sandy beach, nothing else in the picture just the drama of the sea. It was his favourite painting by H.L. Braunston and was hinged to the wall. The painting swung back to reveal a metal safe door in the wall. It was old, very old by the look of the scratches on the green paint. The maker's name on a brass plate could not now be read. The old man inserted the single double-headed key and levered the smooth brass handle to open the door.

Still the old man was smiling as he turned back to his attacker and said: 'There you go, young man. Please help yourself.'

He began to chuckle gently and walked towards one of the chairs by the desk. The attacker moved gingerly towards the open safe. There he could see three stacks of banknotes, each over four inches high. He was vaguely aware of the old man still chuckling, perhaps even quietly laughing, but his attention was drawn to the cash. He reached in and pulled out a stack which he saw were English pound notes of various denominations, fifties and twenties mostly. He couldn't believe his eyes as he unzipped the front of his jacket and stuffed

14

the notes inside. He repeated the procedure with the other two stacks, which he only briefly looked at, just sufficient to realise they were of foreign currency. He didn't care.

The old man was laughing now, really laughing. The attacker was still confused as to why the old man was laughing. What the hell did he have to laugh at? He looked at him but there he was, leaning against the desk and laughing, his head now dropping towards the desk. The attacker zipped up his jacket and was about to leave when he looked back into the safe and saw papers and some envelopes. He pulled them out and quickly scanned them ... a Last Will and Testament for the man, which he threw to the floor; a Last Will and Testament for the woman, which followed; papers relating to the house similarly went on to the floor. Others looked like papers relating to a business of some sort, and then there was a blue plastic folder in which share certificates were neatly placed in clear plastic envelopes. Everything went on to the floor.

Still the laughing continued and again he glanced towards the old man who had not moved from his position leaning against the desk. The only item remaining in the safe was a cardboard box file at the back, and on its side. It was right at the back and was the same colour as the inside walls of the safe, so he nearly didn't see it. He pulled it out and opened it. He saw a cluster of medals all held by their ribbon on a single bar. There were papers and photographs, envelopes, some tied in bundles, all old and smelling musky. They were, the attacker immediately thought, old war medals, and he knew that there was a good market for such memorabilia. He looked around the room and saw an old brown leather briefcase next to the desk. Grabbing it, he threw out the few papers that were in it and placed the box file with the medals inside. After glancing again at the old man he left the room.

He went back to the hallway by the front door and listened. He could now only faintly hear the old man still laughing;

there was no sound from his wife upstairs. The attacker searched for, then turned out, the lights in the hallway, plunging him into almost darkness with only the light from upstairs allowing him to see the front door catch. He slowly opened the front door and looked outside. The rain was now falling steadily, the dripping from the trees making small splashes on the ground. There was no other sound. He noticed then that the porch light was still on, so he pushed the door to and felt for that switch and turned the light off. Now, as he descended the steps to the driveway, he was in darkness and more aware of the rain as it fell on to his head. Almost in a panic, he realised that he still had the balaclava on his head. He ripped it off and stuffed it into his jacket pocket. He was aware of the cash down the inside of his jacket and felt uncomfortable as he walked towards the gates, hoping that the elasticated waistband would be sufficient to hold the notes in place.

The main gates through which he had run just after the car had entered had closed and for a minute he began to panic. He ran to them and saw no lock, then looked at their eight-foot height. It was only then that he saw the small side gate. He found the electric button at the side and heard the click of the electric magnet release the door, which swung open towards him a couple of inches. He pushed his head through sufficiently to see up and down the road.

He knew his way around the town but this area was quite unknown, so he decided to walk down the road towards the town centre, keeping as close to the inside of the pavement as possible and to use the dark shadows of the trees and walls to hide in should a car appear. There were very few cars and he didn't see anybody else walking. Twice he heard the wailing sounds of an emergency vehicle racing somewhere in the distance – as long as they were busy and not around his area he didn't care.

* * *

It took him over half an hour to reach the safety of his twelfth-floor flat that he shared with his mother and was pleased that she had gone to bed, which allowed him time to sort through his haul. He went to his bedroom and used the bedside light to separate the jewellery from the cash. He pushed the box file in the briefcase under his bed for the time being. He hung his wet jacket in the small wooden wardrobe, oblivious to the water dripping on to his dry trousers that hung there. The jewellery he put into a plastic carrier bag then carried it into the kitchen and stuffed it into the bottom of a tin in which all similar bags were kept before usually being used as a liner for the small rubbish bin.

He returned to his bedroom and put the money under his bed mattress then collected the box file and went to the living room. He had one special hiding place that so far the police during their many searches had failed to discover. He carefully took all the china ornaments from the centre of three wooden ceiling-high units and placed them on the worn settee, then removed the various pieces of junk from the cupboard at the bottom of this one cabinet. It had taken him a painstaking ten minutes before he had completely emptied the unit, then carefully he grabbed the shelving and pulled the whole cabinet forward until it was just proud of those either side. Through the small gap he managed to squeeze the box file, which he put on the ground, knowing the unit would cover it when it was pushed back into place. By the time he had replaced all the junk and ornaments he felt drained, both physically and mentally. He noticed for the first time that his hands were shaking, though whether this was through excitement or relief he didn't know. Certainly, he became frightened as he began to realise the length of sentence that a judge would pass for this offence. This was a big jump from his usual street robbery where invariably the drunken victim didn't even report the robbery to the police.

He returned to his bedroom and lying on his bed fully clothed he relived the time from when he entered the house to when he had left it. He was torn about what to think of the old man. What was that all about? The old man had volunteered to open the safe that he hadn't even known about. Bloody hell! That was a first. He began to laugh then he stopped as he wondered whether the old man was all right – had that injury to the head really been serious? No, it was only a shove that made him fall on to the floor and anyway, his missus was OK and she would go and look after him. He focused on what would happen next. Tomorrow he would get a mate to take the jewellery to London to sell as he had done in the past. He always got a better price that way – the greedy thieving bastards in Brighton half the time bought it for next to nothing then told the Old Bill about him anyway.

Within minutes Aaron Brooks fell asleep without a care in the world, just anticipation of what the next day would bring.

Mary had been stunned for a minute by the attack, then as she made her way to the top of the stairs she saw the back of the attacker as he went out the front door. She didn't notice the briefcase he carried as she went down the stairs. She saw the light from the room her husband used as a study and went through the doorway calling his name softly. She gave a gasp when she saw Sir Roger slumped over his desk with blood on the desktop and glistening red in his hair. She ran to him.

'Roger, Roger, are you hurt? Oh God, what has he done to you?'

She gently moved his head and saw the flicker of his eyes and a smile across his mouth as she moved to kiss him on his cheek and to hold his head. She sobbed as she told Sir

18

Roger that she loved him. He didn't respond and his eyes showed very little reaction, which brought back her anxiety. She reached over his desk and telephoned the emergency number asking for the police and ambulance. Mary let Sir Roger rest his head back on the desk while she rushed outside to the Rolls to activate the electronic gates for the emergency vehicles.

Mary had returned to the study after seeing the gates open and after again checking Sir Roger she had telephoned Mark Carter, Sir Roger's Head of Security, to tell him what had happened. She had only just finished that call when the knock on her open front door announced the arrival of two paramedics. The two men, each carrying a case, entered the house and followed Mary's cries directing them into the study. While one paramedic set down his case and went towards Sir Roger, the other gently spoke to Mary asking her various questions about what had happened. His reassuring tone and words meant that all her attention was taken away from the other paramedic who was attending her husband.

Shortly, other calls from the front door were answered by the paramedic attending Mary, and they were joined by a male and female police officer who took in the scene from the doorway for a few seconds before entering the study. After being introduced by the paramedic to the police, Mary showed the police officers into the front room. She was aware of blue strobes dancing over the drawn curtains as she sat on the settee and invited the officers into two armchairs opposite her. Slowly and carefully the officers led her to recount the events and to give a description of the attacker, which the female officer carefully noted in her pocketbook before excusing herself from the room to use her radio to circulate the description. The male officer continued gently coaxing details about the evening's events, starting from where they had been in London. This form of questioning was slower but more methodical and contained detail that might be useful later if the investigation was not completed during the 'hot period'.

This was interrupted when the older of the two paramedics, the one who had attended Mary, entered the room to announce softly that Sir Roger had received a small cut to his head and was suffering from concussion. Although the injury did not appear to be serious, they would take Sir Roger to the Royal Sussex County Hospital for a proper examination.

Other police officers arrived and the female officer again left the room to brief them before returning to Mary and explaining that they would need to examine the bedroom in some detail to gather any forensic evidence the attacker had left behind. Also, if it were possible, could they ask that she change her coat for another so that that could also be examined?

It was some half an hour after Sir Roger had left by ambulance that Mark Carter arrived and was allowed into the front room where Mary was just finishing her account for the police officers.

Carter was, like Sir Roger, over six feet tall and he had a good build, which he maintained through regular sessions at the gym. His boyhood sports of rugby and boxing coupled with his ongoing fitness regime gave him a muscular shape, though he tried to hide this behind his expensive and well-tailored suits. He had an oval, clean-shaven face that was gave prominence to his now-greying short-cut hair. He had been described as a good-looking man in his younger days and even in his mid-forties he had retained his looks. He had an air of confidence about him that allowed him to take control of situations and people without any fuss.

'Mary,' said Carter as he walked towards her, bending to a crouch position and taking hold of her hands, 'What in God's name has happened?'

'We were attacked as we got home from Josephine's gallery opening. It was just one man but he's hurt Roger. He's gone to hospital but the medic said that it's only a slight head wound. Concussion, they think. They may keep him in tonight to check, but I need to get there as soon as the officers are finished with me here.'

Mark half turned on his haunches and addressed the two police officers: 'When can I get Mrs Knight to the hospital? Are you finished?'

The male officer moved forward in his chair and began to put his notebook into his tunic pocket. 'Yes, we have sufficient detail now to begin our enquiries. We have circulated the description of the attacker, but no luck as yet. We have, as you can see, forensic people examining the house and they will take some time. If you are happy, we can either take Mrs Knight to the hospital, while you remain here, or you can take Mrs Knight. The forensic people, I think, will be some hours yet.'

It was decided that Carter would accompany Mary to the hospital. They would wake a neighbour and ask him to look after things should the police leave the house before they returned. A more detailed written statement could be obtained in the morning.

The accident and emergency department was busy with many of the chairs occupied by persons who appeared to be either asleep or under the influence of drink or drugs. Two burly security guards in uniform stood watch and it was they who pointed Carter and Mary Knight to the reception desk. Sir Roger was located in a curtained cubicle, asleep on a trolley. His head had two plasters at the hairline of his forehead, but apart from those he appeared to be resting peacefully. They were barely in the cubicle before a nurse in a starched blue uniform came in and confirmed their identities before telling them the result of the examination. Sir Roger had two small superficial cuts to the head which were of no consequence, but rather more relevant was the fact that he appeared to have post-traumatic amnesia, though it was too soon to say for certain.

'The outcome can depend on many factors' she explained. 'The type and severity of the initial trauma and the age of the person are factors, but in truth we won't know until a few more hours. It may be that we will have to conduct more tests – scans could be needed – but at this time I am really pleased to say that the doctor who examined Sir Roger is happy that the amnesia will be slight. It may well be that, because Sir Roger is generally in such good health, he'll be fine in the morning after a good rest. There may be a brief interruption in the short- to long-term memory transfer mechanism, but we will have to see. I really wouldn't worry; he will sleep now overnight.'

Mary smiled for the first time since the robbery and arranged to return in the morning.

When Carter and Mary Knight arrived back at the Knight's house there were only two vans in the driveway, both showing they were from the Scientific Investigation Branch of Sussex Police. Without any blue strobes or persons in fluorescent jackets about the place the house seemed almost to have returned to normal. But then Mary entered the house and saw the various boxes and portable lights in the hallway. On hearing the front door open and seeing it was Mrs Knight, a man wearing a white disposable one-piece suit came from the study. He explained that the bedroom was now just being cleaned and that they had finished their examination there, but fingerprint dust and tape were being removed. Their work in the study was also nearing completion. Mrs Knight's offer of a tea for everyone was readily accepted, which gave Carter the opportunity to talk to the Scientific Officer.

'Hi, I am Mark Carter. I'm Sir Roger Knight's Head of Security, so am particularly concerned about what has happened here tonight. I was in the job, in the Met for twenty years, retiring as a detective inspector. As head of his security, Sir

Roger will be asking me some bloody awkward questions in the morning. I have spoken to Mrs Knight fairly briefly in the car to and from the hospital. From what I understand the robber pounced on them as they returned home, just after the alarm was switched off and before the front door was closed. So, he pushed or threw, maybe hit, Sir Roger, who fell to the ground here in the hallway. The robber then frightened Mrs Knight so much that she opened the safe upstairs and took her jewellery. There was a scuffle up there but the robber left. How the hell did he know about the safe in the study? How did he open the bloody thing? Obviously, Sir Roger will be able to tell us at some stage, but was the safe forced?'

The Scientific Officer shook his head. 'No, definitely one hundred per cent, the safe was opened by the right key. There is an open desk drawer. Maybe the key was kept in there.'

'Yes but say the robber knew about Sir Roger's safe, why did he bother with the jewellery? And conversely, if he didn't know about the safe, how come it is open and empty?' said Carter quietly, almost to himself.

Over the next hour Carter made sure that all the police equipment was packed up and taken away. He made sure Mrs Knight was asleep in the spare bedroom before he made himself comfortable on the settee in the front room for the night.

3

The following morning Mrs Knight made some telephone calls to Josephine and her friends to explain briefly what had happened. Her first call had been at 7 a.m. to the ward where Sir Roger was being looked after. Initially confused as to where he was, he was now quite awake and asking when he could go home. It was news that had lifted her spirits and given her the confidence to make the calls. Carter was woken by the sound of Mrs Knight's voice in the kitchen and after a quick wash he joined her.

After a breakfast of toast and coffee he used his mobile to call his office at Crawley where he updated his deputy, Don Davies, and told him that he would be away for the day with Sir Roger and Mrs Knight. Carter's appointments for that day were not important and Don said that he could either handle them or rearrange them. Don Davies was of a similar age to Carter whom he had met when he was a detective sergeant in the Sussex Police stationed at Crawley, in the Special Branch department. They had met initially when Sir Roger's business had hosted visitors from foreign countries who had a reputation for wanting to capture industrial secrets from British companies. As Sir Roger's Head of Security Carter met with Don Davies frequently before those visits to ensure that only those industrial secrets that they wanted to be stolen actually were. This game between countries was an accepted fact of life within the industrial and spying community and both men were adept at ensuring that the visits went as planned. Don Davies and Carter had remained friends and on his retirement Don was offered the job as

Carter's deputy, standing in for much of the day-to-day and routine work.

It was after ten when Aaron Brooks woke up and stumbled into the kitchen to make a cup of tea. He used the same dirty mug he always used, It was still on the side where he had left it the previous evening before he had gone out. Neither he nor his mum ever bothered to wash up unless they had to do so. Plates used three days ago were in the sink along with an assortment of mugs and dishes. The work surface was cluttered with crockery and packets of opened food packaging, together with any number of cooking items. Aaron had once described his home to a friend as a shithole and today this would have been a kind description.

Aaron made his mug of tea, leaving the tea bag with the rest of the week's now dried-out used tea bags on an overflowing saucer. He went to the living room and opened a window to release the smoke that his mother had left earlier that morning when she had had her customary three cigarettes and a mug of coffee for breakfast, and switched on the television. In other people's flats in the same tower block the living room was a pleasure to be in, with a south-facing balcony that looked towards and over the city of Brighton, out to sea. Their balcony, though, was barely ever used. Old packets of cigarettes and a few discarded cigarette butts had been wind swept into the corners, together with general dust and dirt. The room itself was of a good size, but was cramped by the ragbag of furniture his mother had acquired over the years, all of it cheap and ill cared for.

Brooks fell into the settee whose cushions had long ago lost their life and spring and put his feet on the glass coffee table in front of him. He lit and drew heavily on his cigarette as he thought back to the previous evening. He was unaware of what was on the muted TV until a picture of the house in Dyke Road came into view, with a male reporter talking into a microphone standing by the shut gates. He instantly recognised the gates and with a flurry he searched for the TV remote, spilling some of his tea on the already-stained carpet. Finally he found it on the windowsill and pointed it frantically at the screen, hearing the words gradually increasing in volume.

'... are appealing for witnesses. Just to repeat the description, a man aged twenty to thirty years, medium build, five feet ten inches to six feet tall wearing a dark jacket and trousers who is believed to have made off on foot. Back to Karen in the studio.'

As Karen began to talk about another item, Brooks used the control to mute her voice.

'Shit!' he said quietly, then louder: 'Shit, shit, shit!' Did the old man die? 'Oh fuck, no, he couldn't have done, it was just a push,' he said to himself. His mind raced around what a murder prison sentence would mean for him. How many years would it be? What age would he be when he got out?

'Jesus bloody Christ!' he said aloud. 'Come on, get a grip, let's think about it.'

He sat there staring into space trying to work things out, trying to get his story straight before the police knocked on his door.

When Carter opened and held the door open for Mary, he saw Sir Roger sitting up in bed propped up by pillows apparently asleep. But at the sound of Mary walking towards him, he opened his eyes and seeing Mary smiled at her.

'Oh love,' she said, rushing to his side and taking hold of his hand before leaning down to him and kissing him on his cheek. 'Oh, darling, I am so glad you are OK. How are you feeling?'

Carter hung back in the doorway and watched the obvious love in their embrace.

'The police came to see me...' Sir Roger said in a steady

26

voice, '...an hour or so ago ... two detectives, asking about what had happened.' He gave a slight laugh then continued: 'I could only remember walking up the front steps and then waking up in A&E. I can't recall anything of what happened. The doctors say that I may have lost my memory from the stress of what happened. What *did* happen, Mary?'

Carter felt like the invisible man and didn't dare move lest he interrupted Mary as she gave a full account of what had happened. Sir Roger was happy that his beloved wife didn't appear to be physically hurt, though he knew she would have dark memories of the incident that could resurface at some time in the future. Sir Roger only started to question Mary when she told him that the safe in the study had been emptied. Some papers and their wills were found on the floor, but the safe itself was empty. Initially Sir Roger didn't appear too anxious, but he suddenly became very focused on what she was saying. His face turned a bright red as she confirmed that indeed everything had been stolen; there was nothing left in the safe at all.

'Not a grey box file?' Sir Roger persisted, a hint of desperation in his voice. 'Right at the back, the same colour as the inside of the safe?'

Mary had to confirm this at least three times before she asked him: 'What was in the box? I thought you only kept some cash in there?'

'Oh, nothing very much,' Sir Roger said as much to himself as anyone in the room.

He then appeared to see Carter for the first time and waved a hand towards him. 'Hi, Mark, thanks for looking after Mary. When I get out of here in a few minutes, are you free for the rest of the day? I need to sort out a few things with you.'

Before Carter could reply Mary interrupted: 'You need rest. I am sure that's what the doctors will say, and in any case who says you can go home just yet?'

'Mary,' Carter said gently, 'would it be an idea if you could

safe but its emptiness didn't surprise him. He sat at his desk and for a moment just looked at the desktop and the few papers that were to the left of where he sat, his to-do pile – he always worked methodically from the left.

'Mark,' Sir Roger said, lifting his gaze to his Security Officer's eyes, 'I have a problem. How big it is I don't know as yet – time will tell. In the safe were a few work-related papers, nothing of too much significance. I can go over those with you and ask Mrs Mountfield to reprint them. A nuisance, but there we are. The cash, I don't know, but I would think there was about ten thousand in sterling and more in foreign currency, mostly euros ... a few dollars as well, perhaps twenty, twenty-five thousand pounds' worth in total. I won't tell the police there was that much. I know Mary wouldn't have a clue how much was in there; it was for entertaining, shall we say.'

He smiled and Carter acknowledged the subtle lie, as he knew very well it was money used to facilitate business ... well, bribes in common parlance.

'It was the grey box file,' continued Sir Roger steadily holding Carter's eyes. Sir Roger had been thinking how much to say and even though he had known Carter for over six years during which time Carter had committed various unlawful deeds on his behalf, he didn't want to reveal all unless he had to. He might not have to yet.

'The box was in the back of the safe, had been there for so many years in truth I forgot about it most of the time; it just blended in. Anyway, the long and short of it is that it contains some old papers, old World War Two stuff. Wouldn't mean a lot to anyone, but it does to me and that is what I really want back. The other things, well,' he paused, 'well, Mary's jewellery is insured, the money is of little consequence and, as I have said, the work papers can be duplicated. I want you to quietly get on with finding that box file and I want all the contents back safe and securely.

I don't care how you do it, or what it costs, just get that box back.' He spoke slower towards the end as if to emphasise the importance of his words.

Carter knew he wasn't being told the contents of the box or the reason they were important – that wasn't his concern. He knew that over the years Sir Roger had given instructions to him that had been as clear, and each time Carter had managed to get the wanted result. He hadn't told Sir Roger of his methods – Sir Roger didn't ask and Carter didn't tell.

'I just don't remember what happened,' Sir Roger said quietly and with a frown, 'just don't remember at all.' He sighed as if resigned. 'What I don't understand', he continued, 'is how did he know that I had a safe in the study and how the hell did he know where the key was kept?'

'Mary was asked just that by the police. He had the jewellery from upstairs and Mary had the impression that he was rushing to get away. You were in the hallway, Mary thinks maybe semi-conscious. Did he have a go at you? We just don't know, do we? And unless your memory does return at some time in the future we may not know until we get hold of the bastard.'

After a few minutes arranging other business matters and telephoning Mrs Mountfield at the Crawley site their business was completed. Just as they were walking to the door Sir Roger could hear the frantic arrival of Josephine, her loud and excitable voice asking many questions without waiting for an answer. Carter and Sir Roger smiled at each other at the sound of activity and walked to the hallway where Josephine flung her arms around Sir Roger's neck.

'Daddy, Daddy!' she wailed. She looked over Sir Roger's shoulder at Carter and they exchanged a brief glance.

Carter bade his goodbyes and left to attend Brighton Police Station in the centre of the city to try and see a detective sergeant who had recently been promoted there from Crawley. DS Terry Harrison had been long overlooked for promotion from the detective constable position he had held in Crawley for over twenty years and having known him for more than five of those years Carter thought it would be a good place to start his own enquiries.

While he smoked a further two rolled-up cigarettes and finished his mug of tea, Aaron Brooks fretted about the news item and seriousness of the implications. His idea of someone he could trust going up to London to sell the jewellery he now thought was not the best; however much he trusted a fence to take hot stolen property, he knew that when the case involved a murder, or even an attempted murder, no person could be fully trusted. The jewellery would have to be put away for another day. Where to hide the jewellery was also decided very quickly – with that box file under the lounge unit. That left the cash. He hadn't fully counted it, but the bundles were larger and contained bigger-denomination notes than he had ever seen before. He guessed there would be thousands of pounds in one, though he didn't know the value of the foreign notes. He wanted to spend the money, that was for certain, and he became excited at the thought of the girls his money would be able to buy. He would fulfil some of his fantasies with them, some of his inner thoughts that he dared not share with others, not even the tarts with whom he had shared lines of cocaine with in the various squats he had visited in Brighton.

He knew that, although he stood nearly six feet tall, he had a very thin body; 'Lanky' had been his nickname at school, and he knew he didn't look too good to the girls. He picked his spots regularly leaving red blotches over his face; at the age of twenty-three he ought to have grown out of that adolescent affliction. In any event, his long face didn't attract many girls and maybe his lank red greasy hair didn't help either. If he had been very honest with himself, he would also have had to add to the list of undesirable attributes the fact that his body invariably smelled due to lack of washing and his breath stank from a lack of brushing cleaning and dental care.

He decided that he would put the foreign notes with the grey box along with half the English money. He would rely on the other half until the heat died down. He would stay at a hotel in London for a few days and he would leave that afternoon. Before then he wanted to make sure that any search of the flat wouldn't reveal the evidence to link him to the crime.

Spurred into action, he thought about his hiding place. True it hadn't been found during the numerous searches of the flat that had taken place, but if the police were to search in connection with a murder investigation he knew it would have to be a more secure hide. He paced around the flat, looking in his and his mother's bedrooms, kicking aside discarded clothing and shoes, and then in the kitchen and bathroom. In films he had seen people removing tiles from bathroom walls and making a hole in the brickwork to create a hide before retiling the whole wall to conceal the activity. He dismissed the idea as he didn't have the skills or knowledge to do this. He returned to the lounge and again looked at the unit under which he had hidden the box the previous evening. It was a heavy unit; it had been there so long that the weight had created grooves in the carpet where it stood; it looked as if it had never been moved. It was a good place he decided, but could he improve it? He decided to remove the unit and look at the situation again. He repeated the same procedure as the night before and then stared at the box file.

Then a thought came to him suddenly. Why not under the carpet? He almost ran into the kitchen in his excitement and found the Stanley knife that he knew was in the kitchen drawer. He returned to the lounge and cut through the carpet at the edges of the two neighbouring units before prising the carpet from the wall edge and folding it back towards him revealing some rubber underlay. He cut this underlay in the same fashion as the carpet to reveal a concrete floor. The idea he had had now became a course of action, he would have to create a space large enough to hide the box, jewellery and cash, in the concrete, and then when the underlay and carpet were replaced all would look completely normal.

Realising that the sound of breaking the concrete would make a lot of noise, especially to the people living below, he tried to think of a plausible reason to give for his actions. This his limited imagination failed to do but then it occurred to him that he should check whether the old lady who lived below was actually in. He quickly finished getting dressed then took the flight of old concrete stairs to the flat directly under his and banged on the door. He could have used the bell that was neatly screwed into the doorframe, but then he had always just banged on doors. He waited for a good ten seconds before banging again, harder this time. Still there was no response, but as he was about to head back upstairs feeling elated he heard a door behind him open. Standing in the doorway was a very old man, always referred to among the residents as 'The Major', as he bore an uncanny likeness to the character once seen in the popular comedy television programme *Fawlty Towers*. Not only did he look like the character but his mannerisms were so alike that the resemblance was striking.

'Mrs Goody isn't in, young man,' the Major announced in a loud voice. 'Gone out, shopping I think she said. Don't know where, probably into town but she didn't say.'

Brooks looked at the Major and the idea formed in his mind. 'Will you see Mrs Goody when she gets back?' he asked, walking slowly towards the Major.

'Yes, of course, young man, she's getting me my paper, always does, well when she goes out,' he said. his voice becoming quieter as if he was unsure that what he was saying was factual.

'Ah,' said Brooks brightening, 'only I live above her and I need to make a bit of noise for a few minutes, so would you tell her it won't be for long, just some banging, say fifteen minutes or so?'

'Right,' said the Major slowly, not really fully understanding why someone would need to be banging and making a noise in their flat. The Council employed people to do that, but young people were a bit strange and the lad who lived upstairs had certainly over the years been a bit strange. 'Right,' the Major repeated, 'making a noise for fifteen minutes, right.'

Without asking any questions or clarifying anything the Major closed his door.

Brooks ran back to the living room and after twenty minutes' work examined the shallow hole he had made in the floor. With the cash and jewellery laid underneath, the box was just pushing the carpet and underlay a bit higher but the effort to create even this shallow hole was such that he gave up on trying to create a deeper one. He was pleased with his efforts though and in no time had replaced the unit and ornaments. The rubble he had knocked out he had already put into plastic carrier bags and the few small pieces he just kicked into and around the carpet. They were soon lost among the dirt already there.

He packed a rucksack that he had used at school many years ago with a change of clothing, then, after leaving a short note for his mother, he picked up the plastic carrier bags and briefcase and left the flat. By this time it was after two o'clock.

He walked steadily through the back entrance of the flats and, as he turned a corner, threw the plastic bags into a small hedge, adding to the rubbish blown there over the past month or so. He looked behind him to see whether he was being followed and didn't see anyone so he dropped the briefcase into a waste bin as he made his way to Ditchling Road, then south towards the city centre before turning right into Viaduct Road heading downhill to the London Road. He continued to the railway station where he queued to buy an open return ticket to London.

4

At the same time that Brooks was settling into his seat as the train drew out of Brighton railway station, Detective Sergeant Harrison walked into the small bar of the quiet Regency Tavern public house, not far away from the seafront. Carter had been there for over half an hour and was on his second gin and tonic, the remains of which he gulped down as he rose to his feet. The two men greeted each other and shook hands before walking to the bar.

'The usual, Scotch and water, Terry?' enquired Carter.

Harrison laughed. 'You've a good memory, Mark. Yes, please.'

As Carter ordered the drinks, Harrison walked towards the table Carter had been sitting at. The bar was in a small annexe to the side of the main bar, with a red-themed decor that included the comfortable chairs that were neatly arranged around the tables. There were no other customers in this bar, and only a few older voices could be heard from the busier bar next door. The windows were set higher than in most bars and the red velvet curtains meant that Harrison couldn't be seen from the outside.

Terry Harrison was forty-three years old, but with his slightly stooped frame and matching dark hair and eyes he looked five years older. As usual, he wore his brown suit with a white shirt and green tie. This was his standard dress for work and, though he replaced the suit and shirt from time to time, the colour combination remained just about the same.

By contrast, Carter was wearing an expensive dark-blue

37

woollen suit with a new light-blue shirt and a dark tie. Nobody would have thought that they were the same clothes he had worn the previous day. He looked younger with his broad straight posture and had the appearance of a fit, attractive and successful businessman.

As he placed the drinks on the table, Harrison eyed his glass and raised his eyebrows. 'A double! Thanks, Mark. Things must be going well for you, or is this on expenses?' He laughed.

'On me for now but who knows come the end of the month when I put my expenses in.' Carter laughed back. 'So, Terry, how's it going down here, a bit different from Creepy Crawley, isn't it? A bit more like the Met I suppose, busy all day and every day.'

Harrison nodded in agreement as he took a sip of his drink. 'Yes, very different. Busy of course and there are more uniform bods around to help out. That's good, but on the down side, God, there are so many high-ranking bosses around that you wouldn't believe it. I reckon there could be almost as many here as there are at Headquarters.'

Both men laughed at that as Harrison continued: 'Not to mention all the young wannabes; Christ, they are all for themselves. Teamwork, never heard of it! Self, self, bloody self. All they talk about is promotion this, promotion that.'

Harrison took a good gulp of his Scotch, finishing it in one as if emphasize his disgust.

Carter stood up and nodding sagely he took Harrison's glass and went to the bar for a refill.

For the next ten minutes Carter listened to Harrison's account of how the job had gone downhill, blaming the youngsters, the bosses and of course the Crown Prosecution Service, or 'Can't Prosecute Service', as he called them. Carter laughed at the right times and offered understanding comments, agreeing with Harrison's views. After another drink Carter thought it the right time to get to the reason for the meeting.

Harrison knew Carter worked for Sir Roger Knight and being aware of the robbery the previous evening had guessed the reason for the meeting when Carter had telephoned earlier that morning.

'Look, mate,' said Carter, leaning forward and lowering his voice, 'I really need to get on top of Sir Roger's robbery. I need all the help I can get.'

Harrison leaned forward so that the gap between them narrowed to two feet and said, 'I appreciate that, Mark. The jewellery I understand was worth over thirty grand and there was also cash, over five thou? But it will be insured, won't it?'

Carter had decided prior to the meeting that he would under no circumstances refer to the box file or to the real value of the cash. He had also decided that he being too keen for information might raise suspicions so had decided to play the sympathy card. 'It's not that really; sure, the jewellery has sentimental value, but the expensive stuff lives in the bank safe. No, it's not the value, it's the hurt he feels. You know Mary was assaulted as well as Sir Roger and that is what has really got his anger up. I'm not joking; he is furious that anyone would lift a finger against Mary, and between you and me he wants this kid's blood.' Realising quickly what he had said he continued: 'Not literally of course, but, you know, he wants to see him go down for it. He's really bloody angry...'

Carter leaned back and knew that Harrison had listened to every word.

Harrison nodded slowly, looked at his drink and took a sip before looking at Carter. 'OK, I am not on that case – I've got the usual crap stuff – but I know a couple of the blokes on the team. I will see what I can find out and let you know.'

The conversation continued for a few minutes before Carter looked at his watch and indicated by emptying his glass that the meeting was finished. They stood and shook hands before Carter left the bar knowing that Harrison would buy himself another drink before returning to the station.

5

Sir Roger remained in bed for two complete days while Mary regained control of the house and started back on her routine of organising their lives. She had always been in charge of the social life they had shared away from his work that until the past year he had devoted most of his time to. On reaching eighty-three years of age he had taken the advice that he had been given for the past twenty or so years – that he ought to slow down his work a level or two and allow others within the company to take their responsibilities.

In Mrs Mountfield he had a secretary, or personal assistant, to use the more current term, who had worked for him for over thirty years. A spinster and now in her early fifties she was an attractive and outgoing person, though she was always very severe on any member of staff who displayed poor manners or behaviour. Sir Roger knew that her reputation among junior staff was quite fearsome and she would not tolerate any behaviour lower than her own high standards. It had been rumoured that one departmental head had said that she had an eye for Sir Roger and even hinted maybe more than an eye for him. The man's life had become so difficult because of her behind-the-scenes manoeuvring that he had left the company within six months without any pay-off. Her revenge had not stopped there, as through surreptitious means she made his wife aware of his affair with a female junior member of his staff.

Sir Roger's trust in her was absolute. She still worked at the Crawley Headquarters of Advanced Electrical and Engineering Group, which was the administrative centre for the whole company. It had twelve factories in the United Kingdom and a further seven on mainland Europe. It was also in partnership with another three companies, one each in America, Brazil and Argentina. Their business was the design, manufacture and installation of electrical equipment with over 80 per cent of the business coming from governments. Despite its size it was discreet, its headquarters sited on the edge of a large industrial estate, surrounded by high concrete walls, with nothing to show the outside world of its true value or the nature of its business. Even Sir Roger Knight's lifestyle displayed that, while obviously a rich man, he had none of the show that most men of his worth would have had.

From his bed at home during the two days he made telephone calls to other Board members and was quite content that the business was being run as he wished. He had confidence in their collective ability and would undoubtedly receive a call from Mrs Mountfield if his attention needed to be drawn to anything.

His only concern was the recovery of the grey box and this had caused him hours of mental anguish. He had weighed up the various options and decided that for the time being he would put his faith in Carter to resolve the situation. One of the options Sir Roger had considered was to tell Carter what the box contained and the anticipated consequences for him if its contents were made public. He had borne in mind that when Carter did recover the box he would surely look at the contents anyway, but after weighing up the advantages and disadvantages of telling him, he had decided that he would for the time being keep his own counsel.

The news from Carter had been disappointing so far. The police were doing everything correctly as far as giving publicity to the offence was concerned, though Sir Roger and Mary had declined any interviews with either the press or television. Descriptions of the stolen jewellery had been circulated to the jewellery trade in general and to those operating out of Brighton's Lanes area in particular. Local beat police officers had visited all the shops that bought second-hand jewellery and the intelligence unit at Brighton Police Station had tasked their informants with asking around their local criminal contacts; an unofficial reward had even been offered to these to ensure an enthusiastic response. The forensic search had revealed very little. Mud marks from the attacker's shoes in the bedroom had been analysed to give the make, model and size of his shoe, but apart from that very little had been learned. No fibres from clothing or the attacker's hair had been recovered and nothing from which DNA could be extracted was found.

The following morning Carter was due to meet with Sir Roger at 11 a.m. to give another update on the police's actions. Hoping for some good news, he telephoned DS Harrison at the police station promptly at 9 a.m. and was disappointed to learn that there hadn't been any further developments in the investigation and even more disappointed that as a result of no promising line of enquiry the team was being scaled down to just one detective sergeant and one detective constable. Carter knew that, with limited resources available and the relentless amount of crime being reported, a scaling-down was inevitable, but in an effort to maintain pressure on DS Harrison he told him that he was to say the least disappointed and that Sir Roger would probably telephone the Chief Constable to request more resources to be put into the investigation. DS Harrison's response was to the point: 'Good luck there, chum, but he's such a tosser and so out of touch with what policing in the real world is about I doubt anything will happen. I will though carry on talking to Matt Southall who's the DS in charge and if there's any updates I will let you know about them soon as.'

Carter had thanked him and said that he appreciated his efforts but it wouldn't be enough for Sir Roger. 'Is there anyone you know, or can you find out, someone I can lean on to show that we mean business, you know what I mean? Like we did with that guy who was selling the wiring a couple of years back, remember?'

DS Harrison had blanched at the reminder – he fully remembered all right. The man had been stealing small amounts of copper wiring for a month from the company delivering to AEEG but AEEG were being invoiced for the total amount. Carter had identified the culprit but the Crown Prosecution Service had decided there was insufficient evidence to mount a successful prosecution and the man had escaped without any punishment. That was until two months later when he was set on while on his way home from the pub one Friday night and given a beating that had necessitated two operations and a three-week stay in hospital. DS Harrison had been the investigating officer and after receiving three thousand pounds in cash from Carter all leads towards identifying the attacker petered to nothing. The case would still have been on file, had that not subsequently been either misfiled or lost.

'Yes, I remember, and don't worry – if there is any news, I will let you know,' said DS Harrison as he ended the call.

DS Harrison remained looking at the telephone for a few seconds and thought over the conversation and wondered what was so special about Sir Roger and Lady Knight being attacked to warrant this reaction from Carter? It wasn't even as if she had received any injury at all; sure, there was the mental anguish but no physical injury. He knew Carter was fiercely loyal to Sir Roger and that he would receive a very handsome reward for any news he could give, so he would do some digging himself in his free time, as long as his officious young female detective inspector didn't get to know.

6

It was after nine thirty that night that Aaron Brooks returned to Brighton by train, wearing new clothes and carrying a new holdall in which there were more new clothes. The clothes shopping he had done in London had cost him some two thousand pounds, but out of the five thousand or so that he had taken with him he thought he had bought well. He had taken the time as well to have a haircut and generally clean himself up, making full use of the hotel's facilities the like of which he hadn't experienced before. Time and time again when he was either soaking in a deep bath or taking a long hot shower he had told himself that this was the lifestyle he wanted. He had seen it on television and in films but now he had experienced it for himself he wanted a lot more of it. Even the girls he had paid for were as good as he had seen on television or read about in the Sunday newspaper – as long as they got paid they seemed happy to satisfy him.

From the railway station to his home was only a mile or so away, but he hired a taxi, and he even gave the driver a tip. Reality struck him as he walked in through the front door and the smell of musty and stale smoke hit his nose and he noted the dust on the table and how old and threadbare the carpets were. He guessed his mother was asleep and when he put the light on in the lounge he saw the empty wine bottle on the glass table that confirmed his initial thoughts. The empty tumbler was next to it and the ashtray was full to nearly overflowing with old cigarette butts.

He looked at the unit and saw that all the ornaments were

as he had left them, reassuring him that his secret hiding place hadn't been found.

As he was looking at the clock and deciding whether to go to bed, DS Harrison received a call on his mobile phone from the duty detective manning the Intelligence Unit.

'Skip,' said the young voice of Adrian Boulton, 'I've just had a call from a bloke who said to tell you he was "Spider". He was at Brighton Rail Station twenty minutes ago when he saw Aaron Brooks getting in from London by train. He said he didn't recognise him at first; he's had his hair cut and got brand-new clothes ... looked really cool according to Spider. Anyway, I ran a check on him and looking at his form he is a street robbery guy, got a load of previous for following drunks at night, then pushing them to the ground and nicking whatever they're carrying. Well, I saw you were dealing with a guy who was rolled the other night down on the seafront, the same night as that old couple were robbed in Dyke Road, and thought you might be interested. Maybe Brooks is your man? Sorry to ring you so late, but to tell you the truth things are fairly quiet here at the moment. If you wanted, I could get a warrant for you for the morning.'

DS Harrison had been half asleep on the settee watching a rerun of some old football match but now he was more alert. It would be a good job for him to solve; there were no witnesses or description of a suspect to go on and he was about to file it as undetected, but if what Spider said was true, Brooks could be a good bet for it. And to make the whole thing better DC Boulton could get the warrant and save him the time and hassle of obtaining one himself from a magistrate in the morning.

He said, 'That would be really good of you, Adey. If you get the warrant, then I'll get in early and go with the early-turn DC and see Mr Brooks.'

They made arrangements for where the warrant would be left together with all the associated paperwork, including a form retrospectively registering Spider as an informant so he could receive a financial reward, even though this was against all the rules.

As he finished the call DS Harrison made a mental note to speak to Adey Boulton's supervisor in the morning. A youngster using his initiative and making a decision – two miracles in one minute, he thought.

DS Harrison arrived at Brighton Police Station at six o'clock in the morning, wet from the walk from his car parked a hundred yards away. He wore his usual brown suit but had on a crisp new white shirt that still had the fold lines showing at the front. He felt good and the weather couldn't dampen his enthusiasm – a chance of a good arrest warranted a new shirt he had thought while shaving.

He ignored the lift and used the stairs to the first floor where the early-turn detective, Rob Watts, was sitting at the table that served as the general enquiry point. He was an old stager, a detective constable in Brighton for over twenty years, someone whom the Americans would call a 'vet', or veteran, a man who could answer any question relating to crime and criminals in Brighton or, if he didn't know, certainly knew someone who would.

DC Watts heard DS Harrison approaching the top of the stairs and looked up from the morning paper he was reading.

'Morning, Terry, watch those stairs at your age,' he said, laughing, 'especially at this time of the morning. Your papers are here. Adey left them, all ready to go whenever you are,' He continued cheerfully.

Due to the length of service it was custom for constables to use the first name of their supervisors, especially in the CID, unless there was a senior officer around when it would have been a 'Sarge' or 'Skip'. DS Harrison smiled at the old-timer, whom he regarded as excellent at behind-the-scenes work. Paperwork and correct procedure were his love and speciality. Thank God, at least someone liked it, he thought.

'Fancy a cuppa first?' asked DC Watts, holding his mug towards his lips. 'Not long since the kettle boiled.'

DS Harrison was tempted to accept but instead said, 'Nah thanks, I'd rather get going and get the scrote while he's still asleep. I suppose he could have a job in London, you know; gone straight and become a commuter.' He laughed as DC Watts made an exaggerated spluttering sound from his mug.

'Yeah right, Brooks has got a job; any bloody job would be the first. His old man never worked before he buggered off back to Ireland but his mum has always worked. I think she's a cleaner down the bus depot. Haven't seen her for years but I think she never took her work home with her, if I remember right.'

'And I put a new shirt on this morning! Don't tell me it's going to get ruined the first day,' said DS Harrison as he watched DC Watts grab his raincoat from a nearby chair and a set of car keys from the board.

They made light conversation on the way to Brook's address with DC Watts driving as DS Harrison checked the warrant's details.

At the block of flats DC Watts parked their car in the clearly marked 'Disabled' bay nearest the entrance and under cover of the canopy. They walked to the main door, which they weren't surprised to find wedged open by a folded piece of card stuffed between the door and its frame. The smell of urine and disinfectant was noticeable but not as bad as in some of the even older blocks of flats about the city. They took the lift to the twelfth floor and seeing no alarm bell DS Harrison used his fist to knock loudly on the door. There wasn't any response and, not caring about disturbing the neighbours who shared the floor, he continued banging until at last he could hear shuffling from behind the door and a young man's voice asking in a whine: 'Who the fuck is it?'

DS Harrison knocked again and bellowed, 'CID. Open the door, Aaron, or I'll bloody break it down. NOW!'

Almost instantly the door was opened and DS Harrison pushed it further open, pushing Brooks backwards. Brooks' skinny body and sleepy eyes put up no resistance and he couldn't help showing a mixture of fear and resignation – body language that every experienced detective recognised quickly and which tended to confirm that they had the right man. Maintaining the pressure and not giving Brooks time to react either physically or verbally, DS Harrison used his frame to tower over Brooks.

'Is there anyone else here?'

'Nah,' replied a sullen Brooks. 'Mum will be at work. What time is it?'

'Nearly half past six. Aaron Brooks, I am arresting you for a robbery on the 17th of September and I've got to caution you, blah, blah, blah ... you know it better than me. Get dressed. We've got a warrant to search this hovel that you call home, so to save us the time and trouble and help us get along why don't you just tell me where any of the money you haven't spent is?'

Brooks was starting to get dressed and felt that it was just about the worst thing that had ever happened to him. He didn't try to analyse how they knew it was him; they somehow did know and he was in trouble; it didn't matter what the duty solicitor would say.

Resigned to his fate, he was on the point of denying knowing anything about any robbery, as was his usual way. He watched as DS Harrison took a ten-pound note from the back pocket of Brooks' jeans that had been in a heap on the floor.

'Done the rest have you?' asked DS Harrison in a more conversational tone.

Something in DS Harrison's manner, his relaxed non-aggressive voice together with a lack of urgency caused Brooks to be puzzled. Even if he had spent all the cash, he would have thought that the DS would ask about the jewellery and even that box with the war stuff in it. Surely, the DS didn't think he'd sold all of that and spent all that money as well? He almost reacted with a smart answer but caught himself just in time and decided to keep his mouth shut, his eyes away from the DS, and continue to get dressed. He was thrown by the behaviour of the two detectives who appeared to be quite happy and satisfied. He expected a sudden fury to erupt from the DS, a slap to his head, shouting in his ear, maybe a push on to the bed before his room was torn apart in a search. He tried to keep a distance but couldn't due to the cramped space. He winced when from the corner of his vision he saw the DS suddenly turn, expecting a blow in the next second but nothing happened. He continued to get dressed as DS Harrison took a cursory look through his wardrobe and drawers but nothing was said.

During this time DC Watts had moved from the bedroom and carried out a visual search of the flat,. He didn't dirty his hands by touching anything, even though both he and DS Harrison had taken a pair of plastic gloves with them.

Brooks was aware that his nerves showed in his shaking hands and his state wasn't helped when he was told that he couldn't smoke, though it wasn't so much the fact that he wasn't allowed to smoke but being told so in an apologetic tone. He decided to just do whatever he was told and offer no resistance or cheeky backchat.

The three travelled down in the lift with Brooks' hands handcuffed behind his back. No one spoke either then or during the ten minutes it took to drive to the Central Custody Suite on an industrial estate north of Brighton near the A27 motorway.

Some older officers with blinkered views thought the system of Central Custody Suites had been introduced as another way of saving money, with prisoners from around an area all being taken to one location where they could be processed.

Others knew that they had been introduced to safeguard the police from false allegations and ensure that they complied correctly to all aspects of the Police and Criminal Act 1984 regarding the conduct of handling prisoners.

DS Harrison stood next to Brooks in front of the raised dais behind which sat the duty custody sergeant. He gave Brooks' details of name address and the reason for his arrest: 'At about eleven fifteen on the fourth of March, on Kings Road, Brighton, on the seafront, I suspect this man, Aaron Brooks, robbed a man named Peter Dobbs, by pushing him to the ground and stealing Mr Dobbs' wallet from his back pocket. At the time of his arrest I cautioned him, to which he gave no answer. I then asked him if he had any of the money left and he indicated his trousers in the back pocket of which I found a ten-pound note.'

The desk sergeant wrote down DS Harrison's words on the front of a large form and without looking up asked: 'Is that all correct?'

Brooks looked quizzically at Harrison and said, 'Nah, I didn't do it.'

'Right,' said the desk officer. 'Is what DS Harrison said right. He told you why you were being arrested, he cautioned you and he found the money in your trouser pocket? Is that right? I'm not bothered whether you are admitting the crime or not, that is for the investigating officers to prove or otherwise; I am only interested in procedures.'

Brooks looked and was genuinely confused by the turn of events. He had been arrested for an offence he didn't commit and he could prove it – only he would have to say where he was.

Brooks elected to say nothing further and also declined the duty solicitor or any person to be informed of where he was being detained. He wanted to get into a cell for a few minutes to put together what was happening; his head couldn't make it out.

Brown, the duty solicitor, was adept at grasping the facts of a case and taking instructions from clients quickly, such that in a morning he could have up to nine clients appearing at different courts. Sometimes it was just a case of giving a client's apologies to the magistrates together with some heart-rending account of what had driven his client to act out of their usual law-abiding character.

After the lawyer from the Crown Prosecution Service had given an account of the offence – the first time that Brooks had heard all the detail apart from the interview with DS Harrison – Brown rose to speak on his client's behalf. He was aware, as were the magistrates, of Brook's previous convictions for similar offences and had warned Brooks that almost certainly the magistrates would remand him in custody to be sentenced by a judge sitting in a Crown Court. Brooks had already resigned himself to this but in fact he didn't really care; he wanted to get started on the sentence so he could finish it and then he would sell the jewellery when the heat had died down. The magistrates duly remanded Brooks in custody for sentencing and he returned to the cells under the court building feeling quite happy. The only request he had when visited by Richard Brown was for his mother to be told about his arrest and the result, though he didn't think she would care very much anyway, in fact probably not at all.

Over the following three weeks Carter persisted in telephoning DS Harrison every other day, some calls encouraging greater effort and a few beginning to sound more threatening with reminders of what Carter had done for DS Harrison in the past. The threats weren't direct or crude, just reminders of how Terry and his wife had enjoyed a lovely holiday in Crete thanks to Carter, and the clothes, and the meals. The message was not lost on DS Harrison who in his own way increased the pressure on DS Southall and his detective constable for a breakthrough or anything which could be interpreted as one. In fact, the leads such as they ever were had gone very cold; none of the jewellery or foreign money had surfaced or even been talked about among the criminal fraternity. Carter had expected that the combined pressure of the police overtly trying to detect the crime and his more unorthodox and covert methods would have at least brought some rat to the surface. The rewards Carter had offered had gradually increased and the circulation of these offers among the second-hand dealers and low life had been extensive.

He explained all this to Sir Roger while they were in Sir Roger's greenhouse. Sir Roger listened as he tended his collection of fuchsias preparing them for summer. Carter was standing by the doorway with his hands deep in his overcoat pockets as he watched Sir Roger carefully concentrating on each plant.

'Do you know anything about fuchsias?' asked Sir Roger without looking up and gently moving the plant he was inspecting in a slow circle as he examined each shoot and firmed up the compost.

'No, never really got into growing plants; my wife tends to look after the flowers,' replied Carter lightly.

'Ah, I remember you saying that before. These plants are my favourites; they can be shrubs or small trees. The first, *Fuchsia triphylla*, was discovered on the Caribbean island of Hispaniola – that is what we know these days as Dominica and Haiti – in 1703 by a French man, Monsieur Plumier. There are over one hundred different species, you know...' He paused as he looked at the shelves stacked with brown pots many of which appeared to have just some twigs sitting in them. 'I've got thirty-odd...'

Sir Roger as always tried to show little emotion and hid the frustration he felt. Mary had recovered from the incident well and had regained her usual confident and outgoing personality; the subject was seldom spoken of between the two. The insurance company had paid in full for the jewellery and the declared value of cash Sir Roger had claimed for as being stolen. While he had made mention of the box file he had stated the contents as personal papers and of no value. The police had been in touch with him and Mary several times, the last to say that they had made all the enquiries they could and that at this time the investigation would have to be put to one side pending any further developments.

'So', said Sir Roger, 'it boils down to the simple fact that Mary and I were robbed and, despite all the combined efforts of the police and you, not one item has been recovered and there is nothing to identify the bastard except for the description that Mary was able to provide. Nothing, zilch, absolutely not one shred of hope, is that right?' His voice was even-toned and didn't carry any menace or threat, but there was an edge of firmness about it that Carter quickly picked up on.

Sir Roger turned to watch Carter and was aware of the other man's unease. Sir Roger had always been well served by Carter and couldn't understand how it was that an unplanned crime could yield no clues or leads despite the combined best efforts of the police and Carter.

Carter found it difficult to look Sir Roger in the eyes as he just nodded his agreement and mumbled, 'Yes, we can't believe it. Just about every crime of this type is committed by an opportunist; they seek and grasp an opening. There is little or no planning because they don't know what they are going to do or to whom. So, he's got away with cash and jewellery, all right. He's going to spend the cash first, probably the English before the foreign, but nobody has talked of any low life suddenly coming into money or spending it around the city's bars. Maybe he'd spend it on drugs, but still word would have got out and I am sure I would have heard. Then there's the jewellery, but again nothing's surfaced. It just doesn't make any sense. OK, the box, why take it in the first place? Sir Roger, you haven't told me about its contents, but the question we have to ask is: did he look in it?' His voice trailed away as he realised that Sir Roger's recollection of that time was still missing.

Sir Roger stopped what he was doing. 'I really don't want to tell you what's in the box; it's very personal, nothing to do with Mary and I should have just destroyed it many, many years ago. Anyway I just want you to keep the pressure on. I know' – Sir Roger raised his hand and smiled – 'I know the chances are slim, but let's just keep going. Not full time, but maybe if you persevere – who knows? – something might happen.'

Carter nodded his agreement before the two men went on to discuss other security matters.

7

The rattling keys and sharp barked orders worked their way towards Brooks who was awake and waiting for his turn. As he lay there he heard his cell mate turn over on the bunk above, making the whole bed structure move an inch to one side before settling back again. A loud clunk as the key was put into his cell door was followed by a clink, as the lock was undone. Simultaneously the door was flung open, crashing on to the side of the bunk edge, again causing the frame to move.

'Up, gentlemen, if you please. Breakfast will be served in the dining hall in just twenty minutes. A full menu available as always,' chuckled Prison Officer Williams as he moved on to the next cell. 'Every bloody day the idiot says the bloody same, "Up, gentlemen, if you please,"' mimicked the Geordie trying to impersonate Williams' broad Glaswegian accent. 'As if we have any bloody choice! Breakfast, I'd love to ram that shite he calls breakfast down his bloody throat.'

Brooks laughed from the bottom bunk. 'You know, you always say the same as well! "Love to ram that shite down his bloody throat."' Brooks heard a light laugh coming from above and saw a pair of hairy and strongly muscled legs appear.

In one movement Steven Sheen landed squarely on the balls of his feet on the concrete floor, the adroitness belying his fourteen stone. He wore only his boxer shorts and pushed the door to allow him to reach the washbasin that was in the small space at the bottom of the bed. The cell was ten feet long and eight feet wide, which meant that it was easier if only one of the two who shared this space was moving at once. The routine had built up over the two weeks since

Brooks had been moved in with Sheen. Sheen's physical build had initially intimidated Brooks but he soon learned that Sheen's aggression was reserved for his time in the gym or when he was practising one of his favourite sports, Thai boxing. Sheen had been in prison for four years and was nearing the halfway stage of his sentence, which meant that parole and release were due, provided he didn't blot his copybook, that was. Over the long hours that he and Brooks had lain on their bunks or sat on the wooden chairs at the small table opposite their bunk, they had got to know each other as well as most do in similar constricted confines, but in reality Sheen had learned little of the offence for which his cell mate had been sentenced to six months' imprisonment. Brooks had said little, as within the hierarchy of prison life, his crime and punishment were on the small scale. In any case, he didn't want to draw attention to himself, so he kept his head and voice down and avoided areas where the landing and wing gangs congregated during free association time.

After washing and shaving himself Brooks had to dress quickly to catch up with Sheen and be ready for the bell that signalled the prisoners could leave their cells and make their way down the landings to the dining hall. At the sound of the bell there was a marked rise in the level of voices as doors opened and men started to file out of their cells. Brooks followed Sheen and joined the throng along the landing. As they were on the third floor they accepted that they would always be last in the queue for the meals.

The routine followed day after day, week after week and month after month. The prisoners either fitted into the system or challenged it whether by railing against prison officers and fellow prisoners or deliberately flouting the rules. Sheen was not one to be seen to be a problem to anybody, especially with his imminent release, and was happy to just go along with what the system demanded of him.

The routine for both men after breakfast differed as Brooks

59

went to the sewing room where he joined others in the boring but historically famous sewing of mailbags. This was a small team as most of the postbags used now were made of plastic in the Far East by persons who earned even less than the prisoners in Lewes Prison. Sheen made his way to the offices where he had worked for the past two years, using his good manners and brains to avoid the mind-numbing experience of working with other lags in the various workshops. He showed respect to all the staff, even though some of them treated him like something caught on the sole of the shoes. He had worked his way up from cleaning the offices to being a general dog's-body refilling photocopiers with paper or ink cartridges, moving furniture or files, or any manner of other menial jobs.

Although he had a neck the size of other men's thighs and arms, his clean-shaven face and ready smile made him unthreatening to the women who made up most of the office staff. His hair was black and cropped, he had no piercings or tattoos and he wore his prison-issue blue shirt buttoned to one below the collar. His black shoes were always polished as smartly as his blue prison-issue trousers were pressed, following the Army method of laying the trousers beneath the bed mattress. He took care of how others saw him and knew that the less of a threat he presented and the more keen he appeared to please, the more likely he would get a good report for the Parole Board. He was even left alone by the gangs who realised that he wasn't interested in joining them, and having witnessed his boxing in the gym there weren't any volunteers to provoke him into a fight.

Brooks had learned that Sheen was a Geordie through and through, tough and hard as were many from that part of England, but at the same time he was educated and streetwise enough to rise above the usual prison types. He didn't try to impress as he had no cause to and he was confident enough within himself to take or leave others as he wanted.

His account of how he had come to be in prison was as straightforward as the man himself. After leaving school with good examination results he had joined the Army with hopes of a long career enjoying the sport and camaraderie of friends. That had ended when he became disillusioned with his Army bosses and particularly with the politicians who insisted on sending him and his friends to fight wars that the English public had little time for or gave support to. He had resigned as a full Warrant Officer and returned to his native city to work as a fitness instructor during the day, and at weekends as a doorman at the clubs in the notorious Bigg Market area of Newcastle. For six months he had enjoyed the life and money that he was able to save towards a small flat in the city centre. One of the perks of his job that he received from some of his regular daytime female clients was the extra-special, private and personal training that he gave when their husbands were not around. One woman had made it clear that her interest in him lay in bedroom physical action as opposed to gym sweat, but that same evening had revealed all to her husband as a way of repaying him for his own infidelities. The hard-headed businessman had then used that betrayal as evidence towards his divorce, citing Sheen and making him a pariah among the fitness instructor community. Sheen's work had dried up overnight and from thereon in he had drifted in a downward spiral until he had been offered a job as part of a debt-collecting team whose methods might be best described as unscrupulous. The television and newspaper exposure of the company he worked for together with the subsequent police investigation had led to every one of the twelve employees being brought before the courts. It was he and his colleague Jimmy 'Toon' Elder who had drawn the most bile from the media, in part because of their brawny looks, and Sheen had ended up being sent down for eight years.

It was while Brooks and the other five in his team were

having a smoke during their afternoon tea break that the subject of 'getting wasted' was raised. Brooks knew that alcohol was a prime commodity within the prison but he had never seen or heard of it first hand during his time. Tobacco, any drug and more recently phone cards were common trade and all were easily available, though at a price. Brooks had no visitors and no one to telephone and he soon found that he had something to trade with, his phone card that he could buy as a result of his sewing wages. As he didn't use his card and he could obtain two a week, he knew that he had a commodity to trade with. He was told that in exchange for the four phone cards he had he would receive a cup of home hooch, a concoction made from the finest ingredients that could be found in the kitchen, including the potato peelings and all manner of scraps. This brew wasn't a cheap one containing liquid fuel from the boiler room or additives from used ink cartridges and, after initially thinking it was a con, he was persuaded to take some.

That evening during the free recreation period he had been escorted to a cell on the mid landing where behind the closed door he was given a cup of clear liquid to drink. After the initial burn at the back of the throat he enjoyed the heat as it travelled into his stomach, though there wasn't any discernable flavour. It was shortly after finishing his drink that Brooks returned to his cell, just as the buzz in his head started to make him feel giddy as the alcohol began to take effect. Sheen was sitting at the cell table reading another Stephen Leather thriller when Brooks walked unsteadily into the cell. Sheen had seen the effects of hooch all too often and showed concern as he helped Brooks on to his bunk where he lay fully clothed until lockdown some fifteen minutes later. Sheen checked on Brooks periodically to ensure that the eyes were still showing signs of life, even though Brooks' speech was slurred.

Sheen was confident that they wouldn't be disturbed and

his parole wouldn't be jeopardised by Brooks' condition, so he took the opportunity to have some fun with the youngster.

'So come on, Aaron mate, what is the score with you? You've never said anything to me about yourself or what you are in for. What's the matter? Don't you like or trust me?'

Brooks moved his eyes towards the figure of Sheen who had moved his chair to be next to the bunk and sat leaning over him. Sheen was smiling as he talked, his voice sounding gentle and caring.

Brooks responded with a smile. 'Course I trust you, and yeah, you are a real mate to me. You've shown me the ropes an' all ... really helped me here.' He waved his arm in a general all-encompassing way. 'Really, really helped me.'

Sheen could hear that the slurring in Brooks' speech was getting more pronounced and could tell by the state of his eyes that he was heading for a major hangover in the morning. He had seen it all too often working on the doors of nightclubs in Bigg Market. He knew Brooks would be close to passing out once the full extent of the alcohol raced into his blood and that in the morning he would have to help him get ready for the unlock.

'Got to hand it to you, Aaron, you are a quiet one. How did you pay for this stuff?'

'Phone cards, four!' Brooks laughed

'To Eddy's guys?'

'Yeah, the bald one; Charlie, isn't it? Got sorted out really good.' He slurred as his head rolled from side to side. 'Not had such a hit since I did a few good lines of quality coke a while ago in Brighton... Wow, what a hit that stuff is,' he rambled. 'This is really good, away, up and away, starting to fly.'

Brooks was lying on his back with his head on his pillow rolling from one side to the other at the same time as his eyes fought to stay open.

'OK, mate, I'll be here to make sure you're all right. You just fly away,' said Sheen laughing.

For a minute there was nothing said by either as Brooks smiled and slowly waved an arm about in an arc while Sheen watched on.

'Do you know, I'm in here for something I didn't do,' slurred Brooks, trying to focus on Sheen.

'Everyone is in here for things they didn't do, mate; well, not that people are going to admit to anyway,' replied Sheen, who was becoming bored with trying to talk to Brooks.

'No, really, really I am, honestly. I didn't know anything about the job I was supposed to have done, it was a fit-up and they think they have won, but they haven't.' He suddenly laughed loudly and half rose on to one arm as he tried to focus on Sheen, 'The stupid lying useless bastards think they were clever getting me for that job, but if only they knew.' He laughed and fell back on to his back, putting his hands over his eyes as if to shield them from the single bulb that was encased in the ceiling fabric.

'Why did they fit you up?' Sheen said, becoming alarmed at how loud Brooks was laughing and worrying it might attract attention from the wing prison officer.

Brooks took his hands away from his eyes and wiped a tear that had formed. His laughing was quieter as he said, ''Cause what I've done before, like to rob people on their way home, just knock into them and nick their wallet or handbag, stuff like that. Only this time I wasn't there; I had moved to another area and was doing something new and that was a real earner. So they nicked me for that job and never found out about the job I was doing at the same time miles away.' He was convulsed with laughter, though the sound wasn't as loud as before.

Suddenly Sheen began to warm to his subject; this was getting interesting. Tales of woe were commonly exchanged among the lags as a way of bragging or 'bigging' themselves, and usually they were boring and transparent lies. This, though, was different; there was something about what he was saying and how he was saying it.

'So what was the job you did then?'

'Changed my habits. 'Stead of drunks in town, I thought of the people who live in the big houses outside. Not a village or something, but on the edge of town. Thought I could get one of them as they got home, might have more on them and anyway it takes the coppers much longer to get there. Anyway, I live about halfway so I could run home pretty quick, and it's all downhill.' His laughing turned to a bout of giggling.

'So, clever, very clever, you go to a new area and change what you do. Clever, but was it better?'

Brooks kept his eyes open, though they weren't able to focus on Sheen.

'Christ was it ever! You wouldn't believe it, loaded, just loaded. Still, can't believe it and they are looking for the bloke who done that with me in here, that couldn't have done it, as I am guilty of the other job, aren't I?' He laughed again.

Sheen laughed and together they spent the next minute rolling around until both had tears in their eyes. Sheen was the first to compose himself.

'So what happened then?'

Brooks slowed his laughing but retained a wide smile as he looked at Sheen.

'Saw a Roller, old guy driving and missus half asleep turn towards a big house. I mean a big house, you know, electric gates that opened as he got there, really big place. Anyway I'm off like a shot after them and just squeeze in the bloody gates as they close. The missus opened the door and the old guy locked the car then followed her and I'm just behind him and hear the alarm bleeping, then it stopped so I just ran in, pushing the guy to the floor. Well, the missus is stunned and takes me upstairs ... no, not for a shag...' Brooks broke down laughing and saw that Sheen appreciated the joke as well. 'No, not a shag, though I've 'ad worse, but she just opens the safe and there's all this jewellery in there. We 'ad a little set-to as I was going, but I legged it downstairs.'

Brooks stopped talking and a puzzled look spread over his face, all traces of laughter had stopped. 'Never have worked out about that old guy, though,' he paused. 'I mean I was happy and just getting out of it, then he says, "What about the safe in there?" and I'm like, what? And the guy just gets up and takes me into his office-type place with a desk and everything. I mean, at first I didn't know what he was doing, then I thought it was a trick. He went into the desk, a drawer and when he put his hand in I thought, "Oh shit, he's got a gun," and I was just about to leg it when he comes out with a key. Then he moves a picture on the wall and behind it is a safe. He just opened it, just opened the safe.' Brooks laughed a little but had a concerned frown on his face.

'What happened?' said Sheen, adding a slight concern to his voice to match the atmosphere that Brooks had created.

'He just sat down and I looked in there and, shit, you wouldn't believe it – stacks of cash, I mean, like three inches or so high, two of them. One was foreign, don't know what it's worth, but it's got some big notes in there, mostly hundreds of those euro things, some fifties as well... Not touched them, just got them hidden for the future. Maybe they'll be worth more when I get out.'

Brooks and Sheen laughed loudly.

'Anyway,' Brooks continued, 'the English notes were over ten grand, over ten grand, and I didn't even ask him for this shit; I mean, I didn't know it was there. You know what I mean?' He looked at Sheen who nodded in agreement.

'There was papers there, just chucked them on the floor and was going when at the back I saw a box, like one they use in offices to keep things in, about so big.' He used his hands to indicate a box about twelve inches by ten inches, though his arms were so unsteady it was only a very rough approximate. 'Christ, there are some weird people about, what they keep in their houses. It's got war medals and stuff in there, all foreign, German I think and old, maybe from the war...' he added slowly as his voice slowed to match the speed of his affected brain.

'What sort of stuff?'

'Just saw medals and things then, looked later at home, papers, lots of them in German I think, not sure as I don't speak it...' Brooks laughed. '...Mean don't read it.' And he laughed again. 'Passports, I remember passports; foreign ones have got fingerprints in as well. Don't trust a photo, them lot, do they? Or does it mean they're all criminals?'

Brooks laughed at his own joke for several seconds, wiping his eyes and nose with the sleeve of his shirt at the same time.

Sheen nodded, not wishing to say anything in case he spoilt the flow. His mind was intrigued by the revelations and he was also wondering if there could be some advantage for him. As an old soldier, he knew the value in war memorabilia – world war mementos could fetch a good price at the right dealer.

'So what sort of stuff, you said medals and passports and other papers?'

'Yeah all sorts, lots of papers; I mean the box is full. I don't know what it is really, just old stuff. Could almost be history, I suppose, but I didn't spend long looking at it.'

Sheen looked at Brooks and was amazed at how quickly he appeared to have recovered from the effect of the hooch he had drunk, though Brooks eyes were very dilated and having difficulty focusing.

'Will it be safe? You know, won't it be found and then you'd be right in it. Just think, if it is found when you're in here, then they'll know you did that job and not the usual one that they put you in here for?'

Brooks shook his head from side to side and his eyes stared unfocused at the off-white ceiling. Suddenly his head lolled to one side, his eyes staring vacantly towards the wall behind Sheen. He was getting worse, thought Sheen, as he saw Brooks struggling to fight off sleep.

'Won't find it, cos I hid it really good, really good. I mean even if all the furniture was taken out they still wouldn't find it.' He gave a quiet laugh as his eyes closed.

Sheen reached and gently shook Brooks' arm. 'Can't be that well hidden!'

Brooks moved his head towards Sheen but his eyes disappeared into their lids.

Again, Sheen shook Brooks' arm and, on getting little response, shook him harder until again his eyes opened.

'Where is the hiding place, Aaron?' asked Sheen quietly.

Brooks appeared to be on the verge of falling asleep so Sheen shook him harder while keeping a smile on his face. His voice changed to a harder tone as he repeated: 'Where is this hiding place then, Aaron?'

Brooks stirred. 'Under the cupboard, under the carpet,' he mumbled, the words running into each other.

Sheen was now very close to Brooks and he could smell the sweet acidic tang from the drink. It made him feel like retching. '*What* cupboard, Aaron? *What* room?'

'Main room...' The words were barely audible now. 'Got to pull the middle one out, never find it,' he slurred again, and again his voice trailed off almost as if it were his dying breath.

'Look, mate, how about I sell the war stuff and we go fifty-fifty? I know a bit about old war stuff and could get a much better price than you. There is a site on the Internet that I can use to research people and medals and things; we can sell them with a known history. We'd get a lot more than at a shop where they'll just rip you off then take a good profit for themselves. You see, the collectors want to put history together and they want to create the story as it was, and believe me, they will pay for something that is good. Fifty, fifty – how about it?'

'K, good' was all the response from Brooks whose voice was now barely audible.

Sheen tried to ask Brooks further questions but there wasn't any response other than the heavy breathing of a man who was dropping into a very deep sleep. Sheen debated whether to undress Brooks a little or move him from where he was lying on his back but decided to leave him alone.

As Brooks drifted further into sleep, Sheen got himself ready for bed all the time thinking that he could be out in less than a week and could get started on the research. He knew of others who had sold World War Two memorabilia via eBay and he could certainly do the research himself, which he would enjoy. As he lay on the top bunk he was lost in thought and barely recognised the automatic turning off of the lights at 10 p.m.

Sheen lay awake for some hours before drifting off to sleep, only to be woken by the sound of heavy boots running on the landing outside the cell. He became aware of raised voices, then shouts followed by more boots pounding outside and on the metal staircase linking the floors above ground level. He looked at his watch and saw that it was already unlocking time and that it would be the ever-cheerful or wind-up Williams who would be unlocking again today as part of his three-day shift pattern. But the sounds were not of him going about his usual routine. There was a sense of urgency in the shouting and the speed of people running, their boots clanging on the metal landing. He heard the words 'Quickly!' and 'Now!' among the ever-increasing noise. Shouts were also coming from the prisoners, adding to the overall chaos that appeared to be happening outside.

Sheen leaned over to look at Brooks, who was still dressed. He could only see Brooks' back – his shirt was out of his trousers and there was a wet mark around the seat; the bed looked wet in the same area.

Sheen smiled – he had seen it many times before when a

soldier had drunk too much and slept so deeply in an alcohol-induced unconsciousness that they had lost control of their bladder.

The noise outside was getting louder. There were raised and urgent voices. Sheen wondered what had happened and hoped that it was something dramatic that would liven up the day for him. He wondered if there had been some sort of breakout during the night. He hadn't been in a prison where an actual breakout had happened, though prisoners allowed home on leave frequently failed to return on time. The rattling of keys got closer and he heard the cell next door being unlocked before urgent voices were raised. Seconds later the keys were thrust into his cell door lock. The door flew back harder than usual banging into the bunk.

'Sheen, Brooks, you OK?' shouted Prison Officer Williams. Williams looked up at Sheen then at Brooks and seeing no response he rushed towards the still figure.

'Brooks!' Prison Officer Williams shouted as he reached him. Saw the wet patch on the bed and had already registered the smell of stale urine, though that by itself was not too unusual a smell in a cell.

Williams pushed Brooks' head, 'Brooks!' he yelled.

No response.

'Oh hell!' he said before turning and rushing to the doorway and shouting, 'Another one here, Medic, cell Charlie 26!'

Williams returned to Brooks and pulled him roughly to lay him on his other side so that his face looked into the cell and towards him. Williams used his forefinger to prise open Brooks' left eyelid and then repeated the process with the right lid.

'Christ!' he said as he looked up at Sheen, who by now was sitting up on his bunk and about to swing to the ground.

'Stay where you are, Sheen,' yelled Williams. 'Get your legs back up and just stay there. Medics will be here in a minute to look at Brooks, but you just stay there until they come.'

Williams left the cell and turned to the right and Sheen could hear him opening the cell next door and shouting out the names of the two occupants.

Just then two prison officers wearing white unbuttoned coats over their prison uniforms ran into the cell carrying a small suitcase showing a large red cross on a white background.

They went to Brooks, and Sheen peered over the top of his bunk to watch as the two medics leant over, consciously trying to shield what they were doing from him. Sheen shifted his position slightly and saw one medic lift the eyelids; even from his position Sheen could see there was no iris at all. The other medic put his fingers to the side of Brooks neck to see whether there was any pulse but from the look they gave each other it was apparent to Sheen that Brooks was dead. They stood and the older of the two, an officer whom Sheen had not seen before, went to the doorway where he used a hand-held radio to talk to the control room.

While he was talking the other medic faced Sheen. 'Did Brooks take anything last night?'

Sheen tried to give a blank face. 'What do you mean, Officer. How is he? Is he ill or something?'

'Don't be bloody funny with me! Did he take anything last night, pills or something else?' said the medic, staring and boring his eyes into Sheen as he searched for the tell-tale sign of a lie.

'Not in here, no,' said Sheen defensively. 'I wouldn't have allowed him. I'm not having my parole buggered up. As far as I know he isn't into drugs, not in here anyway, but don't know what he did on the outside. I'm sure there's nothing in here. What's going on, how is he, why aren't you doing something for him?'

'There's nothing we can do for him – he's dead. There are others, too, and we want to find out what he's taken, so I suggest that, as you're his bloody cell mate and you are looking for parole, you'd better think bloody carefully about what he took, because it wasn't the bloody fish that he had for dinner that killed him.'

Sheen pointed to the bottom shelf above the table and said, 'That's his stuff there, not much and there's little else of his in here, just some stuff that he keeps on the floor under the sink.'

The other medic walked back into the cell with another prison officer whom Sheen knew as Officer Vanguard, a young, lean and very keen officer who did everything by the letter of the manual. As the medics left, Vanguard walked towards Sheen and said in a confident tone: 'Right, you are going to stay there until we get the investigation underway and I am going to sit here to watch you. I suggest you lie back and think about your answers to the CID because this will be a murder investigation.'

'Right sir, OK. I'm just stunned about this. He was a good kid, just got lost, I'm really sorry. The medic said that there were others. What did he mean by others? Not more dead, for Christ's sake?'

'You'll know soon enough what the score is but...'

He stopped talking as a loud shout instantly recognisable as belonging to Prison Officer Williams echoed down the wing announcing that medics were required quickly at cell Charlie 40, which Sheen knew was the last in the wing and was occupied by two young Asian men who were strong followers of Islam. They could always be seen each carrying a copy of the Koran from which they would often quote for the benefit of prison officers if they were being told to do something they didn't want to or wanted to get something special for themselves.

Sheen and Prison Officer Vanguard looked at each other, but nothing was said and Sheen knew that he would gain nothing from asking questions, so decided that the best thing was to lie back and wait for the questioning that would follow later that morning. He had meant what he had said about Brooks; Sheen had been genuinely quite fond of him. Brooks didn't do anything to upset him. He was just a kid who like most in there had had a bit of a hard time, had taken the gamble that crime would pay and found out that this was frequently not the case.

Sheen was worried about the effect Brooks' death would have on him. The death of a cell mate was always going to lead to suspicion of foul play, which left him having to consider what his own account of the evening should be. He reached a decision that he would say he was tired and was just about asleep when Brooks came into the cell. He had feigned sleep so that he wouldn't have to talk to Brooks and had heard Brooks get on to his bunk before all went quiet. Sheen would say that he slept all night and was totally unaware of what Brooks had done during the evening or night. He would answer any and all questions and try his most open face and smile to convince his interrogators that he was telling the truth.

What Sheen was unaware of was that a total of five prisoners had been found dead that morning and a further three were so seriously ill that they were transferred to the Royal Sussex County Hospital in Brighton for emergency treatment. The Sussex Police Major Crime Unit had been informed and Detective Superintendent Dave Wordsley had been appointed as the senior investigating officer. He was a detective with over twenty-eight years' service whose career had taken him to different departments within the criminal investigation world. Known and respected among his colleagues as a hard-working and very thorough investigator, he had received the call while travelling from his home in Horsham to work in Brighton.

He had continued to Sussex House to meet with several members of his team who had also received the call and to check that all the pre-planned administrative measures were in place. The Major Incident Suite was one of three available to the Force at Sussex House and all the dedicated staff were already in position. He knew his deputy senior investigating officer, Detective Inspector Andy Gowen, from several enquiries in the past. They had worked together well and each knew what the other wanted. It was always important that the two leaders got on well as individuals and had personalities that complemented each other so that the whole team could see the leadership was strong.

Andy Gowen was in some ways almost the opposite from his boss, slighter build with a full head of black hair and a soft Welsh accent. He dressed more smartly than his more senior officer, though not in an extravagant or flamboyant manner, but in well-fitting dark suits.

After their initial meeting Dave Wordsley left Andy Gowen to finalise the team and organise the initial actions, to call out the crime scene investigators and sufficient officers to maintain the integrity of at least five separate crime scenes. While he drove to Lewes Prison to meet the uniformed officers and the prison staff he had much to occupy his mind.

As lunchtime approached there was growing unrest within the wing with shouts from the locked-down prisoners, the exception being the cells where the dead bodies lay and where the live cell mates remained under guard. This had been on the instructions of Dave Wordsley who wanted the Home Office pathologist and crime scene investigators to begin their analysis of each cell before persons were moved in or out. Sheen was resigned to what was happening and the delay, content to lie on his bunk and allow time to pass. Killing time was nothing new. He'd spent hours in the Army waiting for senior officers to make up their minds, or being punished by a sergeant on the drill square. It also gave him time to collect all his thoughts.

The next week passed in a surreal way for Sheen. All the

prisoners in the wing had been locked up for up to twenty-three hours each day and many had been moved, as he had, to a new cell.

Sheen had seen his new cell mate Jamie Green at recreation times over the past few months but had instantly mistrusted him, believing him to be a wheeler-dealer wanting to know everyone's business. Green was older than many on the wing, in his fifties and of thin build, with a long thin face that could have been described as scrawny, his dark sunken eyes and thin greying hair accentuating the paleness of his skin. His gaze always moved in a conspiratorial way. Sheen didn't know if Green was an informant or not, and was not prepared to find out, deciding that to not talk to him at all was the best policy.

Sheen had been interviewed and given the account he had decided upon. He had been surprised at the low level of questioning by the detectives who appeared to accept what he said as the truth, but then, who could contradict his words? The police investigation had centred on a find in the kitchen – bottles of a clear liquid that tests showed to be poisonous – and a cell in which quantities of cigarettes, mobile phones and phone cards were found. Several prisoners whom Sheen knew had been involved in the supply of the deadly drink were removed from the wing.

He was surprised, though, that so shortly after the deaths he was back working in the offices, but he got on with his tasks in the same pleasant manner. The staff, of course, knew that he had been a cell mate of one of those who had died and a couple of the women who had a soft spot for Sheen expressed their sorrow at what had happened. Sheen took advantage one lunchtime, when a fifty-plus-year-old female supervisor in the finance department approached him while he was cleaning up a spillage at the office coffee machine. The office was almost empty as most of the staff had gone to lunch; as the rules clearly stated, at least one person had to remain in the office at all times. The woman whom he knew as Miss Cambridge had spoken to him on several occasions when Sheen had cheerfully completed whatever job he had been asked to do and he had always made a point of being polite and respectful to her.

Miss Cambridge watched as Sheen finished wiping the coffee from the linoleum-tiled floor. He dried the whole area carefully, aware that he was being watched. He turned to see Miss Cambridge smiling at him.

'Thank you, Sheen. As always you've done the job well. I think most prisoners would have just smeared the area with water and left the floor wet, waiting for someone to slip on it.' She laughed a little and Sheen gave a smile.

'Why would I want anyone to hurt themselves? You are all very nice people in here and I like trying to help you in my little way.'

'Well,' Miss Cambridge replied, 'you are different from many that we have had in here in the past, that's for sure – everyone says so.'

'I wasn't always a bad boy, Miss Cambridge. What I did was wrong, I fully accept that and realise the debt to society that I have to repay. This has been a real experience for me. I was so sorry when Aaron died... You know Aaron Brooks?' He paused while Miss Cambridge gave him a sympathetic smile and nodded her head, before he continued hesitantly as if choking at the memory of his best friend. 'Aaron had made a few mistakes but we had talked a lot and we both had plans to work really hard at jobs when we finished our sentences. We thought we could support each other. In fact,' – Sheen slowed his speech and slightly lowered his eyes – 'in fact, he had told me I could stay with his mother in Brighton until he was released, but I know Aaron; I bet he didn't ask his mother ... before' – Sheen swallowed – 'before he died. Do you know, Miss Cambridge, Aaron didn't write to his mum or telephone her, not at all? And she hasn't visited. I wanted to write to her to let her know that Aaron was really a good guy at heart and that he loved her, all the things that she'd want to hear – after all, he was her son.'

Miss Cambridge nodded, She had not married or had any children, but had remained at home looking after her wheelchair-bound, frail mother, seeing her primary duty as towards her rather than her personal happiness. She had had a few relationships with men but none in the past thirty-two years. When she'd first started at the prison all those years ago she had received looks from the prisoners as well as staff and at times had quietly been excited by some of the fantasies she conjured in her mind at bedtime. As far as she dare, she even wore clothes that she knew would be provocative – skirts above the knee, blouses that showed cleavage. Now she was fifty-seven years, her clothing was distinctly middle age and her attitude had changed also; she was much more hardened towards the prisoners whom she regarded as capable of just about any trickery or lying if it meant them getting what they wanted. But Sheen was different, she thought. Unlike the others who would have held her gaze as if trying to persuade her of their sincerity, he looked at her, but not in a pleading manner.

'Well,' she said, 'I know there are many formalities that we have to go through but I think it would help Aaron's mother if she did hear from someone...' She hesitated before changing her words from 'like you' to 'a friend. 'Yes, from a friend who could offer her some comfort that Aaron had decided to put his past behind him. Why don't you write to her, give me the letter and I will make sure it is posted to her?' Miss Cambridge smiled at Sheen but didn't notice the ever so slight change in the size of his eyes as his mind registered disappointment that he wasn't going to be given Brooks' home address immediately.

'That would be great, Miss Cambridge, thanks very much. I'll write this afternoon and perhaps let you have the letter tomorrow if that is all right?' he replied brightly.

'That would be fine – I'll make sure that it is in the post tomorrow night. Who knows, Mrs Brooks may even reply to you.'

Sheen smiled at Miss Cambridge and then continued with his duties while Miss Cambridge returned to her desk and busied herself while thinking that she was helping someone who was genuinely trying to reform himself.

8

Sir Roger made a final check of himself in the bedroom full-length mirror, making a small adjustment to his black tie and checking the silk lapels of his dinner jacket for any signs of fluff or dandruff. He also looked through the reflection at Mary who was sitting at her dressing table near the window. She looked immaculate as usual, choosing a pale-blue full-length satin gown which was cut to show her slim waistline. Sir Roger glanced at his watch and noticed that it was seven twenty-five and at the same time saw the headlights of a car entering the driveway at the front of the house. Although he had been advised by Carter to always keep the main gates closed, Sir Roger had decided that he wasn't going to be intimidated by the robbery and was going to carry on as usual, leaving the gates open for the driver who was to collect them.

Sir Roger and Mary sat in the back of the Lexus as it was driven smoothly and efficiently to the seafront at Brighton and the distinguished red-bricked Metropole Hotel where the charity event was to be held. They were greeted in the large foyer by the rotund and happy organiser who escorted them into the grand dining room. The room had been arranged with round tables each seating twelve people with a long table raised on a platform at the front of the room where Sir Roger and Mary would join other notable and distinguished guests. A gathering of over two hundred and fifty people were already milling from the bar area towards their allocated table places as Sir Roger and Mary were shown to their places and presented with a cocktail. At these events when

Sir Roger was to give a speech he seldom drank any alcohol until after he had finished talking; he didn't need the 'Dutch spirit' that many speakers did. Unknown to his audiences, Mary had always contributed greatly to the writing of his speeches by making suggestions ranging from the subject matter, order of presentation and speed of delivery.

There was prolonged applause for Sir Roger as he finished his speech by announcing that his and Mary's personal foundation would be making a large contribution to kick off this year's donations. Mary thought the speech had been just about as perfect as was possible. As the applause slowed, Mary smiled at Sir Roger to show her approval and pride in his speech and also in him. Her love and devotion to him had always been clear, but neither she nor Sir Roger thought it appropriate to make a display of it in public; a smile and a wink was more than enough.

Mary thought that Sir Roger had fully recovered from their ordeal except for one thing that she couldn't just put her finger on. He appeared to be physically strong again and, though troubled about the break in his memory, that wasn't the issue; there was something else. This had started as a small germ when she had walked into his study and overheard part of a conversation Sir Roger had been having on the telephone with Carter. Usually Sir Roger would have just continued his conversation – secrets didn't happen between the two of them – but this time she had the feeling that he had changed the conversation just as he saw her. It was a fleeting feeling that she hadn't paid any real attention to, but since then he had twice closed his study door when he was on the telephone and on a recent visit from Carter the office door had remained shut during the whole of his stay...

She put her worries out of her mind as she watched people congratulate Sir Roger on his speech and thank him for his continuing support. Mary also became the subject of congratulations as people thanked her for all her sterling efforts and helping to keep Sir Roger, who was such a busy man, involved in the charity's activities. Afterwards they danced to a 1950-style swing band and for half an hour they felt like the happiest couple in the room.

It was only later that evening as they both lay in bed, exhausted from the evening, that Mary asked Sir Roger whether anything was troubling him.

'No, not at all. What on earth could be troubling me?'

'I don't know; it's just a feeling that I have,' said Mary as she snuggled closer.

Sir Roger moved his arm around Mary's shoulders and said quietly into her ear. 'Nothing could trouble me at all. I've the most wonderful wife, a lovely daughter, the business is booming and I have my health. Why could anything be wrong when my life is perfect.'

'Business, before your health?' said Mary in a sleepy tone. 'Wrong way round, my darling.'

Sir Roger gave a small chuckle and, having given Mary a peck on the cheek, turned over. For half an hour he didn't sleep.

9

Susan Brooks returned home from the cleaning job that she had continued to do after hearing of her son Aaron's death as a way of occupying her mind. She had been upset on hearing of his death during a visit from a uniformed police officer and accepted the offer of a visit from a prison support officer who had explained the circumstances of the death and of the procedures that had to be followed. In all her life she had never been interested in police television programmes or the newspaper articles concerning deaths and the procedures that happened after such an event. She preferred light entertainment, celebrities dancing, women talking about their lives, soaps whose characters were like her friends. She had no idea of what had to happen until she was led through the labyrinth of bureaucracy by the police family liaison officer and the prison support officer, step by step. It had almost shattered her. Now she felt just sad though not crying all and each day, but sad. She didn't regret not writing to him or visiting him in prison, that she hadn't given him any last words of love and support. She wasn't going to catch the two buses to Lewes to visit him. What would be the point? What would they say to each other? She had briefly thought about writing to him, but what would she say in a letter?

Tomorrow she would attend the crematorium. She would be collected at ten o'clock by the police family liaison officer. She hadn't contacted Aaron's friends to invite them; she didn't even know who they were or how they could be contacted. Anyway, news of Aaron's death had been in the local and national newspapers for some days, even on the main TV news. She had refused to talk to anyone from the media, telling the police family liaison officer that she just didn't want to get involved with 'all that sort of thing'.

She picked up a letter on the mat as she entered her flat. It was neatly hand-written in blue ink on a white envelope, which made a change from all the other letters she had received recently which had all been in brown envelopes with a typed white address label. It was only after making herself a cup of tea and settling down to watch the television that she remembered the letter, though. She tore open the envelope and immediately recognised the paper as being the type used by prisoners. Intrigued, she put her glasses on and noted that someone called Steve with a long prison number had sent it from Lewes Prison. As she read the letter slowly, she could feel, perhaps for the first time since hearing of Aaron's death, the beginning of a tear forming. This man Steve had written that Aaron and he had become friends and together they had decided that prison and crime were not the way of life that they wanted to live in the future. He said Aaron was at heart a decent youngster who perhaps had just gone along with others, following their lead and copying their lifestyles. The letter said that the two of them had talked for hours about what they would do when they were released and how they would support each other. Steve finished the letter by passing on his condolences and hoping that perhaps one day he could visit her, to tell her in person, face to face, what a good lad her son had been.

Susan used the sleeve of her blouse to dab at the edges of her eyes. She reread the letter again, then, as she drank her tea, thought about this person Steve who had signed his name at the bottom of the letter. His handwriting was neat and clear; that was in his favour. She looked at the envelope again and noted that the address had been written by someone else. It was all a bit of a mystery, really.

*   *   *

Sheen was standing at the back of a group of inmates watching the final moves of a chess game between the two finalists of the wing's chess competition. Everyone knew that Pete Thomas would again win; he always won; even starting without a bishop or knight, he would win. Other inmates were watching football on the widescreen television, shouting and abusing the players while others played an assortment of card, board or computer games. The general evening free time was a relaxed time when the prison officers made only infrequent visits on to the floor, preferring to watch either from the doorway or using the cameras that covered all the area.

As the final move was made and checkmate declared to a chorus of 'Well done!' and 'Jammy bastard!' Sheen noted that a warder standing at the doorway was beckoning him. The warder opened the door for Sheen and told him to go to the main wing office as the 'Super' wanted to see him.

Sheen knocked on the door and entered the office with a concern. Visits to the office were for serious matters, not as serious as a demand to visit the Governor, but still not a welcome invitation. He stood in front of the metal desk that was covered with stacks of brown folders each detailing the life story of a prisoner. Two mugs with brown stains near the rims and a telephone somehow managed to also fit on to the desk. 'Super' Prison Officer Thomas looked up at Sheen then reached for the folder on top of the pile. He opened it and read for a few seconds before closing it and replacing it on the pile. Only then did he speak.

'Sheen, your request for parole has been considered by the Board and in their wisdom they have decided to grant you early release pending all the usual formalities. Your interview will be tomorrow morning, ten o'clock sharp, so think about what you are going to do when you leave here. You will need an address to go to and you will be on probation for two years, so any foul-up by you in that time will mean an instant recall, do you understand?'

Sheen barely contained a smile as he replied as expected, 'Yes, Sir; thank you, Sir', before being dismissed and returned to the recreation area.

A beautiful sunny day beckoned in Brighton with the spring sun gaining strength and glistening off the sea and the green minarets of the Brighton Pavilion, but DS Harrison didn't pay any attention to how clean and bright everywhere looked; instead, he saw the start of summer as the time when tourists would arrive in their hundreds of thousands, causing more congestion to the already nightmarish traffic system and the crime rate to almost double. His mood darkened a little further when he saw the parking spaces near the front of the police station were all taken even though it was only half past seven.

'Bloody hell,' he muttered to himself as he set off to tour the streets to find a parking space. Today he had been quite lucky; only three streets away he waited while a woman had finished packing her children into her four-by-four then watched as she manoeuvred at least eight times to get out of her parking space. DS Harrison muttered under his breath still more when she looked back towards him to see whether there was any traffic coming. 'Bloody stupid tart; nothing's coming because you've blocked the sodding road with your bloody beast of a car,' he muttered before reversing straight into the space. This was one of the few roads that wasn't solely parking for residents, though he still checked the sign before he grabbed his briefcase and walked to the station.

After swiping his identity card he walked up the stairs to the CID offices on the first floor and made his way through the large open-plan office occupied by constables towards the glass-fronted offices at the back which was where he and the other three sergeants had their offices. The Detective Inspector had her office between the four sergeants' offices; it was almost like some sort of statement, he had thought when he first arrived after promotion. As he approached his office he heard the forever cheerful voice of Debbie Burrows, a detective constable of six years who was regarded by her peers as one of the best in the room. She had a style and manner, both in terms of her body language and speech, that almost confirmed the non-politically correct caricature of the blonde Essex girl. She was blonde and from Essex, but that was where the caricature comparison ended. She had very good listening skills and absorbed information like a sponge, thinking through the options before opening her mouth. Her sharp mind could recall facts from years ago and she barely, if ever forgot a face. In her time in the CID she had solved many cases that many of her male colleagues could never have but was not regarded as a boring non-stop workaholic. Indeed, her sense of fun meant that she was frequently at the forefront of any social happening and though single and available at the age of twenty-eight she had no constant boyfriend.

'Sorry,' said DS Harrison, 'didn't see you there, Debbie. How's it going? Don't tell me you've been here all night?' He smiled at her as he moved towards her desk that as always was covered in yellow Post-its and various green files.

'Nah, got a phone call from Jack on nights who said that the uniform guys had made a good nick and it would be worth me getting in earlier if I wanted to grab the prisoner. Here I am, and Jack was right – it was a good nick.'

'Go on then,' said DS Harrison, moving in and sitting at the next desk waiting for the story.

'Street robbery, just off the seafront. Gave the punter, a fifty-year-old man, a real shove in his back, knocked him into railings, cutting his face open, breaking his nose and some teeth. He's been to hospital and is downstairs now having his statement taken by the uniform lads. Had his wallet taken, usual thing; cash gone and wallet found in a basement in the next street. The uniform guys got to him quickly and, though he didn't see much of the attacker, he saw enough to give a quick description. Took him for a quick run around in the car, they would say, on the route to the hospital.' She laughed and DS Harrison grinned as he appreciated that the car trip was probably nothing like the quickest route to the hospital, more like a tour of the streets to see if the attacker could be identified.

'Anyway,' Debbie Burrows continued, 'seems that the man pointed out this guy, Dave Harding. The lads stopped Harding and checked him out. He tried to do a runner when he saw the victim in the back of the car and obviously knew the game was up. Anyway only made it a few steps, money in his pocket, rolled up, one hundred and ten quid, exactly what the victim said was in the wallet. And you won't believe it, the prat said there was only seventy quid ... Didn't know how much he had on him – what a loser! His brief will be at Sussex House at ten, so I'll interview Harding then. Let you know how it goes.'

DS Harrison noted that it had been a good arrest and he was pleased that the uniform guys had used their policing skills to catch the robber. After a few more minutes he sat in his office and became immersed in the mountain of papers that awaited his attention.

It was just after eleven o'clock when he received a call on his office telephone. It was Debbie Blower, who sounded a little subdued.

'Sarge, just interviewed this Dave Harding bloke and no problems with the robbery last night, had it all, in front of his brief et cetera et cetera. Gave a full story of what he did and it matches with the victim's account, so I'll check with the Can't Prosecute people and get their go-ahead for a robbery charge. He's living in a doss-house in Regency Square off the seafront, so I'll keep him in custody until the morning.'

DS Harrison was listening to Debbie Blower's account wondering why she sounded somewhat subdued after all a full confession. No room for retraction or denials later; all in all a good morning's work. He didn't feel the need to remind her that his address had to be searched and there were other routine enquiries he would know she would make, so he waited for her to continue.

'The thing is, he said he had done another job, just the same – pushed a guy in the back, in the same street, and got his wallet – but had made it back to Regency Square without being seen. Gave the date as about two and a half months ago. I've searched the system and can only find one job that fits what he says.'

DS Harrison suddenly felt his face redden and his heart beat faster as some sort of sickening wave washed over him. A feeling of dread. He felt his mouth go dry as he realised what Debbie Bowers was about to say. He didn't realise it but he was holding his breath as he gripped the receiver waiting for Debbie Bowers to continue.

And then there it was.

'It was a job that you dealt with. You got an arrest for it, someone called Aaron Brooks from the flats in Hollingdean Road. I've done a quick look at his form and he died in Lewes nick last month, one of six from that dodgy hooch job.'

'But ... but he coughed it, straight away, pleaded guilty, I'm sorry, Debbie, but your man must be trying it on.'

'Why? He didn't have to say anything. I just asked him if there were any other crimes he had committed that we could clear up now and have TIC'd.'

DS Harrison thought how they could get around the problem. It was the first time that he had encountered a prisoner admitting to an offence that had previously been cleared up by another. In the end, he advised Debbie to contact the Crown Prosecution Service and seek their advice.

Sheen had finished his breakfast and cleaned his cell in preparation for going to work. He was especially glad now that he wasn't working as a cleaner in the wings or off to a workshop doing boring carpentry work and listening to the never-ending speculation regarding the 'hooch' deaths. His job gave him a sense of normality and he wasn't going to mess it up.

When Sheen arrived at the offices he saw that the post had arrived and was waiting to be sorted into the various wire pigeonholes in the post room. This was a job that he did without being asked to if one of the junior girls hadn't already done it. As he sorted through the letters, he was joined by the new girl whose name badge gave her name as Fliss. They talked as they sorted the mail until, when the job was done, she returned to the main office, leaving him with the task of delivering the post to the Governor's office.

At 10 a.m. sharp he was marched into the parole office and stood making all the correct 'Yes, Sir' and 'No, Sir' replies at the right time as details of his parole were gone through, after which he returned to his duties.

As lunchtime approached, Sheen was carrying a tray of dirty mugs he had cleared from the desks when he was summoned to the Governor's office by his secretary who, as always, addressed him as though it was the hardest thing she had ever done in her life. He followed her and stood in the 'at ease' position with his hands behind his back in front of the Governor's desk. In just three minutes Sheen was told that the parole date was fixed for the next day, that his day's work was finished. He was to have a meeting with his wing prison officer, who would give him all the details he needed for his release. There had been the obligatory word of advice concerning life choices and the hope not to see him again before he was dismissed with a wave of the back of the Governor's hand.

Sheen was delighted at the news and could barely contain a smile as he walked through the offices on his way back to his wing. There he saw Miss Cambridge preparing to lay out her sandwiches. She always stayed in the office as the duty member of staff to eat her lunch while most of the women took the advantage of an hour to do some shopping in the High Street. Sheen approached her desk and told her his news. She didn't offer the same curt advice as the Governor, but in essence her words meant the same, and, unlike the Governor, she meant hers. Sheen was just about to shake her hand and thank her for her consideration towards him when he suddenly appeared to remember Aaron Brooks.

'Ah, Miss Cambridge, I haven't had any reply from Mrs Brooks – you remember, Aaron's mum, who I wrote to. I really wanted to look her up and actually tell her about Aaron, personally, you know?'

Miss Cambridge looked disappointed at the news as if she too had been let down by the lack of response from Mrs Brooks.

'I'm sorry, Sheen, I know it is a bit of a let-down. Your offer is very kind and I am sure she would have felt better had she met you; perhaps she is just hurting so much, you know, in such grief that she can't write yet. If she does, we will of course forward the letter on to you. We will have your address on file.'

Sheen sighed then tried to look upset, 'It's just, just that I will be going home to Newcastle and I had hoped to see Mrs Brooks before I went; it's unlikely that I will be back down here again.'

Miss Cambridge could see how upset Sheen appeared and deciding to be bold she lowered her voice and looked about the office. 'Why don't you just do something for a minute, then come back and clear up my desk for me.' She smiled at him as she spoke; an unsaid message was sent.

Sheen nodded. 'OK, Miss Cambridge, I'll do that.'

He returned a few minutes later and found in the centre of her desk a single folded piece of paper on which was typed Mrs Brooks' address. Sheen saw Miss Cambridge talking on the telephone at another desk with her back to him; he folded the piece of paper and left for his wing, smiling and thinking of how he would get into the flat.

As he lay on his bunk feigning sleep to avoid any conversation, Sheen was trying to imagine what he had to do in the morning. He had been told that he had to report to his probation officer in the afternoon in Newcastle, which meant catching a train or bus from Lewes to Brighton, then on to London and across the city for a further train to the North-East. He knew he wouldn't be there until perhaps the early evening so he told the wing prison officer he had hoped that the meeting with the probation officer could be delayed until the following day. That was refused as he was told the office would be open until ten o'clock, as it was every night. That meant that time was very tight for him. He weighed up the option of reporting to the Probation, then travelling back down the following day, but that presented more problems. Would the Probation have a job lined up for him immediately; if so, how could he get away? Other people would also notice him missing and altogether it could prove to be very difficult.

Sheen had his belongings, such as they were, packed in his holdall before the inevitable call from Prison Officer Williams, which for his benefit also included a reminder not to be late, said with a smile. Sheen completed the formalities and was shown the door to the prison at 7 a.m. Out he went into a steady rain that had been falling during the night, creating a slight mist. His brown leather jacket had the collar turned up as he crossed the road and started to walk downhill towards where he was told the bypass was, and where the buses ran frequently into Brighton. As he walked with the holdall in one hand he kept the other in his jean pocket holding on to the travel warrants he had been issued with in prison. He had seen the smirk on the face of the prison officer supervising his departure as he handed him the rail warrant from Brighton to Newcastle, via London, second class, one way. He had also been given the money that he had had on him during his arrest as well as the wages he had earned during his term, altogether just over sixty pounds. This, Sheen thought, wouldn't even be enough to pay for a room and meal in a doss-house. He walked quickly, enjoying the freedom to walk and look around where and whenever he wanted. He was looking behind him when he saw the bus coming, which meant he had to run the last few yards to the stop.

The bus had only a handful of passengers as he settled into a seat halfway down the bus. He looked out the window all the way into Brighton intending to stay until the route terminated. The bus made its way through the countryside and past the university on the outskirts of Brighton before stopping at housing estates where the bus filled. The traffic had built up, allowing Sheen to get his first view of Brighton as it made its way past the Brighton Pavilion and down to the seafront where it was more blustery and raining harder than it had been in Lewes. The bus ended its route at the bus station and Sheen found a map near by which told him where he was in relation to the town, but not where the address of Hollingdean Road was. Deciding that he needed to bear the time in mind, he saw that it was now eight o'clock. He walked past the parked buses into a side street in which many light-blue-and-white taxis were parked. He went to the first in line and gave the driver the address of Hollingdean Road without mentioning any specific address.

'The Sainsbury's end OK?'

'Sure.' He wanted to be as inconspicuous as possible as he didn't know how the next hour would go. His first option, of course, would be to be nice to Mrs Brooks and test how she reacted to him. Threats of violence he had also considered, but that was not in his character and again, what would he do if she didn't give in to the threats. He would be pushed towards some sort of violence and anyhow, even just threats would be enough for him to end up back in Prison. No, he would talk to her, try to win her over and offer her half of what he could get for the currency and war medals or whatever was in the box. If that didn't work, then he would get on his way to Newcastle and forget about everything to do with Aaron Brooks.

After paying the cabby he had waited in front of the supermarket under the awning and decided that he would walk along the length of the road to find the flats rather than ask anybody.

He felt nervous as he started walking along Hollingdean Road, passing dilapidated Victorian-style houses until, looking over a low wall, he saw two blocks of flats in the distance. He knew from the address supplied from Miss Cambridge that the Brooks' flat was in one of those. He paused at the entrance of the Hollingdean Depot of Brighton Council as a cleaning lorry entered sending spray from its wheels towards him. He half turned as the water hit his side and cursed. There were few pedestrians on the pavements but a constant flow of cars and buses in each direction as he walked steadily with his head lowered against the rain and his free hand thrust deep into his jacket pocket.

Looking up and in front of him, he saw the twin towers of flats and felt both tingling excitement and a twinge of nerves. The first block had 'Dudeney Lodge' written in bland-looking letters on a wooden board near the main entrance. There were cars parked in the designated parking spaces in front and to the sides of the flats, which he thought were built on about fourteen floors. He walked to the entrance and checked his watch. Twenty minutes past eight. Was he too early? he wondered as he looked at the bank of intercom entry names and the corresponding buttons. He knew the address and after locating the name Brooks on floor 12, he pushed the button. He didn't realise that he had taken a large breath before exhaling as he readied himself for her to reply. For some reason, he was still looking at the button he had pushed and the small grill next to it, willing a reply, and hadn't seen the front door open from the inside as an old couple aged in their seventies came out.

The old lady looked at Sheen and said, 'Don't think half of them are working, luv; they weren't last week when the Council were told about them kids squirting their drinks all over them. Bloody kids, young as eight I reckon, always causing trouble around here. You're lucky the lift is working.'

The old lady remained in the doorway while her husband stood next to Sheen and indicated by holding the door for him to go in. Sheen thanked the lady and walked into the foyer, which was cleaner than he expected it to be, and certainly cleaner and better smelling than many blocks of flats he had visited in Newcastle in his childhood.

The lift was slow, each passing floor illuminated by lights above the door. When he arrived at the twelfth floor the doors opened and he saw four front doors to separate flats. It was immediately obvious that three of the flats were more cared for than the other, which had grease and dirt marks on the door, and through the frosted glass panel he could see a net curtain that looked brownish. The door didn't have any number, so Sheen checked the other three doors and guessed the door with no number must belong to the Brooks family.

He pressed the bell, which didn't ring, so he gave a light tap with his knuckles on the glass pane. He repeated the tapping several times but didn't get any response. He knelt down and looked through the letterbox, and called her name, again without any movement from within. He turned to look at the windows of the other doors and didn't see any movement from them and briefly considered knocking on one to see whether Mrs Brooks was likely to be in now or, if out, whether she would return in the next hour. He realised that his time was short and felt a wave of frustration. He again peered through the letterbox and called out her name, and again he got no reply. He suddenly thought of a TV programme he and the rest of the inmates on his wing had watched some months ago. He had been sitting next to Aaron throughout the programme and they had collectively laughed at the banal advice being given about closing windows and doors and making sure everywhere was locked when you left the house. A thought occurred to him: he remembered how once upon a time front door keys had been hung by string inside the door underneath the letter-box in case you lost your key and couldn't get in. Surely a thing of the past?

'I wonder,' muttered Sheen under his breath as he slid his hand through the opening and twisted his fingers down and against the door. He felt his heart jump as his fingers touched a string, which he slowly pulled through towards him, a key dangling on the end. He checked the windows again of the other front doors and seeing no movement inserted the key and opened the door.

He stepped swiftly into the hallway and closed the door behind him. He could instantly smell stale cigarette smoke and a musty air of dust and grime. He gently called Mrs Brooks' name as he moved from room to room, wrinkling his nose at the different smells that each room gave and looking with disgust at the mess everywhere. He didn't loiter or inspect anything until he entered the living room. He looked at the units and they were exactly as Brooks had described them – three together and along one wall. He took off his shoes and socks before placing the socks on his hands to avoid leaving any fingerprints. Within a minute he had removed all the items from the central unit and then started to pull and drag the unit away from the wall. When he had created a gap through which he could see the carpet he felt his mouth go dry in anticipation.

He leaned through the gap and pulled the carpet back and was pleased to see it was exactly as Aaron Brooks had described it. He quickly pulled out the grey box file, cash and jewellery and laid them on the sofa before replacing the carpet. He didn't want anyone to know he had been there and with nerves stretched he pushed the unit back into its place. It slid back easier than it had been to drag it out and within another minute he had replaced the ornaments in roughly the same positions he had found them. He didn't inspect what he had taken from the hiding place but stuffed them into the bottom of his holdall before replacing his socks on his feet and putting his shoes back on.

He went to the front door and realised that his heart was pumping very quickly. It was the first time he had ever entered somewhere as a trespasser and the first time that he had stolen from someone. He listened at the door for any movement from the foyer and hearing nothing quickly unlatched the front door and slipped out, pulling the door closed behind him. He crossed to the lift and used the call button, but then realised he didn't want any of the other occupiers of the floor to come out and see him, so he made his way to the emergency staircase and walked down the stairs. He made sure that he was quiet, constantly listening for any other person using the stairs. In the event, he made it to the ground floor without seeing anybody and after telling himself to calm down and act normally, he walked away from the flats without looking back. He retraced his steps to the supermarket where he knew taxis would be waiting to collect the shoppers.

For the next nine hours Sheen resisted even taking so much as a glance into the holdall but kept it close on the seat next to him – first in the taxi, then the train to Victoria and Underground to Kings Cross, and finally the train to Newcastle, where he arrived just after six o'clock, just three minutes late.

He walked to the Probation offices and after waiting for an hour in the unswept and draughty waiting area was shown into the usual bleak government office. For the next half an hour Sheen stood and politely answered all the questions put to him by his probation officer, confirmed where he would be living, and agreed to all the conditions that were laid down.

The address agreed where Sheen was to live was with an old friend and his wife in a neat three-bedroom house on the outskirts of the city in the area known as Scotchwood. Sheen and Harry Johns had been friends at school before joining the Army together where they remained inseparable throughout the training and subsequent postings. They had been together whether under enemy attack or drinking in bars, each looking out for the other so much so that they were nicknamed Tom and Jerry after the cartoon characters. Sheen being the larger and stronger was Tom while Harry was Jerry, smaller in build but faster, always managing to beat Sheen in the final few yards of any run. The only part of their lives they didn't share was Jackie.

Harry had left the Army when he married his childhood sweetheart and together they had settled down into their married life, which meant that Harry and Sheen were not able to see each other as frequently. Even after Sheen had also left the Army and was working in Newcastle their paths didn't cross, so it was only by rare prior arrangement did they meet for a drink in a bar. All the same, on his arrest and the surrounding publicity, Sheen had received a call from Harry offering his help and support, including attending court to be a character witness if required.

Harry and Jackie worked at the Nissan car plant in Washington near Sunderland, about twelve miles from their home. He as a supervisor on the production line while she was in the HR department. They didn't have any children, preferring to pay as much as possible off their mortgage on their semi-detached house while living a quiet life away from the night life of Newcastle. They agreed that children were for the future and as they were only touching thirty years of age they were in no rush.

As Sheen arrived at their house and alighted from the taxi, he was met by Harry walking down the short path from his house to the pavement, beaming from ear to ear with his arms outstretched. As Sheen paid the driver, he felt Harry's arms circle his chest in a hug and felt a wet kiss on his neck.

'Steve, you bugger – how are you, mate?' he laughed.

Sheen responded by trying to playfully struggle from his friend's grip and said none too quietly 'God, is this fat bastard the same guy who used to run?'

They both laughed and hugged each other. Harry knew that since leaving the Army he had stopped his exercise routine and with the good regular meals that Jackie gave him he had put on weight. His middle had certainly grown a few inches and some of the once-muscled stomach now hung a little over his trouser belt. His hair was still sandy coloured but thinner and his eyes as fierce a blue, but he had shaved off his 'Mexican bandit'-style moustache and 'goatee' beard to reveal that some weight had also been added to his jowls and neck.

'Bloody hell, Steve, you look as fit as ever,' Harry said, standing back and looking at Sheen from top to bottom, 'not a bit of fat on you, but that is before you have eaten our Jackie's food.'

They both laughed and with an arm around each other they walked into the house. Jackie had been in the kitchen that overlooked the road and, having heard so much about Harry's best pal, had decided to let them greet each other while she watched. She understood straight away that Harry had been telling her the truth when he had told her of Sheen's many sexual conquests. He was a handsome man with a good strong build, his laugh was loud and she saw that he had good white teeth. She waited for the men to enter the kitchen and turning as if seeing him for the first time she greeted Sheen with a handshake and a small kiss to each cheek.

Sheen dropped his holdall on the kitchen floor and prepared to meet Jackie only just in time. It was the first time that he had met her in six years and he realised that she looked much prettier than the photographs Harry had shown him when they were together in the Army. Harry had told Sheen that she was a 'looker' and he now saw what he meant. Although quite short at five feet four inches she had a bright face, dark eyes and an engaging smile. Her dark-brown hair was just longer than her shoulders and was tied into a single ponytail at the back held in place by a bone clip. She had a slim figure shown off by the red V-necked jumper and tight-fitting light-blue jeans. Her make-up was sparing and Sheen would have said that she didn't need any at all.

Harry and Jackie made him feel at home straight away. Mostly the conversation revolved around their times and scrapes they had enjoyed in the Army. There was a lot of laughter over dinner as each man told their stories and drank beer while Jackie had a glass of white wine.

After Harry and Jackie had gone to bed after the television news at half past ten, Sheen made his way to his room and unable to contain himself any longer he opened his holdall's contents on to the bed. His two battered old suitcases that Harry had stored after Sheen's arrest were on the floor by the side of the wardrobe. Sheen could remember each item in there and wasn't looking forward to examining some of them. The trainers and walking boots plus his training clothes would probably not be too pleasant, he thought, as he smelled the outside of each case. 'At least they don't reek,' he said out loud with a smile. He recalled various items of clothing, personal papers, his passport and old photographs and decided he'd open the cases in the morning when he would open the window, just in case his prognosis was wrong.

The cash he flung to one side together with the box file as he emptied the jewellery out on to the duvet. There were loose pieces, a blue necklace with matching earrings that he put together and other necklaces and bracelets that he laid out matching wherever there appeared to be a set. There were several velvet pouches and two velvet-covered boxes, which he examined carefully. He spent some minutes looking at all the sparkling stones, noting the many colours, from clear to shades of blue, green and red. He didn't know if they were real or not; he had heard that many really valuable items were kept in bank safes with cheap imitation and copies kept at home and used for general wear, so what did he have here? Who did he know who could value them? In the back of his mind there was a struggle between whether it was right or wrong what he had done, but the struggle was only half hearted. The old man and his wife would have been paid out by the insurance company so they would be OK – the only loser was the insurance company, and they could afford it.

He turned his attention to the bundles of money. The smaller one was English pounds, which he counted into five one-thousand piles. The other two were of foreign money, which he knew he could easily exchange into pounds. As he counted methodically, he made small piles each of a thousand euros and dollars. He counted eight piles in euro notes with a few left over, and nine in dollar notes, again with a few left over. He didn't know the value of the foreign money in English pounds but he guessed it to be about fifteen to twenty thousand pounds, maybe more. He carefully tied the notes back into their bundles and decided that he would need to unpack all his stored things to find his passport before he tried to exchange the cash. Even then, he would do it in small amounts to avoid suspicion at the banks and travel agents.

He looked at his watch. It was after eleven thirty so he decided that he had all day tomorrow to think further about what he was going to do and also to examine the box and its contents.

* * *

Sheen heard Harry and Jackie moving about in the morning as they visited the bathroom before going downstairs. Shortly after he heard the kettle whistle as it boiled. He wanted see them before they went to work.

As he walked into the kitchen to the smell of toast and coffee he put on a smile. 'Good morning. I thought I'd see you before you went to work. I have to get a move on as well.'

'What have you got to do?' asked Jackie over the top of her coffee mug that she was holding to her mouth with her other hand holding a slice of toast coated with jam.

'Well, I want to try and find a job, and also somewhere to live, so I can get out of your hair. In the first place, it's into town and try the Probation people again; they might have an inside run for a job, then I'll see what flats are available.'

'Flats are not cheap in the centre. Things have changed a bit in the last couple of years; it is expensive there now with all the new building works. You might be better looking south of the river; it's still more reasonable there,' said Harry as he buttered his toast with barely a glance at Sheen.

'Right, I'll do that. Maybe I'll look for work in that area as well then,' said Sheen brightly. 'I suppose there isn't anything where you work, is there?'

Jackie frowned a little and looked at the wall, concentrating. 'I don't know,' she said slowly, thinking about what jobs were available. 'I don't suppose you have a CV, do you?'

Sheen was puzzled. 'A CV?'

Jackie smiled at him. 'I thought not. Look you need to get a proper CV, a work and history report about yourself. It isn't difficult – we can sit down this evening and do it on the computer. Before then, can you list out your jobs, dates started and finished, and what they comprised of – not "in the Army, shooting people",' she laughed. 'What skills you learned, what responsibilities you had, all that sort of thing.'

All three laughed and shortly after Harry and Jackie left for work in their separate cars, leaving Sheen to get showered and dressed.

After compiling the list of jobs and skills ready for Jackie that evening, Sheen contacted the Probation office and told them what he was doing. Keep contacting them, he had been told; keep them informed of what you're doing and they soon lose interest in you. He made various phone calls to friends and people he knew, to let them know he was back and also looking for work and somewhere to live. Just about everyone he knew were law-abiding citizens, something he hadn't thought of until he had been imprisoned, though he was pleased that none refused his phone calls and they all talked warmly to him.

It was late morning when he settled at the dining table with the box file and carefully took the contents out, spreading them over the table. He examined the medals and the corresponding ribbons, recognising the two Iron Crosses, but not the others. He opened a brown envelope that smelt musty and pulled out a bundle of letters that were tied together loosely with string. He noted that the handwriting was small and neat and clearly German. The date on each letter was at the top of the front page; they were from 1938 until 1944 and altogether he counted eighteen letters. He looked at each briefly, scanning the words to see whether there were any that he could decipher or translate; they all appeared to be similarly written. The addressee was 'Helmut' and the sender was 'Deine dich liebende Schwester'.

He opened another envelope and slipped two cards on to the table. Again they were German and again from the Second World War time. A blue cardboard-covered passbook, with a red cross at the top and underneath the Nazi eagle symbol sitting on a swastika and the word 'Verwendungsbuch'. Inside the front cover there was a passport-sized black-and-white photograph of an attractive woman, probably in her thirties.

The photograph was stapled at the top and bottom and there was an ink stamp mark in each corner. He looked through the following pages and noted they were filled with various handwritings on different dates that appeared to span several years.

The other document that he had taken from the envelope was in fact not cardboard, but appeared to be some sort of woven cloth. Again it bore the Nazi eagle, with two words typed above. 'Deut—' He peered closer but couldn't make out the last letters that were obviously in some sort of old script, and 'Reich'. Under the eagle was the clearly typed word 'Kennkarte'. He opened the card and recognised the photograph as being the same woman as in the first document. This appeared to contain personal details of her and he guessed that it was some sort of identity card. He placed them on to the envelope he had taken them from and moved them to the edge of the table.

He opened another brown envelope and gently shook the various documents on to the table. Again he noted they were from the same period and were in German. He gave a quicker look through these documents as they were also printed and written in German. As before, there were black-and-white photographs in two of the documents of the same man who appeared slightly older than the woman. He tried to read the name and thought he recognised one as being the same as the woman had in her documents. 'Probably husband and wife,' he muttered. Several loose pieces of paper were also among the documents and after a further quick examination he replaced them inside the envelope.

He had two more envelopes to open.

The next envelope contained just two documents. He recognised instantly the first as an old-fashioned British passport, which was confirmed by the lettering on the front cover: 'United Kingdom of Great Britain and Northern Ireland'. At the bottom of the front cover was a white inlay on which was hand-written

'Mr R.L. Knight'. Sheen opened the front cover and saw the letters referred to the passport holder as being Mr Roger Leonard Knight. Looking through the pages he saw numerous immigration and visa stamps all dated in the late 1930s, which if he put in order would perhaps be interesting, but not now. The other document was of brown thick paper, almost cardboard in feel with the words 'National Registration Identity Card' written in capital letters under the crest that he recognised as being that of the United Kingdom. He opened it and read that the holder was Roger Leonard Knight. There was a passport-sized photograph that he glanced at and becoming less interested with his findings he put the card with the passport.

As he was replacing the two documents into the brown envelope, a sudden thought occurred to him and with a slight rush of puzzlement he opened both documents and looked again at the photographs. Both were of men, possibly late teens or early twenties, but *different* men. As he studied them side by side, he could see that there were in fact many small differences in their facial features – the shape of the chin was rounder in one; the nose straighter and perhaps more crooked in the photograph in the passport. This face had a slightly harder appearance, the eyes almost boring into the photographer's lens as if defying him. Both hairstyles were similar with side parting and both appeared to be a middling colour, but with a black-and white photograph it was always hard to tell. He studied both documents and the photographs, trying to decide which had been tampered with, but saw nothing to help him make the identification. He felt a little excitement about the find but didn't know what it meant and decided then was not the time to delve further.

After replacing the two documents he sorted though a number of loose documents at the bottom of the box. All appeared to be from the era of 1930s and 1940s and appeared to be odd pieces of paper, cards and some letters, written in a different hand from the bundle Sheen had examined earlier.

He decided to replace the documents, then tomorrow he would ask if he could use Jackie's computer and research what he could. The jewellery he had decided to hide for the time being, burying it in nearby woods, which would be easy to do and safe from accidental discovery. The foreign cash he would change each day in small amounts using that to pay for his lodgings and to get by with before he decided on his future.

10

DS Harrison was at his desk when his mobile phone rang. He saw the caller identified as being Mark Carter and though he was being swamped by paperwork he decided to take the call. The conversation was brief and they arranged to meet later that evening to catch up, which to DS Harrison meant that Carter wanted to know what progress the enquiry was making. Inwardly he groaned – another problem! – and also it would mean he would be late home again, bringing more sarcastic comments from his wife who over the years had become more accustomed to evenings alone than with his company. 'You love the job more than me' seemed to have been her mantra for some years, though it hadn't been as frequent after his promotion. The extra spending money had softened the blow and made things more comfortable for her.

DS Harrison was glad to put the paperwork to one side and, noting that at this time the initial evening rush of traffic leaving Brighton would be easing, decided to call it a day and make for the meeting with Carter. During the afternoon he had made a quick check through the computer system to ensure that there had been no developments in the robbery investigation and that nothing had happened to give Carter an edge at their meeting.

'Bloody hell, Terry, you look more miserable than normal,' said Carter, as he appeared at the corner table that DS Harrison had sat at just a few minutes earlier. Carter gave a slight laugh and seeing DS Harrison had a full glass of beer in front of him, went to the bar to get his own gin and tonic.

'I don't know,' mused DS Harrison, shaking his head slowly, 'this job has changed over the years and nothing is for the better.'

Carter laughed at the musings of an old hand – he wished he had a pound every time he had heard that said by one of the old stagers; it was the same in every police force throughout the country, he presumed. Deciding to offer a little sympathy, he coaxed, 'Your woman DI giving you a hard time?'

'No, not really, she's busy riding another DS this week. No, it's funny really. Tell me, in your years in the job how many times did you have someone admit an offence that they didn't do? And I'm not talking about a tramp in winter trying to get himself in the warm for a few weeks; I'm talking about a street robbery for which he knew he would be sent down, because that is what has happened.'

Carter looked at DS Harrison and shook his head. 'Never, not for that type of thing. Was he a gang member – you know, frightened of someone and wanting to get away?'

DS Harrison took a sip of his drink. 'No, actually he's bit of a loner in many ways. Had previous for the same MO in the same area, down by the seafront. He would probably have come up based on his MO anyway, but we got a call from a snitch who saw him in new clothes et cetera and when I interviewed him he just coughed it. Straight down the line. Got six months because of his previous for the same sort of thing.'

'What's happened then?' said an intrigued Carter.

DS Harrison took a long pull of his beer before saying in a flat tone, 'Another robbery, a week or so ago, and due to some good work by the uniforms a kid was arrested. Had the money on him, ID'd by the aggrieved at the time. Really good work, money recovered, later interviewed by a good young WDC, again with a brief present, and fully admitted it. She asked him if he wanted any TICs and he said he'd done a robbery previously. Gave all the details. No problem until she checked and saw that it had already been cleared by the lad Brooks that I dealt with.'

'What does he say about it, I mean Brooks? I assume you have seen him and asked him.'

'Tricky to do that,' said Harrison. 'He's dead.'

'What?' said Carter, louder than he had intended.

'Died in prison. Not a violent death though; he was one of the lot who drank that home-made stuff. You must have read it in the papers.'

'Yes, I read it. Three have been charged with making it or supplying it and – what was it in the end – six died? Well, interesting, I can see why you are worried. Have you seen his mum, friends – anybody got any ideas?'

'Seen his mum, seen his friends, talked it around the station, asked his solicitor. I don't know,' finished Harrison as he gulped at his beer, draining the glass. 'I thought I'd seen just about everything.'

Carter stood and took the empty glasses to the bar while Harrison sat thinking of Brooks and wondering what he had missed – something, but what?

The two men talked about other matters while they had another drink, and after DS Harrison had confirmed to Carter that nothing had progressed in the Knight case they decided to call it a day.

Sir Roger had fully recovered from the effects of the robbery and had resumed his life as if nothing had happened at all. Initially, he had been worried about the loss of the box and its contents, but as the days, then weeks and now months had passed he had pushed his fears towards the back of his mind. This was a natural process for him, to put bad things behind him, to move on, to look forward – that was how he had been successful in business. Any lessons to be learned would be, but not re-run again and again analysing each and every point. He hadn't told Carter the contents of the box and was glad he had held his silence. It had taken a strong mind to resist the yearning to share a problem with another; a secret was best kept to oneself no matter how difficult it was. He had kept secrets all his life, filing them away in a special place in his mind and, once there, never brought out again and told. He had secrets from everyone, including Mary, deeds from his past that he would never discuss, locked away. He could live with himself and his inner thoughts.

11

Over the following two days Sheen kept himself busy. The jewellery had been buried in a nearby wood in a place that he could easily recognise again using a tree, a telegraph pole and a church spire as the three points to identify the exact spot. He was using the Winthrop Theory which he had learned from his days in the Army and he felt energised by remembering those days. The weather was similar to those days as well, he thought – why did it always rain hard whenever he was working in woods?

Each morning he changed some of the foreign currency, altogether into over four thousand pounds, though nevermore than two hundred pounds' worth at any one time. The afternoons he spent sitting at the kitchen table with Jackie's computer examining the documents and researching what he could. It all appeared to fit together, except for the photographic discrepancy between the two UK documents – this he couldn't resolve. He was satisfied from his research and using the computer to translate those words he couldn't fully make out that the documents related to a married couple. The husband had been in the German Army, gaining bravery awards and promotions until he had been invalided out with honour, after which he had become the Battalionsführer of the Volkssturm. His career could be traced through numerous sites and Sheen became more and more respectful of the man as he chartered his various postings and battles. Honours had been won the hard way, up against the enemy during heavy fighting. The dates and locations he saw also indicated that the fighting was conducted during the harsh winter in Russia when food and comforts would have been non-existent. He noted that there had been two injuries suffered, though he didn't fully understand what they entailed. What he did see was that after the first injury he was in hospital for three months before returning to his unit.

His wife had been a Red Cross Helper and, translating what he could from the Verwendungsbuch, it seemed she had been active on many occasions, tending in the main to victims from Allied bombing raids.

The letters Sheen worked out were sent from her to her brother who lived in Switzerland. Some of the handwriting was just too small and difficult for Sheen to read, so a complete picture of what the letters said couldn't be made. He had learned, though, that the brother was looking after her and her husband's child. Words and phrases punctuated the letters such as 'growing up', 'missing him', 'keep safe', 'better life', but always in the third person, as if she was denying the child was hers. Maybe, Sheen wondered more than once, he had lost the meaning in the literal translation he had made, and the child was her brother's. He had become almost obsessed by his research and once had been nearly caught by Jackie coming home, with the papers spread out across the table. Only once had Jackie made a comment when she used the computer one evening about how many searches Sheen had made regarding Germans and the Second World War. This he had brushed aside by saying he was just bored and surfing the Internet.

That night he lay awake putting the pieces together in his mind. He wondered what had become of the couple after the war when all the records appeared to have finished. Of the brother in Switzerland he could find no trace. Several times he wished he knew how to research the Swiss and German electoral rolls and birth registers and the like, though would they have escaped the bombing and looting? The one pressing point that he couldn't understand was the two photographs:

no matter how he looked at it, the two photographs were of different men using the same name. Why were they in the box? What was the connection between them and the German documents, if there was any? He turned various scenarios over and over again in his mind before he fell asleep.

The next morning Sheen awoke and saw between the partly drawn curtains that dawn was not long away. He hadn't slept for long and, though he knew he was tired, his mind returned again to the box and its contents. Perhaps for the first time he thought of how he had come by them and wondered who had owned them. Aaron Brooks was the key. 'Aaron, old son, why did you take the box? You had the jewellery and cash all of which you could carry easily concealed on your body, in pockets and down the jeans, but the box couldn't be hidden so easily. What was it you said about the job?' Sheen realised he had been whispering to himself but he was now wide awake and sat up. 'You said that you were arrested for a robbery that you didn't do but that it had taken place at the same time as the job you did. There was an old man involved in your job and you had been worried about whether he was hurt. You would have got a lot more time inside if you had been caught for that, so you took the job you were arrested for. Alibi, you said. Oh Aaron, Aaron, how I wish you could speak to me, you little so and so The box, did you know what was in it, did you have a look before you decided to take it as well? Oh Aaron, my boy, I wish you could talk to me now.'

After a small breakfast of toast and cereal he donned his old running shoes and set out for a run around the area. He had gradually built up his running both in terms of speed and distance. Having always been a good runner in the Army, he enjoyed the feeling of exhaustion immediately after a run followed by a lightness in his step for hours later. His other fitness love he had already revived – cycling every day. He had paid over five hundred pounds for a new cycle, explaining the lavish purchase to Jackie and Harry as saying that he had been repaid some money by an old friend. The new cycle was so much smoother than his old, battered one and he was especially delighted by the smooth gears and wide tyres that meant he was able to cover roads and cross-country trails.

That morning he finished his run and decided to continue with his research. But he learned little more than he had already found and it wasn't until mid-afternoon that he again thought of Aaron. 'Alibi!' he almost shouted. 'Bloody hell, come on, Sheen, get your act together.' He turned again to the computer and started doing searches regarding local newspapers in the Brighton area. He quickly found that the local newspaper printed six days a week was the *Argus* and with a little research he was able to find the copies relating to the robbery at Sir Roger Knight's home. As he sat hunched over the breakfast table, totally concentrating on what he was reading, the front door opened and a second later Jackie's face appeared at the kitchen doorway.

'Hi,' she said cheerfully, precariously balancing two large shopping bags in each hand. There was a thump as her foot pushed the front door closed and she walked into the room, dropping the bags on the floor next to Sheen with a sigh of relief. She looked at the computer screen and for a few seconds read the page: '"Old man robbed in his house in Brighton". What are you looking at that for?' she asked, smiling at Sheen.

Sheen had been caught off guard. 'Just reading it, that's all,' he said, feeling guilty and flustered.

'Hey, let me have a read while you put the kettle on, there's a love,' she said as she sat down and turned the screen towards her.

As Sheen waited for the kettle to boil he watched Jackie read the screen, scrolling down in smooth movements. As he was putting the water into the mugs Jackie looked up.

'Come on, what gives? You're not just happening to read a story about an old man being robbed in Brighton ages ago, that's crap. You're up to something or involved in something, aren't you?'

Sheen saw her smile and noted that her words were said softly; this was no harsh accusation. He finished making the tea and sat back at the table. He felt disarmed, unsure of what he could say but no ready explanation came to him.

'It was a job that my cell mate did. He did this robbery, he told me about it and I thought that I'd just look it up and see if he was telling the truth. He died of poisoning in the prison and I was thinking of him, so I just thought I'd look it up, that's all,' he said.

He felt his cheeks flush and lifted the mug to his lips.

Jackie kept her eyes on his, holding his stare. He was the first to blink.

'I am nearly thirty years old and work mostly with men. I deal with disciplinary procedures and complaints every day and have to interview people about what they have said or done. I don't just sit there and ask daft questions and listen to their lying answers. I play a game to myself. I ask them questions that I know the answers to, obvious ones where there is no threat to them. They answer the questions and I look at their face and eyes when they answer. I look at their hands and I look at how they are sitting and whether they move or not. I look at them and then I ask them the difficult questions, where they want to avoid telling the truth. Usually there is a grain of truth in their answers, something for them to build the lie around. In every case, it is easy to see when they are not telling the whole truth, their eyes dart around or suddenly disappear to one side as they try to construct an answer; they start to lick their lips before answering, they move their hands, grip something, move something. I know a guilty look when I see one. I'm just surprised that you weren't looking at porn!' She gave a slight laugh. 'That would have been interesting seeing what turned you on.'

Sheen felt his face flush even more. He was trying to think of something to say when Jackie said, 'Well?'

'Well, what?' Sheen replied

'Let's talk about the robbery thing later,' she laughed. 'Tell me about what turns you on.'

Sheen gave a nervous laugh and looked at the table top; he wasn't used to a woman asking him about his sexual thoughts. Feeling embarrassed, he looked at Jackie and said, 'I don't really know – it just happens, doesn't it?'

Still looking into Sheen's eyes Jackie smiled and spoke softly, 'I've checked the computer to see what you are looking at when Harry and I are at work and you haven't been to any porn sites at all and you haven't had a girl while you've been here. You haven't become a monk, have you? You keep yourself fit and you are an attractive bloke who's had a few girls in his time, well, according to Harry...?'

'I've just been busy, you know, looking for a job and keeping a low profile for the Probation people. They'd be unhappy to see me in the pubs and clubs in the city, wouldn't they? So I'm just taking it slowly.'

Jackie stood and stepped towards Sheen, who looked up as she stood against him. From his seat he could see her looking down at him. He felt her thighs move against his arm and give a slight rub. She put an arm around his shoulder and leaned down so that her face was inches from his. She moved closer, her lips gently brushing his, her eyes all the while staring into his. Jackie slowly moved to sit on his lap, squeezing into him to avoid the table at her side. She gave him small gentle kisses and moved her other arm around his neck. Sheen felt excited and after a few more kisses he started to respond, moving his lips in time with hers. He moved an arm around her waist and put the other across her lap. The kisses became longer and he felt her tongue move between his lips and teeth as their lips came against each others' harder. Their kisses became full blown with each using their tongues to explore the other's mouth. Not sure if he was going too quickly, Sheen moved his hand from Jackie's lap to the centre of her skirt where he could feel her legs pressed together, then to the hem where without any resistance he moved his fingers between her legs.

'Come on,' Jackie said as she stood and pulled Sheen to his feet.

'What about Harry?'

Jackie took two steps backwards towards the hallway and laughed. 'He's at work for another two hours so we have time to have some fun.' Jackie led Sheen up the stairs and into his bedroom.

Sheen felt a trickle of sweat run from his chest around his ribs towards his back and the sheet he was lying on. He arched his back slightly to allow the sweat to reach the sheet.

Jackie made a soft purr as she felt his chest move her head. 'Not bad, not bad at all for a bloke who hasn't had it for a few years. A few more practices and you'll have me waking the dead.'

Sheen laughed causing Jackie's head to bob up and down on his chest and some more of her hair to fall on to his neck.

'A few more?' he said. 'Jackie, we shouldn't have done it this once, let alone a few times more. Christ, what if Harry came home?'

Jackie raised herself to lie on her elbows on his chest. 'Harry is at work. He'll phone when he's on his way home, don't worry ... and don't make a big deal of it, we're only having fun.'

'I'm just surprised,' he said with a grin on his face.

Jackie gave a laugh and sat up. 'You mean at me not being the prim and proper woman you thought I was, the nice loving *boring* wife. You thought I was the forever faithful type, you know, a shag once a week, perhaps two, in the dark, missionary position, saying thank you afterwards even if it was an awful shag?'

Sheen was taken aback by her language. It showed a side of her that in truth he hadn't thought existed. Most of what she had said, he really did think of her.

Jackie smiled at him and sat on his legs facing him. She leant down until her face was an inch from his. 'That's what you thought, isn't it? Come on, tell me the truth and I will know if you are lying.'

Sheen smiled at her and gave a slight nod. 'Yes, I suppose it was. I thought you were a good-looking girl with a great body, but I didn't think for one minute you'd be like this or that I'd get lucky with you.'

'Ah, so much to learn! You're out of practice, but you'll catch up,' she said, laughing.

'We'd better get ourselves ready, hadn't we, just in case,' said Sheen, trying to sit up.

'In case of what?' said Jackie as she started moving her hips. 'Get ready for round two? In which case I'm ready now'.

Jackie's mobile had rung as they were drying each other after their combined shower and ten minutes later Sheen was sitting at the kitchen table watching as Jackie put away the shopping.

'So, come on then, what is that story all about? And don't forget I'll know if you are lying,' said Jackie, cramming more packets of pasta into the cupboard.

'Where to start' Sheen said, looking at the table as he tried to get his thoughts into some sort of order. He decided to tell her the truth.

As he told her she continued to put the shopping away, but every now and again she stopped what she was doing and looked at him closely. He could feel her eyes examining him for whether he was telling the truth or lying.

117

When he told her about how he had taken everything from Brooks' flat and how he had brought it all to Newcastle with him, he expected a verbal lashing from Jackie about bringing all that stolen property into her and Harry's home, but she just listened, her face not showing any feeling or emotion.

'And?' said Jackie, raising her eyebrows as Sheen stopped talking.

He told her about exchanging the foreign money and then about burying the jewellery.

'But what is really interesting is the box file,' he started. 'It's easier if I could show you, but we don't have time and I really don't want Harry involved. He's done well for himself – well, so have you – but you know about this and he doesn't, so it is better if he doesn't know, I think, if you see what I mean.'

Sheen looked up at Jackie and wondered if she understood what he had just tried to say, though to him it had sounded like a jumble of words, not making any sense.

'Don't you think I can keep a secret?' she asked.

The last words struck Sheen. 'You'd better or we're both in trouble.'

Jackie gave a small laugh and raised her eyebrows as if the question she'd asked was still to be answered.

Sheen stopped laughing, adjusted his bottom on the chair and was immediately aware that his actions were being watched closely by Jackie, which disturbed him.

'Harry will be home in a few minutes, so how about another time?' he asked.

Jackie continued to study Sheen for a few seconds and had just continued putting the shopping away as Harry drove on to the driveway.

Sheen tried to forget the Jackie she had been that afternoon, but every now and again he caught her looking at him in a way that made him feel he was under examination. After dinner he and Harry watched a football match on television, yelling their support for Newcastle United and shouting abuse at the referee when a decision was given against their side. Harry fetched more beers from the fridge for them and topped up Jackie's wine glass, which she sipped from as she concentrated on her laptop computer, ignoring the men. As the final minutes of the match were being played Harry was sitting on the edge of the settee shouting at the television while Jackie and Sheen exchanged glances.

The next day Sheen spent researching Sir Roger Knight – the person, his history and the robbery against him, the subsequent police enquiry that had run its course with no arrests. It had confirmed to Sheen that Brooks had been telling the truth but it also raised the question of what the papers he had in the box file related to. That they were connected to this Sir Roger Knight, he felt sure, and he was equally certain that the two English documents showed two different young men. Sheen found several photographs of Sir Roger when he was attending meetings or events and these he compared against the young men in the documents and while he couldn't be sure he thought the passport photograph was not the same person. The identity-card photograph, though, bore many similarities and he thought it could be Sir Roger in his youth.

Sheen was settled at the table with all the papers from the grey box spread out and the laptop computer open when he heard a car drive up. He stretched from his seat and saw Jackie coming towards the front door of the house. Sheen knew it was because of him she was home, but did she want to know more about this business or was it to go to bed?

An hour later after they had sorted through all the papers and Jackie had examined some herself they sat back in their seats. Jackie lifted the remnants of a cold mug of coffee and examined the liquid.

'So what do you think?' he asked.

'I think it is pretty obvious. What you have are papers

that could be very important, or not worth a light. The quickest way to find out whether they are important is to offer them back to Sir Roger, with of course a finder's fee to cover your time and expenses, see what his response is. Maybe he'll be happy to give a few hundred pounds – who knows?'

'Yea, and maybe he'll go to the police and I'll be back inside for handling stolen goods,' said Sheen, not liking the prospect.

'True,' said Jackie slowly. 'But, here is a question: why in all the reports of the robbery was there no mention of personal papers; it was just jewellery and money. And how about this pillar of society who says only a couple of thousand pounds were stolen when it was nearer twenty five-plus thousand.' Appearing to warm to the theme, she continued: 'A further point: he's lied about the money, forgot about the personal papers and having reached his high position he knows he's lying. Come on, you don't get to his position without having a memory and brains – no, something is wrong. Why don't you ring him, see what he says?'

'Christ, this is serious,' said Sheen slowly. 'I mean, this could be seen as handling stolen property and blackmail; I could get years for this.' He shook his head slowly. 'I know it makes sense to just put in a call and see what he says. I'll think about it. His home number is on a website that his missus is on, organising a meeting at a museum or something, so I could make a call. I'm not going to do it from around here, though.'

At Jackie's suggestion, they put together various ideas about what he would say, how strongly he ought to come over and how he should sound confident and authoritative. The first contact, Jackie explained, could be all-important – he needed to assert himself over Knight. They tried to make a plan, a rough one at this stage and each came up with ideas about how to thwart any police investigation. Sheen could use a

120

neighbour's car, a small nondescript Honda. The woman was off work having been injured and would be glad of the cash Sheen would be paying her to use it.

Sheen had driven sixty miles south along the A1 with the prepared script he and Jackie had sketched out the night before. When he pulled into the lay-by he felt as if all the other drivers were looking at him as he manoeuvred into an area just away from the other cars. He switched off the engine and sat there for a few minutes preparing, knowing that he was going to step over a mark from which he couldn't return. He had told himself repeatedly to focus on the job – that was all it was, a job, nothing personal, just a business transaction that wouldn't hurt anyone. The response from Knight would be very interesting.

Sheen was using a new mobile phone that he had bought using a fake identity Jackie had provided him with – an ex-employee at her company who had left to go travelling in Australia. Jackie had other identities that could be used if needed; Sheen was amazed at how quickly and expertly she had thrown her efforts into the enterprise.

Sheen made a final check of the other cars and people in the area before taking a deep breath and dialling the telephone number he had obtained from the website.

The call was answered quickly by a woman, which Sheen hadn't anticipated, 'Ah, good morning, Mrs Knight. I'm sorry to bother you but is it possible to speak with your husband, please?' he asked, sure that his voice sounded nervous.

'Yes, of course, I'll get him. Who shall I say is calling and the purpose?' she replied brightly.

'Smith, insurance business ... nothing to worry about,' said Sheen, using his prepared cover.

There was muffled rustling and whispered words as the phone was handed over.

'Hello,' the voice was deeper somehow than Sheen had

expected. 'I'm sorry, but I thought all the insurance issues were settled. Mr Smith, is it?'

'Yes, we may have settled on the jewellery and cash, but I am interested in the various papers that were in a grey box file. I don't appear to have a value for them, can you help?'

Sheen heard an intake of breath down the phone and after a delay a more hesitant voice said:

'Grey box file? Who are you? You're not from my insurance company, are you?'

'Not the one you have been using Sir Roger, no – I am independent. So can you help with a valuation of everything in that box?' said Sheen, all the while looking around him.

'For everything in that box?' replied Sir Roger.

'Yes, everything, and of course, all the secrets,' said Sheen, barely able to release the last three words. He had thought long and hard about how to imply more than he knew to test Sir Roger without brazenly blackmailing him, or at least without being too crude in making the demand.

Sir Roger answered hesitatingly. 'Ah, I see, yes, all the secrets. How do I know I can trust you, Mr Smith?'

Sheen was a little surprised by the response and wanting to regain control of the conversation, said: 'Sir Roger, we both know what is in that box and I think you do not want the contents to become common knowledge, do you? Now this is our little secret and I will ring you back tomorrow when I expect a reasonable offer. As I said, this is between *us*; you bring anyone else in on your side and the deal will be off and I will put everything on open sale, maybe to the newspapers,' he added as an afterthought.

He switched off the mobile and took out the SIM card, which he broke in half. He disconnected the battery and after a few minutes began the drive back home.

He had barely made himself a cup of tea when Jackie rushed in through the front door, throwing her handbag on to the table and removing her coat. 'Well?' she asked.

Sheen smiled. 'It went well I think. I said what I had and that I would ring back tomorrow to hear his offer. He was shaken, I think; he knew all right what I had, though he didn't ask about anything specifically. That could have been my fault, though, thinking about it; perhaps I should just have mentioned a couple of things and let him ask about everything else. Anyway, I'll ring him in the morning, first thing, get him to get the money straight away and arrange for a meeting at lunchtime to not give him the time to arrange anything with the police.'

'Do you think he will involve the police?' Jackie asked as she refilled the kettle and prepared a mug with a tea bag, 'because I don't think he will. We've talked about this before. Come on, we said that he hasn't told the police about that box; otherwise it would have been mentioned by the police or in the papers.'

They talked about what Sheen would do the following morning and Jackie handed over four more SIM cards that she had bought that lunchtime, together with another four mobile phones.

12

Sheen was dressed in green camouflage trousers and a black T-shirt that he had kept from his Army days. He had left the house before 4 a.m. to make the long journey to Sussex. He kept to the speed limits but even so was pleased with his progress, so that when he pulled off the M1 at the Lutterworth turning and took a right at the Frank Whittle roundabout, he saw that it was only half past seven. He found a parking place among other cars from where he wasn't overlooked and using a new SIM card and mobile he telephoned the Knights' house. He was surprised that Sir Roger himself answered it on the second ring. He introduced himself as 'Smith here. I want to hear what you have to offer, Sir Roger.'

There was a brief delay before Sir Roger answered: 'Five thousand pounds.'

Sheen had wondered what amount Sir Roger would offer and had thought that the opening offer would be low but nevertheless was a little taken back by the speed Sir Roger said it. He and Jackie had spent time trying to work out what valuation Sir Roger would make. The speculation had ranged from a few hundred pounds to thousands. Sheen felt himself getting angry; sure, he didn't know any true figure but the way in which Sir Roger answered left Sheen feeling that he was being taken for an idiot. The answer was too quick, too bland, the tone almost dismissive.

'Rubbish, Sir Roger, just bollocks... Pardon my language but if that is your final offer then I will go to the highest bidder – I don't think I will have any problem with getting a lot more than that.'

There was silence for five seconds before Sheen heard Sir Roger say: 'Fifty thousand then.'

It was Sheen's turn to be taken aback, from five to fifty thousand in the space of ten seconds?

Pressing home, Sheen decided to accept the offer and told Sir Roger: 'Fifty thousand pounds, in used cash by lunchtime today. What is your mobile number?' As Sir Roger gave him the number, Sheen wrote it on to his hand.

'I can't get the money by lunchtime though. Tomorrow at the earliest. Who do you think I am?'

'And who do you think I am? Some prat who's just landed on earth? You had a lot of cash in the safe that you didn't tell the police about, so I'm sure you can get fifty thousand together with just a couple of phone calls – do it. I will ring you in a couple of hours. This is just between us, same rules as before – bring anyone in, I mean *anyone*, and I will withdraw my offer of exclusive rights to you.'

Sheen pressed the red button before Sir Roger could answer. He looked at the mobile and thought he could risk using it again later that day before getting rid of it. Then he noticed his hands were shaking. He held his hands out and thought back to when he was in the Army – even on training exercises he had experienced a touch of the shakes when under pressure. On the other hand, he had always reacted well back then, thriving on the rush of adrenalin and blood around his body, which perversely seemed to make his thinking calmer and give him greater clarity.

Suddenly feeling more confident, he started the car and drove back to the motorway. He needed to find a suitable site to meet Sir Roger and make the handover. The grey box file sat on the back seat of the car, hidden under a coat that the neighbour had left there.

Sir Roger had been unhappy at the terse demand and concerned about the amount of cash that he was expected to find so quickly, but after a phone call to his bank and emptying his safe in his office he comfortably had the money. He had put his mobile phone on charge since the call and now sat in his study waiting for the call from Mr Smith. He had decided straight away that contacting the police was out of the question; he didn't trust them and in any event if all went well and the box and contents were recovered in full, he didn't want them to see, and perhaps question him about, what was inside. He had briefly considered involving Carter in this; he certainly knew and trusted him to handle something of this type but had dismissed the idea – it would be easier and cleaner for him to just hand over the money and get his secret back. Nobody else involved would mean the end to the problem – it would be finished once and for all.

It was just before midday that Sheen noticed two windmills on top of a hill to the east as he approached the outskirts of Brighton. He had checked on the map and noticed that they were set on the South Downs Way, just off a quiet road that ran parallel to the A23 on which he had been driving. He made a diversion through the village of Pyecombe and quickly found the single-track road named Mill Lane that led to the car park in front of the stark white mill known as 'Jill'. The other windmill, of course, was 'Jack' and was of a dark colour hidden behind small trees and bushes, further away from the car park. The weather was dry, the sky overcast and on the hillside the keen westerly wind meant that there were only eight cars spaced around the car park. Five of the cars were closer together and the empty bike attachments indicated that the owners were probably away cycling on the Downs. Sheen assumed they had ridden eastwards, away from the car park and towards what his map showed was another location of interest, Ditchling Beacon. An elderly couple were sitting in a car overlooking the view towards the west and Poynings. In an effort to maximise the feel-good factor of their trip out from home he noted that they had wound down their door windows an inch or so. 'Ah for fresh air!' he muttered under his breath as he smiled at them.

The other two cars were empty and no one else seemed to be hanging around the area either. He turned the car around and drove back down the single track to the main road where he took a right towards Hassocks and the village of Clayton. After only a few hundred yards he saw a pub with a large car park that was half full and he parked in the most congested area. He looked around and couldn't see any CCTV cameras covering the car park; he had made sure that none of the blue road cameras had been on the route either.

Confident that he would not be noticed, he went to the boot, put on his old camouflage jacket, casually threw his rucksack on to one shoulder, and then finally closed the boot again, leaving the grey box under an old raincoat that was in the boot. He didn't intend carrying that with him now, there wouldn't be a straight exchange at this time. He had a slow look around, then set off on foot towards the main road. The map showed a footpath leading up the north side of the hill. After the drive south he could feel the stiffness going from his legs and he took deep breaths of air to fill his lungs to push the oxygen around his body. As he walked he continued to look around him, noting the movement of cars on the main road below so he could gauge what was normal and usual. He knew that by knowing what was normal in any area the unusual could easily be recognised. This was something he had had drilled into him in his Army days, whether he was working in the grim urban sprawl of Northern Ireland or the deserts of Afghanistan. It could make the difference between life and death, lying up under a hedge or in a stream, or in an attic peering through a loosened roof tile. Look, he had been told, ask questions of what you are seeing, why is that farmer moving his tractor just a few yards in the yard, why was the housewife hanging out the washing when the weather was due to rain. Study the routine of where you are, look at animals, their usual pattern or routes, know them and the one time that the pattern is not followed could be the time that something is about to happen. And when you are alone or with a partner and the possibility of being found by men intent on giving you a slow and painful death is very real, you do look, you do question and you do work out what is the usual routine, and what is not. It is the same every time, the same procedure, it was why he had always been just ahead of trouble and part of the reason he was so highly thought of by his fellow soldiers.

As he reached the edge of the windmill car park he looked and saw that nothing had changed. He moved around a corner then took off the rucksack and laid it on the ground while he did a complete turn for a last check of his surroundings. He couldn't see any person walking and the birds were continuing with their steady stream of chirping. In a flash, he dropped to the ground and rolled off the path into the hedgerow, pulling the rucksack behind him with his foot slipped through the webbing. He crawled through the hedging until he was in the centre of wild shrubbery from where he had a view of the car park, then with slow but deliberate movements he took out a scrim netting that he used to cover his feet and the entrance area. He placed his binoculars in front of him by the rucksack and also a mobile phone and the notebook he had with various telephone numbers and notes written in.

Looking at the scene before him he settled down and satisfied that all was in order he waited ten minutes before dialling Sir Roger's mobile number.

He gave his instructions, slowly and clearly to Sir Roger, then had the man repeat them back. He learned what car Sir Roger would be driving and what he would be wearing.

Sheen wasn't concerned whether the police were monitoring the call; they could be but he was certain that if that were the case he would spot them before they could see him and he could just abort.

Sheen monitored the car park for the next twenty minutes during which time a walker had arrived back at the car park and after changing his boots for a pair of trainers had driven away. The old couple remained where they were, though there was little movement from inside the car.

After a further ten minutes the Rolls-Royce entered the car park slowly, almost to the minute on time and came to a stop exactly where instructed. The old couple had turned in their seats to follow the arrival of the expensive car that looked out of place among the cheaper and older cars. Sheen watched as Sir Roger got out of the car. It was the first time that Sheen had seen Sir Roger in the flesh and was surprised by the straight back and fluid movements of the man, considering his age. He was dressed in a checked long-sleeve shirt and brown trousers and brown shoes. Sir Roger stood by the driver's door and held his mobile as instructed.

Sheen dialled by touch, keeping the binoculars held in his other hand focused tight into Sir Roger's face. Sheen was looking at Sir Roger's eyes to see whether they were looking in any particular direction, and also to see whether his lips would give away his speaking into a hidden microphone. Sheen couldn't hear Sir Roger's mobile ring but saw the reaction as he pushed a button and held the phone to his ear. Watching his lips, Sheen saw him say 'Yes'.

Sheen, again speaking slowly, gave Sir Roger further instructions. Sir Roger's head nodded several times as if he understood exactly what he was being told. When Sheen finished Sir Roger closed his phone and stuck it into his trouser pocket. He opened the rear passenger door and removed a brown holdall, which he placed on the rough stones of the car-park surface. He leant in and took out a black plastic

tracking device but there was always the possibility of a tracking device being hidden between two notes.

Within five minutes he had completed his task and buried the empty bin liner under a root of a stinging nettle. He tied the rucksack securely and after a last scan moved back and on to the path. Loading the rucksack on to his back he could feel the weight of the money, something he hadn't really considered before. He retraced his steps, walking at a slow speed to give the impression of a tired walker. His eyes, though, were alert and continuously watching for the unusual.

That night Sheen walked into the house just after ten o'clock and had seen that Jackie and Harry's bedroom light was on as well as the downstairs lights. Jackie was lying on the settee watching a television show that had plenty of canned laughter.

'Bloody hell!' said Jackie, startled by Sheen's appearance. 'Why didn't you call? What happened? I've been worried bloody sick here,' she asked in a whisper. She swung her legs down and leaned forward to push the open door closed, looking at Sheen all the time.

Sheen's face broke into a smile that reached from ear to ear as he flung his arms as wide as possible dropping the rucksack on to the carpet.

'Tra-la,' he whispered loudly, 'smooth as clockwork!' He moved to the door and looked through. He could hear Harry upstairs cleaning his teeth. He quietly closed the door and moved to Jackie and kissed her on her lips, once, for a full ten seconds. He felt her respond as her tongue met his.

He pulled away and still smiling walked a little away from her and pointing to the rucksack, said quietly: 'Fifty thousand in there, all clean, no tricks at all; he just did exactly what I told him, *exactly*. That was what worried me; he was just so, just so...' Sheen's face creased as he looked for the word. '...amenable. I thought it was too good to be true; there had to be a trick. But if there is a trick, I can't see it. I can't work it out at all.'

Jackie was smiling broadly at him. 'Oh God,' she said. 'What are you going to do now. What did he say when you gave back the box file?'

'Well, I told him that I would return it this evening, but I decided in the end that if he would pay fifty thousand as quickly and easily as that, well, why not hold on to it and sell it back to him properly next time.'

Sheen removed his camouflage jacket and sat down in the armchair opposite Jackie. 'I've been thinking about it on the way home. He just did exactly as he was told, from five to fifty thousand and not a peep of protest, just agreed. All the meeting arrangements, no protest, not a hint of protest at all. No tricks at all. Why? Why would he do that? This is the question. I thought it was because it was some sort of trap, you know. But the more I think about it the more I am convinced that he hasn't told anyone anything about this at all; he played it by himself. He believed me when I said that the box would be returned this evening after I had had enough time to check the money properly.'

Sheen stopped talking as Harry's footsteps could be heard coming down the stairs. Sheen and Harry talked football for a few minutes before Sheen explained that he had had a long day visiting some old pals who might be able to get him a job at as a forestry worker in the Midlands...

At the same time, over three hundred miles south of where Sheen was talking to Harry and Jackie, Carter arrived at Sir Roger's house. Mary had retired to have a long soak in the bath before going to bed to finish her book. Really it was any excuse to escape from Sir Roger who after returning from his trip out during the afternoon had been in the foulest temper she could remember for many a year. It was almost akin to those he had during their early days of marriage when the pressure of business overtook her needs at home. She had overheard him almost shouting down the telephone at Carter, instructing him to return from his short holiday in the West Country and to be at the house as quickly as possible.

Carter, too, hadn't seen Sir Roger in quite such a fury, standing there with a crystal tumbler half full of a pale malt whisky, and not his first, Carter thought.

As Carter sat in front of Sir Roger's desk in one of the hard-back chairs, Sir Roger paced his study. He disclosed the events of that afternoon that had led to his fit of temper. He still didn't reveal the contents of the stolen box but stressed several times that disclosure of their contents could bring ruin to himself, and worse. It could also mean that other people that he had known for years could also feel the weight of intrusive enquiries into how their companies had become established. He hinted that the contents related to the early years of his life and especially the manner in which his early years of business success had been achieved.

Carter sat through the explanation without responding or interrupting his boss. He tried to file away in his mind the pattern of what he was being told to create a 'timeline' which would make his memory recall the conversation easier later that evening when he would make notes of what he had been told. This was a habit that he had taken up in the police, to record as much as possible, to assist recall later and also to establish what was said sometime ago that could later be challenged as untrue. Of course, if given direct instructions he would later have the option of destroying or producing the instructions depending on what would be best for him.

Sir Roger drained the remainder of his whisky with a large gulp before half refilling the glass. He didn't offer any refreshment to Carter.

He finally looked directly at Carter with a fierceness in his eyes that Carter would not have believed possible and said: 'I want that bastard, I want that box and everything inside it. I want my money back and I want it all done ten minutes ago. I know more about your methods than I probably should. I do have ears and eyes but, while a couple of times I thought you may have been a little excessive, let me tell you here and now, nothing, I repeat *nothing* you do will be excessive if you get the job done successfully.'

He held his penetrating stare, allowing the words to sink in, and saw that Carter's cheeks began to redden slightly.

'You can have whatever you need, do whatever you like, hire help, whatever. No one must know the truth about this, though; it is our secret and it will remain so for ever. You will be rewarded. I will give you half a million pounds, paid into an offshore account that I will set up for you. I will also make half a million pounds available for your expenses, and anything you don't spend from that you can keep.'

Carter was so stunned that he couldn't think for a few seconds. He almost began a smile when the amounts sank in but instead he cleared his throat. 'Sir Roger, I will start straight away. Would you like me to go through my plan of action with you in the morning?'

Sir Roger by now had tunnel vision, his desire for revenge so fierce that he knocked aside the nagging voice of caution that told him to keep his distance. He was bloody mad, he wanted blood and he was going to make sure that he got it.

'Be here at ten with your plan,' Sir Roger said before draining the glass again and walking towards the door.

The next morning Sir Roger was dressed casually and had evidently, by the small snicks to his chin, shaved hurriedly. They went into the living room where Sir Roger informed Carter that Mary was out for the morning, which Carter took to mean that they could have a full and frank talk, rather than an excuse for why he wasn't offered a coffee.

For the next ten minutes Carter ran through his thoughts and the results of his telephone calls that he had already made that morning. In essence, he was to reinvestigate the initial robbery and to that end a copy of the investigation file would be with him by mid-afternoon. He foresaw that in due course a further demand for money would be made by the blackmailer and to that end he had ordered various pieces of electronic equipment from a trusted source in London. He wanted to place a recording device on the home telephone line besides installing covert cameras in the driveway as well as more inside and outside the Rolls-Royce. In a few minutes he had briefed Sir Roger on what to do when the expected further demand was made.

Sir Roger then handed Carter a piece of paper on which was written in his hand a series of numbers that Sir Roger told Carter would allow him to access a new account established that morning for expenses. The account would allow all types of transfers and cash withdrawals from any bank, anywhere in the world, at any time, without question.

The meeting ended with Carter giving Sir Roger a new mobile telephone that he explained was programmed to his own mobile so that any calls Sir Roger received on it would automatically be relayed, in real time, to his. It was to this mobile that Sir Roger would refer the blackmailer when he called again. The explanation he would give would be that the police knew his usual mobile number and they could perhaps be tracing or even listening in on the calls. Sir Roger was to behave meekly towards any future demands but that this time he needed assurances that the real goods would be exchanged.

The positive action taken by Carter so improved Sir Roger's mood that after the meeting he went to his green house in the back garden to attend to his fuchsia plants. Mary was delighted by Sir Roger's brighter and friendlier response when she arrived home and even more surprised when he apologised for his dark mood of the previous evening. He didn't offer any explanation and Mary knew better than to enquire.

* * *

Later that day, during which he had sorted out the surveillance equipment with an old pal from the Met, Carter had another meeting with DS Harrison, this time at the Black Lion pub on the outskirts of Brighton. He arrived early, so decided to grab a meal and he had just finished his steak when Terry Harrison arrived with his usual worried look.

He refused a drink. 'I could get the sack for this you know,' he snapped. 'I had to get a lad on attachment to photocopy the papers and even though he's as raw as that steak you had' – he waved his hand towards the bloody remains on Carter's plate – 'even he was wondering what the hell was going on.'

'OK,' said Carter, soothingly, 'I appreciate what you've done, and I've got two thousand in the car for you. Does that help your worries?'

Harrison almost smiled when he heard the amount. They had agreed on one thousand earlier that morning when Carter had rung him at home. 'Yeah, guess so, thanks.'

Carter nodded. 'I've got to start at the beginning again and go through everything, follow up all the bits that your lot overlooked or couldn't be bothered to do properly.' He smiled, knowing that the insult would rankle.

He suddenly stopped smiling. Something had occurred to him, something that had been at the back of his mind. 'Terry, you said something before about another robbery that night. The guy said he had done it but in fact somebody else had; I can't remember the details.'

'Yeah, a kid named Brooks ... Alan, no, Aaron Brooks. He had previous for street muggings down on the seafront area and there was one that night about the same time that your man was being robbed at home. He admitted the mugging and went down for it. Later another lad was arrested and admitted the same job. You remember?'

'Look, Terry, why did Brooks admit that job when he hadn't done it. Had he done something else and this job gave him an alibi? Did you ever really look into it?'

sea coupled with general dust and dirt that hadn't been washed away for months. Curtains at the windows hung limply or half drawn, giving the whole house an appearance of neglect, like many similar properties in the square. Carter noted the nearest street light to the house was over twenty yards away and that the front door was slightly set back into the building with the walls giving some shadow towards the door. As he continued walking, Carter looked up at the other buildings in the square, looking to see whether any window was unusually clean, or whether there was a camera in the window looking out. Perhaps the curtains weren't pulled completely or a shadow could be seen to one side of the window; any of these could indicate that a police surveillance operation was taking place. That would be 'sod's law' – the last thing he wanted was to be caught by the police going into the house where a known drug-trafficker lived.

He made a note of where the house was, then walked along the small road that ran behind the houses on the west side of the square. He identified McCall's house and noted the wooden gate set in the high brick wall. Carter saw the fire escape that ran down from the fourth floor of the house into the garden.

For the next hour Carter walked along the seafront and sat on a bench opposite the square watching the movement of people around the area. Ten minutes later he stood up from the bench and walked directly to McCall's house, up the steps and put his hand out as if he had a key. His hand hit the lock at the same time as his foot connected with the bottom of the door and after a short cracking noise the door swung open. He moved into the hallway and pushed the door closed behind him, at the same time fixing back in place the small splinter of wood he had caused by forcing the lock. He stood in the hallway in the gloomy light given by a naked bulb towards the back of the house. He remained still absorbing the sounds and smells of the house and noting the door numbers to the left and right of him.

Satisfied that he hadn't drawn any attention, he moved on the soles of his feet towards the stairs. The threadbare carpet offered little spring to his feet and the wooden stairs creaked with every step. He ignored the first floor and continued to the second where he walked towards the back of the house, shortly seeing the room number he was looking for. Light came from under the door and music was gently playing from inside the room. Carter noted that all the other rooms were silent with no lights showing. He walked quietly past the door to the back of the house and went to the fire escape that would be his emergency exit should he require it. He looked through the window of the door and saw that all was quiet, then returned to McCall's door and gave a gentle knock – just the one. He heard the movement of bed springs from inside then a shuffle of feet before the door was opened. As the door reached a foot wide Carter pushed it hard and immediately stepped into the room.

He instantly took in the room and the man now reeling back from the door. He was the only occupant. The man opened his mouth but Carter quickly put his gloved hand over his mouth before he could make any sound, simultaneously forming his fingers of his other hand into a point, which he pushed into the soft well behind McCall's left earlobe, hitting the nerve.

'The nerve leads to your back,' Carter whispered. 'If it's broken, you will never sit upright again, or stand for the rest of your life.' He pushed the nerve harder and felt the man stiffen. 'Do you understand?'

Carter felt McCall trying to nod but afraid to do anything that would make the pain worse.

He spoke quietly and slowly. 'I am going to take my hand away from your mouth but I will hold on to your nerve. You make sure that you hold on to yours and don't make a sound until I tell you, or it's lying down on a bed for the rest of your life for you. Do you understand?'

141

Again there was a nod and Carter slowly removed his hand from the mouth to under the chin where he gripped the jawbone.

'You had a friend, Aaron Brooks; he's dead I know – in prison. He was in there for a job he didn't do, wasn't he?'

McCall's mind was still not functioning properly, not only from the sudden and frightening arrival of the man whose face he hadn't even seen, but also from his earlier recreational use of very good-quality skunk.

'Please, I'll tell you what you want but please let go.'

Carter maintained his hold. 'Just speak quietly and tell me about Brooks before he went to prison.'

McCall tried to straighten his legs to take his weight, which he hoped would lessen the effect of the hold the man had of him. As soon as he moved, he felt the grip around his jaw tighten even more so the pain in his lower jaw equalled that of behind his ear.

'I only saw Aaron before he went to London; he said he had done something. He was frightened but had some cash that he was going to blow. He didn't even want anything to help him – you know, skunk or coke – he was just getting out of here.'

'What had he done?'

McCall struggled to talk through his teeth, which was the only option with the grip on his lower jaw. 'I don't know, he didn't say. It must have been good cos he was off, but he was scared. He didn't say and I, well, you don't ask, do you?'

Carter was now satisfied that it had been Brooks who had carried out the robbery. 'Where did he stash stuff from other jobs?' he asked.

McCall struggled to open his mouth. 'I don't know. He didn't have one; he only nicked money from wallets and handbags, never anything else, and he spent it all quickly.'

Carter considered this for a few seconds. 'Who else was Brooks friendly with?'

'Don't know – he was a bit of a loner, knew a lot of people but not mates with them, if you know what I mean.' McCall's voice got stronger towards the end of his sentence, his words a touch quicker, both a sure sign to anyone experienced in recognising the immediate build-up of energy before a fight.

Carter had that experience and was ready for McCall's sudden twist of his head at the same time that his hands reached for Carter's testicles and his heel for Carter's shins. McCall was just a fraction too slow and that fraction of a second enabled Carter to move his hand position slightly from just behind the ear to the side of the head and with a quick jerk McCall's neck snapped. Carter repeated the move with another swift thrust and felt no resistance. He gently moved McCall to his bed and laid him down in what would initially appear to someone in a sleeping position. He was careful to touch McCall as little as possible and to hold his body and clothes away from his as cross-contamination of fibres had resulted in many convictions and he didn't want to become another statistic.

Carter looked around the room, noticing the clothes thrown on the floor, the nearly overflowing ashtray with the cigarette tobacco pouch and papers next to it on the bedside table. A small block of resin was at the back of the pouch. A plastic bank coin bag contained some dried chopped leaves . Strange, thought Carter, with all this there wasn't a strong smell of cannabis or even tobacco smoke in the room. He moved to the torn curtains that were pulled together and opened them slowly, again making sure the curtains didn't come into contact with his coat. The window was an old-fashioned sash type made out of wood, which over the years of sea air and general neglect had warped in an open position. Carter gave the top half a push downwards and found it stuck, so reversed the procedure with the bottom half. Surprisingly it slid open upwards silently. Carter gave a smile as he ran his gloved hand under the windowsill and found a hard lump in one corner. As he started to pull this he felt some resistance and then heard the sound of Velcro coming undone. He slowly continued and brought the small package up to the level where he could see it. He was holding another plastic bank coin bag with a long Velcro strip along one side. The bag contained three large white rocks that he immediately recognised as being crack cocaine. Carter looked into the garden and surrounding area and almost laughed out loud as he muttered: 'Silly bastard, oldest hiding place in the world.'

He dropped the package on to McCall's chest and, after closing the window, made for the door. He silently went to the fire escape and, as he had expected, found it unlocked. It was obviously used as a way in and out to avoid the front door, he thought.

Sir Roger looked again at his watch and decided as the hand moved towards midnight he would have to make the call. It would be 8 p.m. in Luján, some seventy kilometres south-west of Buenos Aires, the time when he knew people would be home from work. It was the telephone call he knew he should have made immediately after the robbery but which he had delayed in the hope that the grey box and its contents would be recovered. Even now he had hesitated, delaying making the call while Carter was actively pursuing the blackmailer

He still couldn't understand why he had kept all this stuff all these years. When he was young, it had been bravado, some kind of ego-trip, or perhaps even a kind of insurance for him. He hadn't looked at the documents for many years but he could remember each and every one of them, each and every page, and over the past few months since the robbery he had thought about them every day.

He took a deeper breath and lifted the receiver. His notebook with the number was open on his desk and as he finished pushing in the last digit he closed the book. He heard several

144

clicks before the ringing tone and almost immediately a man's voice that he recognised.

'Señor Mayer, good evening. It is Sir Roger here.'

'Ah, Sir Roger, a most unexpected pleasure to hear from you. I trust both you and Mary are well?'

'Yes, we are both well. I hope that you and Señora Mayer are well,' said Sir Roger as brightly as he could.

'We are both well. Shortly to sit down for dinner, Sir Roger.'

His accent was pure English, each letter and word correctly pronounced. Sir Roger knew that Señor Mayer could speak as fluently in Spanish and German and almost as well in French. The comment about dinner was a polite way to get Sir Roger to cut to the chase; there was no going back.

'Señor Mayer, I'm afraid that I have a problem that I have tried to resolve but at the moment it is still outstanding and out of respect for you and the other associates I thought I would show you the courtesy of bringing you up to date.'

Sir Roger took another breath and was aware of silence as Mayer waited for the reason for the call to be made clear.

'Señor Mayer, Mary and I were the unfortunate victims of a robbery here at the house. The thief showed some violence to us and he was able to steal from our safes. Most of what was stolen is of no consequence, jewellery and money, but there was a box containing some personal papers of mine...'

Again there was silence at the other end of the phone line as Sir Roger continued. 'The personal papers were historical and why I still had them, I cannot explain. I received a demand for money to buy them back from a man and of course I paid the money as instructed; it was fifty thousand pounds. I have my security manager, Carter, investigating and he is also in contact with the police. I just wanted to let you know that we are doing everything we can to recover the papers and of course we will pay whatever it takes to ensure their safe recovery. I will then – I give my word – destroy each and every piece of paper.'

Sir Roger waited, hoping the explanation would be accepted, though in his heart he knew it wouldn't be.

'And what exactly do these personal papers consist of,' said Señor Mayer in his cultured voice and without any emotion.

'They relate to my years in Switzerland, Señor Mayer, when I was living with my uncle. Among the papers were letters from my mother to my uncle.'

'And that is all?'

'No,' Sir Roger knew this was the moment that would decide his, Mary and Josephine's futures, 'Also there were some records relating to my father, his decorations for bravery and citations, his medals. Also, I'm afraid was my passport and the passport of Roger Knight.'

He waited as his words were received and the implication was quickly digested. Sir Roger knew that only Señor Mayer could command total respect from him, even fear and it was with a mixture of both that he waited until Señor Mayer spoke evenly again.

'Sir Roger, this is very disturbing news. It could have repercussions for everyone. The papers must be recovered immediately. I will repeat myself this once, I mean *immediately*. I expect to hear from you within twenty-four hours that the papers, all the items you mentioned have been recovered, that they have been destroyed and that any person who has seen them or knows of them or has any idea about them will never talk of what they know. Have I made myself clear, Sir Roger? If you fail, you can expect us to take the matter under our control. Now, I have been impolite, I have forgotten to ask after your beautiful daughter Josephine. I trust she is as lovely as ever and enjoying her new art gallery, which I am told has been a success.'

Sir Roger could almost feel a knife being pushed into his stomach and turned slowly. The words were so innocent but at the same time so explicit.

'Señor Mayer, she is well and you are as always well informed – her gallery is doing well. I will try everything to bring this whole matter to an end – immediately, as you say. I will telephone you tomorrow night at the same time. I am so sorry, Señor Mayer, for causing the problem and also for having to worry you with it.'

Sir Roger would have added further apologies if he hadn't heard the click as Señor Mayer replaced his phone.

Sir Roger poured himself another whisky. At the thought of the danger into which he had put Mary and Josephine he felt his heart beat faster. He willed this 'Mr Smith' to contact him again. He didn't care about the money. He would not only sanction Carter to do whatever he liked to the man – he would happily assist.

14

Carter awoke in his hotel room and after ordering a Continental breakfast from room service dressed and began work to finish reading the two files he had obtained from DS Harrison. Both contained nothing of real note and after finishing them he sat back to consider his next move. Sunday morning, he thought, not a good time for getting people at work, but a good time for catching people at home on their day of rest. He had considered seeing Mrs Brooks previously but had dismissed the idea as being of little point. What could she have told him? After all, the place was searched by the arresting officers at the time of Aaron Brooks' arrest and nothing had been found.

Carter suddenly almost smacked himself in the face as it dawned on him that Brooks had been arrested for a street robbery in which only cash was stolen, so the police would only have been searching for money, not for a grey box with war memorabilia. 'Damm and blast!' he said as he started to put all the paperwork away into the room safe.

Ten minutes later he parked his car in the Sainsbury's car park and walked the same route to the block of flats that Sheen had taken a few weeks before. He pushed the intercom button and was surprised to be answered just a few seconds later by a lady's voice who sounded happy to have a visitor. He heard the electronic buzz as the front door to the flats opened and he was even more surprised to find the lift working. In his years of working in the Met Police he had found a lift working in a tower block on probably only a handful of occasions.

As the lift doors opened he saw the flat door open and a small woman, with a thin build and in her late forties, standing in the threshold. She was wearing a buttoned-up blouse and a pair of jeans, no make-up and no footwear. As he walked towards her, he held his outstretched hand towards her and gave her his warmest smile.

'Good morning, Mrs Brooks; it really is so nice of you to see me.'

Mrs Brooks took his hand, her hand small in his. As he got closer, she almost leaned away to look up at his face.

'Come on in,' she said, leading the way into the lounge which was only slightly cleaner these days than when she and Aaron lived together. She indicated the settee to Carter as she dropped into the armchair opposite the television, which was still on, though the sound was turned off. The room was smoky, which annoyed Carter; his suit would smell of her smoke for days. He sat and smiled at her.

'Mrs Brooks, thanks again for seeing me. I think you have been visited by the police recently as it appears that Aaron admitted to an offence that he hadn't committed. Somebody else has admitted doing that crime. However, there was another crime that evening and it appears that Aaron committed that one. A lot more was stolen in this crime and my job is to recover what I can. Now I don't work for the police. I have a free hand to do what I want – to pay for information, for instance.'

Carter stopped talking to allow the last words to sink in. Mrs Brooks nodded her head and flicked ash from her cigarette into the already three-quarters-full ashtray.

'You see, Mrs Brooks, there was a lot of cash and jewellery stolen and also a grey box, about this size.' He indicated the size of the box file with his hands. 'The grey box contains some old papers, from the Second World War. Now...'

'Look, mister,' she said, leaning further back into the armchair, 'Aaron did something that night. When he got back

149

I was in bed but I heard him moving about. Now what about this reward?'

'Well, why don't you tell me everything you know, and who else knows and then I can think about how much the reward should be,' said Carter, leaning back and crossing his legs, trying to appear relaxed and confident.

'How much are we talking about, mister?' Mrs Brooks said, her eyes held steady on Carters'.

'Mrs Brooks,' said Carter, 'I don't know yet as I don't know what you can tell me. If it leads to the recovery of the stolen property, then it will be substantial, several thousand pounds, in cash and you won't have to sign for it.'

He smiled sweetly. Inwardly, he could feel that excitement building up; he felt that this could be when he received the news that could break this case. He held his smile but noted that Mrs Brooks' face didn't change at all.

'How do I know you will give me anything? You're not the police. I didn't catch your name but you've taken me by surprise by coming here on a Sunday morning.'

Carter leaned forward and took a wallet from his suit inside pocket. Keeping his eyes on Mrs Brooks, he opened the wallet and took out four fifty-pound notes. He also allowed the wallet to remain open.

She was the first to break eye contact. He knew she would – money did that to people. He leaned forward and put the notes next to her ashtray. 'That is just for you seeing me on a Sunday morning,' he said. 'And' – he pulled out a further two fifty-pound notes and laid them on top of the others – 'that is because I didn't have an appointment.'

Mrs Brooks smiled and leaned forward to stub her cigarette out at the same time as she straightened out the notes.

'That night I was in bed, not asleep and I heard him come in. I knew he didn't have any money and was surprised he had been out in the evening. It was raining, and without money where was he going? I thought to myself. He had been in trouble before and I thought he was probably up to no good and I was going to get up and have a go at him, but then he'd start and we'd end up shouting and slagging each other, so I just listened. He was in his room for a time then I heard him go in the kitchen and I heard the old biscuit tin open. He's hid stuff in there before, you know what he'd stolen. Anyway the tin closed and he went in the lounge. Didn't hear the telly get switched on, that was bit strange and he was in there for a while before he went to bed.'

Years of listening to prisoners confessing their crimes had taught Carter patience, and experience had told him to let the person continue without interrupting them. His heart was beating a little faster.

'Anyway, I got up in the morning, I work down the bus station, a cleaner down there, have been for years. So I was making my tea and I thought I'd look in the biscuit tin. We don't have biscuits in it; it's for the carrier bags you know, somewhere to keep them tidy.'

Carter almost laughed at the thought of her and Aaron Brooks keeping the place tidy.

'And I knew straight away that there was something in there as it was heavier. I saw some jewellery, quite a lot of it, all sorts, some loose and some were in small bags, velvet ones. That's all I know – what is that worth?' said Mrs Brooks as she leaned forward and lit another cigarette.

Carter felt himself deflated by the suddenness in which she had finished her account. It was too sudden, too quickly concluded.

'Well, that is quite useful, Mrs Brooks. You didn't mention any of this to the police did you?' He took another four notes from his wallet and put them casually on top of the others.

'Of course not. After Aaron died I wasn't going to help them, was I? What he'd done he'd done, and that's the end of it.'

151

Until money appears, Carter thought. He leant back again and appeared to be nonchalant as he casually asked: 'And then what?' This was the clinching question, he knew. If she denied knowing anything else, he would perhaps reach a dead end. On the other hand, if she continued there could be more to learn.

'I put it all back and went to work. When I got home he'd left a note, gone to London and the jewellery had gone. A few days later he got home, I was in bed and when I got home from work the next day he wasn't there – he'd been arrested.'

Carter sat there and stared at her. The smile had left his face. 'Mrs Brooks, I have given you five hundred pounds – now that isn't all, is it? I've been fair to you. I've told you that you will be rewarded and I've given you some money just for seeing me. Now let's stop playing games, shall we? Go back and fill in the missing bits, all of them please.'

Mrs Brooks had felt confident talking to this man who appeared to be pleasant and good-looking. Now she felt a change in his demeanour towards her; his voice had changed and instead of the laid-back listening style he had become more direct. Not threatening as such but his nice gentlemanly attitude had vanished. She was a little apprehensive.

'Look, I don't want to get into any trouble. I've told you more than the police. He did have the jewellery and then it went when he did.' The ash fell from her cigarette on to her lap and she made no move to clear it. She looked down at the money already on the table as though she was thinking.

'Mrs Brooks,' Carter said as he fully opened his wallet and pulled out ten fifty-pound notes, which he laid into a pile on his knees. He gathered the money in his hand and leaned forward slowly. He put the new cash on top of that already on the table.

'Now, please continue.' He sat down but instead of sitting back in a relaxed manner as before he remained perched on the edge of the settee.

Mrs Brooks felt a little uneasy and then seemed to make a decision.

'OK, the night I saw all the jewellery, I saw a blue brooch and I kept it for myself, thought I deserved it.'

'Please let me see it,' said Carter.

Mrs Brooks got to her feet and put her cigarette into the ashtray and went out of the lounge. Carter stood and looked out of the window and admired the view to the sea.

Mrs Brooks came up to him and held in her palm a brooch that Carter immediately recognised as being one that had been stolen from Mary Knight.

'Do I get extra for finding this?' Mrs Brooks asked.

'Mrs Brooks, you will get extra for this. Now, please can we sit down again and you tell me the rest of what you know.' Carter smiled at her as he walked back to the settee and waited for her to light another cigarette as she stubbed the previous one out. She remained standing at the far side of the room next to the window.

'I don't know anything else, honestly,' she said.

Carter sat there and thought of where he had arrived in the investigation. He had confirmed that Brooks was the robber, he had had the stolen property here and after a few days in London he had returned before being arrested for the other robbery. He went to Prison where he died. The demand to Sir Roger had been afterwards, so either Aaron Brooks had an accomplice or Mrs Brooks knew a lot more than she had said. The question was how to play it from here. The five hundred pounds wasn't important; more money could be given without any problem if it produced the result he wanted. He was beginning to really dislike this scruffy woman, but he needed more from her.

'Mrs Brooks, please think carefully. You have been very helpful so far. You say that when you heard Aaron come home he went into the kitchen and you found the jewellery.

Mrs Brooks gave a slight gasp as she saw the hole in the concrete and it became clear to her that Aaron had used this as his hiding place for the property he had stolen. To Carter it felt like a breakthrough, though in reality it took him only a step forward. He looked at Mrs Brooks and knew that she had not known of this hiding place. He pushed it all back and replaced the pieces on the unit. He didn't speak, allowing the silence to reach into Mrs Brooks. As he finished, he added the brooch to the letter.

'Tell me, Mrs Brooks, Aaron used that as his hiding place, who else knew about it?'

'I swear, I didn't know that was there,' she replied, her voice sounding panicky.

'Mrs Brooks,' said Carter, 'I asked who else knew about it – who else comes here?'

'No one comes here, no one at all,' she replied.

She started to walk away and had made two steps before she felt an arm around her throat and her head jolted backwards. She didn't hear the snapping of her neck; it was too quick. Carter laid her on the carpet then collected the cash from beside the ashtray. He looked around the room before returning to the settee and turning the cushions he had been sitting on over. It was crude, but perhaps the forensic examination wouldn't be as thorough as it ought and in any case he was going to get rid of that coat later that day. After a final check he walked towards the front door and saw the key hanging on the length of string. He pulled the key off and dropped it on to the ground, knowing that it could confuse the police enquiry.

Sheen moved his arm and looked at Jackie's face inches from his, her eyes staring into his. She was smiling. 'See, I said you'd get better with more practice and in a week's time you will be the best I've had.' She laughed gently and kissed him.

Sheen responded to the kiss then moved to kiss her neck as she slid on to her back.

'I've had a good teacher, but you and Harry were childhood sweethearts so what do you mean? Have you been unfaithful to him before?' he said quietly.

Sheen stopped kissing her neck and look down into her eyes.

'A few times. I live my life and as long as Harry doesn't find out I don't see how it matters; it's not as if I'm looking for love, is it?'

Sheen was seeing Jackie in a different light. He did not feel proud of what he was doing but every time he thought he would tell Jackie it had to stop she would look at him in such a way that his resolve, such as it was, faded. Now he realised what a hard woman Jackie was, but he couldn't help himself. She was his lover and his accomplice. He kissed her on her lips, long and meaningfully, before rolling on top of her for the slow, gentle lovemaking that had replaced the fast and furious sex that they had enjoyed earlier.

15

'Anything happening, mate?' said Tony Bell as he rushed into the office that overlooked the Thames. His jacket was already on its way through the air towards his desk as he walked towards Micky Robert's seat at the main desk by the window.

'Not much, typical Sunday really, lot of traffic coming in but all going sweetly,' said Micky in his typical upbeat voice.

Both men were in their fifties and had worked for MI5 for many years, in different departments and in various roles. Neither had achieved promotion or gained any real recognition but each had been steady in their careers. Sunday working for them was just part of their shift system and being on the desk was a role that each liked as the time went quicker when they were busy. Micky had been looking forward to going home punctually but knowing that Tony was his relief had resigned himself to being late, so he was surprised and happy that Tony was on time, and as he got out of the chair Tony jumped straight into it.

'Just some routine messages, all in their piles for distributing later,' said Micky, indicating the various piles of paper at the back of the desk. Although most of the work was done by computers nowadays, paper still seemed to proliferate – just answering the telephone seemed to generate acres of the stuff.

Tony looked out of the window at the fine river view before reading through the various messages. Nothing would be important, he knew; anything of worth would have been sent immediately via computer to the departmental duty officer, or in very sensitive cases they would have been telephoned to attend to the duty room to handle the matter themselves.

One of the skills of an intelligence officer is seeing some innocuous piece of information and recognising that that piece could fit in somewhere else to help complete a picture. 'Thinking out of the box' is a modern-day expression for what has always been regarded as 'just doing the job'. The difficulty for a good intelligence officer is not over-reacting to everything; there isn't sufficient time or resources to do blanket coverage, and nothing can ever be one hundred per cent guaranteed. The information has to be read, thought about and researched all in double-quick time, either to be acted upon or filed pending any further linkage.

Early that evening an incoming message on his computer terminal made Tony sit up a fraction and reread the message:

```
From:     ACC 3/4 Berlin
To:       London, Duty Team for action as
          appropriate
Subject:  Sir Roger Knight

Had routine message from BND contact. SIGN
(Argentina) monitored telephone conversation
between Sir Roger Knight (England) to Señor
Mayer (Argentina) to effect that Sir Roger
and wife were robbed, papers stolen that relate
to Sir Roger Knight's childhood. Very apologetic
to Snr Mayer who issued threats of consequences
should the papers not be recovered in 24 hours.
(Sunday evening 23.59hrs - London)
     Have asked for update, will forward, END
```

Sir Roger Knight was a name that anybody in MI5 recognised as he was a major industrialist and businessman with contacts and friends in the highest circles. While he didn't court publicity, his name was frequently mentioned in connection to some new government contract or his being appointed to a working party of some note. Tony Bell didn't know much about Sir Roger Knight but a quick search of the database enabled him to build a pen picture within minutes that included the robbery report. More intriguing now was the connection between the papers relating to his childhood and this Señor Mayer.

Señor Mayer produced a negative result on the computer search, which in itself didn't really surprise Tony. Still, this 'Mayer' was of interest to SIGN, the Argentinian Secret Service, formally known as the Servicio de Inteligencia de la Gendarmería Nacional, so he was a 'person of interest'. The fact that 'personal papers' were mentioned suggested that he probably wasn't a business contact, and a further search confirmed that. The Argentina business contacts were listed in Sir Roger's file, together with a short pen picture of each. The final pieces of the jigsaw that compelled Tony to dig further was that the information was passed from SIGN to the German Security Service, the BND, and that whoever had received and read it within the BND had seen good reason to pass it on to the British intelligence officer ACC 3/4 in the Berlin Consulate.

Tony knew that the person currently performing that role was Patricia Langdon. He had known and worked with Pat, as he knew her, even though she was employed by the SIS or MI6, MI5's sister intelligence organisation. Practices had changed radically within the intelligence world in the last few years and now the two organisations were pretty much compelled to share their information and intelligence. It was after this edict that Tony had met Pat, working with her on a drugs importation gang that had links to the British arm of an international terrorist organisation. They had spent time working out of the same office and had spent many hours together on observation posts. He knew of her professionalism and respected her as a person, so had full confidence in her following up with the contact as soon as possible. He sent back a short formal note, acknowledging her message and detailing that he was going to forward this original to the person holding the designation D6/1, to whom further correspondence should be addressed.

'Come on, you know the score, it's Sunday evening. I'll try and get it done first thing in the morning but it's impossible to do it now,' said DS Harrison in an exasperated tone.

Carter had expected the response because he knew police officers who acted as prison liaison officers rarely worked at weekends and even if they did it would be unlikely that their prison counterpart would have been working, too. But by making the request now he was ensuring that Terry Harrison would be making the necessary telephone calls first thing in the morning. Carter had read the letter from 'Steve' twice and noted that the envelope was in a different handwriting, meaning that maybe 'Steve' hadn't known where Brooks lived, though a check in a telephone directory would have told him, as would a visit to the library to look in the Register of Voters, the Brooks' address. There was nothing further that he could do that evening so he decided to have dinner followed by an early night.

Just around the corner from the Metropole Hotel where Carter was about to enjoy his dinner a girl named Chloe was knocking on the door to McCall's room. This was the fourth time she had called that day and now she was becoming desperate for a rock that she had ordered two days before. She had knocked quietly not wishing to wake him up if he was asleep but now, though, she was getting desperate. It was Sunday evening and she needed to have a good night before the week at work that lay ahead. As a trainee law clerk at the local magistrates' court she was finding the pressures and demands made upon her harder and harder to meet. Then there was the matter of her final exams, the evenings she had to spend reading books and researching the

Internet for 'Stated Cases', completing dissertations, all of which were now just a few months away. She needed that rock! She knocked harder on the door. Still there was no reply, no sound from within the room. She was in a dangerous position, she knew; she had known it for months now. Every time she visited him there was the risk that the police would find her there buying her rock. It would mean the end of her career, her reputation, perhaps even the relationship she had with her parents.

Another knock and a call of his name and, again, no reply. That was it, she couldn't stay here; she had to go and attempt to find a guy called Pete or Phil, she couldn't remember his name, but he sold crack from a house near the hospital; she could walk there in fifteen minutes if she got a move on. She walked out of the emergency exit and down the metal stairs and through the unlocked back gate into the small road that ran behind McCall's house.

Sir Roger was not looking forward to making this call, but the news from Carter had at least been a move in the right direction. At least he had recovered a piece of jewellery to show who the thief was and now it was a matter of tracking down any friends or associates who might be the blackmailer. He had a small whisky, which he sipped just as Señor Mayer's voice sounded on the other end of the telephone. Sir Roger updated Señor Mayer, trying to make his voice sound as positive and confident about resolving the problem as possible, but he was met with a curt reply and the telephone being replaced. Señor Mayer had not interrupted but he was obviously not pleased.

At five thirty on any morning the Poole Valley bus depot by Brighton seafront was an interesting place to watch. As the cleaners began their tasks of cleaning the insides of the buses, the ticket office and other public areas, the early-risers waiting for the first buses and coaches to open started to arrive. Some people slept on the few benches in the open air, either having missed their rides the previous evening or fearful of missing the first ride out. Some just slept there because they had nowhere else.

Jim Hannigan had been the cleaning supervisor for sixteen years before becoming the early-turn manager for the depot. He knew the regular customers, the homeless people who quietly wandered off, the drivers, the ticket office staff and the cleaners. He knew who would be early for work and who would be late. He knew who would be drinking tea and where they would be. He knew who would report sick. He knew the depot and was proud of his job.

By six o'clock he was concerned, as not only had Susan Brooks not reported for duty, there hadn't been any telephone call giving an explanation. This was unusual for such a reliable lady and as a result he looked up her personal file and telephoned her home. There was no reply and though he tried every five minutes for the next half-hour there still wasn't any reply. By now it was becoming very busy at the depot, with buses and coaches leaving and arriving every minute. Crowds of commuters arrived at the depot on buses and coaches, walking against the tide of commuters trying to get to their transport. To an outsider it looked chaotic, but Jim had witnessed this for so long he took it in his stride. For the moment he decided that maybe there had been a misunderstanding with Susan's shifts; maybe she was taking a day off that hadn't been recorded properly on the rota sheet, or maybe ... Anyway, he would find out tomorrow morning what the reason was when she turned up for work. He had a lot to do now.

Monday mornings were busy also at the Knight residence off Dyke Road. Mary always wanted to make sure that her plans for the week ahead were in place – her various meetings, coffee or afternoon tea with friends, her two bridge sessions and, of course, her visits to the museum. Mary Knight was a busy and organised woman who these days, after Sir Roger's virtual retirement, had nearly a free rein as to her schedule. She was finalising her plans with Sir Roger in the kitchen over a cup of coffee and a slice of toast when the front gate intercom sounded.

Mary looked at the clock. 'Barely eight,' she said as she rose and walked to the small screen in the corner. 'I expect it's the postman, though I'm not expecting anything.'

The small black-and-white picture showed a man at the gate, but there was no car in sight. He wasn't a postman, but he did look very smart in a suit.

'Are you expecting anyone?' she asked Sir Roger without taking her eyes from the screen

'No,' he replied almost absently.

'Hmm,' said Mary as she pressed the button, allowing the gate to open. She liked this new toy that Carter had installed after the robbery and still enjoyed playing with it. She used the console and selected camera 4, then used the small joystick to pan the camera down the driveway so the man was in the centre of the screen.

'Auto-focus ... come on!' she muttered before calling out to Sir Roger: 'Will you get the door, please.'

Sir Roger took a last mouthful of toast and headed to the front door, which he opened just as the man reached the top step.

The man was perhaps thirty years old, well built and smartly dressed in a dark-blue suit. His light-blue shirt was immaculate and his patterned tie tied into a perfect knot. His shoes were black and well polished. The man didn't smile as he stood in front of Sir Roger.

'Señor Mayer has asked me to call on you this morning and to have a talk about your problem. Señor Mayer has further instructed me to resolve the problem quickly and that is what I do, that is my job. May I?' he said, indicating the hallway.

Sir Roger was caught off guard by the calm, well-spoken but assertive man and meekly stood aside to allow the man to step into the hallway. Sir Roger closed the front door as Mary came through from the kitchen.

'Er ... Mary,' Sir Roger started to say but was interrupted by the man, who strode towards her with his hand extended.

'Caldwell, James Caldwell. I work for an associate of Sir Roger and am here to talk with your husband, if you don't mind.'

Mary was also a little taken aback and found herself shaking his hand without realising what she was doing. 'No, of course not. I was ... well, in a few minutes planning to go out, but I can stay if you wish. Cup of tea, coffee, er ... Mr...?' She asked haltingly.

'Caldwell, and no thank you. If you don't mind, I think it would be best if we can start straight away. We have a lot of ground to cover and time is important, to all of us I am sure.' Caldwell smiled at each in turn and raised his eyebrows towards Sir Roger.

'Yes, of course,' Sir Roger and Mary said almost in unison before Sir Roger opened the study door and gestured for Caldwell to enter.

Less than half an hour later, just as Sir Roger was finishing giving his account of the whole affair, Mary called out from the hallway:

'Off now, back before lunch.'

Caldwell hadn't made any written notes but was listening intently.

'OK, Sir Roger, where is Carter now? I would like to meet him to find out what plans he has and to catch up with exactly what he has done so far.'

Sir Roger telephoned Carter and told him to come to the house as soon as possible, which he did twenty minutes later. Sir Roger hadn't given Carter any explanation and Carter for his part didn't think it the time to question Sir Roger. As he arrived at the house he saw that the front double gates were open and that, though Sir Roger's Rolls-Royce was in the driveway, Mary's car was missing.

Carter sighed as he parked in the space Mary usually parked her car in. What was the bloody point of all that CCTV equipment, he thought, if she willy-nilly left Sir Roger with just a wooden door between him and who knows who. He pushed the bell and looked at the camera hoping that Sir Roger would check the monitor in the kitchen before opening the door.

But Sir Roger opened the door within seconds and before Carter could say anything Sir Roger gestured him into the house. Caldwell was standing just to the side and behind the door where Carter hadn't been able to see him.

'Carter, my name's Caldwell.'

Carter spun on his heels and was instantly balancing on the balls of his feet as if expecting some kind of attack.

Caldwell smirked. 'Good reflexes, Carter, but it wouldn't have done you any good if I had a gun, would it?' As if to prove a point, Caldwell pointed his index finger towards Carter and curled his thumb. 'Bang!' he said quietly. He walked back into the office without saying anything further and was seated before first Sir Roger then Carter joined him.

Sir Roger made the brief introduction before telling Carter to bring them both up to date with everything he had done. Carter told them about the enquiries he had made, about obtaining the files from DS Harrison and then the visits to McCall and Mrs Brooks. He finished by saying that as soon as he knew who this person named 'Steve' was, he was going to pay him a visit too.

It was Caldwell who spoke first. 'So McCall and Mrs Brooks, what are they going to say about you. McCall will be arrested for drugs at sometime and could tell the police, and Mrs Brooks, well who knows, at some stage someone may ask her about her son and how she's coping with her grief, a local newspaper type of personal story, anything like that?'

Carter looked at Sir Roger and saw two steely cold eyes looking back at him. Carter gave a slight shrug. 'I killed them, and neither will say anything.'

'Very clever,' said Caldwell. 'So to cap it all we now have the heat of the police investigating two deaths, obviously linked deaths. Well, Sir Roger, I want to know about any and every move that you or Carter make. Every tiny thing I want to know about and straightaway, any calls, anything. I am in contact with Señor Mayer day and night and I can tell you that after I have told him what has happened so far it is unlikely that he will be happy. I am going to London now. I have an art gallery to visit this afternoon; it is supposed to be a very interesting one.'

Sir Roger blanched.

'Please, we're doing everything we can. You can see that. I've said it doesn't matter about any money of mine; just please, do not hurt Josephine.' Sir Roger felt broken as tears formed in his eyes. He knew he could not beat this man Caldwell and certainly not Señor Mayer. He knew that any threat made by them would be carried through.

Carter faced Caldwell. 'I don't fully understand what relationship this Señor Mayer and you have with Sir Roger, but I know that if you hurt a single hair of Josephine's I swear you will both pay for it!' His face was red with anger and his hands were balled into fists.

Caldwell gave a faint smile and kept his voice devoid of emotion. 'Carter, get Sir Roger to acquaint you with the facts before you make stupid threats that you have no ability to carry out – not against me, and certainly not against Señor Mayer.'

Caldwell looked directly at each of them before slowly and deliberately turning and walking from the office. The front door closed quietly and it was several seconds before either Sir Roger or Carter moved.

'Sir Roger...' began Carter before Sir Roger raised his hand in a silencing motion.

'Mark...' Sir Roger looked up with tears forming in his eyes. 'Don't please, don't try and fight them; you don't know what you are letting yourself in for. No one can beat them, believe me.'

'But, Sir Roger, they can't just make threats against you like that.'

'Oh yes they can.' Sir Roger's voice barely carried to Carter. 'They can.'

Carter sat down opposite Sir Roger, his mind racing. Just who was this Señor Mayer who could frighten Sir Roger?

Andy Foster had caught up with most of the weekend messages and had held individual meetings with his eight staff in the D6 team that he led, ready for the mid-morning meeting he would have with the heads of other teams. Nothing dramatic was happening within his team, just the fairly routine work of monitoring potential industrial espionage targets and the movements of some potential activists who could be conspiring to steal secrets. There was one interesting development, however – Tony Bell's notes about Sir Roger Knight and his very odd conversation with Señor Mayer. It was the curtness that the man had shown towards Sir Roger that was strange; most people were a little in awe of him. But this man showed him no deference at all; there was even the hint of menace in his voice. He had tasked D6/5 to follow up with enquiries into Señor Mayer and also to examine Sir Roger's home telephone records and any mobile telephones held by him and Mary. Routine work for D6/5 which wouldn't take him long, just an hour or two – maybe useful, probably not – but that was what old-fashioned intelligence work was about.

Carter had decided to leave the Metropole Hotel. What Caldwell had said was true, he knew: the police would be starting two murder investigations and they might quickly find the link. The one person who could cause Carter concern would be DS Terry Harrison, though he felt that he would keep quiet, as he also had a lot to lose. DS Harrison would have to admit everything they had done previously as well as what he had done for Carter in the past few days – that would mean imprisonment along with an end to his marriage, no job or prospects of a new one, no home and no pension. Harrison, at least, would remain quiet.

16

Jackie had returned home from work at lunchtime and within minutes she and Sheen had torn each other's clothes off and climbed into his bed. After they were spent, they lay together loosely, sweat running between their bodies that were barely covered by a single sheet. Sometime later Jackie rolled on top of Sheen and looked directly into his eyes.

'I'm thinking of leaving Harry,' she said quietly.

Sheen took a second to absorb what Jackie had said. It was right out of the blue,

'What?' was all he could think of saying. 'Why? Not because of me?'

'Of course it is because of you, but not just you. Don't get me wrong – look I like you, maybe a lot, but there is more to life than me going to work, OK that's not that bad, but coming home, evenings here watching the telly. Sometimes I get out and have a bit of excitement, but I want *more* excitement. Look at you. Been in prison. Now, you've got money, more to come, jewellery to sell, freedom, excitement, adventure ... You'll bugger off somewhere and I'll just drop into the old routine again. You've given me something I've wanted and I'll not get it with Harry. All he wants is to pay more of the mortgage off, then get me pregnant.' Jackie shivered as if the whole idea repulsed her.

Sheen didn't know what to say. It was a bomb that he hadn't seen coming. True he had thought more and more about her and he loved their time together, but he always felt guilty about Harry. He had never wanted to break up their marriage; he thought they were a perfect match.

'What are you thinking of doing then?' he asked.

'Once we get some more cash from Sir Roger, why don't we just sell the jewellery and bugger off abroad, travel, buy a motor home and just go where we want. Let's have an adventure together. This time, give Sir Roger the stuff back, but get another fifty thousand, then he'll be happy; we'll have the money and we can all get on with our lives.' Jackie was now sitting up. She had spoken with passion and Sheen felt her energy and commitment but he avoided looking her directly in the eyes. Her body was still glistening and he looked at the shine above her breasts.

'How do we go about telling Harry?'

'We can either face him and have it out face to face, or we can leave him a note – I don't mind either way.'

Sheen felt a twinge. Harry was his mate, it wasn't right, but then again what he and Jackie had been up to wasn't exactly right either. He didn't know if he could face Harry and tell him. He wasn't frightened of Harry physically; Sheen was fitter and stronger, and he was also a natural fighter.

He pushed his hands across his head. 'OK, Jackie, this is fast, you know. I didn't see this coming at all. Why don't we just think about it for a few hours, you know, talk it through. There are things to think about. What if Sir Roger won't pay any more for instance, or what if he's gone to the police? Perhaps we should just dump the stuff, or send it back to him – we've got that fifty thousand and I've another twenty or so in cash one way and another. The jewellery is worth a bit more, but I don't know how to sell it – we can't just walk into any old jeweller's shop and say "How much?", can we?'

Jackie sat back, taking the sheet with her, folding it around her chest.

'OK,' she said slowly. 'Let's start at the beginning. My leaving Harry, no big deal really. He's got his mates, he'll have the house and his car; he'll meet other girls in a few weeks and probably have one moved in within six months.'

Sheen smiled as Jackie continued: 'So we ask Sir Roger for another fifty grand. Perhaps we send him some of the stuff back through the post, a reward for last time and a taster for what he will get back if all goes well. Then we get that fifty, so over a hundred thousand – that's a lot. Then the jewellery we just leave for a rainy day. The weather is good, we are young, we get on well – let's just go for it...'

Sheen found himself nodding in agreement and smiling. It was all so straightforward. 'There are a few things to think about – what about my probation officer? If I don't report in, he'll revoke the parole and I'll be back inside. I don't know, Jackie, it's just...' He took a deep breath.

'Don't be a spineless sod as well; I thought you had more about you,' Jackie said forcefully.

'OK, OK, let's just spend the next day making sure that we have everything in place,' Sheen conceded, holding his hands up.

'No, we get dressed now, we pack and then we are gone. If Harry gets home before we go, then fine – I'll face him; if not, I'll ring him this evening,' she said as she bounced off the bed and began walking out of the bedroom.

Sheen lay there hearing the shower start, then decided that he would take a shower. He felt excited by the turn of events but not without some unease. This had the potential to turn out badly, he thought, but Jackie was a lovely woman and it was true that they could have a lot of fun together. Where on earth did that idea of travelling around in a motor home come from? he wondered; he'd never heard it mentioned before.

That afternoon Carter answered his mobile just after two o'clock. It was DS Harrison apologising for the enquiry taking so long and starting to explain the reason. Carter cut in.

'Terry, just give me the name and address.'

DS Harrison read out the full details. 'Stephen Sheen with a release address at the home of Mr and Mrs Johns, Harry and Jackie, of Carmichael Road, Scotchwood, Newcastle. His probation officer is Paul Lambert of Newcastle Probation.' He gave him a rough description from his photo.

Carter wrote down the details on a sheet of paper torn from a note pad, cursing when he heard the address was in Newcastle. As soon as he finished the call he rang Sir Roger.

'Did the Mr Smith have any sort of accent, Sir Roger?' he asked.

There was a few seconds pause. 'Yes, come to think of it, there was – North-East I think, certainly northern ... why?'

Carter told Sir Roger about what he had learned from DS Harrison and explained that he was driving to Newcastle straight away.

Sir Roger was thoughtful as he switched the phone off. He would tell Caldwell about the development later, after Carter had made contact with Sheen. He knew this was against the order of Caldwell and so, by proxy, Señor Mayer but he needed to get this mess sorted out and he wanted to be there when it was finally sorted.

Andy Foster finished his meeting and returned to find a yellow Post-it note sitting in the middle of his desk. The note itself just directed him to the D6/5 desk occupied by Peter King but its position suggested the urgency. As Andy Foster arrived, Peter looked up and completed a final few taps on the keyboard. They were the only two people in the office and as a result they were able to talk at the desk instead of retiring to a closed room, as protocol demanded. Andy sat on a chair on the other side of the desk, Peter turned the computer screen so both had a view of it.

'Well, Andy, here's something worth looking at a little more, I think, though at the moment I am still waiting to confirm some points. Without any speculation, what we know are the following facts.' He pressed a key and writing appeared on the screen.

'One,' said Peter pointing to the top line, 'Sir Roger and Mary were robbed in their home; they reportedly had jewellery stolen from an upstairs safe and cash stolen from the safe in Sir Roger's study. I have read the police investigation final report, done by a Detective Sergeant Matt Southall, an experienced officer. It looks as if the robber took Mary upstairs to ransack the safe for her jewellery, then as he was leaving he came across Sir Roger in the hallway and seems to have pressurised him into revealing the existence of a further safe in Sir Roger's office. All the usual enquiries were made, good attendance and so on, but in the end the robber wasn't identified and no property has been recovered. DS Smith makes a comment that he learned from a fellow DS, a Terry Harrison, that a chap named Carter had also been very busy making enquiries and he had also failed to identify the robber or recover any property. This Carter is Sir Roger's Head of Security, an ex Met DI. An interesting character, it seems. I had a little word with a contact in the Met Special Branch who knew Carter many years ago. Said Carter was verging on being over-enthusiastic in his investigations. He was a real result getter and had a good reputation for catching thieves, though his methods were questioned by some of his superiors. Carter retired from the Met early and took on the job with Sir Roger.'

Peter King scrolled the screen down a few lines then looked closer. 'Two, the chap named Mayer is of German extraction and he, his friends and family have been under constant, though casual, scrutiny by the German authorities for some years. It appears from what is known that the Argentinian National Security maintain a regular monitoring of his and his associates' activities. Basically, Mayer's father resettled in Argentina after the war, together with some others. It is generally thought that they had stolen funds of one sort or another that they have used to run successful businesses ever since.'

'What sort of information is this? What is the provenance?' enquired Foster.

'Well, some of it is dated in the 1950s, the stuff about the activities of some Germans who set up home in Argentina after the war. Nazis, we assume. Difficult to know the true provenance – the information hasn't been graded, as we would do today. In essence, though, it appears that Señor Mayer – and this is graded information – is on the Boards of three companies who have large contracts with the Argentinian Government. They also have ties with five German companies, who in turn have governmental contracts with Germany and Spain.

'Now the interesting thing is Sir Roger's business interests. In short he has his fingers in a lot more pies than he claims. Over the years he has set up a lot of separate companies, completely independent of each other and with nothing to do with his main company at all. They are all shown as having their Registered Office at one address, that of his accountant.

'OK, next fact: Señor Mayer is in very close contact with a chap called Pierre Cahout, an international wheeler and dealer. His role is to move money, stocks and the like from one country to another, investing in companies or funds, through tax-efficient countries where the records get muddled or even lost. The Argentinians are especially interested in this aspect. Through the German source I've requested further details about Señor Mayer, his full telephone billing and anything else they can get about his contacts, especially in the UK. I am in the throes of accessing Sir Roger and his wife's bank accounts and I should have them by late today. Now what else is there?' Peter scrolled down further. 'Ah yes.'

He looked up at Andy and leaned back in his chair, crossing his arms behind his neck. 'After the robbery Carter installed a digital CCTV system at the house. I thought just to cross the *t*s and dot the *i*s it would be worth checking, just for visitors or whatever. I think we can access it, but I will have to speak with the tech boys in B for their expertise. Do we have your authority to do that?'

Andy Foster was certainly interested. 'Yes, you do. It might prove useful.' After a few seconds pause he continued: 'Peter, are you staying with this today; it may be something or nothing but I would like to get this squared as soon as possible.'

Peter King nodded in agreement. 'No plans for this evening. My girlfriend is away with her pals, a hen night in Blackpool – God help us all,' he laughed lightly. 'I'll be happy to see this through. I'm on top of the missing wife of the Tory MP; she's shacked up with another MP, a Labour one. Little did hubby know they've been at it like rabbits and have been for over a year. He got told just about two hours ago now and will be looking for a less prominent role in the meantime. Imagine the giggles in The House from the Labour rank and file.'

Both men laughed and Andy was still chuckling as he sat at his desk and unlocked his safe to get on with his papers.

17

Sheen had packed his holdall with clothes, which only took half the space but covered the box file that sat at the bottom. The bundles of cash he put into the side pockets, which he then zipped closed, keeping just two thousand or so pounds on him. They had decided that they would use Jackie's car and three times she went to it to put a suitcase and two large holdalls in the boot. Sheen was a little down at the thought of what Harry would think when he got home and couldn't bring himself to make rejoinders to Jackie's light-hearted jokes. It was still two hours or so before Harry was due home when they finally closed the front door and, with Sheen driving, headed for the main road that would take them south.

They had decided that they would head for Sussex and stay somewhere locally but not in central Brighton. Sheen drove steadily and together they talked through their plan, Sheen offering the more steady approach while Jackie was full of energy and bravura. On the A1 dual carriageway Sheen stayed in the outside lane, leaving a good space between himself and the car in front, while driving at a steady seventy miles an hour. As seven thirty approached, Jackie said that she was ready to call Harry and give him the news. She said it almost with a kind of glee that again made Sheen think of how his buddy, soon to be ex buddy, would take it.

As Jackie pulled her mobile from her handbag, Sheen told her that he didn't want to listen. They decided to fill the car with petrol and then park in another part of the services where Jackie could make her call. His guilt was strong and after paying at the kiosk he drove into a near-vacant parking area facing the lorries whose drivers were either asleep or inside the building having their dinner. As Jackie started dialling, Sheen left the car and walked towards the kiosk. Jackie watched him while finishing dialling then sat back and listened to the ringing tone.

Five minutes later Sheen returned towards the car, unpeeling a packet of cigarettes he had just bought and putting one cigarette into his mouth as he reached the car. He lit the cigarette, recoiling as the taste of tobacco reached all corners of his mouth. As he got in the car he exhaled and saw Jackie looking at him with a broad smile. She held out her hand and took the packet and cheap lighter from him and keeping her smiling eyes on him she lit a cigarette for herself.

'I haven't smoked for God knows how many years,' she said, drawing a lungful of smoke in.

Sheen exhaled again and wound his window down and grimaced as the smoke blew back in.

'I haven't ever really smoked. I just thought it might help relax me. I feel a bit tense right now.' He half laughed. 'Don't know why I'm feeling tense – running away from my probation officer, so a recall to prison is on the cards, blackmailing an old man, stealing stolen property, stealing my mate's wife – what the hell have I got to be stressed about?'

He drove off, joining the motorway traffic again. 'Can you steal stolen property?' He threw the rest of his cigarette out the window and looked at Jackie who was struggling to supress her rising laughter.

'Move back,' she instructed as she leant in front of him and tossed her cigarette out of Sheen's still-open window. 'Harry took it quite well really, I think. He did say a few words, like "fucking bitch" and "fucking bastard" – that was us he was referring to.' She laughed out loud.

Sheen was trying to concentrate on his driving. 'What did you say to him?'

Jackie was still laughing as she sat back in her seat. 'I said that you and I were going away together, that we had been together, sexually, for a few weeks and that I wanted a bit of fun and excitement in my life instead of him. I mentioned that he was boring the arse off me and that I would be in touch one day about selling the house and sorting out the money side. That's when he lost it a bit ... well, quite a lot really. Not crying. He wished us well or something like that, saying we were two bastards who deserved each other. He wouldn't cry on the phone, probably won't at all, though the Scotch will get a hammering tonight I think.'

Jackie leaned over to Sheen and kissed his cheek at the same time moving her hand slowly up his groin and grinning at him. 'No regrets on my part. Any on yours?' she purred as she nibbled on his earlobe.

Sheen relaxed his shoulders and smiled. 'No, no regrets, but if you keep doing that with your hand we'll have an accident and then I'll have regrets. That would make Harry happy.'

They both laughed as Jackie returned to her seat and searched for a music station on the radio.

Sir Roger was about to sit down for dinner when the bell at the gate rang. He moved towards the CCTV screen and immediately saw Caldwell standing there looking directly at the camera, as if defying Sir Roger or Mary to refuse him admission. Sir Roger immediately felt apprehension and fear. He reluctantly pressed the buzzer and watched Caldwell get back into his Jaguar car and drive forward as the gate opened. Sir Roger walked towards the front door and on the way called to Mary that he had a visitor and for the dinner to be held back.

He stood in the doorway as Caldwell got out of the car then locked it with a press of the key and start up the steps towards him. Caldwell kept his eyes squarely on Sir Roger and ignoring Sir Roger's outstretched hand gently pushed Sir

Roger back into the house. He kept his hand in the small of Sir Roger's back as he guided him to the study. As Sir Roger turned, Caldwell spoke slowly and deliberately:

'So, Sir Roger, bring me up to date with things.'

Sir Roger felt intimidated but he wasn't going to show that he was afraid of him. 'Nothing to tell. Carter is out there trying to make progress, and I'm about to eat my dinner.'

Caldwell took out his mobile phone and while scrolling down sat in the chair that Sir Roger always occupied, behind the desk. Becoming angry at Caldwell's rude and arrogant manner he was just about to say something, but in that instant Caldwell lifted his hand towards him and pressed the mobile against his ear.

'Señor Mayer, I am with Sir Roger who says there is nothing to bring me up to date about and that I am preventing him from eating his dinner.' Caldwell grinned at Sir Roger and after a few seconds said, 'Yes of course Señor Mayer.' He handed the mobile to Sir Roger who stood there as if in a trance.

He heard Señor Mayer's soft tone and although Señor Mayer was speaking slowly Sir Roger missed the first several words. He did hear enough though: his daughter as of that moment was in the care of Caldwell's friends and she would remain in their care until such time as the matter was fully and successfully resolved.

Sir Roger took several seconds to understand what was being said to him, but then it dawned upon him.

'This has nothing to do with her; she's an innocent Señor Mayer, please,' he heard himself almost pleading as his mind whirled at what was being said.

'So perhaps you will give me the information. What has happened, what has your man Carter found out?' Señor Mayer asked evenly.

Sir Roger was almost crying. 'Carter has the cell mate's details, the cell mate of the robber, the man Brooks. He's on his way to see him now.'

There was quiet for a few seconds during which Sir Roger wondered whether Señor Mayer had rung off.

'You were told quite clearly that Caldwell was my representative and that he was to be told of any new developments as and when they happened. You were warned about your daughter and yet you took the decision to go against my express wishes, so the consequence will be all yours. You have already jeopardised the lives of many by your actions, by your directly disobeying the order to destroy totally any link with the past, absolutely any and every link. You didn't. The consequences are that we now have to take actions to prevent authorities from investigating the whole organisation. Tell Caldwell everything and do not disobey again, or it won't be just your daughter who will enter our care.'

Sir Roger felt a little faint and was sure that the blood had drained from his face. Caldwell smirked and indicated the chair. 'Why don't you sit down, Sir Roger, and make yourself comfortable while you tell me exactly what Carter is up to and where, though I understand he is driving north at this exact moment.' Caldwell smiled and saw Sir Roger's eyes betray surprise.

'My daughter, where is she? What is happening to her? You haven't hurt her, have you?' Sir Roger said fiercely. 'If you have hurt her, believe me you'll pay.' He kept his eyes on Caldwell's hoping that the hate and venom he felt towards the man would show, and perhaps make him at least a little apprehensive as to the consequences of his actions.

But Caldwell stood there with the same smirk on his face, totally unfazed by Sir Roger's outburst. He clicked his tongue, as if he had reached a decision and smiled at Sir Roger. 'She is safe. She has been taken to a house in the country and will be given three square meals a day – that is, unless you screw up again. In that case, the meals will stop, just like that, no food, no drink either. Can you imagine how she will cope with no food or drink, Sir Roger? A few hours and she will be hungry; a couple of days and she'll be crying and her body aching. She's been told that she is where she is because of you and that only you can solve her predicament. Imagine her in pain knowing that and imagine what she will feel towards you, her hatred. Oh, and of course, should things go badly, imagine the pain when she dies.'

Sir Roger hated Caldwell more with every word he spoke; it wasn't just the words, but the manner he had as he said them. He was deriving pleasure from making the threat, gloating and challenging Sir Roger to do something about it. He couldn't and he knew it. He knew that any threat made would have been agreed to by Señor Mayer.

Caldwell continued: 'Of course you wouldn't have mentioned to Mary anything about this mess you have caused, would you? You wouldn't have told her of the many lives that could be ruined by your stupidity and your disobeying direct orders? Oh no, well perhaps sweet Mary should be brought into the loop and told why her daughter's mobile isn't working – what do you think, Sir Roger. Shall I call her in here?'

Sir Roger slowly shook his head from side to side. 'No, Mary doesn't need to know anything. She doesn't know anything about my youth or my parents or about my business dealings. She doesn't know about what was stolen – as far as she's concerned it was just her jewellery and some money.'

Sir Roger looked up and slowly told Caldwell what Carter had said that afternoon during the telephone call. He felt as if all his years had suddenly caught up with him. As he finished talking, Caldwell abruptly turned and left the study. Sir Roger hurriedly got to his feet and rushed towards the study door, worried that Caldwell was going to find Mary, but the man had already left the house. Sir Roger went to the kitchen to open the electric gates. He watched on the CCTV screen as Caldwell turned right, away from Brighton and the coast and towards the roads that led to the North and Newcastle.

*   *   *

As Jackie had predicted, Harry had reached for the bottle of Famous Grouse and, after three large glasses gulped down in under an hour, had broken down and cried. He felt betrayed by the two people in the world whom he thought he could trust the most. He hadn't seen it coming; there hadn't been any clue that he could recall, no furtive smiles between them, no brushing against each other or trying to engineer time together. He and Jackie had had sex three times in the past week, three times! – what was she thinking when they had been in each other's arms? By ten o'clock he had finished crying and almost three-quarters of the bottle of whisky. He was sitting in the armchair that they joked about as being 'his', the one directly in front of the flat-screen television. He was still in his work clothes and hadn't washed that evening, as was his usual practice. He hadn't eaten and the whisky had began to take its toll.

Now though he had finished with his name-calling, he thought of how he would start taking his revenge. Work, he thought, he would phone them first thing. She worked in HR, she was used to sorting out other people's lives ... Well, he would sort hers all right. Goody-two-shoes, that was how she was thought of by the bosses who had promoted her twice in the past three years ... Well, he was going to put them straight about what a two-timing lying bitch she was. See what they did about her when they knew. He smiled as he remembered Sheen was on probation. He would enjoy telling them what he had done, running off with his wife ... That should earn him a recall to prison. His mood lifted a little as he poured himself another drink. He didn't have to work in the morning so he didn't care how he would feel then.

*   *   *

At ten o'clock Sheen and Jackie were drinking also, but in a small bar of a village pub they had booked into just half an hour before. Jackie had continued teasing Sheen as he drove south until, having had enough of her teasing him with her tongue and hand, he had suggested they find somewhere to stay. They were still behaving like two love-struck teenagers when soon after they had registered for their room. Sheen had paid cash for the room and within a minute of being alone they were naked on the bed, giggling and kissing. Sheen felt relaxed at last, his tension replaced by excitement, his confidence once again high, as it had been in his youth. He was behaving without any thought for the consequences. He didn't care about anything or anybody else – Jackie captivated him. Her strength in thinking through what alternatives they had when they dealt with the 'old man', as they called Sir Roger, her single-minded approach of leaving Harry and her excitement for their future together had rubbed off on him. He felt someone who could be strong, someone he could rely on was alongside him. He felt energised, not exactly as he had been in the Army, but along those lines. His thinking was clearer now that he felt no guilt. Jackie had been right when she had said, 'Forget the past and let's live.' She had probably said those words over twenty times in the past few hours and he had initially responded cautiously, but as her enthusiasm had increased so his arguments had fallen by the wayside.

After their quick and frantic lovemaking they had showered together before going down the stairs to the bar. Their entrance had caused the three men playing cards to stop their game as they looked at the newcomers. They had looked at Sheen and would have noticed his muscular build, but would have spent longer looking at Jackie who wore a shorter than knee-length blue skirt that when she sat on a stool at the bar rode up to reveal half her thigh. She sat facing the men, resting her left arm on the counter while Sheen stood in front of her with his back towards the men. Jackie was smiling happily and Sheen responded, aware that the men were looking at Jackie who was enjoying the flirtation. He asked whether she wanted to sit at a table but with mischief in her eyes she had said that she was comfortable where she was. She toyed with her vodka, a large one on the rocks, swirling the ice while making light talk to Sheen who was enjoying his pint of bitter. They had decided against a meal in a restaurant in favour of baskets of chicken and chips that the landlady was serving to them at the bar.

As Sir Roger was climbing into bed, Mary looked up from her book. 'Is everything all right, darling?'

Sir Roger had kept conversation with Mary to a minimum and in fact had spent most of the evening in his greenhouse pretending to carry out essential care on his plants to avoid any awkward questions. Throughout their marriage he had always tried to be honest with her and on the few occasions that he had lied to her he had felt guilty for days afterwards. He had been torn about how he should handle the threat against Josephine. He had done nothing all morning trying to work out what would be for the best – for her, for Mary and, of course, for him. He cared less for himself but knew that without him Señor Mayer would not hesitate to use whatever means to resolve the problem. Sir Roger had decided mid afternoon to try to telephone Josephine but of course the mobile went straight through to voicemail. So it was true – they had already taken Josephine. He had cried then, until he heard Mary arrive home when he had quickly gone to the greenhouse to pull himself together. He had decided that he wouldn't tell Mary anything; the news of Josephine would devastate her. And then he would end up telling her that his whole adult life had been a lie. Their marriage wasn't legal and that every anniversary had been a sham, a lie. He couldn't do that to Mary.

'Fine, just got a small problem concerning work. It's nothing, though perhaps I have a touch of something that is making me feel a bit lethargic.'

He smiled at her and seeing that she wasn't fully satisfied with his answer he added, 'Honestly!' as he bent over to her and gave her a kiss on her lips. She responded slowly to the kiss, her eyes never leaving his, as if waiting for the real answer. Three minutes later Mary had turned off the bedside light and Sir Roger lay in the darkness thinking of Josephine and hoping that she wasn't being mistreated.

18

Josephine had finished crying and her anger had subsided as she tried to put her thoughts into place. Why this had happened to her, she didn't know, and neither the woman nor man who had kidnapped her from the gallery that afternoon had spoken more than a few words between them during the time they had been with her. She tried to recall exactly what had happened and what she knew; knowing that, if she could work *that* out, it might help her to figure out what was going to happen.

It had been a normal day in the gallery; she had no pressing appointments and until mid-afternoon she had only had three friends visiting her for the usual chat. No serious customer had been in and from where she had been working towards the back of the gallery mostly on her laptop hadn't seen people looking through the window. When she was in the gallery she often saw people out on the pavement looking at some of the paintings towards the front and she had learned that making a waving gesture towards them frequently lured them in. As she had a wide range of work displayed with a corresponding wide range of prices, this method had successfully sealed several sales. Her mobile phone, too, had been quieter than usual; she didn't have any social plans for that or the next evening so no one was ringing to make arrangements or discuss what they would wear. She had eaten the salad she had bought with her coffee from the sandwich shop on the corner of the street at lunchtime, and then went back to looking at the new art exhibitions that were opening across the country.

She had been absorbed in viewing an exhibition that was due to open the following week when the door to her gallery had opened and a man and woman had entered. The woman had smiled at Josephine and walked directly towards her, one hand outstretched as if wanting to shake her hand. Josephine recalled that she had stood and walked a step or two towards her when the man had said something. She paused and tried to think what he'd said but his words didn't come to her. She continued her train of thought: the woman was reaching her, but there was something odd about her, Josephine thought, and instantly she remembered – it was her left hand outstretched, her right was in the handbag, A tan-coloured bag, leather or similar, and then that hand came out. It was at the same time that she had started to shake the woman's left hand. The man had suddenly appeared by the woman. He was quite large, not fat, wearing a jacket and a jumper beneath. A flurry of movement, a blur, a sharp prick in her neck, her hands being held together by the man in front of her. The woman was behind her. Her head swirling, fainting, hot and cold, then ... then nothing, nothing at all until a short while ago.

She tried to move. Her left wrist hurt; she remembered that it was held in a metal grip that made her wrist more painful when she moved it. There was a chain – it went from the wrist bracelet to the wall where there was a metal plate. Her right hand was free; it hurt around the wrist but she was able to feel about her. The place was not just dark but black dark. She felt frightened; she shivered but she wasn't cold. She was sitting on a bed and when she shifted her weight the bed springs creaked a little. The mattress was soft with a blanket at the bottom of the bed. She was fully clothed, her boots, shirt, jumper and jeans, still there. Her head ached, not enough to make her cry, but on another day, at her flat, she would have taken a paracetamol, maybe two, with a glass of water. Water, she was thirsty, her throat was dry.

How long had she been here? What was the time? She felt for her watch, not there; she used her right hand to search her pockets ... nothing in any of them, not even the back pocket where she kept two twenty-pound notes for emergencies. Her coat she had worn to the gallery that morning? She felt around her – no coat. Her mobile phone she remembered was on her desk next to the laptop, being charged.

Josephine pulled the blanket over her boots. Her instinct was to take the boots off – she was on a bed after all – but she felt angry. 'Bugger them!' she muttered. Who are they? she asked herself. Why her? She didn't have any enemies. Her gallery pictures? Of course, that would be it – they were stealing the paintings and sculptures in the gallery; they had just gotten her away so they could take them in their own time. 'Bastards!' she said quietly, but, she thought, at least she was insured against theft. At least when this ordeal was over she would be able to buy more items to replace the stolen ones. That wouldn't be the end of the world, she thought. Just got to keep calm, she said to herself, not provoke them, even help them if it would finish this ordeal quicker and get her out of here.

Her mind wandered to what the man and woman looked like. Ordinary, she thought, thirty, perhaps forty years old. She tried to picture their faces – what did they look like? The woman had smiled at her, just an ordinary face. Wearing a hat, no a type of beret, perhaps. Josephine tried to remember the colour – was there a pattern on it? She became more active, the pain in her head receding as she tried to think hard about the beret, or was it another type of hair covering? Hair? Didn't see any, she thought. Clothes? Didn't notice. She'd been too busy looking at her hand, the left hand, the wrong one. So many questions that she was asking herself and she didn't know the answers to them.

* * *

The man was kneeling in front of the fire poking at the last pieces of material to move them into the flames. The plastic from his jacket had melted before bursting into flames while his jumper and trousers had burned steadily. The beret worn by Wendy Baxter who was currently in the kitchen had been one of the first items on the fire. A trouser suit under a long coat that she had been wearing earlier that day in the gallery had also gone into the flames.

They had arrived at the rented house in Devon just after five o'clock that afternoon and had easily carried the still-unconscious Josephine into the cellar that had been prepared for her arrival. They had rented the house only the previous day after receiving the call from Caldwell. Wendy didn't need to ask what was wanted or what she had to do to prepare it. She knew the kidnapping would take place in London and that the best location to hold someone was at least one hundred miles from the kidnap scene and away from prying eyes. That meant finding a property as secluded as possible but within a community area rather than out on moorland, for example. A cellar was best, but an outhouse or loft would do depending on any neighbours in the vicinity. Wendy had immediately drawn a circle on a map of at least a hundred miles' radius from London, and then looked at the options available. Finally she had decided upon Devon and for the next three hours she had used the Internet to search for rental properties, using Google Earth to check their environs. Subsequent phone calls had eliminated several and she finally narrowed the possibilities to a list of four, each of which she was prepared to visit that evening or the following morning.

The woman who had turned up unexpectedly at his farm asking to rent the old cottage had pleasantly surprised the farmer who owned the property, Mr Roy Jenkins. He had advertised it for several weeks without any response and had resigned himself to losing the money that he sorely needed to prop up the farm. She had explained that she and her husband lived in London but had been burgled so many times that they now wanted to get away for a few weeks to think about their next move. She appeared somewhat timid and perhaps traumatised by the experience, and over a cup of tea she had told him that they both worked from home, so a quiet location would be ideal. The spot in between the villages of Newton Poppleford and Budleigh Salterton was just perfect, she enthused. Those views across fields, and the sea just a few minutes away at Budleigh! It would give them just the space and relaxation they needed.

Mr Jenkins had told the lovely woman who had introduced herself as Ann Turner that the house had been a project of his wife, but she had succumbed to a cancer just a month before the house had been ready, and though still raw from her passing he had pushed on to finish her project. This would be the first time that it would be rented and he was pleased it was to her. Such was 'Anne's' happiness that she even gave Mr Jenkins a quick peck on the cheek before she took an envelope of cash out of her handbag.

That same afternoon she had prepared the cellar, sweeping away the dust then moving a single bed from one of the bedrooms into it. She used a new electric drill to make holes in the cellar wall, into which she screwed a base plate through which she then threaded a heavy chain. She had sat on the bed herself to judge the length – there had to be some movement but not enough to allow their victim to move away from the bed. She had bought tinned soups and microwavable ready meals, for three people to last a week. She had visited a large DIY supermarket where she bought a quantity of disposable all-in-one white suits of the type worn by builders and police forensic officers together with thin latex gloves. She worked all evening until she had everything as ready as she could. Only then did she telephone Caldwell to say that all was ready for the 'guest' and gave him the location.

The following morning Wendy had driven to London and

met with a man she only knew as Michael. He was thirty-five years of age, of large build and wore a black jumper under a plastic bomber jacket. The jacket looked leather, though on closer inspection it was shiny and could not therefore be real leather. If anyone had looked in Michael's wardrobe at home, they would have seen a further three jackets of exactly the same type, all new, hanging in a line. On a shelf next to the jackets were three identical jumpers, all still sealed in their cellophane wrapping.

Wendy had her preferred method of lifting someone, a drug that she had been introduced to some years ago while working in Central America, administered in the neck for quickest results. It had been straightforward to administer the injection; the same distraction had worked twice before for her and Michael and Josephine had reacted perfectly, taking her eyes off of Wendy at the crucial time when Michael had spoken.

Immediately after the injection Josephine appeared to be in a daze while being able to walk normally. Between them they had led Josephine out of the gallery holding an arm each and put her gently into the back seat of Michael's nondescript grey saloon car that he had left outside. Michael had driven while Wendy sat with Josephine in the back seat, who, if anyone had seen her, would have seemed just to be asleep. Michael and Wendy were both aware that the amount of CCTV cameras situated in London was greater than any other city in the world, which meant that if the alarm was raised their movements could be tracked in 'real time'.

Michael drove slowly in the traffic, away from London, taking the M4 motorway heading towards Wales and the West Country. From the M4 at Newbury he swung south on the A34 road to Southampton on the south coast. In a side street they moved from the grey car to a light-blue one that Michael had put in the street during the night. Michael knew the grey car with the keys left in the ignition wouldn't stay there long. It would be spotted by a youngster before nightfall and taken on a joyride before being set on fire later that night. The fire would destroy any evidence. Following Wendy's instructions he had driven along the main roads towards Devon while Wendy had monitored Josephine's condition. An antidote was on standby in her handbag should Josephine's breathing become laboured or her skin colour show signs of great stress.

They reached the farmhouse as darkness fell and after a cursory look around she and Michael were able to carry Josephine into the house and down the stairs and on to the bed. After searching and removing any and every item from her pockets, her watch and stud ear rings they had locked her left wrist into the shackle. Wendy had then made a final check and left the cellar knowing that from past experiences Josephine would wake from the heavy sleep with a painful head and little memory of what had happened. She estimated that Josephine would come to around ten that evening, which would give them time to destroy their clothing, don the white suits and a fresh pair of gloves and have something to eat before checking on her later.

19

Peter King was checking the time on the top of his computer and saw that it was a few minutes after ten when he noticed a new message had been sent to him. He had spent the evening looking at bank accounts and company accounts held by Sir Roger Knight and had become more and more amazed at what he found. Millions of pounds had been put through accounts of his companies, all in small and steady amounts over a number of years, nothing large enough to draw attention, nothing to alert anyone from the Inland Revenue or Customs. He had looked at where all the money had gone to and saw that the majority had been transferred through offshore accounts into tax safe havens, beyond the reach of the British authorities. He had made a note to try and trace exactly what activities the companies did that enabled the funds to pass through unnoticed. It was definitely a style of money-laundering that major criminals used – he would pass on the information to the specialist investigation team in the morning as it had greater contacts and access than he had. He had made a note for Andy Foster to that effect when he decided that he would finish for the evening and grab a pizza on his way home.

At that moment he saw the message blink at him and automatically pressed the button to open it:

```
From:    ACC3/4 Berlin
To:      D6/5 London
Subject: Sir Roger Knight
```

Further intelligence from BND contact. SIGN has monitored telephone calls to and from Señor Mayer (Argentina).
To man in England, 'James', two calls:
  Asking for 'James' to be on standby for work the following day – agreed to
  Giving details of girl Josephine, daughter of Sir Roger, working at a gallery, Mayfair, London, asking that she be taken as a 'guest' for a few days, perhaps a week.
[Graded as A1]

To Señor Mayer, from man called 'James' and believed from voice the same person as above;
Asking Señor Mayer to speak with Sir Roger – Señor Mayer speaks with older man, believed to be Sir Roger (Knight – not confirmed). Señor Mayer states Sir Roger's actions have caused many problems for him and his associates. States [translation by SIGN]: 'Sir Roger, listen carefully. Josephine is in the care of Mr Caldwell's friends and will remain in their care until such time as this matter is fully and successfully resolved.'
Stating his guest had arrived safely and was being looked after, with out problem.
[Graded as A1]

ACC3/4 comment   There is a delay in receiving some communications, but SIGN and BND aware of the implications of content and will try to speed up. Contact at BND says SIGN are prepared to share some intelligence direct with London if situation escalates. To be confirmed, will advise.
  Regards

Peter King reached for the telephone and reread the message while waiting for Andy Foster to answer.

'Andy, sorry to bother you so late but I was just packing up when another message from ACC3/4 came through. Thought you'd like to hear it as things are obviously moving with Sir Roger. Hang on and I'll read it to you.'

As he finished reading the message he heard his boss sigh. 'So they have kidnapped Josephine. Has that been confirmed by any other source?'

'It is the first I've heard of it. Nothing urgent has come from Sir Roger's house, either his landline or mobile. The monitors would have said as they know the brief and what we believe could happen. I haven't had time to check with the Mets yet, but somehow I doubt Sir Roger would have contacted them.'

Andy Foster agreed but nevertheless it would have to be checked properly in the morning. He was thinking through the ramifications. They had knowledge of a girl being kidnapped but, if they told the police, firstly they would blow open the fact that they had been monitoring Sir Roger's telephone calls and, worse, they would be betraying the trust between the international intelligence agencies – which is that what they learn by covert means must be protected. If the sources and intelligence were disclosed, SIGN wouldn't talk to either MI5 or MI6 again. Currently, it didn't deal directly with the UK security services, though they knew that BND would be forwarding the intelligence. It was a tricky situation and Andy Foster decided that he wasn't on the right pay scale to resolve it. He would pass it on in the morning – he would get into the office just after six o'clock to get himself fully up to speed.

'Thanks, Peter' he finally said. 'I'll be in at six-ish. Can you send through to me what you have got so far. What time will you be in?'

Peter King knew the dilemma that Andy Foster was in and

understood what he would do. Passing the buck was something that intelligence officers tried to avoid, but this was definitely one such occasion. 'No problem, sending it through as a message now. I'll be in about six as well. Goodnight.'

Andy Foster replaced the phone. The fact that Josephine had been kidnapped wasn't his main concern, as the implication was that as long as Sir Roger's problem was resolved she would come to no harm, other than a few superficial mental scars perhaps. There were two problems, however, that were important. Sir Roger was a distinguished and respected man and he was personally known to many leading politicians of all parties. He'd had dinner with the now ex-Prime Minister and had even turned down a position in the Lords. His main, bona fide company had government contracts. If he were found out, if the truth became publicly known, it would cause huge embarrassment to the Government, both past and present.

He poured himself a small brandy and sat in the armchair by the fire. His wife had just gone to bed, so he knew he could sit with his thoughts for a while.

OK, he thought, let's put this in perspective. The press find out about Sir Roger and what happens? Well, he reasoned, MI5 had known about it as long ago as 1952 and over the years they had kept quiet about it. Why? To save face and to have the benefit of having Sir Roger's company work for the Government on contracts that were cheaper than its competitors'. So MI5 and the Government had been involved in a cover-up ever since then. He shuddered at the thought of the witch-hunt that would ensue and he knew full well that as current Department Head he would be the one to be the scapegoat. He finished the brandy with a gulp and set the balloon on the table before rising and making his way upstairs to bed.

Carter remained seated in the driver's seat of his car and from his slumped position he could doze and at the same time see any movement at the car park entrance. He had parked deep in the shadows under a large tree over an hour before after receiving calls from Sir Roger and Caldwell during which he had been told by both men that he was to wait for Caldwell before doing anything, and that he was to do exactly what Caldwell said. This had immediately annoyed Carter but any protest he knew would have been immediately rebuffed. He had seen Sir Roger cowed by Caldwell and he knew greater forces were at work. He was to give responsibility over to Caldwell and support him. Very well, he had thought, that is what I will do.

He sat up as he saw headlights enter between the two closed warehouses, briefly causing him to close his eyes to avoid his night vision being impaired. The car had now turned off the headlights and was moving towards him with only its sidelights on. Carter guessed it would be Caldwell. The timing was about right but nevertheless he didn't want to become a victim of a gang of youths out looking for trouble. Almost immediately, he slipped invisibly out of the door (he'd removed the courtesy light long ago) and sprinted towards a low hedge. This he had planned when he first selected the meeting place. Caldwell had something about him, a smooth manner and voice that Carter found somehow intimidating. From his crouching position he was able to push gently into the hedge while watching the twin sidelights approach his car. He was over twenty yards away, which would give him a head start should it be needed. He guessed that he was as good a runner as Caldwell, plus Carter had scanned the area before so had a better idea of which direction he would head for.

He heard the soft rubbing of the tyres on loose chippings from the tarmac and heard the car slow and stop ten feet away from his. Caldwell opened his driver's door. The sound was quite distinct, but the courtesy light didn't show, which impressed Carter. He heard Caldwell walk towards the Carter's

Ford Mondeo and could just make out the figure approach the driver's door. Confidence began to return to him as he heard Caldwell's voice:

'Carter, where are you? We need to talk.'

Carter cupped his hands together over his mouth when he replied, hoping to disguise the exact location of the voice.

'What is going on, Caldwell?'

'We're working together now. No more one-man murder wave. Together we will sort this mess out,' Caldwell hissed.

Carter could see Caldwell walk a few paces back towards the direction he had arrived, then turn in a square of three paces on each side. He waited for fifteen seconds before again through cupped hands saying: 'Just what is going on?'

Caldwell stopped walking but Carter could imagine his head would be moving as he scanned Carter's likely position.

'You heard Sir Roger – we are to work together whether we like that arrangement or not, and you are to do as I want. That's what's going on.'

Carter knew Caldwell was right. There was no threat in his voice, just a statement of fact, so he stood up and walked slowly towards Caldwell.

Hearing the slight scuff of Carter's shoe, Caldwell turned and made out the faint figure moving towards him. 'Ah, very good. Didn't notice you at all. Well done! Taking the light out of the interior and using the cupped hands – very good – I'm impressed.'

Carter was a little taken aback by Caldwell's patronising praise. 'Come on, Caldwell, you're a slimy bastard and I wouldn't trust you as far as I could throw you'.

Caldwell smiled to himself, knowing he had the upper hand. 'We are going to do this together. If you mess me around or question my decisions, then you will be out, and I do mean "out". This is way out of your league. You have done good detective work to get this far but now we know who we are looking for we need to work differently. We've got to find him, get the property back and then deal with him as necessary. With your record to date I'm thinking that I will do the first two points while you're better suited to the third.' He paused two seconds before adding, 'Though this man isn't a druggy or an old lady, is he?'

Carter stopped eight feet or so away from Caldwell and felt his face redden in the dark, belittled at Caldwell's words.

'Now, Carter, how are we going to conduct ourselves when we go and see Sheen and Mr and Mrs Johns?'

For the next two minutes they discussed options of what they would have to do. They would quell the Johns before taking Sheen, search the house and, if all went well, would leave with all the recovered property and Sheen, leaving the Johns couple in the house under threat of reprisals should they discuss what had happened with anyone.

Carter and Caldwell each drove steadily for a quarter of an hour before parking their cars a hundred yards or so from the Johns' home. The house showed lights upstairs and downstairs, though the curtains appeared to be drawn. Carter tiptoed around the side of the house so he could view the back garden while being readily available to assist at the front door should there be a fracas. Caldwell rang the bell and for a few seconds there appeared to be no reaction from inside the house. Then there was an oath before the front door was opened and light from the hallway illuminated Caldwell.

'Hello – Mr Johns, is it?' Caldwell asked brightly and without waiting for any response. 'So sorry about it being late but I would like to have a word with Mr Steven Sheen who is staying with you.'

Harry Johns was drunk, not falling over, but enough to be slowed by the alcohol. 'A word with *Mr* Sheen?' he said with ironic emphasis on the 'Mr'. 'Mister soddin' Sheen and my wife have gone, buggered off. Who wants to know?'

There was a slur to the words and Caldwell felt the force of a mixture of whisky-sodden breath and saliva.

Carter appeared at Caldwell's shoulder as Caldwell said in a friendly voice. 'Could we talk to you inside, Mr Johns, it is rather confidential.'

He gave Harry Johns a smile and slowly moved forward into the house followed by Carter. The living-room door was open and Caldwell walked into the room, taking a quick glance into the kitchen on the way. Carter stood at the foot of the stairs, looking upwards, his ears straining to hear the sound of someone moving.

Harry Johns closed the front door and joined Caldwell in the living room. 'Who are you?' he said slowly as if trying to pronounce each word carefully.

Caldwell turned and said in a gentle voice: 'Mr Johns, I work for a man who Mr Sheen took money from and didn't give what he was selling in return. We want to speak with Mr Sheen to sort out this misunderstanding.'

Harry Johns looked at Caldwell, then moved back to the armchair. He picked up his glass which was virtually empty. He took the remainder in a gulp, then holding the glass he pointed it at Caldwell, 'When you've had yo…ur word, let me know 'cause I want a word with the bastard…' His voice got louder, the words a little quicker and the slur stronger. 'And I want a word with that bitch of a wife as well…'

Carter entered the room and with a little nod towards Caldwell he sat on the settee and faced Harry Johns.

'Harry, what's going on? Are you saying they have both gone, that they're having an affair?'

'True, bloody true! Gave him a home … We've been mates since before the Army and this is what he's done, gone off with my wife. Just got the phone call this evening from her, bitch.' He shouted the last word. 'Bitch, bitch,' he repeated. 'Bloody bitch.'

Carter nodded and said nothing, allowing Harry Johns to

vent his anger. Caldwell stood still and allowed Carter to continue.

'Harry, we've got to find them and as soon as possible. I am with the police. They are in trouble when we find them. Can you help us, please … give us any ideas of where they might be?'

Harry Johns looked at Carter and despite being drunk he could tell that he wanted to catch Sheen and his wife as soon as possible.

Harry Johns nodded. 'Can give you names, friends of them both, in the Newcastle area … Got some paper?'

Carter pulled a small notebook from his inside coat pocket and unhooked the pencil that was attached to the binding. Harry Johns leaned over and clinking the bottle on the edge of the glass poured himself another finger of Scotch.

For the next five minutes Carter wrote down the names and addresses that Harry Johns dictated in between sips of his drink. Caldwell said nothing, just watched and listened as Carter gently coaxed information about the individuals and their relationship to either Sheen or Jackie. Caldwell was impressed by the way Carter smoothly, gently and methodically teased information out of Harry.

'Just a couple of more things, Harry. Does Jackie have her own car?'

'Yeah, a Nissan.' He gave the make and registration number. 'That's what they took, how they went, it's not here,' he said, trying to put the words into the correct order.

'And mobile phones, Jackie and Sheen?' enquired Carter, still writing down the index number of Jackie's car.

'Yeah.' Harry closed his eyes and recited the number. 'He hasn't got one, not that I know of anyway.'

Glancing at Caldwell, Carter said: 'Harry, could you tell my friend here what Sheen has been up to since he's been here? Has he taken all his things? Perhaps it would be an idea to have a proper look around in case he forgot something.'

Caldwell picked up on Carter's affable manner and smiled

at Harry. 'Perhaps we could look in the rooms upstairs, Harry.'

As they stood up, Carter pulled out his mobile phone and after scrolling a few names he pressed the button. It was answered on the third ring.

'Terry, sorry it's late, but it's rather urgent. There's a good drink for you in it of course. I need a full check on a Nissan car. Got some paper?'

Carter heard DS Harrison mutter under his breath but ignored the sound. There was some rustling of paper and he waited until DS Harrison said 'Ready'.

Carter read out the registration number of Jackie's car and her mobile phone number then asked for a full printout of the mobile phone record. DS Harrison was about to protest but Carter, knowing what he was going to say, said, 'Terry, I also want cell site analysis of the mobile, where it is now and where it has been since this afternoon.'

Carter smiled at the silence and wasn't disappointed when DS Harrison inevitably complained that he was asking for him to break the law and his pension would be on the line for doing this.

'Terry, there's ten in it for you. I shouldn't have to be doing this if your lot had done their job properly in the first place.'

Harry Johns and Caldwell re-entered the room while Carter listened to DS Harrison's whining voice. 'You are a bloody detective sergeant, Terry; an ANPR check is straight forward for you as is the mobile cell site analysis. It's basic police work.' Without waiting for a reply he ended the call and saw Harry Johns looking at him.

'I heard that. Well done! Get the bastards, but I want a bit of them afterwards. Oh, do you want photos of them?' asked Harry Johns.

He found some photos of both Jackie and Sheen, which he handed over to Carter.

Carter and Caldwell smiled at each other and Caldwell said, 'Thanks for all your help, Harry. So sorry about what that Sheen has done to your Jackie. He's a bad one and after we've finished with him you'll be welcome to whatever is left.'

20

Chloe pushed her fingernails around the edge of the fire door and pulled it open slowly to avoid any noise. She was pulling the door closed, again slowly and quietly, when she saw a person backing out of McCall's room. The light was poor – the one bare bulb gave little light and what light it did give was barely reflected from the grubby walls and carpet. Chloe was pleased: McCall was in and at last she would be able to get some decent gear at a reasonable price. She moved quickly towards McCall's door and as she reached it she saw that it was a girl who was backing out. Sensing before seeing Chloe, the girl turned and stood frozen to the spot as Chloe joined her. Chloe was smiling as she reached the doorway, but seeing the girl's face she stopped smiling and looked in. McCall was lying clothed on his bed, asleep except that he looked ashen-faced. She looked at the girl and Chloe's mouth opened to ask a question, except she knew the answer without asking. The girl nodded and stuffed her hand deeper into her jean pocket, the other still at her mouth. Chloe noted the hand movement and holding hers out said, 'Give!'

The girl looked at Chloe. She didn't recognise her and noted the clean clothes, well-groomed hair and make-up – not the usual kind of girl, like herself, who visited McCall.

'Give, now!' repeated Chloe.

The girl stared at McCall then at Chloe and back again to McCall. Her mouth opened and Chloe could just about hear her words: 'He's dead.'

Chloe looked at McCall. 'How did he die?'

The girl looked at Chloe and shook her head from side to side. 'Don't know – overdose I expect.'

Chloe's hand was still outstretched and seeing it the girl withdrew her hand from her jean pocket. In her hand she held two polythene bags. Chloe took them and after a quick examination saw that they contained skunk and cocaine rocks. She looked at the girl, who nodded at Chloe and looked down at Chloe's hand. Chloe's first instinct was to take them for herself. She looked past the girl down the rest of the hallway and couldn't see or hear any movement.

'Who else knows about this?' she whispered.

The girl shook her head from side to side. 'No one I think. The door was locked and I had a key. We were old friends ... He trusted me, no one else, just me.'

Chloe made her decision. 'He's dead, there's nothing we can do for him, so why don't we just share what's here and clear off? Let someone else find him?'

The girl looked frightened. Chloe set about dividing the bags and after a few seconds handed one to the girl. 'That's half.'

The girl took the bag and put it into her jeans.

'Lock the door and don't say a thing,' whispered Chloe. 'I've never been here and you've never seen me.'

With that she turned and walked to the fire door. Within half a minute she had gone down the fire escape, across the garden and was in the street. She was aware that she was shaking and saw that the polythene bag was still in her hand. She stuffed it inside her small handbag that hung from her shoulder. She knew that what she had done would mean the end of her career, if she was ever found out, but at that moment she didn't care. What she had would help her get through her exams and then she was going to stop taking drugs, for ever. Honestly.

The other girl returned to her basement room and looked at her polythene bag. She had truly loved McCall when they had been together but she couldn't continue to stand by and watch him having sex with girls who were desperate for drugs. He didn't even give them a discount – it wasn't even part of the deal. She had pleaded with him but in the end he had told her to go. They had remained friends but as she never used her key when she went to see him he had obviously forgotten she had one. She cried.

She remembered how she had found McCall. He hadn't answered his door, he hadn't been seen by some of the regulars, and didn't answer his mobile. He could have been arrested of course, but he only dealt from home and everyone said the police hadn't been to the house in ages. It was then that, sensing something was wrong, she had gone to the house to again try and find McCall. After again getting no reply to her knocking and gentle calling through the door for him she had used her key. She had seen dead people before, several in fact and all from overdosing. They looked as if they were asleep, as if they had just dropped off and were in dreamland and McCall had the same look. His face was ghostly white, not only because he didn't spend time in the sun, but because the blood had had time to drain from the upper part of his body to the lower side. His hand had felt cold.

The polythene bags were on his chest. So odd, she couldn't understand that at all. She thought of him, alone in his room, cold, alone. She stopped crying, wiping her nose and eyes on her sleeve before leaving the basement flat and walking to St James's Street, a main road with plenty of people walking about even at that time of night. She dialled 999 and told the emergency operator that a man called McCall had died from a drug overdose and was in his room in Regency Square. She replaced the receiver and left the telephone box and walked quickly home. 'God bless!' she said and then her mood brightened as she thought of the contents of the polythene bag the girl had given her.

* * *

It was just after 3 a.m. that DS Harrison was awoken by the mobile phone on his bedside cabinet. He used the mobile as his alarm clock and his first instinct was to turn it off, turn over and have another five minutes' sleep. Then he realised it wasn't the usual tune; it wasn't the alarm, it was an incoming call.

'Bloody hell!' he muttered thinking of Carter.

He took the mobile to the landing before answering it to avoid disturbing his wife. She thought it wrong that a policeman should work all day, be on call all night and then be expected to work the following day. *And* they didn't get paid for being on call! DS Harrison listened to what he was told, alert now he knew that it wasn't Carter but the duty detective constable at Brighton Police Station. A telephone call had been received, from an anonymous female, about a guy named McCall who died from an overdose. DS Harrison had inwardly groaned and felt like saying, 'So what?' but the constable went on. The attending doctor had examined the body and believed that McCall had died, not from an overdose, but from having his neck broken. The duty detective superintendent had been consulted and was attending the flat and wanted the local on call detective sergeant to attend also.

DS Harrison sighed and knew he had no choice. It would be a long day, the first of several, perhaps fifteen hours, maybe longer so a shave and shower before going in would mean he would feel fresher for longer. He started to get himself ready, as quietly as possible, though he knew his wife would wake up. The name McCall didn't mean anything to him, just another druggie who had met his end, probably at the hands of another druggie.

At five thirty, Jim Hannighan watched the cleaners gather together in their usual groups, getting their cleaning gear together before they went to their allotted jobs. Again he noticed Susan Brooks was missing and after making sure that all the tasks were properly assigned he returned to the office to check that no messages had been received from her. Later that day he planned to visit her and see why she wasn't coming into work.

Josephine hadn't slept very well, drifting off for short periods then lying awake trying to get back to sleep. She was hungry and thirsty and even with the blanket tucked under her chin she was cold. She estimated that she had been there for some hours and at one stage during the blackness she had called out, very loudly for several minutes, but without any response. She was becoming scared at the lack of response and thoughts entered her head of what if she had just been left there to die. Would she ever be found?

Josephine didn't know that it was just after seven in the morning when she heard a bolt slide, then a door being opened, allowing light to enter the blackness. She sat up quickly and saw that the light was illuminating stairs down to the concrete floor of her room. The walls were all plain concrete, as was the floor. There was nothing else in the room except a single bulb hanging from the ceiling. As she finished scanning the room, she saw a pair of white trouser legs descending the wooden stairs. Then as more of the body came into view she could make out that it was a person encased in a white fabric all-in-one suit, carrying a galvanised bucket in the right hand. The left hand was holding on to a wooden rail but Josephine was unable to determine the sex of the person, let alone any features. The person stood at the bottom of the stairs while their eyes adjusted to the darkness before moving slowly towards Josephine, checking the chain was still attached to Josephine's wrist and the other end to the wall. The person stopped next to Josephine who remained sitting on the bed.

'Who are you and what are you doing to me. Why am I here?' Josephine exploded. The one-piece suit covered the person's head while a fabric facemask concealed most of the face.

The person didn't say anything but put the bucket on the floor and took out a paper bag and a small bottle of water from the bucket. The figure dropped both on to the bed then turned and walked away towards the stairs. Josephine was close to tears with frustration and again she shouted: 'Who are you? Why are you keeping me here?'

The person's steps didn't falter as they started up the stairs and went from Josephine's view. Quickly realising that she was about to be plunged back into darkness she grabbed the bag and bottle of water. She had just opened the bag to see homemade sandwiches in it when the door was closed firmly and the bolt slid back into place. Josephine was about to scream when the bulb hanging from the ceiling came on. It was a very low-wattage bulb that cast a low gloomy light around the room but at least it was an improvement on her conditions. There were two rounds of sandwiches, a cheese and tomato and a ham and tomato, both in sliced white bread. Josephine hated sliced white bread, preferring brown wholemeal, but so pleased was she at the prospect of food that she started eating quickly. She sipped the water and, looking at the bucket on the floor, squirmed at the thought of that being her toilet.

As she ate, she tried to think positively. The food and drink was a good sign – well, not a *bad* sign. Didn't it mean they wanted to look after her, keep her well fed instead of just keeping her alive? Why homemade sandwiches? Wouldn't it have been more usual to have bought them? Was there a reason they were homemade, such as, perhaps, they weren't near a shop. But petrol stations sell them – they're everywhere, aren't they?

'Oh God,' she said aloud. 'This could drive me mad. OK, let's forget the sandwiches. Water...' She picked up the plastic bottle and turning the top felt the plastic security strip break.

'The water's been bought, it's not a bottle filled from a tap. OK ... oh for bloody hell's sake!' she said louder, exasperated by her not working out any significance. She continued to eat and thought of the person, dressed in the one-piece suit, complete with hood, just like the forensic police officers on TV. 'Why a face mask?' she asked herself quietly, then just aloud enough for her to hear herself she said: 'To hide their identity.' Her heart jumped. 'That's it. I know them, or at least I would recognise them.' She finished the first sandwich and took another swig of water from the bottle before starting on the second sandwich. 'If I know them, why would they kidnap me?' She thought for a moment. 'Because of blackmail, for money, from Daddy.' That made her feel almost elated. 'Of course, they are people who I can recognise, people who are giving me food to keep me nourished – that's why he or she didn't say anything. I would recognise their voice. They don't really want to hurt me; they just want money, which Daddy will pay, and then the whole ordeal will be over.'

Josephine felt quite relaxed having reached a conclusion and, with her spirits raised, she finished her sandwich and lay down to sleep. Time passes quicker when you are asleep.

21

It was nearer to half past seven when Andy Foster left his office and called for Peter King to join him in the cafeteria where, after their early start, they could get a breakfast. Andy had spent over an hour reading all the work prepared by Peter King, stopping his reading only to print off relevant pages. He was due to brief Sir Peter Webb in his office at 9.30 a.m. Sir Peter was one of the longest-serving officers in the Service and was held in high esteem by all who had known him during his long and distinguished career. Such was his persona that even as he reached retirement age it was thought by many that he would continue working one way or another, even if he 'officially retired' and his name removed from the internal directory.

Andy had placed the papers into a new folder, unmarked, and used the stamp from his desk drawer to mark the front cover 'Secret'. He placed the file into his safe while he went for breakfast, where he listened to Peter King, who briefed him further on information he had learned that morning.

At nine thirty sharp Andy was sitting in front of Sir Peter's desk and for the next twenty minutes he recounted the facts, indicating, where appropriate, the relevant hard-copy pages. Sir Peter asked few questions until Andy had finished talking. Sir Peter rose from his black leather swivel chair behind his large solid-oak desk and moved towards the window. Due to his status, his office overlooked the Thames, and from his top-floor position he could see over the trees that lined the pavement. He had a splendid view, as he was fond of telling people, but at that moment he wasn't looking at the view;

he was thinking of the problem that had been handed to him. He had worked out various implications and scenarios; none of them very good for the Service, or for him.

His mind made up, he turned to Andy, 'Thank you for bringing this to my attention. I would like – Peter King, is it?' Andy nodded. '–to continue with all his intelligence gathering. Please pass on my compliments at what he has achieved so far. I will pop down and see Sir Roger this afternoon, have a word and see what he has to say. I don't think we will involve any other agency at this time. I would like you, Andy, to keep on top of this, find out what "James" is up to and of course, if anything is learned about where Josephine is, well I think we have the resources to return her to her father, don't you? Let's try and keep this in house, shall we?'

'Yes, sir,' replied Andy while at the same time thinking, 'Oh Christ!'

Jackie and Sheen had been the only guests at breakfast. While Jackie was content to eat toast and coffee, Sheen enjoyed a large fried breakfast. They had both slept well and had planned to leave about ten o'clock for the remaining trip to Brighton. This, Sheen estimated, would take about three hours. If Jackie had been thinking of Harry and how he would feel this morning, she didn't say anything about it to Sheen; indeed, she was, if anything, even livelier and happier than usual.

DS Harrison was in a gloomy mood, which was a frequent state these days especially after only a few hours' sleep. He had been to McCall's house and met the detective superintendent, who had already spoken with the doctor who had discovered the broken neck. She was unable to say anything further about the cause or time, just that she thought death had occurred over twenty-four hours previously. She explained that she hadn't examined the body any further; she would leave that to the Home Office pathologist whose expertise was far in excess of hers. She had been glad to have been released from the scene so she could return to her bed and get some sleep before morning surgery.

DS Harrison had been detailed to organise the call-out for a major incident room to be established and he had driven to Sussex House, where all such murder enquiries in the county were based, to make the arrangements. Remembering Carter's call earlier that night, and finding himself for the moment alone, he took the opportunity of requesting the cell phone analysis for Jackie's mobile as well as entering her car details on to the police National Computer and the Automatic Number Plate Recognition system, or ANPR as it was known. He had waited to see whether the search for movements of her car would be immediate, but as there was a delay he had decided to leave it and check again later in the morning. He had felt guilty sitting at the computer entering the details and had prepared an excuse if he were discovered. In the event, he had time to himself before the major incident team began assembling.

The first team meeting into the death of McCall got under way, DS Harrison sitting in the middle of the long table with Detective Superintendent Dave Wordsley, as senior investigating officer, sitting at the head. The cause of death would not be known until the post-mortem examination that the Home Office pathologist would conduct that afternoon and which the detective superintendent had asked DS Harrison to attend. Attending post-mortems was probably the least favourite job that DS Harrison could be assigned; he hated the smell of the place; let alone having to witness the actual examination of the body. He still couldn't understand why a detective had to attend as the pathologist would call into Sussex House after the examination with her findings on her way home to London.

The intelligence team attached to the investigation were already reading through the list of McCall's criminal convictions and his known associates. It was during this detailed look at his background that it was discovered that he had at one time been a 'Registered Informant', or a 'Covert Human Intelligence Source' as they were politically correctly called. He had lived in Brighton all his life so the number of people known to him was large, most would have to be eliminated from the enquiry by interview. Harrison sighed – it would be a very long day.

Carter and Caldwell had met in the restaurant of the hotel at seven, as agreed when they had arrived late the previous night. They had a list of Sheen's and Jackie's friends in the Newcastle area and together with the help of a GPS Route Finder had divided the names into two halves that would enable both men to concentrate on smaller areas. By eight o'clock Carter had spoken to three people who were friends of Jackie and each had been shocked when told of her elopement with Sheen. None had been aware of the affair and none had seen her for some weeks, nor could they suggest where she might be. This was basic police work, thought Carter, as he looked at the next address and worked out the quickest route.

Caldwell had taken a longer time to drive to his area and had seen only two couples, and with just as little success. He knew the likelihood of finding people in during the day was less than in the evening but he was determined to carry on until the task was finished. He tried to think of what he would do in their circumstances. Where would they go? He was pleased that Carter had been able to access a police officer straightaway to begin the trace on Jackie's mobile phone and car. At least it showed that Carter had attributes other than killing drug dealers and defenceless older women.

By eleven o'clock Harry Johns was feeling a lot better and after a shave and shower had forced some dry toast and black coffee down. He decided to ring Jackie. He wanted to find out whether there was any chance of her returning. They would put this whole mad episode behind them and get back together again; they could make it work. He sat in the same chair as the previous evening, the chair that Jackie had always sat in when he and Sheen had been watching football. His empty glass was still on the table next to him; the empty bottle lay on its side on the carpet. He dialled her number and heard it ring.

Jackie picked up her mobile from her handbag in the car footwell and seeing the caller sighed.

'It's Harry. I'll take it, then tell him not to call again.'

Sheen nodded and continued to concentrate as he drove through the roadworks on the M25.

'Yes?' Jackie said curtly into the phone.

Harry had given some thought as to what he should say but hearing her tone he knew that she was not likely to be returning to him. He went through the motions anyway. 'Just wanted to check that you are all right, you know.'

'I'm fine.'

'Look, can we talk? This isn't right. We love each other, and we are the original childhood sweethearts.'

'There's nothing to talk about Harry. And by the way, I fell out of love with you a long time ago and just put up with your boring ways while I waited for someone exciting to come along, and now he has.' Jackie looked at Sheen, gave him a broad smile and touched his thigh.

'Jackie, it's just temporary. It's just lust, not love. Come on, we can talk it through.'

'You're not listening, are you, Harry. Stop your whining and don't call me again. I have nothing to say to you, except...' She paused. '...You're pathetic!'

'You bitch,' he said slowly. 'Well, you've made your bed so you can bloody well lie in it. I know about the blackmail, and the cops will get you, I'll see to that.'

Jackie was stunned. 'What?'

'Yeah, so clever aren't you and bloody Sheen? Well, the

cops were here last night and I told them everything about you two; they know the lot and they'll get you wherever you go. I hope it's today and you both rot in hell.'

'Cops? Come on, Harry, there weren't any cops – that's bollocks,' she said, her voice trembling as she looked across at Sheen for support.

Sheen had started to speed up on exiting the roadworks but after hearing what Jackie said he automatically took his foot off the accelerator and looked at Jackie who had a mix of worry and fright in her eyes.

'They were here all right. Told me you and him had blackmailed an old man. They've already started looking for you and they'll get you today – no matter where you go.'

Sheen was now driving in the inside lane behind a large lorry that he was only watching with one eye, his other concentrated on Jackie. She was beginning to panic.

'What do you mean they'll get us today?' Involuntarily she looked around as if the police were already there and about to pull them on to the hard shoulder.

'They've got means, smart arse; computers can trace anything these days, cars, mobiles, anything.' Harry was feeling happier than he had done for hours. 'So, darling, have a nice long holiday in prison. Shame, lover boy, will be in another one.'

Jackie hadn't heard the last insult; she had heard too much already and she was trying to understand the full implications of what Harry had said. She pressed the red button to end the call.

Turning to Sheen, she said, 'He said the police are on to us – we're wanted for blackmail.'

Sheen didn't reply but saw Jackie tapping into her mobile phone.

'Tracing cars?' she said to herself, then a few seconds later: 'No, that's no good.' Again she tapped in several letters and again she shook her head. Sheen didn't say anything. His mind was everywhere, except on his driving.

For the next few minutes Jackie kept typing on her mobile, stopping to read then typing again.

'There's lots on tracking, fleet tracking, real time, Automatic Vehicle Location, GPS tracking. Jesus!' she exclaimed. 'Smart phones are a nightmare. Listen to this. It says they "log the position of the device at regular intervals in their interior memory" – blah blah – "In some private investigators cases, data loggers are used to keep track of a target vehicle. Data pushers are common, used for asset tracking, personal tracking and vehicle tracking..." Fuck!'

'Chuck the bloody thing out, now!' Sheen shouted.

Jackie didn't hesitate and immediately lowered her window and threw the mobile out. Sheen, looking in his mirror, saw the lorry following was a good hundred metres behind and guessed he wouldn't have seen what it was that Jackie had thrown from the car. He thought quickly. 'Vehicle tracking, got to be easier than phones I suppose. All those cameras on blue posts. We've got to get rid of the car.'

As Sheen was wondering what to do with the car he saw the sign for Gatwick Airport as the next exit in one mile. 'We'll dump the car at the airport. When they find it they'll check the airlines to see where we've gone but we'll take the train to Brighton.'

Jackie was still recovering. 'What about hiring a car there?'

'No good, they'll check that after finding your car, and anyway if we have another car they can just track that one. At least, they won't know which train we're on.'

'They'll know we are going to Brighton, though, won't they? Cos of the old man. I mean why else would we be here? We could have flown from any airport; we've passed loads on the way down here.'

'Yes, so we'll have to be quick. We've got two phones that they don't know about. They can't track them, so we'll have to think fast and act fast.' He smiled at her reassuringly.

Jackie brightened immediately. 'Yes, that's right. Let's get on with it and then we'll go.'

'There is another alternative,' said Sheen as he watched the countdown markers for the exit. 'We just send the stuff to the old man and clear off; it will be returning stolen property to him and us getting a reward.'

'Don't be daft,' Jackie laughed. 'You're not serious, are you?'

Sheen laughed and shook his head. 'No, just saying.'

An hour later the couple were on the slow train to Brighton, quietly discussing their plans.

DS Harrison returned to his desk and switched on his computer, at the same time letting out a sigh. He was not looking forward to the afternoon; he would forgo lunch – seeing a post mortem on a full stomach was never a good idea. He took a quick glance around the room – everyone was concentrating on their own computer screens and, apart from the tapping of keyboards and the gentle hum of the air conditioning, there wasn't a sound. His computer came to life and he entered his password a flashing envelope in the top left corner indicated emails were waiting to be read. The database opened and he put Jackie's car number into it. Immediately the screen changed: '10.54 a.m.' it read in the left column. The next column showed the location. There was a long list of entries which he skipped until he reached the bottom one which read: 'M25 east, half a mile west of Junction 9.'

His eyes shot open. 'Bloody hell' he muttered, 'They're coming here.' He looked at his wristwatch – 11.53 a.m. – then read the bottom line on the screen: '11.00 a.m. – SYSTEM UPDATING – 1 HOUR APPROXIMATE.' There was a contact number in case of emergencies.

DS Harrison clicked on the envelope that was still flashing, almost demanding his attention. There were nine new emails. Finding the one he wanted from the IT and Telephone

Investigation Department, he opened the email. Beneath Jackie Johns' mobile phone number and home address was a list of times and locations. He looked at the last line, which indicated that the mobile was located within an area south of the M25, close to the M23, just north of Gatwick Airport.

DS Harrison pulled his mobile phone from his jacket pocket and speed-dialled Carter.

Carter was just about to leave his car to try another address when the call came and after hearing what DS Harrison had told him, he immediately called Caldwell and told him. At the same time as he was talking, he was swinging the car back towards where he had earlier seen the signs for the A1, which led south towards London and then the south coast. Caldwell did likewise and shortly he was nudging ninety miles an hour in the outside lane of the two-carriageway road, his headlights full on to intimidate drivers in his way.

Carter was ahead of Caldwell and also driving as fast as he could, using the horn and flashing his lights to move vehicles from his path. He made a short call to Sir Roger who had been sitting in his study at the time. He relayed Sheen's position and also the fact that it probably meant Sheen and Jackie Johns were on the way to Brighton. He could expect another demand from them and he should stall them, using any method he could. He and Caldwell were on their way.

Sir Peter Webb sat in the back of the Range Rover as it was expertly driven, quickly but without attracting attention, towards Brighton. The front seats were occupied by Jonny Allen, the driver, who was normally part of the A4 Surveillance Team, and Bill Hardcastle, an old-time member of the Technical Team whose knowledge of all things technical were legendary within the Service. The briefing of Bill had been short – it was just a simple matter of planting a listening device in Sir Roger's study that could be heard in Thames House. The device was to pick up every word, not use any connection to a hard telephone or mobile line – easy for Bill, almost impossible for anyone else – and oh, it had to be placed covertly, without Sir Roger knowing about it. Bill had packed a few small devices each no larger than a small matchbox into a formal briefcase and been ready for Sir Peter within five minutes.

Sir Peter had said barely a word since the start of the journey as he cast his mind back over the years he had known Sir Roger Knight. He remembered the first time, in the 70s, perhaps 1973 or 1974, at a reception for business leaders who had government contracts. Plain Roger Knight he had been back then, a rich and powerful businessman, shy of any limelight, but who nonetheless had agreed to help MI5 in a covert operation against a so-called friendly nation. The whole thing had gone very well, very well indeed. He, Sir Peter, had earned recognition for it, which in part had helped his promotion in 1975, a first step up the ladder. He had met Sir Roger many times since, also his charming wife Mary and their daughter, the delightful Josephine. He thought of her for a few minutes, how she had grown up and how she was a quite beautiful young lady the last time he had seen her. That was over five years ago. He thought of her for another minute wondering how she was coping and hoping that no harm would come to her. She really was sweet, but the reason for his journey wasn't her, it was for another reason. He forced himself to think of Sir Roger's predicament. What a fool he had been keeping such material, what an idiot! But it was now a case of damage limitation, as they say.

Sir Roger looked at Mary who was holding her mobile phone and making a growling sound. He knew what the reason for it was but he said, 'What's the matter, darling?'

Mary didn't look up. 'Why doesn't Josie answer. I couldn't get through last night and I've tried three times today and she won't pick up; it just goes to answerphone.'

Sir Roger had tried himself and knew the reason the mobile wasn't being answered. 'I expect she has lost it somewhere.'

'I've tried the gallery number as well and there's no reply either,' she said in an exasperated voice and ending her call.

Sir Roger sat at the kitchen table hoping that lunch would soon be ready. Since the call from Carter he had stared at the papers on his desk; none were important, just routine minutes of meetings that had been sent to him, more as a way of making him feel he was still at the helm rather than for his input. He couldn't stop thinking of Josephine, his daughter, the love of his life apart from Mary. What would they do – injure Josephine, hurt her in some way and show him what they had done? He felt physically sick ... For the first time in his life he was helpless.

Sheen and Jackie had spent their time on the train talking and agreeing on what they would do. They felt certain after Jackie's conversation with Harry that they would have a limited time to act if they wanted to get more money out of Sir Roger Knight. They had decided to get off at the station before Brighton proper, London Road it was called. There would be fewer cameras and officials there. Sheen speculated, correctly as it happened, that British Transport police were based at Brighton and he didn't want to walk straight into them.

From London Road station they walked downhill towards the main road into Brighton. Sheen wheeled Jackie's suitcase with his holdall on top while carrying another holdall in his other hand. Jackie carried another holdall. Within a few minutes they spotted a hotel that looked as if they could stay there without drawing attention to themselves. The hotel was painted white with a small car parking area at the front. Within a couple of minutes they had completed the formalities and found their room, which was on the first floor at the front of the hotel. They looked around the room.

'Not exactly what I would like for you, but when the old man has paid up, it will be the Hilton for you in the future,' said Sheen, taking Jackie in his arms.

'Hilton, Mr Sheen? What's wrong with the Savoy or are you being tight?'

He laughed. 'The Savoy it is,' he replied and kissed her.

Jackie responded to the kiss but pulled herself from his arms.

'Not now – we've things to do. You'll get what you, and what I, of course, want, when it's all done,' she laughed.

Sheen started to rummage through the side pockets of the holdall pulling out bundles of notes while Jackie sat down and switched on the television. Sheen had counted out five thousand pounds which he was breaking into five bundles to put in his pockets when he became aware of the news on the television. A man had been discovered in his bed-sit the previous night and the police were investigating how the man died. There were suspicious circumstances, it seemed. Jackie changed the channel as Sheen stood up and put a bundle of notes on the bed beside her.

'Right, I'm off. Don't forget what you've got to get and let me know when you're done.' He bent down and gave Jackie a kiss on top of her head.

'OK, darling, I'll be on my way in ten minutes.'

After Sheen had gone Jackie went to his holdall and found the remaining bundles of cash. She looked at them, weighing them in her hands before placing them in the room safe in the wardrobe. The box file she put into a drawer of the dresser, covering it with her underwear.

Carter and Caldwell were now together and at a steady ninety miles an hour were making good fast progress towards the south coast. Caldwell had rung Wendy Baxter to find out how her guest was, and on being told 'Fine' he had said that he hoped it would be over that day or perhaps the next.

22

Jim Hannighan finished work promptly at two thirty and drove to Hollingdean Road approaching the flats where Mrs Brooks lived from the same direction that Sheen had. He found the front door to the flats propped open by a brick, though no one was around, and took the lift to Susan Brooks' floor. For five minutes he had banged on the door and shouted through the letterbox without getting any reply, before a door behind him opened and a small old lady with grey hair and holding a walking stick looked at him.

'I'm trying to see Mrs Brooks; she's not been to work,' he explained.

'No love, I know. I always hear her leave in the mornings when I'm making my cup of tea. She closes the door quietly, but I still hear it. Then the lift, I can hear that coming, the doors open, then close, then I hear it go to the bottom ... Nothing wrong with my hearing.' She spoke with a firmness that belied her frail-looking frame.

'Do you know where she is? Has she gone away?' Jim Hannighan asked, standing upright.

'Not heard her since Sunday morning. She had a visitor, a man, never heard his voice before. He went not long after and not heard her since,' she replied.

'I know she lives alone these days, after what happened to her son. I'm worried about her.'

'Well, I haven't heard her or anything. See if the key is hanging from the string,' she said.

Jim Hannighan was puzzled for a minute but saw the old lady pointing towards the letterbox and it became clear. He eased his hand inside and used his fingers to search but couldn't feel any string. 'No,' he said, straightening up. 'Nothing there.'

'Perhaps you should call the police then, dear, and let them have a look.' She was now standing on the landing and looking more concerned herself.

Jim nodded as he reached for his mobile phone and rang the emergency number. Closing down the mobile after giving all the details he said, 'Ten minutes and an officer will be here.'

In fact, it was only eight minutes later that PC Hawkins stepped from the lift to find Jim Hannighan finishing the cup of tea the old lady had made for him. After explaining the reasons for their concern, the officer tried to slip a plastic card into the lock before resorting to using his metal-expanding baton to break the glass in the door. He reached in and gesturing for Jim Hannighan and the lady to remain outside the flat he stepped into the hallway.

PC Hawkins noted the smell – the place had a musty, dirty odour about it. Stale cigarette smoke and something else. He found Mrs Brooks in the lounge and recognised straightaway that she was dead. He didn't move towards her but instead returned to the landing. After explaining to Jim Hannighan and the old lady what he had found, he ushered them into the lady's flat while he made a confidential call. He passed the details to the Force Control Room, who immediately passed them on to the duty detective inspector at Brighton Police Station.

Sir Peter Webb announced their arrival at the gate intercom and a very surprised Mary opened the gate to let the car in, calling to Sir Roger who was in his study. He joined Mary at the front door as Sir Peter strode from the Range Rover with Bill Hardcastle a few steps behind. After giving Mary a peck on each cheek, he warmly shook Sir Roger's hand. Turning slightly and holding out his arm, he said: 'Bill Hardcastle; Bill, Sir Roger and Lady Mary.'

Hardcastle shook hands before they went into the house, leaving the car and Jonny Allen in the driveway. Jonny was used to killing hours when on surveillance and preferred to be alone rather than listening to Sir Peter's posh voice. The remainder of the party went into the lounge.

After ten minutes' catching up with family matters and a cup of tea, Mary sensed that there were important matters to be discussed and left the men to it, saying that she would be at a friend's house.

After Mary had left, Sir Peter asked Sir Roger directly: 'Roger, you *are* in a bloody mess, aren't you, old chap?'

Sir Roger hadn't bought Sir Peter's excuse for 'popping in' but was surprised by the brusqueness of the question. Sir Roger had been thinking of how much to say and how much could Sir Peter and his boys and girls already know. He decided to say nothing, but lowered his head. He could feel tears welling up and he squeezed his eyes close.

'Roger, don't blubber – that won't get us anywhere, will it? Our priority is to get Josephine returned and for you to get back your stolen property, though of course that will have to be destroyed. As it should have been years ago.' Sir Peter's voice took on an edge and his eyes bore into Sir Roger's misty eyes. Sir Roger knew that Sir Peter had been a tough operator over the years in the Service and that he could be quite cold and ruthless when he had to be.

Sir Roger broke the eye contact first and nodded. For the next five minutes he told Sir Peter – almost – everything that had happened and what the enquiries by Carter and Caldwell had achieved. He made no mention, of course, of Carter's visit to either McCall or Mrs Brooks.

Sir Peter said something quietly to Bill Hardcastle, who got up and left the room.

'Bill will get some pictures of chaps that we know and perhaps you will point out this James Caldwell fellow?'

Bill nodded and left the room.

Sir Peter asked Sir Roger various questions to fill the time but there was little he had to learn. He concluded by asking: 'So, you are expecting another demand from this Mr Sheen. I suggest you pay him and make sure you get everything back. I'm sorry to say this, but I know you will understand. Señor Mayer may be a very angry man but there are angry men in London, too. It's crude, but let us for a minute think of the consequences of Señor Mayer finding out about the other companies you own and the various bank accounts that he is unaware of.'

Sir Roger couldn't control his surprise at what Sir Peter had said – how had Sir Peter found out about his private dealings? There were only two people who knew everything and an accountant, surely, wouldn't reveal confidential matters like that.

The room was quiet. Sir Roger had come to terms with Sir Peter knowing of the private affairs, that he would address in due course, but he was becoming angry with what amounted to another case of blackmail. God, he thought, to be blackmailed by scum like Sheen was one thing, but by a member of MI5. He stared at Sir Peter, not caring to hide the loathing he now felt for this man.

The silence was broken by Hardcastle returning to the room. He was holding his mobile. He moved to Sir Roger's side and held the phone for him to see the screen – a photograph of a man. Sir Roger shook his head. Hardcastle pushed a button and the picture was replaced by another. Again Sir Roger shook his head. They were on the twenty-third photograph when Sir Roger's eyes widened as he recognised the face of James Caldwell.

'Yes, that's Caldwell.'

Hardcastle spoke quietly into his mobile, then listened for a few seconds before thanking the caller and closing down the phone.

Sir Peter rose from his chair. 'Sorry about how we have to be about this, old chap. It's an all-round nasty state of affairs that has the potential to cause a lot of upset to many people. Skeletons ... well, they need to stay where they lie; they do not get brought out. I think you understand.'

Without shaking Sir Roger's hand, Sir Peter strode from the room followed by Hardcastle. Sir Roger remained in his chair and listened as the car doors slammed and the engine started. The sound of the car horn brought him back to reality and he went to the kitchen to operate the gate opening. It was then that he couldn't control his tears any more.

Sheen had been buying items in various shops in the Churchill Square shopping complex before buying a copy of the local *Evening Argus* and having a coffee. He found what he was looking for and made a call from his mobile to the number shown in the advertisement. He drank up and hailed a taxi to take him to the address he had been given.

Jackie had also been in the city centre shopping and having bought what they had agreed necessary she took a taxi back to the hotel to await Sheen.

DS Harrison had not enjoyed the post-mortem but he had at least managed to stop at a café for a late lunch on his way back to Sussex House and the major incident suite. He was immediately met by Detective Superintendent Wordsley and after informing the detective superintendent of the result of the post-mortem, death caused by a breaking of the vertebrae in the neck, the superintendent remarked that another body had been found that afternoon. DS Harrison was so tired he could barely show any interest. Let that be somebody else's problem, he thought.

'... hadn't been to work,' the superintendent was saying. 'It was her manager from Poole Valley who raised the alarm. After her son dying in prison as well. We will have to keep an eye on what they are doing there as I understand her son was an associate of our man.'

DS Harrison still wasn't interested but the superintendent was still pushing on. 'Aaron Brooks was her lad's name,' he said.

DS Harrison felt his head move and jaw drop before he could control either. 'Aaron Brooks?' he heard himself say.

'Do you know him, Terry?' the superintendent asked with more urgency than DS Harrison wanted to hear, knowing that he was about to become involved in this other enquiry as well now.

'I nicked him for the robbery he went to prison for, that's all.' He had images of WDC Debbie Burrows sitting at her desk that morning all those months ago, telling him that the robbery Brooks was in prison for had been committed by another man. Then followed images of Carter talking about the false admission made by Brooks. Oh God, the files he'd given Carter – no, not given, *sold* to Carter. DS Harrison felt light-headed as if he was going to faint as the enormity of his position struck home. And even that very morning he had misused the Police National Computer. He felt giddy.

'Are you going then, Terry?' he heard the superintendent ask.

'I'm sorry. Got lost there a bit, tired and hearing about Brooks, *Mrs* Brooks. I'm shocked.'

'OK, but if you can help them for a few hours, see if there is any link-up with ours. We'll get both rooms talking to each other in due course, but an early heads-up could be helpful,' said the superintendent as he started walking towards his office at the end of the corridor.

DS Harrison remained rooted to the spot for a good minute. He was convinced that the end was in sight for him, especially after the car and mobile phone checks he had made that morning. They'd throw the book at him for all the disciplinary offences, but only after he had faced trial for being an accomplice to murder, no *two* murders, he corrected himself.

* * *

Jackie was in the room when Sheen knocked on the door. They made a cup of tea using the room's facilities and discussed what each had bought that afternoon. Everything had gone to plan and they were ready to take their next step.

Carter received a call on his mobile phone as he was negotiating the Heathrow Airport turn-off on the M25; the traffic to the airport was gridlocked by an accident and he had to swap lanes to make progress. Caldwell was immediately behind him. The news from DS Harrison wasn't a huge surprise for Carter – true, it could cause problems if the lines of enquiry were right but he knew there would be no evidence, just circumstantial. Terry Harrison was his concern, though – listening to him whine about how he shouldn't have got involved, how his career was finished and how hard prison would be for him. Carter had thought about suggesting Sheen and Jackie Johns should be put in the frame for the murders but decided against it. It was only when he reminded Terry of the cash he had had that the whining lessened, though he could tell DS Harrison still wasn't happy.

Mary had arrived home to find Sir Roger with red eyes; he'd obviously been crying. She knew that it was connected to the visit from Sir Peter and like Sir Roger she hadn't believed his story about 'happening' to be in Brighton. Seeing Sir Roger now, she felt sympathy for her husband and put an arm around his shoulders as she sat on the armrest of his chair.

'Tell me, darling – what's happened?' Then as a thought struck her; her free hand went to her mouth. 'Oh no, not Josephine?' she gasped.

Sir Roger slowly shook his head, 'No,' he said.

'What is it then?'

'Can't tell you, dear. Leave it to me, It's my mess and I'll sort it out.'

'No, I won't leave it to you, Tell me what is wrong. You're in a hell of a state. What did Sir Peter want?'

Sir Roger sat looking at the carpet, seeing nothing and no one, just hearing Mary's words. 'Mary, leave me alone, please; it's nothing for you to worry about. Business.'

Mary pulled up and took her arm from his shoulder. Standing in front of him she said strongly, 'I am not leaving you alone until you tell me what is wrong. Business? You're retired and everything is going well in any case; they can handle anything there, so that's not the reason, is it?'

'It's complicated. Let me handle it.'

'Handle what?' she fired back at him, positioning her hands on to her hips.

Sir Roger looked up at Mary. He loved her, more than anyone. Seeing her standing there with a determined, almost angry look nearly edged him into telling her the truth about the lie of a person she had been loving and living with for all these years. But he dismissed the idea.

'I'm just not feeling my best at the moment. Sir Peter wanted to discuss a small problem with me. Things aren't helped by Josephine not answering her phone. I'll have a gin and tonic and perhaps an early night. I'll get myself together for the morning when I'll sort everything out.' He looked up at her, trying to look her in the eye so that she would be more convinced of what he was saying.

'I don't believe you, Roger; you are just brushing me aside and I am not happy about this at all,' she said as she stormed from the room, closing the door with a solid thump. It wasn't quite a slam, but she had used more force than she had ever done before.

23

Sheen was just finishing the last letter and concentrating on the red felt-tip pen in the plastic moulded letter as the bathroom door opened. Jackie stood there wearing a new pair of black jeans, a roll-neck black pullover, and a black woollen hat, which hid all her hair. She smiled and said, 'Not *too* chic?'

Sheen laughed, thinking she looked lovely and how the clothes showed off her body, especially her waist.

'And?' he asked.

Jackie looked at him. 'Oh!' She rushed to a brown bag still in the bathroom, reappearing quickly with a white latex glove on each hand and carrying a small pair of leather gloves that she put over the latex. 'Now?' she said.

'Perfect,' he replied, 'though you look so sexy someone may remember you.'

She laughed and looked at what he had been doing while she got herself ready. It had been so strange to her, to change her clothes without having a shower, or wash, no cream or make-up of any description and even not to clean her teeth. The reason he had given her though was sound and in these matters she would always agree with his views.

Picking up the single A4 sheet, she looked at the red ink and read out loud: 'Here is one Iron Cross, examine back, and 5 letters. £100K used notes, no tricks and ALONE. Will call a.m.'

'Succinct and to the point,' she said.

Sheen cleared up the plastic mould he had used, the pen and the remaining sheets of paper from the pad he had used, putting them all into a carrier bag. The plastic mould stuck out so he snapped it into two and wrapped the bag closed. All would be thrown into a rubbish bin that evening.

Jackie saw that his clothing was exactly the same as hers; they could, apart from their size, have been twins, she thought. As they cleared up the room and made sure that the contents of the box were in the safe together with most of the cash, the news on the television played in the background. Neither paid much attention to the local headlines about two bodies having been found. But then the report passed to a girl wearing a large dark coat that glistened in the light but persistent rain. She was standing outside a block of flats.

'Another body was found this afternoon at a flat in Upper Hollingdean Road, that of a woman believed to be about forty-five years old. A neighbour described the deceased as a quiet woman who worked as a cleaner at the bus depot in the city. She had had a traumatic time recently when her son accidentally died while in prison. Police say that a post-mortem will be held this evening by a Home Office pathologist at which point the cause of death may be established. At this time the police have refused to confirm the identity until relatives have been traced and informed.

'The police have established a major incident room for each of the deaths, and a source has revealed that the son of the deceased lady and the deceased man from Regency Square, identified earlier today, were known to each other.'

'Thank you, Esther,' said the anchorwoman in the studio.

Sheen stood still. 'Jackie, that woman, she's Aaron Brooks' mum, I'm sure of it. She lives in that block of flats, is about that age and her son died in Prison.'

'Oh come on, that could be any number of women...' Her voice trailed off as she saw Sheen's worried frown.

'Jackie, you don't think that, do you? Aaron knew this McCall fella, too, they said. It can't be a coincidence – it can't!'

'So you're saying that one or both are because of – what? – the stuff you've got?'

'Look, Jackie, two people have been murdered in one city at around the same time. One of them is the mother of the person who took Sir Roger's stuff; another is his acquaintance. Then we have these two blokes calling on Harry as well. I don't believe it's the police at all. They're after us and they're not … nice!'

'So, do we just send it all back. That would stop them coming after us, wouldn't it?' said a slightly nervous Jackie who was beginning to wonder what would happen to them if they were caught.

Sheen looked into space as he tried to put his thoughts together.

'What we said on the train about going ahead, I still think we should do it, get as much as we can from him, let him have his stuff back and then we can disappear. We can do it. If we stay ahead of them, we'll get away with it. You've been the driver for all this – are you having second thoughts now?'

Jackie looked at Sheen. She broke into a big smile and slowly shook her head. 'No, let's do it, as we planned.'

After packing a small rucksack for each of them, Sheen put on a light-blue and yellow anorak while Jackie put on a red raincoat that she too had bought that afternoon. The outer clothing hid the dark clothing they were wearing as they passed through the empty foyer and into the car park. Sheen touched Jackie's arm to steer her to a small dark-blue Vauxhall Astra parked near the entrance.

'There she is,' he said, using the fob to unlock the car. There was a small metallic click as the doors unlocked, but the four-way flasher he had disabled after buying the car that afternoon. The interior light was also disabled, the bulb removed. They threw their rucksacks into the back and turned right to head away from the city centre. They drove north on the A23 road past The Pylons and took the left turn towards Burgess Hill. Sheen continued until he turned into a small lane signposted to a village named Clayton. There he found a parking space among some other cars.

Sheen turned the engine off then pulled the throwaway mobile phone out. Sir Roger's number was already listed and he pushed the green button. He was aware that Jackie was watching his every move.

'Hello.' It was Sir Roger's voice.

Sheen looked around. It was dark and no one was around that he could see.

'Mr Smith here, Sir Roger. Listen carefully. Go back to where you went before, look in the bin, and follow the instructions. You have until 10 p.m. to do this.'

Sheen pressed the red button.

'Right, let's go,' he said, opening his door and taking off his anorak.

Jackie had removed her coat and was just behind him as they each put on their rucksacks and headed away from the car and towards the footpath that Sheen had seen on his last visit to the 'Jack and Jill' windmills. This footpath was parallel to the one he had previously used, set higher and with a few more bushes and scrub grass on the edges. He kept a good steady pace but was anxious to avoid either of them developing a sweat. It took fifteen minutes before he saw what he was looking for – a blackberry bush large enough for someone to hide in. He bent down and used his feet to make a hole at ground level towards the centre of the bush then extracted himself.

'Good luck!' he whispered as he gave Jackie a peck on the cheek.

Jackie was more than nervous – scared would have been closer to the truth had anyone asked her. She remembered what she had been told earlier, rucksack strap around an ankle, hands out front, and feel your way forward. She did this while Sheen, crouched next to the bush, strained all his senses as tried to work out whether anyone was around. Several times he winced at the noise Jackie was making, but he didn't say anything – her confidence had to be increased, not hurt. He reached into his rucksack and walked thirty yards away before lying on the grass and switching on the night-sight, one of a pair he had bought that afternoon. They had cost three hundred pounds a piece but were probably the best he could have got 'off the shelf'.

He focused on the bush where Jackie was lying and was satisfied that she couldn't be seen. He hoped that she had organised herself quickly and had her night-sight focused on him. He gave her a thumbs-up and blew her a kiss before standing and making towards the path. The path was a stony one, which made more noise, but with care he knew that he wouldn't be heard more than a few feet away. He wanted to avoid the grass as with a dew any footprints could be identified by someone who knew what they were looking for.

Using his night-sight, he returned to the car park that he had been to before and, having located the rubbish bin, he took an envelope from his pocket and laid it on top. He quickly went through the car park, away from where he had hidden previously and took the South Downs Trail uphill. The stone path was uneven and he had to take care; a sprained ankle and they would be in trouble. He walked for ten minutes before taking to the field to his right, walking directly away from the path. He again turned to his right and walked for a further ten minutes. He found a wooden post with a small mound of earth topped with grass and lay down. Using his night-sight he could see the car park and the rubbish bin. He checked his position by slowly looking through 360 degrees, until, satisfied, he pulled the black rubber sheeting from his rucksack and slowly drew it over him. Now for the wait, he said to himself.

* * *

Sir Roger had listened to the call and recognised the accent. Immediately the call had finished he dialled Carter.

Carter didn't know the area that Sir Roger was talking about but after a minute had located it on his car satellite navigation system.

'We're an hour away,' he said, 'maybe a little longer, but we can come in from the north, so if you go at 9.45 p.m. we should be in position. Just follow any instructions but have your mobile on so you can talk and I can hear what you're saying. I'll tell Caldwell. Any changes and I'll get back to you.'

Carter told Caldwell of the call to Sir Roger and what he had told Sir Roger to do. Caldwell agreed and they talked about their strategy while still driving through the evening traffic.

Sir Roger had just finished his call when Mary joined him in the study. She was about to ask him whether he wanted a drink but seeing him putting his phone on the table she became suspicious of what her husband was up to.

'Who was that you were talking to?' she asked with an edge to her voice.

'Oh, Carter,' Sir Roger said dismissively.

'What about?' Mary persisted.

'Just business.'

'Right,' she said as she sat down on a chair, 'explain to me *exactly* what the business is.' She stared at him with more defiance and aggression than Sir Roger had ever seen.

'Bloody well tell me, Roger,' she almost hissed.

He shook his head. 'Not now – I have to go out,' he said, rising from behind his desk.

Mary was up in a flash and moved to block his way.

'Not until you tell me what is going on,' she almost shouted.

Sir Roger walked towards Mary and stood very close to her. 'Not now, I said. Move away.'

Mary jutted her chin forward and stood as upright as she

could. Her body language making it clear that she was not going to move.

'Mary, please darling, I'll be back soon and then we can sit down and I'll tell you my problem. It's nothing for you to worry about, though.' He smiled as best he could but took each of her arms in his hands and tried to move her.

Mary couldn't believe what was happening – he was manhandling her! Her anger exploded with a force that she wouldn't have believed possible. 'What the hell do you think you are doing? How dare you try and push me out of the way.' She struggled and freed her arms from his hands and regained her position. 'Sit down and tell me – now!'

Sir Roger was caught in a situation he knew could only get worse. Drastic measures were needed.

He raised his voice at her. 'You don't understand. I have to do something – it's for both of us, *all* of us.'

Mary rocked back a little. He had never raised his voice to her like this. She made her decision. 'Right, if you won't treat me like your wife and insist on keeping secrets from me, I'm going to stay with Josephine for a few days.' She turned before he could say anything and this time she did slam the study door after her. She stormed upstairs to pack some clothes and toiletries, then raced down the stairs expecting for Sir Roger to be at the bottom imploring her not to go. But the study door was still closed. She slammed the front door and ran down the steps to her car. She started the car and at the same time pushed for the gate to open. Racing the engine, she ground into first gear and sped from the driveway on to the road.

The altercation was relayed to Andy Foster, who in turn telephoned Sir Peter Webb. He was at home and, judging from the background chatter, had company.

'Well, he's in a pickle, isn't he?' he mused. 'At least with Mary gone, it should clear the way for him to be available for the ransom demand. I wonder what this man is going to do next. Andy, keep a steer on this, will you? If it looks like going pear-shaped, stop the material being made public. I'll have a meeting with the DG tomorrow and get him to issue a D-Notice; the PM will agree, I'm sure. Thank you. Keep me informed, please.' Without waiting for any reply he replaced the receiver and forgetting the whole unsavoury business rejoined his dinner guests. A delicious pheasant pie was being served and he had the exact wine to accompany it. He waved an apology and sat down.

Andy Foster wasn't happy with his boss. The whole situation was beginning to get out of hand; he couldn't get to Brighton in time and, even if he asked for the local Special Branch to help, by the time he'd briefed them of the most basic facts it would be too late. He would just have to sit it out, not drink any alcohol and sit by the phone.

It was just before a quarter to ten that Sir Roger rang Carter. Sir Roger was parked in a lay-by a half-mile south of the turning to the windmills and Carter had by this time made his way on foot to the edge of the car park and hidden himself by a gate that gave access to one of the mills. Caldwell had taken to a field a hundred yards from Jackie's position. He had surprised her by coming from behind and had kept to a crouch until he neared a crest in the field when he had lain flat and used his elbows to 'leopard-crawl' forward. Jackie had watched him all the way, nervously keeping a finger on the automatic call to Sheen if she was discovered. From his position Sheen had watched Carter and immediately marked him as a fit man and of some strength, but one who hadn't served in the military – he didn't have a clue about covert movement, shape or silhouette.

Sheen saw the headlights swing up the single track towards the windmill car park. Sir Roger was within time. Sheen wished he had made an additional preparation but he hadn't thought of it at the time of their planning. He would remember for the next time.

'Just approaching the car park now,' Sir Roger said into the microphone linked to his mobile phone. 'Nothing else in the car park,' he continued. Sir Roger pulled the Rolls-Royce into the same area that he had parked in previously. It was very dark – a covering of heavy cloud was hiding the moon. The interior light illuminated him when he opened his door, watched by four sets of eyes. He left his door open to allow the light to show him the rubbish bin and he found the envelope on top. Recalling what Carter had told him previously, he held the envelope in one corner. It felt heavier than expected and something shifted its position within the envelope. He returned to the car and sat in the driver's seat.

'Got the envelope. Opening it now by the one corner.' There was a slight sound of the envelope being opened by a knife. 'Inside, an Iron Cross, five letters and, er, a single sheet of paper. Hang on ... In red felt-tip pen is written: "Here is one I.C., examine back, and 5 letters. £100k used notes, no tricks and ALONE. Will call a.m."'

Obeying Carter's instructions, he placed the items on the passenger seat and started the engine. He had been told to return home and await Carter and Caldwell sometime later.

Carter broke the connection with Sir Roger and rang Caldwell's mobile phone. As he used the mobile phone, the screen light illuminated and he could be seen by Sheen. 'Amateur,' Sheen muttered under his breath. Sheen could just make out that Carter was talking, though he couldn't hear any words.

Jackie was watching the man Caldwell through the night-sight and saw him move a hand before moving the hand to his ear. She had thought it strange until she caught sight of a small thin line from his ear into his top pocket. She smiled, Sheen would be pleased by her noticing that. She would also remember the other points that Sheen asked her to look out for – how did anyone she saw behave, were they good at their job – all sorts of examples he had given, though she could only remember the general theme.

Caldwell had ended the call with Carter by saying that they would remain in position for at least an hour as he felt the 'bastards', as he called Jackie and Sheen, would be there to watch Sir Roger. Caldwell knew that Carter was not very good at this type of work and so had been happy enough for him to blunder on, probably to be seen by the bastards. After an hour Carter rang Caldwell. Carter was cold and felt his clothes were cold and damp. Although a sportsman, he wasn't used to keeping still in one place and had felt his muscles tighten in the cold and static position. He was relieved when Caldwell suggested that Carter go to Sir Roger's home; he would stay for another hour before leaving in the hope of catching the bastards.

Sheen saw Carter leave and wondered whether he could risk phoning Jackie. He wanted to speak to her to be reassured that she was all right. But he knew that that would be unprofessional; they had worked out their rules of engagement and they needed to stick to them.

Jackie lay and watched Caldwell. He barely moved and at times appeared to be resting his head in the crook of his arm.

Sir Roger saw Carter arrive at the gate on the CCTV monitor and opened the gates just as Carter had been reaching towards the intercom. The house was silent apart from the ticking of the wall clock in the kitchen. It showed twenty minutes past eleven.

Carter had barely warmed up, even though he had had the car heater on during the fifteen-minute drive to Sir Roger's house. In the kitchen, the envelope, letters, Iron Cross and the single sheet of paper with red felt-tip writing were spread across the table.

Pouring water from the kettle into a mug for coffee, Sir

Roger said, 'I've made arrangements for the money to be ready for you to collect at 9.30 in the morning.'

Carter nodded. 'Caldwell's going to give it another hour before coming. He thinks they may have been there watching you.'

Sir Roger grunted his agreement and handed Carter the mug of coffee.

'Mary's gone', he said flatly, 'to stay with Josephine.' His face looked grim but a sad smile appeared.

Carter stood there, shocked. 'Mary, why?' he asked surprised.

'This whole mess. I can't tell her; she knows nothing about any of this; it would break her heart,' he sighed. 'I've led her on with lies all our married life. I'm afraid it will all unravel and we'll be disgraced. I'm old so it doesn't matter to me so much, but for her...' He left the sentence unfinished. 'And Josephine, how can I ever face her again? How could I have done that to her?'

Carter still didn't understand what the papers meant. He had spotted the Iron Cross. He picked it from the table and looked at it. Turning it over, he tried to read the inscription. He couldn't.

'My father's,' Sir Roger said quietly.

Carter looked at Sir Roger then back to the medal. He put the medal gently on to the table and picked up the letters. He saw they were in German, too.

'My mother's letters, to her brother, my uncle, with whom I lived during the war.'

Carter was looking at Sir Roger. 'But I don't understand. They were German ... Were you adopted?'

Sir Roger exploded almost with rage. 'I am German. It's a long story, one it's best you don't know. Forget it!' He sat down heavily and held his head in his hands, his back and neck jolting as he cried.

Carter stood watching his boss, the strong man now sobbing. *German*, he thought, what the hell is going on? He thought of Caldwell and this Argentinian man, Señor Mayer, and the hold they had on Sir Roger. Carter knew that it was all connected and as he thought about it the picture became clearer in his mind. He sat down at another chair at the table and with some reluctance patted Sir Roger's shoulders. He wasn't the best at showing emotion and he felt uncomfortable showing some support and comfort for the man he so respected.

Jackie had been quite comfortable lying still and watching Caldwell. It had almost amused her, she watching him while it should have been the other way around. She had grown in confidence; it was an adventure and she trusted Sheen to have put her in a safe place. She knew roughly where he was and that he could respond to an emergency call from her within a minute or two. She had taken her finger from the mobile some time ago. Wondering how long Caldwell would remain in his place, she suddenly had a thought: what if he was going to stay there all night and then Carter return in the morning. They would be seen she was sure.

Having seen one of the men go, Sheen wondered how many others there would be watching Sir Roger. He didn't think there would only be one. Perhaps there would be two but, if they were any good, maybe three. On the whole, though, he reasoned that there were two. Only two sets of headlights had been unaccounted for, both showing in the main road shortly before Sir Roger had arrived. One had been the man he had been watching, and he had now driven away. The other car he had lost a couple of hundred yards further on towards Burgess Hill, which meant the occupant or occupants could be in Jackie's area.

Satisfied that there wasn't anybody else in his area, he began to move, slowly retracing his route. It was only after he had completed the route back to the path where he had bushes as cover that he dared stand up. He used his night-sight device to scan the whole area from his high position, quartering the area and methodically working his way along lines towards the distance. He continued this process, picking out Jackie's bush; she must have had had a good view of the area that he had been unable to see. He was just about to pass on to the next area when he saw an outline – a head? He checked the surrounding ground and there were no similar shapes. It was a man, he thought, not a rock. There were flint rocks everywhere but the larger ones had been ploughed or moved to the edges; this one was in the middle of grass. Suddenly the shape was gone. Sheen scanned the area but it was nowhere to be seen.

Jackie had seen the man check his watch twice in the last five minutes before he had crawled backwards a few feet before standing and walking openly down the hill.

Sheen watched. This could be a bluff, he thought, openly leaving to flush out any watchers. He decided to wait another twenty minutes.

Caldwell arrived at Sir Roger's house about the same time that Sheen had joined Jackie. They exited the bush and slowly crawled over the wet grass for fifty yards until they were over the ridge and could go into a crawl down the hill to their car. Jackie's muscles had warmed up during the walk, but she would feel stiff later, probably, Sheen explained, because she had been lying in an unusual position due to her being tense.

When they arrived at the car, Sheen made Jackie stay fifty yards away in the shadow while he went closer, taking in the other cars in the area. Like his, they all had moisture on the glass and bodywork, which indicated they had been there for as long as his, but he still walked slowly past them all. When he reached his car he sharply dropped to his hands and bent under the car to check for a tracking device, or worse. He was absolutely sure that neither would be there and that the car was as yet unknown to Sir Roger's men.

He gave a short flash of red beam from his torch and shortly after Jackie joined him. Sheen started the car and slowly drove away from the area, stopping twice at the end of a bend following a straight piece of road, but no car followed them. He drove back to the hotel and together they made their way back to their room.

When Caldwell joined Carter and Sir Roger in the kitchen he examined the items still laid out on the kitchen table. He left the kitchen and stood in the hallway where from the kitchen he could be heard speaking into his mobile. Both Carter and Sir Roger listened as he gave, they presumed, Señor Mayer a full update of what had happened. It appeared that Señor Mayer listened without interrupting, speaking only a few words at the end of the call.

When Caldwell returned to the kitchen the three men sat down and discussed what had happened and what they would do. Caldwell was pleased that the cash would be ready so early in the morning, as it would give them more time to prepare their ambush.

24

Andy Foster switched on his computer just after seven in the morning after another poor night's sleep and another early start. In his inbox he saw an email from the duty officer, forwarded via Peter King, relaying details of Caldwell's call to Señor Mayer the previous evening. Obviously, the office door had been open and the listener in Thames House was able to hear all Caldwell's words. Andy forwarded the message in full to Sir Peter Webb.

Due to the time available he decided that he would take two members of the A4 Surveillance Team with him to Brighton in an effort to see what Sir Roger did.

Mary had arrived at Josephine's flat the previous evening and let herself in using her key. She had called for Josephine before looking in both bedrooms and the other rooms for any signs that Josephine was still staying there. She was very worried and upset both about the mystery of Josephine missing and the argument with Sir Roger; she felt strangely alone without him. She sat on a breakfast stool in Josephine's kitchen and could have cried, but she knew she had to think clearly – her life was suddenly upside down which was a situation she was unaccustomed to. She gave a large sigh and put the kettle on for a cup of coffee.

She went to the fridge to get the milk. The smell of curdled milk immediately hit her and she quickly poured the soured milk down the sink. Pieces of curdled milk stuck in the drain covering and she turned on the cold water to wash it and the smell away. This wasn't like Josephine. She never wasted anything but she was scrupulous about keeping things fresh. Mary checked the date – three days beyond the expiry. The curdled milk, not answering her mobile and not answering the gallery number – it was as all out of character. Just like Sir Roger's behaviour was out of character. As she made the link in her mind, she suddenly felt very alone.

Josephine had slept a lot since she had been in the room. It was an uncomfortable bed and position that she was forced to adopt but she had been able to make herself warm, at least enough to sleep. Twice she had been half asleep when a white-overall-clad person had come into her room and exchanged the bucket and left food for her. She had a meal of scrambled egg on toast with a cup of coffee as her second meal, then her third meal had been a meat pie and vegetables. Each time she noted that the food had been cut up into mouth-size bits and a plastic spoon left on the tray for her. With each visit she tried to ask questions of her captor, trying the reasonable approach of talking quietly and politely at first, but then resorting to shouting and swearing when that failed. But all to no avail, She could still think no further than that she had been kidnapped for a ransom, a ransom she was sure her father would pay.

The sound of the bolt being drawn back again brought her back to reality. Again, the figure in white overalls appeared, a tray in one hand and a bucket in the other. The same procedure as before – the bucket on the ground and slid forwards with a foot, the tray put on the floor next to the bucket, a quick glance towards her and the used bucket quickly lifted away. This time, though, Josephine had put the tray from her last meal at the foot of the bed to see what reaction she would get – maybe an instruction which would at the least give some clue as to their identity. Instead, there was a swift smack to her head and before she could react the tray had been lifted from the bed and the figure was walking towards the stairs leaving Josephine feeling the side of her face. It had been a slap, a hard one. Josephine felt like crying, not from the pain but the shock of it, the suddenness of it and the rising feeling of despair.

Jackie and Sheen had been lying in bed talking over the previous evening's events and what they had learned. There were, they agreed, two watchers, and they had certainly not been police, who would have had more people there and others in back-up positions, as well. They must be working for Sir Roger directly, they surmised. They had watched the local morning news and heard that the murders of McCall and Mrs Brooks were being linked by the police investigating the crimes; both victims had died as a result of having their necks broken. Reluctantly, Sheen told Jackie that he believed that the men shadowing Sir Roger were probably responsible for the murders. Jackie had had to reluctantly accept the possibility and became frightened. Sheen, though, was just disgusted, feeling loathing for anyone who could coldly kill a woman and drug user, neither of whom would have stood a chance. He was going to make the old man pay. Jackie had been bolstered by Sheen's strength of conviction and felt her fear subsiding.

Both Carter and Caldwell had stayed at Sir Roger's house, so at nine thirty in the morning Carter had accompanied Sir Roger to collect the one hundred thousand pounds in cash from the bank. The withdrawal, as arranged, was handled personally by the manager. Caldwell shadowed them, standing in a bus stop some fifty yards away, watching for any person taking an interest in Sir Roger. By mid-morning they were back at Sir Roger's house waiting for a telephone call from 'Mr Smith'. They sat in the lounge in silence, each man waiting in their own way, willing the call to come.

Carter's telephone vibrated in his trouser pocket. It was

DS Harrison. He answered, well aware that Sir Roger and Caldwell would be listening to his side of the conversation.

DS Harrison was agitated and for nearly a full minute told Carter about the precarious position he was in. He was sure to be found out, he said, bound to be, had to be...

'Terry, calm down.'

DS Harrison was barely listening and continued with his tales of woe until Carter could stand no more. 'Shut up, you prat.'

There was silence at DS Harrison's end.

'You've been well paid for what you've done and I've told you that there is more for you later. That's the way it is.'

DS Harrison's voice grew quieter. 'I'm scared' was all he could say.

'Grow up! There's nothing to worry about; you'll be fine.'

There was silence for ten seconds before DS Harrison said: 'Their car has been found at Gatwick Airport, in a short-term car park. The ticket was in the car, but nothing else at all.'

Carter thought for a minute and turned to Caldwell. 'Car's been found. Gatwick. It's clean.'

He addressed Harrison again. 'Terry, have you checked the flights and car rentals?'

'For Christ's sake, I am working on two murder cases – what the bloody hell do you think I can do? Start phoning round seeing if they have caught a flight and checking for car rentals?'

'Terry, it is quite simple; just use your brains for once.' His tone was cold and flat with the edge of threat just hidden from the surface. 'You are looking for a murder suspect and Mrs Brooks' son was in prison – who was the cell mate? McCall is linked in by the style of death. So, make your own enquiries and find out that a bloke called Sheen was released to an address in Newcastle. Get the locals to interview Johns. Find out Sheen and Johns' missus have scarpered, and then find his car at Gatwick Airport. Then do what we bloody well tell you to do and check the flights and car rentals. Also while you are at it, get the CCTV checked. Do it, Terry, or believe me your worst nightmare will come true and quicker than you would believe.'

Carter pressed the red button on his mobile before DS Harrison could respond. He looked at Caldwell who gave a slight grin as if he was enjoying seeing Carter under stress.

Carter looked at Sir Roger, perhaps seeking some sort of support, but a blank face looked at him.

Sheen returned to the car where Jackie had been sitting in the driver's seat. The rain continued to drizzle as had been forecasted by the television weatherman, which actually suited them. They had spent over an hour studying a street map of Brighton and Hove with Sheen working out various routes that they would insist Sir Roger take to ensure that he didn't have anyone accompanying him.

They were making the running and had decided that they would do everything on their terms. Sir Roger would play the game, in which case in a day or two he would have all his secrets back and they would have enough money to last them for several years. Or, if he didn't play ball, they would reconsider their options.

'OK,' said Sheen, examining the map and drawing a small arrow by the side of a road, 'he'll come up here by car. There are plenty of places to park. He'll leave the car, go to the telephone box and retrieve the message taped under the shelf. The instructions will tell him to walk to the railway station, go straight to the passenger bridge and use that to get to Hove Park Villas. He's got to be walking quickly. Anyone following him will have to use the same route as it's too far to cross the railway lines anywhere else. We can have a position a hundred yards away and watch Sir Roger. We can make him walk along this road...' He studied the map again. 'Hartington Villas. So, let's recap and see if it works.'

Sheen folded the map and pointed to Dyke Road. 'He'll drive from his house, up Dyke Road. I don't think there is any point in watching the house; we'd stand out and in any case if someone is shadowing him they could already be down the road, so I don't think it's worth it.'

He looked at Jackie who was also studying the map and nodding in agreement.

Sheen continued moving the map so a new area became the focal point. 'He'll drive to the roundabout and take the slip road on to the A27, heading towards Lewes. We'll need to see him there – that's me. I'll be in the other road, car out of sight with a clipboard etcetera.'

Jackie grinned. 'Hard hat and fluorescent jacket, Mr Sheen, very fetching.'

Sheen returned the grin without looking up from the map. 'I'll wait until I've seen the cars following him, say about ten, writing down their numbers, then I'll ring him and tell him there's a change of plan and he's to park in the Asda supermarket in Hollingbury. That's here...' He indicated an ink dot on the map. 'You'll be there, at the bus stop we went to this morning and you make a note of the cars that appear in the area. Don't forget,' – he looked at Jackie – 'they may be cute enough to abandon a car and run into the car park.'

Jackie looked at Sheen and again nodded in agreement. 'I'll be watching the road as well.'

'OK,' said Sheen, 'you call me when he's there and we'll give him ten minutes sitting there before I call him again. This time I'll direct him to the seafront, at the roundabout by the pier, tell him to take the left ... second left,' he corrected himself as he traced the seafront road, '...and park away from other cars at the far end of the road, where it's a cul-de-sac. I'll see him and any other cars following him.

They may suspect that he'll be met there or ordered into the Marina, which he can get to by walking and using the footpath.'

Jackie remembered the area from earlier that morning and knew where Sheen would be. 'Won't he get fed up with being told to go here and there?' she asked. Perhaps Sir Roger would just get fed up and return home.

'He got what he wanted last night. He knows we are not playing and that we are going to do the deal this time. He wants the rest badly; he'll do what we tell him. If those two blokes last night are any good, they will have cottoned on to what we're doing and they will have to be a man short – one up front still following Sir Roger, the other hanging back. So, we give him a minute there, not enough time for anyone following him to abandon their car and run to a spot to see him, before we tell him to go to the telephone box in Goldstone Villas. He'll take the message and you'll be at the station to see him before catching the train to Portslade. I'll be in Hartington Villas. I'll watch him go past then I'll drive and pick you up outside Portslade railway station. We'll see what we have then.'

He looked at Jackie who was smiling. 'And we do this tomorrow?' she asked.

'No, we do our own run tomorrow, to make sure of the timings. If all goes well, we do it the next day. It'll also give him a day extra to think about things.'

'It'll also give him and anyone with him another day to prepare,' Jackie said quickly.

'Yes, but they won't know. The first phone call telling him to go towards Lewes on the A23 and wait for us to ring him with instructions will mean that they won't be able to do much preparation. Then he'll be told to follow our route – they can't plan for that.'

'And you expect just two men, in one or two cars, not more?' she asked with a little concern.

'We know two men saw your husband and two men were at the windmills last night. Could be the same two, or could be that there are four of them. With any luck we'll find out. We'll also find out how good they are and get a decent look at them.'

'And if he is followed, what then – we up the price?'

'That's what we agreed, but we'll see what happens. If he is followed, then we'll go back to the drawing board and work on another scenario – again which suits us and not him.'

Sheen folded the map and put on his seatbelt.

Jackie started the car and drove towards an area of Brighton well away from the centre, where CCTV cameras covered every inch of road and pavement. They had clothing and props to buy so that the next day's rehearsal would be as realistic as possible and they'd be able to check their timings. Sheen was especially anxious that Jackie would be able to catch the train as he didn't want her recognised by any of Sir Roger's watchers, which was why she would also need a change of clothes and hairstyle between her positions.

25

'Good afternoon, Sir Peter.'

'Good afternoon, James,' replied Sir Peter Webb as he walked up the concrete steps from the pavement towards a discreet wooden door behind which stood James. Sir Peter was the only member of the club who insisted on calling him by his full name; he was Jim to everyone else. Of course, it was expected that Sir Peter would address him as James; he had done so for the past twelve years ever since James had started working as the doorman.

The club was not advertised at all; there was no plaque or any marking to make the gloss painted black door any different from the others in the small backstreet in Mayfair. The two front windows, like the other houses in the street, were covered by net curtains, and Jim watched the street from the right-hand window, ready to open the front door immediately he recognised a member arriving. The club was for a select number of people who worked in positions where discretion was paramount and where meetings could be held without any fear of publicity of any kind. Each member was expected to never mention even the existence of the club; it was for all their benefits and each member could be relied upon to keep the secret. The membership currently consisted of 107 men and, although two previous Heads of MI5 had been women, at this time there were no female members.

The club was staffed by a small number of ex-Servicemen who had served with distinction and had been vetted to the highest 'Developed' standard. A minimum of seven staff were on duty at any one time – three to cook, two to serve, one to answer any calls or bookings, and Jim. The number of members visiting each day would probably be no more than four in the morning, six for lunch, a few in the afternoon and no more than ten in the evening. The restaurant was in fact the original dining room of the house and the 'smoking room', as the lounge was now called, was the original drawing room. The club allowed smoking on its premises as it wouldn't have been acceptable for people like their members to be standing outside the back door in the small garden smoking a cigarette or cigar.

Sir Peter removed his blue overcoat, which James took from him, then walked into the lounge to be met by the only other guest, Sir Richard Bradshaw, whom he had arranged to meet at one o'clock for lunch.

The room was large, square and dimly lit even during the day. The furniture was all of dark wood and there was a dark-red thick-pile carpet and long deep-red velvet curtains. Armchairs were arranged around small tables in clusters with more at the perimeter that could be added where and when necessary. Small table lights gave a limited bright area and there was no sound except for the ticking of the grandfather clock that stood proudly against the wall behind the door. The old stone fireplace sat empty with all signs of the roaring winter log fires swept away.

Sir Peter joined Sir Richard and ordered a gin and tonic; Sir Richard already had a drink on the table.

They had known each other for some years and shared many friends, and though not friends in the social world they had met many times at events usually associated with their work. For the first ten minutes they made small talk, catching up with their respective news before each studied the menu that was ostentatiously 'British', featuring dishes made from the finest seasonal products purchased daily from Borough Market. Both men quickly made their selections for a first and main course, to be accompanied by a glass of claret.

Protocol called for the topic that had brought the men together to not be discussed until after they were seated at the dining table and had started their meal.

'In a nutshell,' said Sir Peter, 'we have a situation that we cannot at this time in all honesty say we have under control, and therefore we have to have a contingency in place should the problem escalate. It may necessitate our asking for a DA-Notice to be issued, I'm afraid.' Sir Peter took a bite from his toast on which he had generously spread country pâté, allowing his opening words to be considered by Sir Richard.

'Mmm,' was Sir Richard's response as he chewed his food. However, a frown appeared on his forehead that indicated to Sir Peter that the request would have to be strongly worded if it was to be agreed to.

'It concerns Sir Roger Knight,' Sir Peter said.

'Oh!' Sir Richard said surprised. 'What on earth has the old devil been up to – not youngsters, surely?'

'Good gracious no, nothing like that,' said Sir Peter quickly. 'No, no. In fact, in many ways he isn't the actual problem; it's the repercussions that are the problem – for all of us. In essence, he has a secret that was known to the Service back in 1952, and then...'

'What?' interrupted Sir Richard, unable to hide his surprise.

Sir Peter finished his toast and pâté, sipped his wine and sat back in his chair.

'Just after the war the Service quite by chance discovered Sir Roger had a past, a history that – shall we say – presented the Service at the time with a choice – to keep the secret or expose it. The decision made was to keep it and shortly afterwards of course we used our knowledge for our benefit, not just ours as in the Service, but also our sisters who live in that modern monstrosity on the river. The government of the day knew, of course; in those days they were privileged to anything like that in case there was a need for denial. As you appreciate, politicians can say what they like in Parliament.'

Sir Richard dabbed his mouth with the linen napkin and smiled.

Sir Peter went on: 'Well, over the course of his very successful career and life he has been invaluable to us all, an extremely important asset able to travel the world and with access to so many areas, so much so that, as you know, he was knighted.'

Sir Richard nodded. He had met Sir Roger several times and was aware of how he had built up a small electronic business into a large company with many government contracts, mostly from the Ministry of Defence. News that he had been an asset – an informant the police would call him – did, however, come as something of a surprise to him.

'Interesting, Peter. Is it the asset that you wish to protect,' he asked, 'or the original secret?' He smiled suavely.

Sir Peter was about to answer when the waiter appeared to clear their plates, so he sipped his wine in the interim.

'Sir Roger wasn't born as an Englishman,' he finally said. 'He is in fact a German whose real name I have in truth forgotten, but in any case it's irrelevant. He spent the war years living with an uncle, his mother's brother in Switzerland. His father was in the German Army. He served with distinction in Russia among other places – he was decorated and injured, twice I think – but along with others he was aware that the war was being lost. Well, he was eventually withdrawn from frontline action to serve in some civilian capacity. He looked to the future and believing, quite correctly, that the Russians would sooner or later plunder what they could as they occupied his country he and his friends decided to get in first.' Sir Peter smiled. 'So that is what they did and, from what I understand, they weren't too particular what they plundered as long as it was of value and could fit in a rucksack.'

Sir Richard raised his eyebrows, not immediately understanding the relevance of the rucksack.

Sir Peter saw the eyebrows raised. 'The goods were carried from Germany to Switzerland by foot and all year round –

over mountains for Heaven's sake. Still, it was well worth the effort. In this way what would be today measured in millions was smuggled out of Nazi Germany. The uncle in Switzerland, a lawyer by profession, had contacts through whom he could either sell some items or have them transported elsewhere – that elsewhere being generally Argentina. Sir Roger was just a youngster, of course, but he seems to have been a bit of a climber, besides studying electronics at university, so he undoubtedly took a part in the smuggling. Anyway, as the outcome of the war became clear and Germany descended into chaos, his father, mother and their associates managed to leave the country just in the nick of time. They made their various ways to Argentina where the funds raised by Sir Roger's uncle were all safe and sound.'

Sir Peter saw their main courses being carried towards them so halted his account. Both men were pleased with their respective choices: Sir Peter's game pie looked and smelled delicious while Sir Richard's roast lamb with rosemary sauce was as good as ever. Both men ate some of their food before Sir Peter continued.

'So we're in Argentina 1945/46. There's lots of money, both there and in Switzerland; the only question was what to do with it. Remember they didn't want to draw attention to themselves – the Argentinian authorities had allowed them to live there after all but didn't want everyone to know about the arrangement. The obvious decision, of course, was to start businesses in safe countries, legitimate businesses that could grow through their own efforts and with a drip-feed of money from either Switzerland or Argentina. The Service found out about this in 1952, I don't know how. One such company was a fledgling electronics company operating out of small premises at Gatwick, before the airport was built there. The rest is, as they say, history. Profits were inflated by the extra money fed into the company, expansion followed, as did contracts with the Government. I should add that I believe the contracts were on very favourable terms for us, though of course not too bad for him either. It was a *comfortable* arrangement.'

Sir Peter concentrated on his food, allowing Sir Richard to finish his meal and reflect on what he had said.

'Well, is that too bad? I mean, I can understand where you are coming from but I'm surprised that you are asking for a DA-Notice for that. I suspect the "DA" is to prevent something else, am I correct?' asked Sir Richard.

Sir Peter finished his meal and wine. 'You will recall that I said Sir Roger is a German national?'

'Ah yes, so how did he get the name?' Sir Richard asked as he too finished his wine.

'There was an Englishman named Roger Leonard Knight who travelled quite extensively just before the war spending all his inheritance that he received. His parents had both died overseas, in Africa, I believe. He somehow turned up in Switzerland and died there, so our man assumed his identity. A solicitor in England was employed to make sure all the necessary arrangements were made and, hey presto, Mr Roger Knight began his life as we all know him.'

Sir Richard listened carefully weighing up what was said and knew that there was a question that had to be asked, and he feared that he knew the answer. 'How did the original Roger Knight die?' he asked bluntly.

Sir Peter had hoped he wouldn't have to cover that point, but he wasn't surprised that Sir Richard had picked up on his omission. 'There is a note in the file. Frankly, I am surprised it's still there – he was murdered by the new Roger Knight. Apparently he admitted this in an early interview by one of the Service men who recruited him. Admitted it, so the slate was clean as it were. In those days, of course, the death penalty was in force so an admission on the understanding that it would be covered up was a great incentive.'

'I see,' said Sir Richard, 'and what has caused the problem now after all these years?'

'You may recall Sir Roger and his wife Mary were robbed in their home a while ago. Among the property stolen were souvenirs of his father's war career, letters from his mother to his uncle, personal papers relating to his mother, and, quite crucially, the original Roger Knight passport and his ID card. One had the original Roger Knight photograph, the other the new Roger Knight photograph.' Sir Peter fell silent as the waiter approached their table to clear their used plates and to offer the dessert menu.

The men discussed the likelihood of the papers coming to light and when Sir Peter explained that Sir Roger was being blackmailed for their safe return Sir Richard had asked why the police weren't dealing with it, though Sir Peter knew the question was asked 'tongue in cheek'.

They took coffee in the lounge where Sir Peter told Sir Richard of the recent events that had led them to believe a 'DA' might be required.

Sir Richard said, 'I can understand your position and do sympathise. The "DA" would have to be agreed by the PM before it could be put forward. It would have to have a status beyond the usual gagging of the media what with the Internet these days. Of course, the notice would stipulate immediate imprisonment for anyone involved with making its disclosure, forfeiture of assets and, of course, no representation at all, at any stage. Quite drastic but I will speak with the PM and get back to you, Peter.'

Sir Peter knew there wasn't any point in asking whether Sir Richard thought the PM would agree, Sir Richard hadn't managed to gain his position by speculation but by application of hard facts, as and when they had suited him, of course.

26

Carter had made scrambled eggs on toast for lunch for the three of them but they barely said a word to each other during the meal. It wasn't because of any great dislike or disagreement, but after the debrief of the evening before and the collection of the cash that morning each man had wanted to think through their own, and collective, options.

As Carter cleared the plates into the dishwasher, the telephone rang in the hallway. Sir Roger picked it up and saw Carter and Caldwell draw towards him so they could hear what the caller had to say. They stood a foot away on each side of Sir Roger.

'Roger, I'm at the gallery' was all Carter and Caldwell heard of Mary before Sir Roger turned and walked a foot or so away from them. They in turn retired again to the lounge.

'And it's closed, locked up. I have been ringing the bell and have been to the neighbours. I've spoken to people who know Josephine very well and they say they haven't seen her in days. A couple of them have rung her mobile and got no reply. A girl who works in the coffee shop knows Josephine and says it's really unusual for her not to call in for a coffee and a salad at lunchtime. She just assumed Josephine had gone away.'

Sir Roger had been thinking of Mary all morning, more than of the blessed blackmailers. He had had enough of telling her lies but was torn as to what he could tell her. It needed to be enough to win her over, but too much and the consequences would be dire for him, and, more importantly, for Josephine.

'Mary come home and we can talk.'

'I tried to do that last night.'

'I'll tell you what the problem is and what we are doing about it.'

'I stayed at Josephine's flat last night. The milk in the fridge was off. It must have been days old and the place had an unlived-in type of chill about it. I'm seriously thinking of calling the police to report her missing.'

'Mary, just come home. Don't go to the police and I'll explain things to you.' A hint of desperation had crept into his voice

'You can tell me now,' Mary said, her voice becoming much sterner than Sir Roger had heard it before.

'Not over the phone; it's complicated and I need to be sure that you understand the whole picture – not just a sentence or two, please.' He felt tears beginning to form and heard his voice suddenly sound every one of his years.

Mary didn't answer at once but listened to what Sir Roger had said, but more importantly she could hear in his voice the desperation and the tears. She tried to think. Calling the police, she knew, would probably not help anyway – Josephine was a grown-up woman. She had every right to go 'missing' for a few days, after all. Mary felt vulnerable, Her daughter was missing and her husband, once so strong and decisive, was now almost pleading with her to return home. She knew he needed her. 'OK, I'll come home but I want to know everything – whatever the problem is I want to know.'

Sir Roger had been facing the front door in the hallway, near to the spot where he had fallen and hit his head during the robbery. As he turned towards the lounge, he was saying, 'I'll tell you everything, I promise.' He saw Caldwell standing in the lounge doorway shaking his head from side to side, slowly. A slight 'tsk, tsk, tsk' sound came from his mouth in time with each turn of his head.

Sir Roger replaced the handset and knew Caldwell had heard certainly the last bit of the conversation. He turned to

Caldwell: 'I'm going to tell her that I'm being blackmailed, that Josephine has been kidnapped and I'll show her the money for the ransom – she'll believe that.'

Caldwell stopped moving his head and without taking his eyes from Sir Roger he pulled his mobile from his trouser pocket. He used the same hand to press some buttons and still keeping Sir Roger fixed in his glare he lifted the phone to his ear.

'Señor Mayer, I am sorry to ring you. Sir Roger is planning on telling Mary that Josephine has been kidnapped and that the one hundred thousand pounds he collected from the bank this morning is for the ransom. I suspect that Mary will perhaps wonder why the police aren't involved and that could lead to her being told too much. I thought you'd want to know,' Caldwell finished. His eyes still hadn't blinked, as he looked Sir Roger directly in the eyes.

Caldwell listened for a couple of seconds then offered the mobile to Sir Roger, who took it and slowly lifted it to his ear. Sir Roger looked at the floor, giving in to Caldwell but not caring; he knew Señor Mayer wouldn't be happy.

'I think', Señor Mayer spoke softly, 'that you should follow Caldwell's instructions. There's room for another guest, I understand, and while Josephine is being looked after to a better degree than otherwise might be the case, Mary, being older, might not find it so comfortable. Indeed, I would have to ask that she be made very *un*comfortable. Pass the phone back to Caldwell.'

Sir Roger did as he was told and walked slowly into the lounge, past Carter who hearing the conversation in the hallway had risen to stand at the lounge door behind Caldwell. Caldwell muttered a few words into the phone before closing it down and heading towards Sir Roger again, straight past Carter. Sir Roger was about to turn around to sit down in the armchair when he felt a hard smack to the side of his head. His ear rang and he tumbled forward into the chair, hitting the back with his face. His nose took most of the impact. Caldwell grabbed him by the shoulder and swung him around into the chair. Another stinging smack followed, making the other ear sting.

Caldwell had anticipated Carter's move and was prepared for the lunge coming towards him as he deftly stepped to one side and lifted his heel up quickly into the area he thought Carter's knee would be. There was a gasp as the heel caught Carter's kneecap, and before Carter could react Caldwell had turned and punched Carter very squarely in the stomach, knocking all the air from him. Carter doubled up with his head facing the carpet so he didn't see the side of Caldwell's hand descend on to his neck. He felt the sudden numbness in his neck and was unable to control his fall to the floor. He fell at Sir Roger's feet and slowly turned on to his back, still doubled up with his arms across his stomach. Caldwell moved to the settee and sat down in an extravagant show of calmness, as if what he had done in the last ten seconds was as easy as swatting a fly. He sat back and crossed his legs.

'When Mary gets here, Sir Roger, you and Carter will shut up. You will not make a sound. Do you both understand?' said Caldwell at the same time as he reached down for his burgundy-coloured briefcase. He saw both men nod and heard both manage a 'Yes' before he took his eyes from them. He swivelled the two combination locks on his briefcase and opened it, the lid hiding the contents from Carter and Sir Roger. Carter was trying to move, to get on to all fours, when Caldwell told him to stop and stay where he was. Carter obeyed and was looking at Caldwell when Caldwell gently closed the lid to the briefcase. In his right hand he held a gun, an automatic with a bulbous end that indicated a suppressor, or silencer, as it was commonly known. Carter looked at Caldwell, then the gun, and back to Caldwell. He half expected Caldwell to be smiling or sneering, but instead his face was devoid of any emotion, as was his voice.

'You will both do exactly as I say. Carter, you are entirely expendable, so especially you, behave yourself. Sir Roger, Señor Mayer would rather that you stayed alive to complete the transaction, but, if you happened to be no longer with us, Mary or Josephine, I'm sure, would be happy to help us – with a little persuasion. Señor Mayer is tired of this complication you have brought to his life and his patience is wearing very thin.'

Caldwell stood and put the gun down on the seat cushion while he fitted a leather holster under his arm. It was a fluent movement, the holding straps perfectly fitted. He placed the gun into the holster and sat down. 'Carter, your killing two people doesn't impress me at all. I have killed many more and the manner you killed them doesn't impress me either. Your clumsy and predictable attack towards me just then will be the last time that you try that sort of thing, do you understand?'

Carter was still in a half-crouch, still reeling from the pain from his knee, stomach and neck. He was used to fighting but now regretted his actions. He was looking at Caldwell and knew that his life was hanging by a thread.

'Yes,' he muttered, before adding, 'Sorry, it was you attacking Sir Roger – I had to defend him; he's my boss.'

Caldwell smiled,. 'He might be *your* boss, but Señor Mayer is *the* boss, the boss of everyone – Sir Roger, you, me and my colleagues who have Josephine as their guest, *everyone.*'

Carter knew there was no point in arguing; he knew that what Caldwell had said was true.

Sir Roger knew only too well what Señor Mayer was capable of. And this man would do whatever he was told. He was curious.

'So where do you fit in?' he asked Caldwell. 'I know why I'm in Mayer's power, but why are you his henchman.'

Caldwell suppressed a smile. 'My grandfather was a colleague of yours. My father introduced me to Señor Mayer, just at the time I was working for myself, just becoming established and known in the rather small area of business that I work in. The skills and expertise that I had, well, Señor Mayer thought I could bring them to the organisation.'

'Skills? What skills?'

'My skill, Sir Roger, is getting a job done. Any job that Señor Mayer asks me to do, I do, and by whatever means necessary. In this instance, Sir Roger, my job is to make sure that everything is recovered, that the money is not handed over, and that no one who has seen or knows the contents of your grey box will talk about them. That is my job, and that is what I will do, with or without you, with your help or not. It really doesn't matter to me. You tell Mary and I will kill her. You tell Carter here and I will kill him. The blackmailers have already doomed themselves...'

'But what about Harry Johns, Caldwell,' Carter interrupted, eager to find a chink in this man's armour. 'We talked to him – he could identify us to the police.'

Caldwell looked at his watch and smiled at Carter. 'Harry Johns was devastated by his wife leaving him, especially for his best friend. What do you think he did last night while we were at the windmills?'

Carter looked blankly at Caldwell.

'Poor old Harry drank nearly a bottle of whisky, like he had when we spoke to him, then he wrote a short note, "I can't live without her" – you know the sort of thing. Then he put a rope around his neck, tied to the bannister, and fell off a chair. It's very sad, but there you are.' Caldwell's voice had an almost hypnotic effect on Carter and Sir Roger.

'Now that we have put our cards on the table, why don't you, Carter, go and make us all a nice cup of tea while we wait for Mary to arrive.'

Carter got to his feet slowly and walked from the room giving Caldwell a wide berth.

* * *

DS Harrison was feeling uneasy at the afternoon meeting with Detective Superintendent Wordsley as they went methodically through the agenda, discussing the various lines of enquiry and setting priorities. This meeting was only for the senior investigating officer and his deputy, which is why the two men were sitting alone at a table, each with their blue A4-size books in front of them in which all police notes were kept.

Little had been learned of any real substance – no witnesses had come forward and even the times and dates of death were uncertain. It was what joined the two victims that occupied the detectives' minds – though for different reasons. That the murders were connected, there was no doubt at all in the mind of the pathologist whose initial report was on the desk between them – the method used, the height of the assailant, the strength used and the lack of resistance by either victim all pointed that way.

Efforts to trace the female caller who had alerted the police were proving difficult, too. The telephone box used didn't reveal much in the way of fingerprints or DNA material, but at least it was covered by the CCTV system. An officer had trawled through the tape and found the caller, but the quality of picture was so poor that it could be any one of dozens of young girls. However, the officer was now searching every camera in the city centre and was hopeful of recognising the female on a camera somewhere else.

'So at the moment we've got no suspects,' Detective Superintendent Dave Wordsley said flatly.

DS Harrison knew that this was the time and he took a deep breath. 'Perhaps we should look closer at what connects the victims.'

Detective Superintendent Wordsley looked at DS Harrison. 'I thought the intelligence unit had checked that.'

'Well, I was thinking, McCall is a drug dealer, well known in the area and' – DS Harrison pulled a sheaf of McCall's antecedent history from the back of his book – 'a few years ago he was checked with Aaron Brooks, the late son of Mrs Brooks, late at night. They were searched and nothing found on either of them.' DS Harrison looked up from the page he had been referring from and leaned back into the blue-upholstered chair.

Detective Superintendent Wordsley said, 'I knew there was a drug relationship, or maybe, a drug relationship between Mrs Brooks' son and McCall, but Aaron Brooks died in prison some months ago; it was in the papers and on local television, too, so it was known. Why kill Mrs Brooks. What could she have to do with her son's activity if he had died some time ago?'

'Maybe the connection could be through an associate, a friend, maybe even a cell mate of Brooks' – you know, someone he was friendly with – and they attacked McCall for some reason, then Mrs Brooks. Could there have been something valuable hidden in that hiding place they found at Mrs Brooks' flat, something that Aaron had stolen and hidden there?'

Detective Superintendent Wordsley thought of various scenarios but he also wondered what had prompted DS Harrison to think of this. It wasn't like Terry Harrison to come up with theoretical ideas; he hadn't shown very much initiative before. He reached for his pen and started to write in his book.

'OK, Terry, there may be merit in that line, I'll write it as an action and give it to the intelligence unit to work on. Could be interesting.'

DS Harrison felt flustered and knew he had crossed a threshold over which he could never return. His whole career and almost certainly his marriage were now in the lap of the Gods.

Carter had managed with a little difficulty to make them each a cup of tea and then sat in an armchair next to Sir Roger while Caldwell still occupied the settee. There had been little conversation in the past hour or so. The dislike Sir Roger and Carter had felt for Caldwell from the word go was now joined by pure terror.

Initially Caldwell appeared confident, sitting with his legs splayed in front of him, but as the time ticked away, something about him changed. He wore an almost apologetic look, as if he was sorry for his actions and the threats he had made. Carter continued to study Caldwell without making it obvious, but there was a real difference in his demeanour. Carter decided the time was right. Caldwell's eyes had been on the floor for over ten minutes; he was probably in some sort of inner turmoil, Carter thought.

When he spoke his voice was soft and quiet but it could have been the sound of a gun going off such was the reaction of both Caldwell and Sir Roger.

'Look, we all want the same thing – we're in this together – so it would be better if we got along. Let's put our differences to one side and nail these bastards. The waiting is tense enough without all this as well.'

Caldwell's eyes had shot up to Carters' as soon as the first word was spoken, examining him for any signs of insincerity or trickery, but seeing none he took a breath and opened his hands towards them.

'Yeah, I agree. Sorry about what happened earlier and what I said. We're all, as you say, tense.' He paused for a second before continuing: 'Sir Roger, when Mary comes home why don't I tell her that Josephine is being held but hasn't been harmed, that I've seen her and that I'm the go-between, the negotiator. It's a business matter from years ago, too complicated to talk about, but it should all be settled in a few days. The police aren't involved because it would almost guarantee the kidnappers panicking and we'd lose some of the control we currently have.'

Carter and Sir Roger both sat up straighter as Caldwell spoke, his words making some sense to both of them.

Caldwell continued: 'I can say that I have seen Josephine. I don't know where as I was blindfolded, but she was OK. I can set a scene that will satisfy Mary, well, as far as any mother could be satisfied in the circumstances.'

Sir Roger listened and thought it might just work. The explanation would be better coming from Caldwell, someone Mary barely knew, rather than from himself who she could tell when he was not being fully truthful. They talked further about what could be said and what picture they could give Mary that might satisfy her fears, at least enough to prevent her from contacting the police,

Mary used her hand-held electronic device to open the gate and had parked the other side of the three cars in the driveway. She felt disappointed at seeing the three cars; she had hoped that it would be just her and Sir Roger, to be able to talk without anyone else there. She felt a little cheated and immediately knew that she wasn't going to get the explanation she wanted.

Mary strode into the lounge just as Caldwell was putting his jacket on and was pulling the shirt cuffs through the jacket sleeve. He was the first to address her.

'Can I apologise, please, for the distress and trouble that has been caused to yourself and Sir Roger.' He tried a sympathetic and at the same time a little embarrassed smile. 'Please,' he indicated the settee he had been sitting on.

Mary was bristling and, ignoring Caldwell, walked directly over to Sir Roger, standing directly in front of him and looking down at him unsmiling.

'OK, Roger, let's have the explanation.'

Sir Roger sat back in his chair and looked up at Mary who was staring intently at him.

'Mary, you know James Caldwell here. He's from an insurance company, a specialised insurance company.'

'Can I explain, Sir Roger?' Caldwell interjected, then without waiting for any response he continued: 'The fact is that the company I work for deal with negotiations between two sets of people. What has happened is that a person from a long time ago has a grievance against Sir Roger, a business grievance, a dispute that was long forgotten – by Sir Roger.' Caldwell felt awkward talking to Mary's back as she continued to stare down Sir Roger. She was listening and at the same time not showing an inch of relenting on her anger.

'Anyway, the upshot of it is that this person asked Sir Roger for a ridiculous amount of money as compensation, a sum far out of proportion to the grievance. Sir Roger quite rightly refused to pay and threatened to take legal action against the fellow. That was that, for a few months, then out of the blue Sir Roger heard again from this fellow saying that he had taken Josephine and would keep her until such time as he received his compensation.'

Caldwell saw Mary tremble but she didn't turn around.

'Sir Roger contacted us, and I was appointed to resolve the matter and to ensure Josephine's safe return. I'm afraid it is a bit cloak-and-dagger stuff that people cannot always handle, and so we decided – well, it was I in truth who asked – that you not be made aware of Josephine's position.' He paused for a moment, letting Mary assimilate what he had said.

'I have seen Josephine. She is being treated as a guest and I mean, as a guest. I was taken to what appears to be a lovely house, I would guess in the country somewhere. I was blindfolded for obvious reasons. Josephine was in a lounge chatting to a young woman of a similar age – they were like two friends. It was in all honesty quite surreal; I have never seen a situation like it before.'

'Josephine has been kidnapped?' Mary said at last.

'Well, yes,' answered Caldwell. 'That is the official term.'

Mary turned on him, her face bright red. 'Our daughter has been kidnapped, and you're saying that's just the "official" term. What are you bloody well talking about? She's been bloody well kidnapped for Christ's sake,' she shouted with all the force that she could muster.

Carter had been sitting in his seat quietly listening to Caldwell's explanation. It was all going quite well, he thought, until Mary's explosion; it was something he had never seen or heard before.

Sir Roger just sat still, relieved that Mary's eyes weren't penetrating his any longer and that the focus of her anger was Caldwell, though he suddenly wondered how Caldwell would react.

'I'm sorry,' Caldwell continued. 'It isn't easy to explain and my choice of words may not have been the best, but I want to assure you that Josephine is very well. She told me that she has a room which is nice and clean; she can have a bath or shower whenever she wants and she has three meals a day. She obviously sent her love to you both and was sorry because she feels somehow responsible for the hurt you must be going through. I told her that Sir Roger only had been aware of the event and this pleased her; she didn't want you to know, Mary.'

'You knew?' she turned sharply towards Sir Roger.

'Yes, of course. I just couldn't tell you though.'

Mary looked at Carter, who gave a faint nod and looked at the carpet. He suddenly realised that there was probably a mark on his neck as a result of Caldwell hitting him there and lifted his head. He looked at Mary to see whether she had noticed anything but her attention was already back on Caldwell.

'So where are the police? They normally deal with kidnapping. You know who took her, tell them his name, and they'll arrest him and have her back in a couple of hours.'

'We can't risk it, Mary. The police, well the boys in blue are truly excellent at many things but in all honesty they aren't that capable in this type of situation. The situation needs careful handling. It really is to our advantage that they aren't involved, and at the moment things are going very well. I have a lot of experience in these matters and I've never failed yet.' He smiled reassuringly.

Mary stood facing Caldwell, then suddenly she held her hands to her face and started to softly cry.

Sir Roger climbed from his chair and went over to her, wrapping his arms around her shoulders as he pulled her into his chest. The sobs came steadily as Sir Roger gently held and stroked her. Caldwell looked at Carter and smiled smugly. Carter had to return a flicker of a smile. He was impressed but at the same time the coldness of the lies sent a shiver down his back. After that performance, he believed Caldwell was capable of anything.

Peter King took the call and after listening for a few seconds and making a scribbled note he thanked the caller and immediately went to Andy Foster's office.

'Andy, listening have just been on...' He waited for Andy to look up from whatever he was doing and focus.

'They have had a couple of calls,' he continued. 'Nothing further from the blackmailers but there was an interesting one involving Señor Mayer. They could only hear one side of the conversation – the whole transcript should be through shortly. There has also been some sort of falling out between the men. Mary's gone home, too, having been promised by Sir Roger that he would tell her everything. They couldn't hear what was said to her – they must have been in the lounge – but they did hear Mary shout.' – King looked down at his notes. ' "Our daughter has been kidnapped, and you're saying that's just the 'official' term. What are you bloody well talking about? She's been kidnapped for Christ's sake," That may not be the exact wording but it's the gist of what was shouted, though of course we don't know to whom.'

'Mary knowing could be a problem,' thought Andy out loud. 'Oh dear.'

Peter King said nothing for a second or two, allowing Andy

Foster to digest the ramifications of what he had just told him. 'Also Andy, I'm not sure yet but I hope to get confirmation tonight – this James Caldwell, we think he could be an ex American Special Forces type of man who went bad. The person we hope it is was born in America but schooled here. His father was a diplomat, a minor one but with the status of a diplomat. The son, through his father, was seconded to the DEA and saw service mostly in Central and South America. I won't give you a full brief now; I'll wait until it is confirmed then get hold of you then.'

Andy Foster felt a shiver of anxiety. American, son of a diplomat, ex Special Forces gone bad – how much worse could all this get?

Sir Peter Webb had been driven home by his usual driver and was preparing for a casual evening in front of the fire reading a book that he had started the previous weekend. His wife would be out as she was every Thursday visiting someone or other; Sir Peter didn't really listen to her explaining her movements. He found his dinner in the fridge and the note on top that told him how long he had to put it in the microwave to reheat. While the meal was heating through he added a log to the fire, bringing the embers to life. He had drawn the curtains and was preparing to carry his book into the kitchen where he could eat his dinner and read at the same time when his mobile phone rang. He silently cursed and picked it up: 'Andy F.'

'Hello, Andrew.'

Andy Foster smiled to himself – only his parents had called him Andrew. 'Sir Peter, I thought I'd better update you on the Sir Roger situation.'

For the next three minutes Andy Foster read the transcribed phone calls and what had been heard in the house. Sir Peter made the occasional 'mmm' sound every now and then as he considered the latest events in the Sir Roger Knight household.

'And, we have now identified the man Caldwell. I'm afraid it isn't good, Sir Peter.' Sir Peter heard a shuffling of papers. 'Caldwell is in fact Burt Schneider, aged thirty-two years, born in Washington, DC. His father is Kurt Schneider, a career diplomat who for seven years was stationed at their embassy here in London, passport and visa section. Burt went to private school here from the age of nine when his father was first posted here, and stayed on for two years after his father returned to Washington. It looks as if he was a good pupil, bright and gained a whole host of top-quality exam passes. Strangely enough, he didn't go on to university, either here or in the States. We've learned from a contact that he joined the American Army, served two years, then resigned after an incident that we don't seem to be able to find out about. His Army record has been removed from the database apparently, according to the same contact. The next time he appears on the official American files, he's working for the DEA in Columbia, and this is a year or so after he left the Army. The contact thinks Dad probably got him into the DEA, but that's speculation. Again the contact is unable to learn much about his career in the DEA. One thing did emerge though: Schneider was in Columbia when twenty-three men and women were murdered at an illicit drug distribution camp. Details are sketchy, but the contact says his source was very hesitant to talk about the event, save to say that Schneider had a reputation for being trigger-happy and enjoying hurting people. The matter was never reported. Peter King, as you know, is a whizz on computer searches but there is nothing at all relating to this incident, so whether it is true or not we cannot verify. Anyway, that was the last time Burt Schneider came to notice as far as the Americans are concerned. Peter has made further searches and can trace flights Schneider made, until eighteen months ago. Many of the flights were transatlantic, but there are a total of nine visits to Argentina, seven from Europe direct and two from the States, via Brazil.'

There was more shuffling of papers.

'Searches on James Caldwell show a passport, British, though there is no record of it ever being used. There is a National Insurance and National Health number for him, a driving licence, but no trace of him ever owning a vehicle or renting one. Likewise, no traces in the financial or banking world whatsoever. That's about it, Sir Peter. We can read what we like into it but our guess is that he is some sort of enforcer, possibly a hitman working for Señor Mayer. Which leads me to the question: do you want us to get him arrested by the police or left alone?'

Sir Peter made another 'mmm' sound as he thought the matter through. 'Bloody mess this one, could turn very nasty – a case of dammed if we do and dammed if we don't, provided anyone finds out of course. I think, Andy, that for the time being we'll keep our powder dry and keep it in house. Perhaps you and a couple from your team could base yourselves in Brighton, be on hand should things get messy, be able to clean up if necessary. I'll speak to the DG in the morning but I'm sure that is what he will want.'

'OK, Sir Peter, we'll be down there first thing in the morning unless you want us down there tonight,' said Andy, hoping that the answer would be for the morning. It had been a long day and he wanted to get home for a rest.

'Oh, tomorrow will do Andy. Keep in touch, won't you?' Sir Peter pushed the red button to end the call without waiting for a reply from Andy Foster.

About the same time that Andy Foster had rung Sir Peter Webb, Mary was putting a plate of Welsh rarebit on to the kitchen table. The plate was not lowered gently, but almost dropped, causing one of the slices to fall from the plate. She put a jug of tap water into the centre together with four tumblers and made no attempt to serve either water or rarebit to any of the three men. The atmosphere was tense with

Mary barely suppressing her anger and frustration at the men: her husband for blatantly lying to her, Carter for not telling her, and Caldwell because she just had a plain nasty feeling about him. Mary had seen and heard many smooth-talking liars in her life and, though she couldn't pinpoint the exact reason, she felt Caldwell fitted into that category.

Mary sat down, poured a half tumbler of water and crossed her arms. Sir Roger offered the rarebit to Carter and Caldwell, who each took a slice, while Carter poured the three men their drinks – all conducted in silence.

Mary was the first to break the silence, turning to Caldwell. 'So, you've seen Josephine and she's having a good time, with freedom and good meals, even though she has been kidnapped and is being held against her will. Are you saying she is being held as a prisoner or not, because to me it sounds as if there is no reason why she can't telephone or why I cannot speak to her. If she doesn't know where she is and you say you don't know where she is, as you were blindfolded when you were taken there, what harm can be done?'

Caldwell was becoming irritated by Mary's attitude. She was a damned lot more shrewd than he liked and becoming more and more persistent with her questions.

He smiled. 'Mary, I am hoping that I will receive a phone call very shortly and I will ask that very question. It is a very reasonable request.'

'How do I know she is being treated well, as you say?' she fired back, a little too harshly.

'I can only relay to you what I saw myself,' he replied, trying to maintain his smile.

Mary looked at him for a good ten seconds, which Caldwell found a little unnerving. 'In this age of the Internet why can't we do some sort of link-up, so I can see for myself, Mr Caldwell. The kidnappers do sound rather agreeable, after all.'

Sir Roger shifted slightly in his chair, which was noted by

Mary. Something wasn't right, she thought. I'm hitting a nerve here, catching the lies. A feeling of alarm grabbed her as she tried to shut out the thoughts that Josephine was hurt or in pain and they were lying to hide the facts from her. 'I really do think the police ought to be contacted, then, Mr Caldwell, you will be able to assist them with what you know.'

Caldwell felt a sudden urge to grab hold of Mary and tell her to stop being such an interfering bitch, that it was her husband who had caused all the problems, that her bloody precious daughter was being held, manacled to a wall, in pitch black and was using a bucket as a toilet. He wanted to tell her that her husband's stupidity had caused the deaths of two, maybe three, innocent people and the two blackmailers would also die, all because of him. He wanted to shout at her that her life with Sir Roger was built on lies, on the murder of an innocent man, on money stolen from people during a war when millions of people died. To shout to her that her privileged, rich lifestyle was all built on lies; her jewellery, her gowns, the Rolls-Royce, the big house, holidays, daughter, *everything* was built on lies created by the man whom she loved. He wanted to ask her what she knew of this man sitting quietly opposite him and next to her. What he was really like. He didn't.

'Mary, as I said I am hoping that the kidnappers will contact me this evening. If they do, then what I will do is,' – he held up his hand and bent a finger with each point he was making – 'firstly, ask if you and Josephine can have an Internet link of some description, by Skype or FaceTime; if that is refused, then, secondly, a phone call – that would seem reasonable to me; or thirdly I'll ask if I can see her again, to perhaps take a photograph of her and record a few words, to reassure you. I think one of those requests should be met and, Mary, I will do all I can to get the assurance you want.' He tried a confident and comforting smile, but Mary's mind didn't register it; she was thinking about the options Caldwell had stated. He had sounded sympathetic to her demands; she would have to agree to let him try, though there was still something she didn't trust about him.

Mary nodded her agreement and then stood up, stating that she was going to have a bath.

As soon as Mary was heard to close the bedroom door there was almost a collective sigh around the table. Sir Roger sat there looking at Caldwell. He had heard all the exchanges and knew that Mary would demand proof; she wouldn't be fobbed off with a lame excuse, though he did in a way have to admire Caldwell for handling Mary so well. Sir Roger had feared several times in the past hours that Caldwell's mask would slip and a mistake would be made. Sir Roger knew any slip would instantly be picked up by Mary and then all hell would be unleashed. He was pleased that so far the account was just about holding together. He was almost on the point of praying that the blackmailers would make contact with him.

Caldwell broke the silence by standing and walking from the room. He was in his shirt sleeves, having earlier replaced the gun in his briefcase. He carried the briefcase with him as he went into Sir Roger's study. He closed the door and made the call. It had been a close shave with Mary; he had had to think on his feet. He rang the number shown on his screen as 'W' and waited for the third ring when it was answered.

Wendy Baxter was in the living room at the cottage, the fire had recently been stoked up and she was watching television while Michael was resting upstairs in his bedroom. One of them was always awake downstairs, ready for any callers or problems with Josephine. They had both been surprised at how compliant she had been since their arrival and it had been an easy task to look after her.

She accepted the call but didn't say anything.

'Hi, it's me,' said Caldwell. 'I've got a problem this end

279

and I need to speak to the girl and get a photograph of her all smiling in pleasant surroundings, or her mother is going to force us to have her there as well, which I'd prefer not to happen. How about later tonight, could you make the necessary arrangements?'

'Yes of course,' replied Wendy.

'Give me a ring in an hour, will you? I'll arrange things this end.'

'OK,' replied Wendy as she closed the call. She walked upstairs to wake Michael. They had work to do, which she was grateful for, as child-minding had never been on her wish list.

Sir Roger sat at the kitchen table and watched as Carter unwrapped a small metal clip, no wider than a thick elastic band of the type that post delivery people use to tie bundles of letters together. Carter slipped a bundle of one thousand pounds from its paper wrapper then slipped the notes into the metal clip. He replaced the paper wrapper over the clip and checked the appearance. He reached down to his bag and brought out a small black plastic box, no larger than three inches square on which there was one metal rocker switch with 'On' and 'Off' marked at opposite ends. Next to the switch and taking up most of the remaining space was a small black screen. Carter moved the switch to 'On' and watched as the small screen flickered to life. A bar ran down the right side and a red dot was blinking at the very top. The rest of the screen was white except for a similar red dot blinking in the centre.

Carter walked from the room watched by Sir Roger and Caldwell. They could hear him open the front door and feel the fresh air rushing in. Carter went down to the gate and noted that the red dot on the bar had moved downwards a little, while the screen was changing colour a shade. Satisfied, he re-entered the house just as Mary came down the stairs looking at what Carter was holding in his hand. He muttered:

'Tracking device, Mary. We're covering all eventualities; we are desperate for Josephine to be back safe and sound as soon as possible.'

Mary had known Carter for some years and, although she had never been close to him, she had liked him. He had been like a friend to the family, doing a lot more than his job description detailed, and certainly he had been like a rock in his support of Sir Roger. She gave him a weak smile: 'Thank you, I know you will.'

Carter pressed her arm gently in his hand and led her into the kitchen where she saw the bundles of cash. There was a realisation that all that money was for her daughter to be home safe and sound. She felt guilty then, her behaviour was wrong, she had reacted badly towards each of the three men; they were really nice men trying their best, to keep the secret from her and then to resolve the problem without involving her. She said quietly in a croaky voice as the words struggled to be formed: 'I want to say sorry, to all of you. I'm upset and didn't think of what you were all doing for Josephine. I'm sorry for doubting you.'

Carter and Caldwell watched as Mary and Sir Roger held each other.

They were drinking coffee that Mary had made for them when Caldwell's mobile rang. He answered it, aware that the three pairs of eyes were watching him. He was a born actor.

'Hello, Caldwell here,' he answered in a formal manner.

Wendy spoke quietly so Caldwell had to strain to hear: 'Everything will be ready when will you get here.'

Caldwell waited a few seconds and, continuing in his formal manner, he said, 'Look, Josephine's family have a right to know that she is being well looked after. I have assured them that is the case, but I do think we could do more. What do you think of some sort of an Internet hook up?'

There was silence.

'I see,' Caldwell said as he turned and looked at Mary.

'Then a phone call – Josephine could use your phone and Mrs Knight mine. You can monitor the call to ensure that nothing untoward is said.'

Again there was silence. Caldwell had to suppress a smile; his acting was really very good. 'OK, then I am afraid that the third option will have to be met. I will come to see Josephine. I will take a photograph of her and also record a message from her to her mother, and I'm going to insist on this. Her family are going through living hell. The money is ready for Sir Roger to deliver anytime. I could even bring it with me, tonight; I can leave here in five minutes, just say where I have to go.'

Wendy heard what she wanted to: 'Leave in five minutes'. That meant he'd be with them in less than four hours.

Caldwell listened to the silence, nodded his head as if in agreement at what he was being told, then said, 'OK, I understand all of that. But why can't I bring the money with me and take Josephine back with me?'

Again he listened to the silence and continued the pretence that he was being told something. In an exasperated tone he said, 'OK, OK', then pushed the red button.

Letting a lungful of air out gently, he turned to the three people watching him. 'They don't want the money as it isn't theirs to have. It belongs to someone else, they say, and they are paid just to look after Josephine. In fact, this is a method I have come across before,' he lied, thinking on his feet and enjoying the challenge of making it up as he went along. 'It was in Ireland a couple of years ago. The people looking after the hostage didn't know who they were employed by; they just looked after the guy – in that case it was a man – and when told, they released him unhurt. In fact, he was in excellent condition, all things considered.'

Mary's mood had brightened, so taken in was she by Caldwell's performance. 'Thank you' was all she could say as she left the kitchen and went to the bedroom.

Caldwell was as good as his word to Wendy. Within five

minutes he had left the house and was heading for the A27 dual carriageway that would take him westwards towards Devon, and Josephine.

Peter King received a transcript of what the listening device in Sir Roger's study had picked up from Caldwell's conversation with Wendy Baxter. He telephoned Andy Foster and he in turn updated Sir Peter Webb.

Caldwell had made good time and was on the approach to Newton Poppleford just before midnight. There had been little traffic and the journey had taken just over three hours, as he kept the Jaguar at ten miles an hour over whatever the speed limit was. He wasn't concerned that he might get caught by a speed camera for the fine involved, but because it would be evidence of where his car had been at a certain time and perhaps could even identify who the driver was.

Michael, meanwhile, had visited the cellar, where Josephine had just fallen into a light sleep. Wendy stood near by watching for any signs of resistance from Josephine as Michael approached her. Sensing someone near her, Josephine had suddenly woken up and as her eyes had seen the white-clad figure next to her had tried to sit up. Michael was on to her before she knew what was happening, lying on top of her with his arms around her. She couldn't struggle at all, even though she attempted to dig her boot heels into the mattress. His weight meant she could gain no leverage and her boot slid over the blanket uselessly. She hadn't seen the other figure approach as her view was blocked by the man on top of her but now she felt a pin-prick to her upper arm. Within a second she felt a little drowsy and then she fell into a deep sleep.

Michael had carried the unconscious Josephine over his shoulder upstairs to the lounge and placed her in the armchair. Due to her state she slumped to one side but Wendy Baxter was able to tie her ankles together. Wendy Baxter could smell how dirty and grubby Josephine was and noted that the clothes she was wearing were dirty and creased. Her face was ashen and her hair, lank, greasy and dirty.

For the next two hours, while the effect of the drug kept Josephine unconscious, Wendy Baxter worked meticulously to clean Josephine up, washing and then blow-drying her hair, applying make-up including eye-liner, blusher to lipstick, and dressing her in an almost new light-pink jumper of hers. Josephine was then looked at from every angle until they were both happy that in any photograph she would look well and cared for. They both knew that they had just completed the first and easy part; the difficulty would be when Josephine woke up.

Both Wendy Baxter and Michael were sweating in their all-in-one white suits and took it in turns to go to the darkened kitchen where they could stand by the open back door to cool down. They had a rule that at no time could a light be put on in a room unless every curtain or blind was drawn. They did not want anyone, a nosy neighbour or even a burglar, seeing them in their white suits.

It was Wendy Baxter who was taking her turn at the back door when she heard Michael call her. Josephine was waking up. Wendy Baxter carried in a plastic beaker with water, which she offered to Josephine. Josephine tried to sit up properly but was hampered by her tied ankles. She came to her senses after thirty seconds and realised that she was still being held as some sort of a prisoner or hostage. The fact she was upstairs in a comfortable room, her ankles were tied together, but both hands free gave her hope. She accepted the water and gulped it down. She had a headache and asked for more water and, while Wendy Baxter fetched another glass, Michael remained in position behind Josephine's chair.

*   *   *

Caldwell drove slowly through Newton Poppleford. There was no one about at that hour; the local pub and restaurants had been closed two hours, not that there would have been many people about anyway. The streetlights cast an orange glow down the main street reflected from the puddles and wet pavements. The rain had stopped a while ago but the sky was full of heavy clouds promising more rain that night.

He found the turn towards the cottage and slowly drove with his sidelights to reduce the chances of him being seen by anyone. He reached the cottage and stepped from the car, unaware that Wendy Baxter was watching from an upstairs window having been alerted to Caldwell's approach by a sensor placed in a hedge by the road three hundred yards away.

She was downstairs and opened the front door as Caldwell approached. They stood in the hallway and whispered to each other out of hearing of either Michael or Josephine.

Caldwell breezed into the lounge. 'Hello, Josephine. Lovely to see you and I must say you are looking well. Your parents will be pleased.'

Whatever Josephine had been expecting, this was certainly not it – she looked up and could not help smiling, her natural pleasantness coming to the fore. In that instant and before she could work out what the sound was, Wendy Baxter had fired three camera shots from Caldwell's mobile phone.

Caldwell kneeled to the side of Josephine and said in a comforting tone that a doctor might use when delivering bad news to a patient: 'Josephine dear, your parents are obviously very concerned about you and I am here to arrange for you to go home. Wouldn't that be just great?'

'I just want to go home, please' was all she could say.

'I'm sure you do and you know your parents love you very much, don't you?' he said, still smiling at her.

'Yes, and I love them as well. Please, when can I see them again?'

'Very soon. I must say you are looking very well. Is that a special perfume you are wearing?' He leaned forward towards Josephine and smelled the side of her face. 'Mmm, very nice,' he said as the camera gave another short clicking sound.

Josephine was reacting too slowly to comprehend what was happening, her mind just about catching up, but still two seconds behind. She had just realised what Caldwell had said and hadn't yet registered the photograph being taken when he suddenly sprung up and sat on the side of the armchair, placing an arm around Josephine's shoulder. He squeezed her shoulder and she looked up at him. Again the sound of the camera. As she was registering the previous sound, Caldwell had moved again and this time he tickled her sides with his hands. Josephine's reaction was the same as most people's – she laughed throwing her head backwards and raising her hands. The camera clicked and clicked again.

Caldwell looked at Wendy Baxter and saw that she nodded to him; they had what they wanted. He stood up and strode from the room without a backward glance.

He and Wendy Baxter stood in the hallway looking at the pictures and listening to how Josephine sounded on the mobile phone. Satisfied, he thanked Wendy and let himself out of the front door.

27

The downpour that Caldwell had driven through on his return to Brighton had persisted and was as strong as ever at eight o'clock when Sheen and Jackie sat in the hotel restaurant eating their breakfasts. Sheen as usual plumped for the full English fried breakfast while Jackie had a selection of fruits, cereals and a slice of unbuttered toast. They didn't speak much at breakfast.

It was still raining at ten o'clock when Sheen parked the car in a dirty parking area, the uneven ground creating vast puddles of grimy water. He had driven past the Knight house to familiarise himself with the area and had then driven the route he expected Sir Roger to drive when he received his instructions. As Sheen got out of the car into the blustery weather, he zipped up his waterproof fluorescent jacket and picked up his clipboard. He walked the thirty or forty yards to a position in the car park where he could stand with his back towards the way Sir Roger would arrive and afford him a view of the direction he would travel. He satisfied himself that he could easily see and record numbers of cars, and after ten cars had gone past he walked slowly back to his car and removed his outer clothing.

He telephoned Jackie and was pleased that she answered at once. She confirmed she was at the bus stop on the road leading to Asda, which gave her a view of the road in both directions leading into the supermarket parking area.

Jackie was wearing plain black trousers with boots into which were tucked the trouser bottoms, a large black windcheater and a dark-brown woollen hat under which she had tied up her hair. She carried an Asda shopping bag in which she had three toys and a cabbage that she placed on top of the toys so that the bag appeared full of shopping. No one would give her a second glance; she was just a shopper waiting for a bus.

Sheen drove into Brighton past the imposing church of St Peter's, which some locals referred to as the unofficial Brighton Cathedral and continued past the Brighton Pavilion to the roundabout in front of the Palace Pier. He took the first exit, heading east towards the districts of Rottingdean and Peacehaven. Had he taken the next turning on the roundabout he would have driven parallel to his route, along Madeira Drive, a straight road over a quarter of a mile long that ended in a cul-de-sac near the Marina where a footpath links the two. He drove to where he estimated the cul-de-sac was, then turned into a crescent-shaped road on his left.

Safely parked in between two vehicles, Sheen collected a brown long mackintosh from the boot and added a cloth cap. He crossed the main road and took up a position by the wall, which afforded him a view out to sea but more importantly of any traffic heading towards the cul-de-sac area of Madeira Drive. By looking to his right he had a clear view westwards along Madeira Drive towards the roundabout at the Palace Pier. He leant on the wall, trying to look like a visitor might on finding themselves with such a view on a wet morning.

He checked his watch and noted the time. He would expect Sir Roger to be arriving in about five minutes' time, so he walked westwards slowly noting that his view of the cul-de-sac area was not as good the further away he walked. He was concerned that from the main road he was too far from the lower road to read the car registration numbers, but there was a walkway between the roads, running along the length of the roads. He saw some concrete steps that led to the walkway. Two minutes later he was on the walkway under the position he had been in when he first looked over the wall.

'Perfect,' he said as he looked at cars passing beneath him. The whole set-up pleased him – although he knew that under the walkway was a pavement that he couldn't see, the road was his priority.

He checked his watch again and waited for a further three minutes, noting the movement of traffic and the parking areas beneath him.

By this time Jackie had returned to the main car park area of the Asda supermarket and had telephoned for a taxi, which arrived a couple of minutes later and within ten minutes she had paid the taxi fare at Hove railway station. She entered the booking hall and used a machine to buy a ticket for her journey to Portslade, then stood at the doorway as if waiting for someone or just wasting time. She telephoned Sheen, who answered as he negotiated traffic along the seafront towards his position in Hove Park Villas, which is the road on the north side of Hove railway station.

Having heard that Jackie was in position, Sheen knew that they were ahead of schedule and had time to spare, a comforting position to be in. Also Jackie had shown initiative and had checked on the next day's timetable for trains to Portslade. A Saturday timetable was usually different from the weekdays one but fortunately there was a train just five minutes later.

Sheen found a parking place in Hove Park Villas and walked southwards to where the footbridge arrived at the end of the road. He turned and looked back from where he had come and planned the instructions he would give Sir Roger to follow: 'about a hundred yards to the junction, crossroads, shops on the right side up to the crossroads and a solid white three-storey building on the left side of the road', He walked along the pavement opposite the shops, imagining he was Sir Roger following the instructions. 'Cross the road here and walk in the other road on the left pavement. I will see you, hear from my accomplice that you aren't being followed, drive up to you, pick you up and then away.' He felt elated – the plan was coming together.

Sheen stood where the following day he planned to park his car, the end parking space in Newtown Road, just yards from the crossroads. He settled into his position and waited for Jackie to call him to say that Sir Roger had arrived at the telephone box where she would have left the message for him to cross the footbridge and the route he would then walk.

Jackie made the call to Sheen from the ticket office doorway, simply stating that she was off to catch her train.

Sheen waited a full three minutes, which was more than enough time for Sir Roger to be at his position. Mentally, he ran through the rest of the scenario including Sir Roger's actions, Sheen taking the bag and going to the boot to transfer the money into his rucksack, passing a hand-held metal detector over each bundle as he did this. Sir Roger would have been given his box; he would be looking through the contents ensuring that everything was there; it would be. This would take no more than thirty seconds before Sheen would have transferred the money, taken the holdall to Sir Roger, putting the box in it and leaving Sir Roger on the pavement, Sheen would drive off. He would use a route to take him back to the main A270, turn left and be at Portslade railway station ten minutes later where Jackie would be waiting.

Sheen smiled. It would work, he thought, provided Sir Roger wasn't being followed; if he were, then it wouldn't. The only change he would have to make in the morning was when he picked up Sir Roger; he would be wearing a white woollen head covering which he could pull down into a balaclava to hide his face. Would Sir Roger try and attack Sheen? if he did, then Sheen would use a length of hose wrapped around a metal bar that he had prepared and which was at the side of his seat.

Sheen returned to his car and slowly drove the route, seeing the large white-painted houses to his left and smart terraced houses to his right along Wilbury Avenue. The Drive was a busy road, but a left turn wouldn't be a problem. Traffic lights could be problematical but also gave him options. On the whole, Sheen felt happy with his and Jackie's planning.

Friday morning was the time when Sir Peter Webb liked to finalise things so he could enjoy a leisurely lunch at a restaurant then be driven home in time for a relaxed drink to prepare for the weekend. He was especially looking forward to this weekend as they had two couples as house guests, both senior civil servants with whom he had been at school. Their careers had taken different paths but they had remained friends and enjoyed their social time together. Their wives also got on well and they would happily leave the men after dinner to enjoy their brandy or port and their storytelling while they went to the lounge and caught up with gossip.

On this Friday morning Sir Peter could only see one item that could upset his plans, Sir Roger Knight, and it was about him that he was going to see the Director General himself to brief personally.

The DG, as everyone in the Service knew him, was an affable man who though well connected had risen through the ranks earning promotion and respect through his ability at the job. He had served in various departments over the years and had been regarded as the man to put into a difficult situation, whenever an individual or a group raised the threat. He was liked by his staff and spoke gently and slowly, considering his words with care. His manners were impeccable as befitted his upbringing, though in his younger days he had been rather boisterous and some had doubted whether he would grow up to make the grade. He was also a career man at MI5 and the reputation of the Service was paramount to him; its integrity and honesty he would protect at any price.

It was what Sir Peter had feared when he finished his briefing – the DG was not a happy man and was, as he said, 'very concerned about the reputation of the Service'. This he repeated while holding Sir Peter's gaze. Sir Peter outlined the planned actions and assured the DG that all was being done that could be and that he personally would be available at any time for Andy Foster to contact for advice or guidance.

This had not truly placated the DG, though he could see no point in pursuing his concerns with Sir Peter, as this had in truth been a disaster waiting to happen. What had surprised the DG most was the disclosure by Sir Peter as to Sir Roger's true background; he had not known or even suspected that Sir Roger was anybody other than the one everyone knew.

Sir Peter had left the meeting slightly subdued and unhappy.

Sir Peter's mood was in stark contrast to that in the Sir Roger household where before breakfast Caldwell had shown Sir Roger and Mary the photographs of Josephine that had been taken the previous night in Devon. Mary was especially delighted at one photograph, that of Josephine laughing with her hands in the air. Caldwell noted when he looked at the photograph there was a faint shadow just discernable on the edge. Damn, he had thought when he first spotted it. That was a close shave; he'd just got out of the way of the camera after tickling her.

Just three miles away from Sir Roger's happy house an unhappy detective superintendent Wordsley sat at his desk. The rain was striking the window of his office situated next to the major incident room, which was in full working mode. He thought of the telephone call he had just received. He had met Detective Sergeant Terry O'Brien twice and both times had been impressed by the softly spoken Irishman who learned his facts before he spoke. Perhaps it was this that troubled him.

The call had arrived shortly after the morning team meeting had concluded and before the detective superintendent had to leave for Police Headquarters at Lewes where he would update the Head of CID and the Assistant Chief Constable (Crime) on the progress of the enquiry and the lines of investigation that were being followed. Because his thoughts had been on other matters, he had at first not understood what the implications could be of what DS O'Brien had told him. It was when he asked DS O'Brien to repeat the information that he had quickly got his pen and started to make notes. It was now that he was reading his shorthand notes and clarifying them that he wondered what he should do.

The note was quite short and written in his own hand: 'DS O'Brien DIU (Divisional Intelligence Unit), Friday, 9.45 a.m. Research PNC and Sussex Systems show DS Harrison has accessed records of McCall and Aaron Brooks prior to deaths.' He underlined the word 'prior'. He continued to read his own handwriting: 'was AO' – he expanded the letters, 'Arresting officer for AB' – again expanded, 'Aaron Brooks'. Not much, he thought, but enough to concern him and of course why didn't Terry mention it to him? That was his worry and he would take his time to think of what, if anything, he should do about this information.

28

Saturday morning dawned for Jackie and Sheen with the sound of rain overflowing from a guttering above their room and falling on to a car roof somewhere under their window. They were finished with their usual breakfasts by eight o'clock and checked out of the hotel by half past.

Jackie was initially fed up with the weather which seemed to have consisted of rain or grey clouds for weeks, but Sheen had brightened her mood by pointing out the advantages it gave them regarding their outer clothing and choice of locations. The rain could be their friend today, he had said. With the prospect of one hundred thousand pounds being in their pockets within two hours, they had a positive attitude.

Sheen dropped Jackie at the Asda supermarket, then drove to his selected car park near the golf club. He changed into the outer clothing previously worn yesterday – it was still damp – then checked the time and at exactly ten o'clock he made the call to Sir Roger's home.

Sir Roger was in the kitchen joining in with everyone clearing away the breakfast debris when the telephone rang in the hallway. He answered it.

Sir Roger listened then confirmed his mobile phone number to the caller. He appeared calm and listening intently to the caller before saying 'OK, I understand what you say.'

He turned to find all three watching him from the kitchen doorway. He nodded at them. 'It was Sheen. He told me to leave immediately. I'm to drive towards Lewes on the A27 alone. He emphasised the point twice.'

Sir Roger looked at Caldwell, who was already moving towards the lounge. Sir Roger followed him in and saw Caldwell pick up the canvas bag which contained the cash, sling his blue overcoat over his arm and grab his briefcase. 'OK, Sir Roger, as we discussed. I'll drive in front. You have the other mobile open at all times, cash on the front passenger seat, keep talking about where you are, what you see. Carter, you behind, at least three cars and let's just do as Sheen says. After he's got the money you come back here, Sir Roger; Carter and I will see Sheen. Don't forget, Sir Roger, to take your time in everything, double-check before you pull out, and when you get the material, check it's all there, slowly.'

Sir Roger knew all the instructions and had rehearsed in his mind what he had to do. He took the holdall and giving Mary a quick peck on the cheek and a soft squeeze of her arm he headed for the front door that Carter held open.

Caldwell drove out of the house first and headed towards Dyke Road. Sir Roger counted to thirty and followed in the Rolls-Royce. Carter counted to ten before following Sir Roger, just catching a fleeting glimpse of the Rolls now and again and allowing other cars to come between him and Sir Roger. Sir Roger adjusted the mobile phone and started to talk, saying that he was approaching the roundabout at the top of Dyke Road. He was going to drive straight on, to the next roundabout and then take the right turn towards the A27 dual carriageway towards Lewes. He took the first roundabout and through the wipers could make out Caldwell's Jaguar ahead, approaching the second roundabout. In his mirror he noted Carter was about five cars and fifty yards behind him. He continued his commentary and at the second roundabout he turned right towards the A27 dual carriageway.

Sheen was in place and looked at the time. About right, he thought, as he read and wrote the index numbers of the following ten cars. He telephoned Sir Roger's mobile.

'Carry on the A27 and take the Hollingbury exit. Park in the Asda car park and await instructions.'

Sir Roger replied. 'OK, understood.' He repeated the instructions so Caldwell and Carter could both hear.

Neither Caldwell nor Carter were surprised by this instruction. Sheen clearly wanted to change things to keep Sir Roger and any one following on their toes.

Jackie received the call from Sheen and continued sitting at the bus stop, choosing to sit near a mother with three children for extra cover. She had a list in her hand and to any casual observer would have looked like she was just ticking off items of shopping. In fact, she was nervously writing down the index numbers of the cars that followed the blue Rolls-Royce into the supermarket car park.

Sir Roger drove around until he found a parking space away from the entrance area, aware that Carter was still waiting for him to park so he could select his own space. He didn't see Caldwell's Jaguar but had the feeling that Caldwell was watching everything. He waited in the car, becoming more and more nervous, examining each new arrival in the car park and flicking the wipers to clear the windscreen every ten seconds.

His mobile phone rang. He answered and heard Sheen give new instructions: he was to drive to an area called Dukes Mound on the seafront. He confirmed he knew the location, then instantly regretted what he had said. He should have asked for directions, should have asked where it was.

Caldwell walked quickly to his Jaguar, avoiding the deep, muddy puddles in the car park. He started the engine and driving one-handed made his way towards the exit using his satellite navigation to find out where the new location was. Sir Roger waited another thirty seconds before making his way to the exit, with Carter two cars behind him.

Sir Roger drove steadily in the slow traffic towards the Brighton seafront and noted that the rain had at last stopped, though more grey clouds were moving quickly in from the west. He checked and saw Carter behind him as he turned into Madeira Drive. He saw Caldwell driving slowly a hundred yards ahead.

Caldwell was on edge. Making Sir Roger go to different locations was good. Sheen knew what he was doing. This could make a good location for the exchange. Caldwell imagined Sheen appearing from the Marina, along a footpath, making the exchange quickly in Sir Roger's car before running back to the Marina where he could either hide or drive on to the main coast road half a mile away. 'A good spot, Mr Sheen,' he said quietly to himself. He pulled over to the nearside into a coach parking space. There were only two coaches parked and he was able to pull in between them. He walked from his car towards a grass area, leaving his overcoat in the car – a running chase could be a possibility. He called Carter and explained the position and at the same time squeezed his arm against the side of his chest to check for the familiar feeling of his weapon neatly tucked in its holster. He found some bushes and ignoring their wetness moved into the middle where he could see eastwards towards the cul-de-sac.

Sir Roger drove along Madeira Drive eastwards, keeping to the twenty miles an hour speed limit and checking that Carter was behind him still. He was a hundred yards behind but without any cars shielding him. Sir Roger passed the coaches and was surprised to see a Jaguar car parked between them. He resisted the urge to look around for Caldwell and as he reached the end of the road he slowed, gently bringing the Rolls to a stop.

Carter had seen Sir Roger's brake lights and pulled over into a parking space. There were few cars parked this far along the road but his ordinary Mondeo car made him feel that he wasn't drawing attention to himself.

From his vantage point overlooking the road Sheen had

watched the occupier of the Jaguar arrive and park before making his way towards the bushes. Although the person could be connected to Sir Roger Sheen, he thought it more likely that the man was just going to relieve himself. He saw the Rolls approach him then pass on towards the cul-de-sac and he also saw a Mondeo car pull into a parking space. From his position he couldn't make out all the numbers of the index plate but he made a note of those he could. No other cars followed for a minute.

Sheen called Jackie and confirmed that she had arrived at Hove railway station and had taped the instructions under the shelf of the telephone box. She was now in position at the entrance to the station and had a clear view of the road and telephone box. She had changed her black windcheater for a thin red jacket and the brown hat for a fashionable cap that cast a shadow over the top of her face. The hat and windcheater were in a waste bin next to the telephone box.

He rang Sir Roger and gave him the location and method of receiving the instructions.

Sir Roger relayed the phone call from Sheen but made no move to start the car; instead he counted. At twenty-seven he saw in his mirror the Jaguar car that had been parked between the coaches perform a U-turn and head westwards. He reached thirty, started the Rolls and slowly performed a three-point turn in the road, and followed the Jaguar.

Carter knew that his position was quite isolated so waited for one car to follow Sir Roger before doing so himself, informing Caldwell that the three were in convoy.

Sheen watched all of this and had a feeling in his gut – it was too much of a coincidence, he thought, these other two cars, each occupied by a single male driver, too much. He telephoned Jackie and quickly relayed what he had seen and gave her the part index number he had obtained of the Mondeo. He checked his list of cars at the roundabout; it was there and just as he was about to say this, Jackie said loudly, 'I have it, Asda!'

Sheen thought of the Jaguar. Both he and Jackie checked their sheets and tried to recall the cars they had seen but neither could recall the Jaguar. Sheen said to carry on as planned at the railway station but if they saw either the Jaguar or Mondeo cars then Sheen would abort the pick-up of Knight.

Caldwell had parked his car fifty yards down a side street then walked towards the railway station and, passing Jackie, entered the ticket office. He saw a man in the corner examining a timetable pasted to a wall, with his back to him. 'Check,' he said to himself, 'early to mid-thirties, five ten high, medium build, innocent, not Sheen.' He took a position where he could pretend to buy a ticket and at the same time see the telephone box; he was only four feet from Jackie. She was aware of the good-looking man standing near her and fleetingly wondered if it would help her cover to talk to him, but decided against the idea.

Caldwell saw Sir Roger park his car in a side street, then a minute later saw him appear on the main road and walk towards the telephone box. The holdall he carried looked heavy. Caldwell had picked up the mobile phone that was on an open channel to Carter and Caldwell, slipping it into his overcoat pocket.

Carter had been about to follow Sir Roger when he had turned from the seafront but was caught by the traffic lights turning red forcing the car in front of him to stop. He had no choice but to sit and wait for the lights to change; any running of the lights would not only draw attention to him but risked involving him in some accident, so he waited. He knew Caldwell was in position and that Sir Roger was to carry the money and therefore would be walking slowly, but he felt frustrated by the delay.

Sir Roger collected the note and read it aloud while

pretending to use the handset in the box. As a matter of habit he looked through the glass but couldn't see either Caldwell or Carter. He replaced the handset and walked directly towards the footbridge.

Jackie was watching the street, noting the cars in her mind when she suddenly felt a hard push in the back, causing her to stumble forward into the door frame as a man pushed past her. She looked at the man at the same time as Caldwell did. Her reactions were slower than his and he started forward after the man who was walking directly towards Sir Roger. Caldwell was ready – he willed the black-haired man to grab Sir Roger's holdall and dump the rucksack at Sir Roger's feet.

'Go on!' he muttered to himself, walking another two steps forward. He was preparing to run forward when the man carried on past Sir Roger. Having made towards Sir Roger, Caldwell was committed to continuing in that direction. He would turn and follow Sir Roger after a count of twenty.

Sir Roger had seen the ginger-haired man push a lady at the ticket office door and watched the man approach him. His heart had raced at the prospect of Sheen doing something or saying something, but even as he approached him he saw the man's vacant eyes. He had felt comforted by Caldwell's sudden appearance and his quick actions in following the man. Sir Roger saw the steps of the footbridge and made for them.

Sheen was sitting in his car on the forecourt of the small office block in Newtown Road, with a small car between him and Hove Park Villas; he was happy with his position.

Jackie called Sheen and told him that Sir Roger was starting up the stairs and wasn't being followed. She hadn't seen any Jaguar or Mondeo cars and she was going to her platform to catch the train, which was just pulling in.

'Good luck, darling,' she said as she closed her mobile phone and turned towards the platform.

Caldwell reached 'twenty' then abruptly turned around and walked back towards the railway station. The lady in the ticket office had just turned and was walking towards the platform.

'Nice body!' he muttered to himself before he once again turned his attention to Sir Roger whose legs Caldwell could see ascending the steps.

Sir Roger was physically fit for his age and had always been a keen walker but, though the holdall wasn't too heavy for him, the tension of the morning was starting to make him feel tired. When he reached the top of the steps he was pleased to see the bridge level out over the train tracks. He kept a good even pace.

Carter was frustrated by the old man driving the car in front of him who had moved slowly through the traffic lights then driven so slowly that Carter had seen a set of lights in front of him change from green to red as they approached. He banged the steering wheel with his fist in frustration and looked through the set of lights towards the railway station, but couldn't make out Sir Roger or Caldwell from that distance.

Jackie's train was still at the station as Sir Roger stepped off the last step. Taking in the surroundings and people, he began to walk as he had been told. There were a few people visiting the shops on The Parade in Hove Park Villas now that the rain had stopped. He was aware of people but didn't see anyone paying him any attention. He kept up his pace.

Caldwell stood on the steps near the bottom of the footbridge and used the metal work to give him a view of the street. He was happy that nothing would happen to Sir Roger in this area as too many ordinary people were around. He felt excited though. The cul-de-sac at Madeira Drive had presented a good opportunity but now he could feel the time and place was closer. He could feel his blood quicken and muscles tighten as had happened previously when the moment of action was arriving; he again felt the weapon secure against his side. He started to follow Sir Roger at a slow pace, keeping away from the road and close to the buildings.

Sheen saw Sir Roger appear and stand at the edge of the road, looking both ways before crossing to the shop side of Hove Park Villas, then again cross Wilbury Avenue and start to walk along the pavement. This meant that as Sheen drove next to Sir Roger and opened the door Sir Roger could get straight in and Sheen could drive off the way Sir Roger had been walking. Exactly to plan, thought Sheen, who continued to watch Sir Roger. The grey box file was on the back seat of Sheen's car and for some reason he chose that moment to instinctively look at it. It was a half-second glance but in that exact moment Caldwell appeared to Sheen's right, standing at the crossroads. Sheen's hand had turned the key to start his car and he was watching the back of Sir Roger as he pulled forward. He glanced to his left and right to make sure that no car was approaching and then saw no more than ten feet away a man standing on the corner. Sheen's eyes locked on Caldwell's and in that instant some sort of message was telegraphically exchanged. A basic recognition took place, each man knowing in that instant who the other was. Sheen gunned the car on to the road. Sir Roger was fifty yards ahead and, if the pick-up was quick and neatly performed, he could still drive and be away from the man on the pavement.

Sheen had driven no more than fifteen yards when he dared a glance back at the man on the pavement. It had been two seconds at the most but in that time the man had started to crouch and his right hand was inside his jacket.

Sheen instantly recognised the movement and position but couldn't believe what his eyes were telling him and his senses were screaming at him. Panic struck him as he put more pressure on the accelerator pedal, making the engine scream – but his speed didn't increase. It was a flat speed and Sheen instantly knew he had to change gear. He wasn't watching the road ahead as he was staring at the unbelievable sight behind him unfold. The man was now fully crouched with his arms extended in front of him. Sheen heard a metallic bang sound as something hit his car followed instantly by the back window being shattered. Sheen understood exactly what was happening and his natural reflexes took over. He changed gear again amid more sounds of the metal of the car being struck and looked forward.

Sir Roger alerted by the sound of the racing car engine had stopped walking and was in the process of turning around when the car driven by Sheen screamed past him with glass falling from the back. The car took the corner on quite literally two wheels and went from view, though the engine noise could be heard for another five seconds. Caldwell straightened up and holstered his weapon. He had counted six shots and knew that they were all within a foot of the driver, but he knew they hadn't been close enough. They had all missed him.

Sir Roger looked back down the road. He saw Caldwell striding towards him. No other people were about.

Caldwell felt his anger approaching boiling point. 'Where's Carter?' he shouted at Sir Roger.

Sir Roger just stood there and dropped the holdall to the ground. He knew that the exchange had been about to take place, he could feel it. He looked into the road and saw some slivers of glass. He couldn't understand what had happened – why had the car driven past him, and why at that speed? Caldwell was approaching him then suddenly stopped and swivelled in a circle before running back towards the railway station.

Caldwell's mind suddenly went back to the woman in the ticket office – it was Jackie Johns, Sheen's girlfriend. It was the same woman in the photograph shown to him by Harry Johns. He took the steps three at a time then ran over the footbridge. He heard a whistle and took the flight of steps down five at a time holding on to the handrail to prevent himself falling over. He reached the bottom and ran towards the ticket office bumping into some people who in the blur he couldn't have said were male or female. He didn't hear their shouts as he crashed through the ticket office area and on to the platform. The train was moving and gathering pace as he ran alongside it looking for a way to board it.

'Shit!' he shouted as he saw that it was a train with electronically controlled doors.

'Stop!' he shouted at the top of his voice and he saw the train driver's head appear from the front of the train.

'Stop!' he shouted again and saw the head disappear back into the cab area.

Caldwell was near the end of the platform and had passed three-quarters of the train's length. He stopped running and the train continued past him, the windows containing faces staring at the spectacle of a man outrunning a train. Some faces were amused; one youth even waved at him; some were looking concerned; only one face looked alarmed – even scared. Her. He had a one-second timespan to see her, and her him. As with Sheen, there was an instant mutual recognition, then she was gone.

Sheen slowed as soon as he had taken the corner, narrowly missing an oncoming car as he tried to regain control. His heart was racing and he noted that his hands were shaking on the steering wheel. He felt breathless and in a state of shock as he realised what had happened – the man on the pavement had been shooting at him. With relief he saw the lights ahead change to red and he slowed to a stop while checking his rear-view mirror for any sign of pursuit.

'Jackie!' he shouted as he reached for the mobile phone, speed-dialling her number. Jackie had picked her mobile up and was about to ring Sheen when his call came through.

There were people near her but she didn't notice them as she answered Sheen's call.

'The bastards were there,' he said quickly. 'The Jaguar man was following the old man and fucking well shot at me!'

Jackie was stunned. 'Shot?' she said before realising that she was speaking too loud. and that a woman was looking at her. Jackie turned her head towards the window and cupped her other hand around the phone. 'Shot?' she repeated in a whisper. 'Yes, he hit the car but not me; he's broken the back window. I'm on my way. I'll be a couple of minutes. Wait inside until you see me.'

'He was on the platform.' Jackie said as a shiver ran down her spine.

Sheen was surprised that the man had made a link between himself and the train. 'OK, don't panic! We're well ahead of him. See you in a minute.'

He hung up, not waiting for a reply. He needed to concentrate on his driving.

Caldwell contacted Carter to explain that the girl Jackie was on the train and the man Sheen was driving a blue Astra car. He wanted Carter to get to the next station as quickly as possible in case they were meeting there.

Carter looked at the map on his satellite navigation and headed towards Portslade railway station. He saw that a road ran from north to south at the station where the rail lines ran east to west; the road would be closed by electronic barriers while the train was in the vicinity.

He rang Caldwell. 'We may be in luck. There's a level crossing there.'

Caldwell was listening to Sir Roger saying that he was returning to his car and would go home. He sounded a mixture of weary, angry and frustrated.

Caldwell ran to his car and realised that both he and Carter were on the south side of the rail lines, the same side that Jackie would alight from while Sheen would be on the north side, trapped by the level crossing.

* * *

305

Sheen found the station and immediately realised that the train arriving was the train that Jackie was on and that she would have to wait for the crossing barriers to be lifted. He pulled into a space on a yellow line drawing attention from a shopper who appeared to shout something about not parking there. Sheen ran to the crossing barrier and stood with the other pedestrians. There were flashing red lights and a shrill sound to indicate the barrier was down, though the cars that were held in the queue of course were aware of it.

The train pulled into the station and Sheen could see the driver in his cab taking a mouthful of a sandwich or something. Sheen scanned the faces of the people waiting on the other side of the barrier; nobody appeared to be looking around for someone. He could only stand there and wait for Jackie.

There was a sudden hooter sound from his right that caught him by surprise, followed by a whooshing movement of air before the noise of a train travelling eastwards passed him. He could hear the metal against metal sound as the train's brakes were applied and the train pulled into the platform his side of the tracks.

The time appeared to drag; it had been thirty seconds since Jackie's train had stopped. A look at the faces the other side of the rail lines, those at the barrier – still the same.

'Jackie, come on!' he said under his breath.

Carter had found the approach to the station and due to the long tailback of traffic waiting at the barrier had decided to abandon his car in a side street in the first available place. He ran back to the main road then set off at a gentle run for the hundred yards that he had to make to the rail barrier. He didn't want to rush too much now; it was important that he could see her or him before they saw him. He saw the crowd at the barrier and looked at the people walking from the station. He saw her. She was running towards the barrier and he was no more than sixty yards from her. He slowed to a walk so she wouldn't notice him.

Sheen saw her as Jackie pushed to the front of the people at the barrier. She looked scared but saw him and gave a quick wave to acknowledge him. Sheen was again looking beyond Jackie, waiting to see the man who had shot at him. Still the train sat at the platform. Sheen cursed to himself – this had been a good plan until that man had arrived and shot at him. If it had gone properly, he would have completed the exchange with Sir Roger and by the time he got here the barrier would have lifted and Jackie would have been ready to be picked up on this side of the tracks.

Suddenly something caught his eye. Behind the crowd at the barrier was a man walking towards them, walking quickly. Sheen's brain immediately analysed the situation. Why are you walking quickly towards a crowd who are held at a barrier? Why not slow down? After all, you will have to wait.

A whistle sounded. Sheen looked to his left. The train driver had his head out of the window. Sheen looked forward. The man was only twenty yards from Jackie. Jackie was looking at Sheen. She looked scared.

'Now!' Sheen shouted at the top of his voice. 'Now!' he repeated again, watching Jackie's face to see if she heard and understood what he was shouting. He waved his hand to indicate 'Come here!'

Carter was still looking at the area where Jackie had pushed to the front and was shielded by the crowd from his view. He heard the shouts of 'Now!' but didn't see who had made them or Sheen's arm movement. Carter glanced behind him and saw Caldwell running at full speed and only fifty yards away. Carter indicated Jackie's position with his arm.

Jackie heard and saw Sheen. People were turning to look at her. She looked left and right. The train was ever so slowly beginning to move. There was no panic – the train would be past in thirty seconds then the barrier would rise and she could meet up with Sheen. But, Sheen had shouted. No time to wait. Without a look anywhere Jackie grabbed the barrier with both hands and using her arms as leverage vaulted the barrier. There were shouts and gasps from people both near her and also from those around Sheen. Jackie didn't look at the train that was moving toward her and gathering speed, but after landing and bending double to gain maximum power from a standing start she ran straight at Sheen...

Everything was a blur. There were many noises, shouts, screams, a loud train horn, train brakes, more screaming and shouting. The distance wasn't far and within three seconds she was approaching Sheen who had his arms outstretched reaching for her. Jackie crashed into the barrier, arms flailing towards Sheen, who grabbed her and dragged her over the barrier. There were shouts all around him from women and men, their tones and words angry. Jackie's feet made contact with the ground just as Sheen was turning and starting to walk almost backwards dragging her with him through the crowd. He bumped into people but he didn't see who and nor did he apologise. Some people ill-naturedly tried to obstruct his path but Sheen's face showed such determination that they soon gave way and he was able to get free from them quickly.

He started to run towards the car, dragging Jackie with him. He opened the passenger door and almost threw Jackie into the seat. He ran around the back and noticed some small round holes in the bodywork. He had only just sat in his seat when he started the engine and drove with screeching tyres northwards and away from the barrier. Neither spoke as he drove quickly away, before slowing down as he joined the main road.

Carter and Caldwell stood among the crowd, watching the train that had initially stopped because of Jackie's actions now roll forward over the road. The wheels thundered on the lines, making a clicking noise as they passed over a rail joint. It seemed to be passing so slowly, their view of the other side totally obstructed. When the train had passed there was a normal scene facing them. The crowd's excitement had instantly gone after the two protagonists had left the area in the screeching car. Carter and Caldwell waited until the barrier had risen and the people from both sides were crossing the tracks. Knowing their quarry had got away, they still felt compelled to check the area in case there was an unexpected gift for them, such as Jackie and Sheen having an accident in their haste to drive away. But there was nothing – everything was normal. They spoke for a couple of minutes before walking back to their cars.

'It was a trap, Sir Roger. We were supposed to be lured after the girl while Sheen was going to get the money from you. He wasn't going to carry out the exchange fairly; that's why he got her out of the way. We were distracted, sure, but he was just lucky. What we need to do now is plan for what they do next.' Caldwell finished talking and took a gulp from his mug of coffee.

He, Carter and Sir Roger had been in his study for over fifteen minutes as each of them had gone through what they had seen and done that morning. Carter had at one point said they had been 'outsmarted' by Sheen, which had brought an instant rebuke from Caldwell. If Carter had been quicker at Portslade railway station it would all have been different; even if Sheen had got away, they would have got *her*. Sir Roger had acted as peacemaker, though he didn't feel like doing so. He was feeling low and frustrated. He could see Caldwell's point of view, but somehow he had thought that after all the running from location to location the exchange would have been made.

* * *

309

Sheen listened to Jackie's garbled account of what had happened. The events had taken Jackie into shock, he thought. He was able, though, to cross-reference what she said with what he had seen and the picture had become clearer to him.

'Well, we know something for sure now. The old man has two men with him, one maybe both of whom are armed. And they sure as hell aren't police.'

He saw Jackie suddenly turn towards him. He felt her anxiety mounting.

'I think there is more than we think to all of this,' he said, waving his left arm in the general direction of the back seat on which only the grey box file sat. 'We know there is some sort of tie-up with Sir Roger and the Englishman in the passport and that Sir Roger is part of the Establishment, but to actually try to shoot me ... kill me – bloody hell, that's way too much. And I don't think it is to do with the money either,' he finished as he looked at the road signs.

Burgess Hill. This he remembered on the route he and Jackie had taken from Gatwick to Brighton on the train ... how long ago? He took the turn.

Peter King got hold of Andy Foster on his mobile phone and was relaying what he was reading from his computer screen. The typist was very quick as the conversation in Sir Roger's study was transcribed only just after real time. Andy was making notes but at the same time using his skills to try and recreate the scene between the three men in the room. It had been a frustrating morning and Andy's temper had been beginning to boil. Why hadn't they received quicker notification of the call to Sir Roger was one of several complaints he had, though in truth he knew from his experience that a foul-up could be rectified in time.

At the conclusion of the call he telephoned Sir Peter Webb and relayed the conversation to him. They both expressed shock at Caldwell's admission that he had fired six rounds at Sheen, though Sir Peter did remark that it was a shame none had found Sheen. All they were interested in was recovering the incriminating material and if Sheen had died then his body would never have been found – they'd make sure of that – and the matter would be closed. They would have to monitor Sir Roger more closely and they discussed how they might do that.

Sheen and Jackie had driven into the town centre of Burgess Hill, a small town in Mid Sussex making its way without any fanfare. The main street turned into a pedestrian precinct but at the top of the street on a road leading out of town Sheen found signs to the railway station and a small road beside it led it to an empty car park where on a weekday commuters to London and Brighton left their cars; today there was only one car occupying one of the twenty or so places. Sheen and Jackie got out of the car and together they inspected the rear of the car where they counted four small holes made by the bullets. Jackie was alarmed. The back window was bad enough but that was a shattered mess – what she was looking at were four clean holes. Sheen examined the holes without saying anything, then lifted the boot lid. The holes corresponded with holes in their bags and holdall that were in the boot. It was the density of the bags and clothing that had prevented the bullets travelling further. Two of the holes Sheen noted were in direct line to the driver's seat.

'Right,' Sheen said, 'we have to have a plan and I suggest we make it somewhere safe. It will take them time even with the police's help to find the car if we leave it here, probably not until Monday if we are lucky, so I suggest we take what we need and leave the rest here.'

Jackie was still looking at the holes and thinking of what might have been. What if that man had been in time to get on the train. What if Sheen hadn't shouted at her to cross the barrier. What if one of these holes was in Sheen?

She was numbed by the experience but felt relieved that Sheen was thinking rationally, so she agreed by nodding her head.

Sheen turned the car around so that the back of the car faced the wall and in the narrow space started to rearrange their bags. They could manage with a suitcase for Jackie and the holdall for him, but what about the holdall of cash? He stuffed some of it into his jacket pockets, gave some to Jackie so that she could do the same, and then put the remainder in Jackie's suitcase. Then he used a T-shirt from his holdall to wipe the interior surfaces of the car. Time was important to them; they had to make time and room between them and Sir Roger and his two men. Satisfied he had done what he could, he reached for the grey box.

Suddenly he heard Jackie say: 'No, leave it. Let's phone Sir Roger, tell him where the stuff is and let him have the damned thing, and all it's bloody secrets.'

Sheen backed from the car holding the box. He held it in front of himself, towards Jackie. 'Look, he was prepared to pay one hundred thousand pounds for this, one hundred thousand pounds! No argument from him. He's desperate for it. This is our future.'

'Our future is dead – that's what it is,' she retorted sharply.

'No ... no it's not. OK today was close, but we didn't expect a gun, did we? It never even crossed our minds.' He looked into her eyes as he continued: 'We take this, we think about it and, if we decide to carry on, then he will really pay. A last chance but it will be on our terms, in our own time and, thanks to today, with advanced knowledge of who we are dealing with. It has nothing to do with the police. These are criminals, gangsters who tried to kill me. I'm not going to let them win that easily. We are now forewarned and so, forearmed. We know what we are against. Let's at least think about it.'

He waited for a reply. Jackie didn't say anything but gave

a shrug of her shoulders. Sheen stuffed the box into his holdall and zipped it closed, then thought of his plan, unlocked Jackie's suitcase, removed two pairs of shoes and put the box in before locking it again. He put the shoes into his holdall and picking up both he smiled at her.

'Come on, this is the first day of our lives. Let's move.'

He was laughing and Jackie nervously joined him. They walked up hill to the main road and bought tickets from the machine before going to the platform. Ten minutes later as they sat on the train in a near-empty carriage Sheen explained his plan. Jackie listened and after asking a number of questions, which Sheen answered quickly, she agreed to it.

Sir Peter Webb was looking forward to lunch after the morning's clay shooting at a local farm and at which he had scored many more clays than his two male guests. The weather had been fine and he had relaxed to allow his aim and firing movement to be comfortable which gave him greater accuracy. The grounds of the farm were extensive and, as Sir Peter was commiserating on a 'bad luck' winging of a clay to his friend, he felt his work mobile phone vibrate in his pocket. Somewhat startled by the interruption, he made his apologies and walked away to the edge of the trees that surrounded the area and where he was out of earshot.

It was Sir Richard Bradshaw calling. Sir Peter was concerned – a call on a Saturday when neither man should be working was exceptional.

'Hi, Peter,' he began. "Fraid I've some rather bad news for you. That DA-notice, I mentioned it to the PM and he rather, well, to be frank, won't have anything to do with it; said not on his watch. Tried to persuade him but as you know he's one of these idealistic sorts who don't understand the real world. Wouldn't hear me out, I'm afraid. Nothing I can do on that front, which I know could be rather difficult for you – sorry.'

Sir Peter could feel blood draining from his face. The DA-Notice refused, couldn't be true. 'Richard, he can't refuse it ... the damage...' He left the sentence uncompleted.

'I'm really sorry, I really am. Of course, he's making a mistake but I can't really go behind his back. He'll find out and then where will I be?'

Sir Peter was stunned. Such an ordinary and straightforward procedure was blocked by a kid who'd never done a day's work, who'd never been at the sharp end... He couldn't finish his thoughts as he suddenly became aware that Sir Richard had said 'Sorry' once more and hung up.

Sir Peter took a deep breath and called the DG, not something Sir Peter wanted to do, especially on a Saturday.

He explained the development to the DG and for the next minute had to listen while the repercussions that were obvious were detailed to him. Sir Peter twice assured the DG that the matter would be resolved without any publicity, even though he thought that his voice didn't sound over-confident about that eventuality.

Next he called Andy Foster and told him the same story.

The plane was on time and they were able to relax on the two-and-a-half hour flight. Within half an hour of landing at Malaga airport Jackie and Sheen had recovered her suitcase and were at the car rental desk finishing the paperwork. Outside the terminal building the weather was sunny and warm which added to their feeling that events would now be changing for the better. Before departing Gatwick, Jackie had bought herself a laptop and had used it to find and book a hotel where they could stay for the next two nights while they prepared their plan. As they settled into the car she directed Sheen to take them to the Hotel Beatriz in Fuengirola, a half-hour drive from the airport.

*   *   *

After the events of the morning Peter King had been called by Andy Foster and asked to man his desk as they were now having to try and find Jackie Johns and Sheen's whereabouts. Peter King had gone into the office as quickly as he could and had started searching on various databases, some of which he wasn't an authorised user for, including various CCTV systems. On a hunch – and illustrating why he was considered a specialist in such matters – he had searched the databases at Gatwick Airport based on where Jackie and Sheen had left their car previously. He didn't have any details of the car they were using but he tried a search of passengers, which is how he identified the flight they had taken earlier that afternoon to Malaga. He called Andy Foster and then resumed his searches as he tried to identify where Jackie and Sheen had gone from the airport.

It was just before seven that evening that Andy Foster introduced himself to Sir Roger Knight and Mary. He gave Sir Peter Webb's name as a reference and at his request asked to speak with Sir Roger alone in his study. He had been formal towards both Carter and Caldwell and had asked them to remain in the house so he could talk to them later.

Andy Foster sat in front of Sir Roger's desk in the same seat that Sir Roger had sat in all that time ago when the robbery had been taking place. He explained to Sir Roger that he was fully aware of the morning's activity and gave some details to emphasise the point, leaving Sir Roger to ponder how so much detail could have been learned.

'So, we know what happened and Sir Peter is at the end of his patience,' said Andy Foster. 'Your man Carter has been incompetent and Caldwell is a liability that, to be honest with you, we could do without,' he continued. 'What we want is for you to act alone, without those two, and for you to carry out any instructions that you are given. No tricks, no underhand dealings, just pay up and recover the items. That is it, Sir Roger, and I am telling you this is a direct request from Sir Peter and above. If and when any contact is made, please inform me straightaway and, as I say, fully comply with any instructions.'

Sir Roger was aware the word 'request' meant 'order' and that to disobey would not be tolerated by the Service. He knew that he had become little more than a pawn in the events, told what to do by others – something he hadn't had during his life. He was on the receiving end of orders whether from Señor Mayer, Caldwell or, now, Andy Foster, all of whom he had to obey for the sake of Josephine. Well, so be it, but one thing that concerned him was that if Caldwell was told he had no further part to play, this would cause great problems with Señor Mayer. Sir Roger told Andy Foster that while he would fully comply he had reservations that Caldwell would just walk away so easily.

'Leave him to me. I'll persuade him and if needed, Señor Mayer too.'

Sir Roger was startled by the mention of Señor Mayer's name. It was obvious that the Service had somehow been following their every move.

Andy Foster remained seated while Sir Roger left the study. A minute later Caldwell entered.

'Good evening, Burt,' said Andy Foster in an amiable tone. 'Please do sit. We have a little matter to discuss.' Andy Foster had watched Caldwell's face at the mention of his first name and saw the shock register before he regained his composure and walked around the desk to use Sir Roger's chair.

Caldwell smiled. 'Was that a mistake? My name is James.'

Andy Foster returned the smile. 'Not a mistake, Burt, son of Kurt ... Rhymes rather sweetly, doesn't it?'

Caldwell lowered his head in a sign of deference.

'This whole mess, caused by Sir Roger, is in danger of causing us as well as Señor Mayer a lot of embarrassment.' Andy Foster said.

Caldwell could not prevent his body from giving a sharp

movement at the sound of his employer's name, something which Andy Foster did not fail to pick up. Two nil, he thought. 'This is not for discussion or argument: Sir Roger will from now on act by himself, without any backup from you or Carter. He will follow all and any instructions that the blackmailer gives him.'

Caldwell's smile had gone and his eyes narrowed as he listened to Andy Foster's words and delivery. Caldwell wasn't enjoying this interview with a man he'd never met or heard of before but who obviously not only knew what was happening but also had the authority to dictate how matters would proceed.

'Carter will be told that his services are no longer required and that he should take a holiday – somewhere where he can relax and forget this whole situation. You, however, will work with me and together we will catch the blackmailers and recover all the items. Once I am assured that all the items are there, then what you do with them, and the blackmailers too, is a matter for you. Sir Roger will be told that you are no longer involved, so this is just between the two of us.'

He smiled at Caldwell and saw that his smile was being returned. Andy Foster stood and extended his hand over the desk, which Caldwell shook.

'Deal,' was all Caldwell said. Andy Foster told him what he was to tell Sir Roger as he left the house, and where they would meet later.

Andy Foster waited for Caldwell to leave before telling Carter in the presence of Sir Roger that his work was finished and wished him a happy holiday, which would be at least three weeks in duration. Sir Roger had already agreed all this with Andy Foster, so the protest from Carter was muted; he knew when he wasn't going to win any argument. He said goodbye to Mary who was taken aback by the news.

Andy Foster had left the house immediately after Carter, leaving Sir Roger with Mary who began questioning him the moment Andy Foster had closed the front door. Sir Roger explained that the Government were now involved and that Caldwell would continue in an advisory capacity while Carter was not needed. Mary expressed her doubts regarding Carter – he had after all been at Sir Roger's side all the time and had become a friend to the family – but Sir Roger pointed out that the new man Andy Foster was Sir Peter Webb's choice. It was for the best, he assured Mary, but she continued to have misgivings.

Caldwell called Wendy Baxter for a report on Josephine. He was told that immediately he had left the effect of the drug on Josephine had worn off and that they had to carry her screaming back to the cellar. As they were carrying the struggling and screaming Josephine down the steps, their grip had failed at one stage and Josephine had fallen to land on her back. That had subdued her and she was then carried on to her bed and her wrist manacled back to the wall. She had been sullen all day and when the food and drink had been given to her she had threatened to throw the bucket containing her toilet over them. They had simply taken the bucket away, which had resulted in Josephine asking for it to be returned, promising not to make the threat again. 'Don't let her have the bucket back until she's soiled herself, then give it to her,' Caldwell said. He then told Wendy that Josephine would be with them for at least a few more days. He couldn't say how long but as they were getting well paid for their services he didn't think they would care how long it would be for.

Peter King found Sheen's rental car after trawling through the car rental firm's records then looked for it on the airport's CCTV system. He could see the car leave the car park and join the flow of traffic towards the main dual carriageway that ran parallel to the coast from Gibraltar to Barcelona, but then lost sight of it. He searched the Malaga CCTV, the

318

road camera system and the cameras to record speeding vehicles systems but without finding their car. The systems in that area of Spain were often old and about half of the cameras weren't working, meaning that Peter King was unable to do more that night. Instead, he would look to cover Jackie Johns' bank account to see if any withdrawals had taken place and telephone the major hotels in the Malaga area to try to identify their hotel.

Armed with the news from Peter King, Andy Foster met Caldwell where he had said – the foyer of the Grand Hotel on the seafront at Brighton.

Caldwell was pleased that Andy Foster had turned up, as he was going to have to report to Señor Mayer later that night and wanted to give at least some positive news. He wasn't going to mention his firing a gun at Sheen or the sighting of the girl on the train as either could suggest that there had been some mistakes.

Andy Foster told Caldwell that they were both booked on the first flight to Malaga in the morning, 7 a.m. from Gatwick Airport. He had also made reservations for them to stay in the Grand Hotel for the night – a car had been arranged to collect them at four thirty in the morning. Foster brought up the delicate matter of Caldwell's passport and Caldwell opened his briefcase and – keeping the contents shielded – produced his UK passport.

'Genuine, I can assure you,' he said with a chuckle.

After saying good night and confirming the meeting arrangements for the morning both men went to their rooms in the hotel. After very little sleep the previous night Caldwell was tired and looking forward to at least some sleep but he had to dispose of the gun. He had been surprised that Andy Foster hadn't quizzed him about it or asked for its whereabouts, maybe he thought, he didn't want to know too much in case some of the trouble could stick to him.

Caldwell set his alarm for 3 a.m. and slept on top of the bed to prevent himself from falling into a very deep sleep. His mobile phone woke him and he showered and dressed quickly. He carried his briefcase to the underground car park where his Jaguar was and within five minutes was driving along the seafront road towards Portslade. He had noticed a scrap-metal yard next to the road after he and Carter had been caught by the barrier. He needed to dispose of the gun. He didn't care really if it was found; it wasn't traceable, his fingerprints and DNA weren't on the weapon, so if somebody could use it, why not? Besides, if the police ended up investigating the shooting the finding of the gun in the scrapyard could lead them a false trail.

At the scrapyard he left the engine running and used his ears to search the area, surprised that a guard dog wasn't on the site. Satisfied, he reached under his seat and pulled the gun out before throwing it underarm over the wire towards a pile of already sorted metal. There was a metallic cling sound followed by another and another as the pile of metal shifted under the sudden impact of the gun. Caldwell had expected some noise but was taken aback by the amount. He was relieved when the sounds finally stopped. He looked around to see whether the noise had alerted someone or an animal but all appeared quiet. He drove back into Brighton and parked his car in a large car park, leaving the ticket tucked into the sun shade. He locked the car and used his mobile phone to let Michael know where the car could be collected from. Michael would make the necessary arrangements later that day and Caldwell would never see the car again. He was sitting in the hotel foyer when Andy Foster came down and settled their accounts before joining him in a waiting Range Rover for the drive to Gatwick Airport.

The evening before had been warm and Jackie and Sheen had enjoyed sitting out on the hotel patio having drinks after their meal in the restaurant. They had found a corner table away from a wedding party who were in high spirits and were able to talk quite openly, though they kept their voices low. They looked out over the gardens adorned with brightly coloured flowers with the sea in the background and felt the gentle heat that helped them relax. They had discussed all the events of earlier that day and after her initial objections Jackie had agreed with Sheen that Sir Roger deserved to feel the shame that publication of the documents would bring upon him, though they still didn't fully understand just why what they had was so valuable. They talked about what could be done but neither really knew how to do it; besides, as Jackie had pointed out, whom could they now trust? It was just as they were finishing their drinks Sheen looked at Jackie and said:

'I'm all for upping the price to two hundred and fifty thousand pounds, especially after being shot at. Call it compensation for my fear and damage to the car.' He smiled.

Jackie took a quick breath and had her mouth open for a couple of seconds before any words came out and then they were spoken in a hushed whisper. 'Two hundred and fifty thousand; he'll never go for that. No, that's far too much and, anyway, he'll have those men with him. I don't want to die and I think they are capable of killing us. Why not post the whole package to a newspaper and let them sort it out; we've got enough money to last a while.' She looked at Sheen waiting for his response, hoping that he would at least think about the dangers.

In fact, Sheen had been thinking of the dangers posed by continuing with the demand.

'We said before that it could only be done if the situation was completely in our favour, if the odds were firmly stacked for us. So how are we going to do that? By planning, that's how. We found them today, they didn't find us; they cocked up their jobs, we didn't, we did everything right. Think of it from their point of view: the pick-up for the exchange would have gone ahead had that bloke and myself not eyeballed each other. They messed it up. He fired a gun! That could have been part of their plan but maybe it wasn't; either way the ball's in our court. I don't see why we shouldn't go for it. Especially over here, if we find the place and dictate the events; if we plan it as well as we did today, we can do it. We can minimize the danger, especially now they have shown their hand with the gun and shooting at me. We didn't even think of that, did we? So now we know, as I said before: forewarned is forearmed. An old expression the sergeant used to tell us in the Army.' He gave a small laugh.

Jackie was again comforted by the confidence that Sheen showed and felt her confidence raised by his words. He wasn't treating her as someone who would just do as he said; he encouraged her to air her views and several times her questioning of him had brought a positive response and a rethink of the plan. They were too tired to discuss anything in depth that night and decided to go to bed. They agreed that a lazy morning would suit both of them; perhaps a training session for Sheen in the hotel's exercise room, followed by his favourite breakfast. Jackie opted for a lie-in, a long sleep, followed by a long bath and perhaps room service for a light breakfast.

29

They had slept with the bedroom window open, allowing the breeze to gently flutter the curtains and the sound of the rolling waves to soothe them into a deep sleep. Now they were awake and after a gentle lovemaking they were laying in each other's arms. Sheen saw the time was approaching half past nine. He showered quickly and dressed in a pair of shorts and an old T-shirt, slipped on his trainers and, giving Jackie a kiss, left the room for his exercise session. Jackie got out of bed to draw the curtains and close the window to create the perfect sleeping conditions for her. She was asleep again in minutes.

Caldwell and Andy Foster each had carry-on luggage and were walking through the arrivals area when their mobile phones rang. After the usual 'Welcome to Spain' message, Andy Foster noticed that he had a voicemail message. As he closed the call, he smiled at Caldwell.

'Our friends hired a car here yesterday, have the details and I think it would be a good idea if we hire from the same place and speak to the staff. Jackie is a good-looking girl, and Sheen is probably memorable to some women, so maybe someone there will remember them.'

Caldwell looked quizzically at Foster.

'Maybe overheard conversation, like where they were going to?'

'Yes, maybe,' said Caldwell.

The staff didn't remember either Jackie or Sheen. Nonetheless, Foster hired a Volkswagen Passat saloon car, which would be comfortable for both of them and be fast enough to drive quickly if needed. They decided that they might head for Malaga and drive along the hotel area in the hope that they might spot Jackie and Sheen, a long shot but in the absence of any further information from Peter King in the office it was worth the chance.

They hadn't reached the main area when Foster's mobile rang.

'Peter.'

'Andy, they're staying at the hotel, I'll spell it for you – B E A T R I Z. It's on the seafront at Fuengirola, just on the west side of the castle. The main seafront is on the east side of the castle.'

'Right, Hotel Beatriz on the seafront at Fuengirola,' Foster repeated for Caldwell's benefit, who was meanwhile spreading out the complimentary map from the car rental company on his lap.

Foster congratulated King on his good work and closed his phone. Caldwell looked up from the map and gave instructions on the quickest route.

'Half an hour max,' Caldwell said as he sat back in his seat. He didn't have a weapon with him but was confident that his unarmed combat skills would be more than a match for Sheen. Andy could take care of Jackie. He wished they could be on the afternoon flight home and then he could be heading home to Washington the following day.

As Andy Foster was driving towards the hotel, Sheen was finishing his running and starting on the cycling machine, which he set for a hard twenty-minute workout. He was sweating a lot – it was the first rigorous exercise he had done for some days – but he was enjoying the feeling.

Jackie slept well for a further half-hour before she woke, ordered a Continental breakfast and took a bath. She checked the time and knew there wasn't any rush. She heard a knock on the door and the muted voice of the waiter telling her that her breakfast was outside the door. She called out in Spanish for the tray to be left there; she would collect it after her bath, then nibble at the breakfast while she got dressed.

Caldwell was looking out of the window watching the reckless driving of the locals, who overtook Andy Foster then immediately turned off. It reminded him of rush hour in Washington or New York – that is, if the traffic ever moved fast enough, he thought. The traffic, though, was light compared even to England and they made good time. Soon they saw the hotel on the other side of the carriageway but following Peter King's instructions they had to continue for a further mile before heading back on the sea side of the road before they could turn into the entrance.

Sheen alighted from the cycle and looked at his performance as judged by the computer. He was surprised at how well he had performed; maybe he wasn't as unfit as he had thought. He wrapped a towel around his neck and looked at the sweat-stained T-shirt and shorts, dithering over whether to have a swim before returning to the room or fetch Jackie so they could swim together. In the event, he decided that he would just have a slow stroll through the grounds and then re-enter the hotel from there rather than go around to the front and use that entrance.

Foster parked the car and, as agreed with Caldwell, he approached the reception desk that stood in the middle of the large and imposing foyer. To one side were a number of comfortable chairs arranged around coffee tables where people were sitting using their laptop computers, the bar in that area was closed. There were three large settees opposite the reception counter, each occupied by a number of people who were obviously golfers, judging by their bags strewn around them. There was a queue at the reception counter and Foster joined it. Caldwell strolled into the foyer and walked around the golfers, casually looking at each of them before heading towards the coffee tables. Just outside on the patio where Jackie and Sheen had enjoyed their drinks the previous evening a couple were leaning over the railings watching the people below as some swam in the large swimming pool while others sunbathed on recliners near the flower beds.

Sheen had walked through the pool area in the garden and saw a gate that led to the promenade by the sea. As he wasn't in any hurry, he decided to change his route back to his room. He went through the gate and casually walked along the promenade, keeping the hotel and gardens to his left. He couldn't see into the hotel grounds but knew that in less than a minute's walk he would reach the edge of the grounds when he would turn left again towards the front of the hotel. He enjoyed the cool-down that the stroll was giving him and took time to stretch his leg muscles. He walked up the side of the hotel and again left at the front, with the car parking on his right. He continued along the front of the hotel towards the main entrance then skipped up the steps and into the foyer. He saw a queue at the reception desk and the golfers in the settees, who were beginning to stand and gather their belongings and golf bags. He turned to his left to head down the stairs, ignoring the lifts, which would take him to the ground floor. From there he would walk past the restaurant to the other building, which is where the hotel rooms were. His and Jackie's room was on the fourth floor.

He knew Jackie had wanted to use the laptop and as the coffee table area was the hotel Wi-Fi space he systematically combed the area searching for her. He didn't see her, but his attention was drawn to a man wearing a suit walking towards the glass doors leading to the patio. A suit? It was Sunday and everyone was wearing casual clothing. He looked at the back of the man as he went out to the patio. Something stirred in his mind. An alarm bell sounded in his head. The man turned to his right, giving Sheen a profile of the man's face.

'Jesus bloody Christ,' he said under his breath.

He scanned the foyer at the same time as moving towards the lifts further to his left. In the queue, five people or so from the front, was a man in a suit. An old couple in front of him were smiling at him, American possibly? Got to be together, he thought – two suits, one in the reception queue and one looking. He ran the three steps towards the lifts and picked up the white internal hotel telephone. His fingers nearly misdialled in his haste. The phone rang. A long ring, then silence, followed by another ring.

Sheen's heart was beating as fast as at any time he had been running or cycling.

'Come on!' he muttered. From his position by the lifts he couldn't see into the foyer but he knew that anyone going to his room would have to pass him. The phone was answered.

Trying to speak slowly and calmly, he said, 'Jackie, pack the holdall with the money, the box and some clothes for me now. The man who shot at me is in the hotel. Meet me at the exercise room. Do it now!'

He didn't wait for any reply, but his heart jumped as from the corner of his eye he saw movement towards him from the foyer. It was a man and in a fraction of a second Sheen had moved to the balls of his feet and drawn back his right arm, his fist clenched, just as the man turned the corner from the foyer. He was the older man from the queue, the possibly American man. He *was* American – he called to his wife to hurry as a lift was coming; the accent was strong.

Sheen turned and hurried down the stairs towards the exercise area, thinking that the suited man in the queue would now be at the front, asking the receptionist which room he and Jackie were staying in.

Jackie flew around the room. Her suitcase was tipped on

to the bed and the money thrown into the holdall together with the grey box file. She didn't know what clothes to take for Sheen, but she grabbed a handful and threw them on top. She squeezed her feet into her trainers and didn't stop to tie the laces as she ran to the door.

Foster had spoken patiently to the old American couple while Caldwell checked the foyer, the pool area and examined each occupied sunbed but without seeing either Jackie or Sheen. Foster had asked the receptionist for Jackie and Sheen's room number and, after a polite refusal to give the information, the receptionist had offered to telephone the room. Foster had explained that it was a surprise for the couple who had married just last week and thought they could hide here on a honeymoon. He had laughed so as to relax the receptionist but, fearing that would not be enough to garner the information, he had palmed a fifty-euro note over the counter. The receptionist with a deft movement collected the note and, placing it into his trouser pocket, said quietly: '4219.'

'Key?' asked Foster.

The receptionist shrugged his shoulders; it was against all the rules, but he had already broken a major rule that could get him sacked. He saw a further two fifty-euro bills and after a few taps on a keyboard he handed a card over the counter.

Foster smiled and thanked the receptionist then turned and found Caldwell standing against a wall scanning the front-door area. He told Caldwell the room number and together they checked the route to the room and started towards it. They passed the lifts but opted to take the stairs down the one flight to the ground-floor level, the same as that of the outdoor swimming pool and exercise room, following the steps Sheen had taken thirty seconds or less previously. They followed the signs into the block where all the rooms were located. Room 4219 was on the fourth floor. Caldwell pressed the lift button. There were two lifts working from the button: the floor indicator showed one lift was descending past the third floor while the other was stationary on the fourth floor. A fire-exit door was next to the lifts and out of curiosity Andy Foster opened the door and peered up. As far as he could see the stairs went to the top of the building, perhaps seven floors, and from the silence no one was using them, which didn't surprise him. He allowed the door to close by itself as a ping sound indicated the lift was arriving.

Jackie had run from the room, nearly bumping into a cleaning lady's trolley laden with sheets and toiletries. The cleaning lady looked at the back of the running Jackie and shook her head. 'Mujer loca!' she mumbled.

Jackie had reached the two lifts and pushed the button, watching the lights that indicated two lifts were ascending towards her. A ping sounded and Jackie was ready as the doors began to open. She didn't wait for them to fully open but rushed in knocking into two people, the holdall falling from her grip on to the lift floor.

'Jeeze, lady' the American man said followed by his wife's exclamation: 'What's the hurry, hun?'

Jackie mumbled an apology and watched as the two Americans got out of the lift talking to each other about there not being a fire and how rude the young lady was. Jackie's lift took longer than usual, she thought, to reach the ground floor. She heard the ping sound, gripped the holdall and waited for the doors to open. She rushed out of the lift and headed for the corridor. The lift doors next to her lift had just closed as Jackie rushed past it, unaware of the occupants.

Caldwell and Foster stood patiently as the lift ascended to the fourth floor. When they got out they looked at the room locator sign and headed towards room 4219. In front of them were the two old Americans still talking to each other about that young lady and her rushing as if the hotel was on fire. Foster didn't hear what they were talking about – it just sounded like two old people having a squabble. Caldwell saw the cleaning lady about to move her trolley and gave her a smile. It wasn't returned.

They approached room 4219 and for a second paused before Foster put the card into the door handle slot. There was a click sound and a green light. He pushed the door fully open and ran into the room. Caldwell stepped into the room and closed the door behind him. He remained at the door and saw immediately to his left was the bathroom; it was in darkness. The bedroom was directly in front of him, though he could only see the foot of the bed and along the wall, which had the television and desk. The television was on. The curtains were half drawn leaving the room in semi-darkness.

Foster opened the wardrobe doors as Caldwell peered into the bathroom. The light was just sufficient to show nobody was in there, even if they were hiding behind the door and plastic shower curtain. He joined Foster in the bedroom and saw the upturned suitcase on the bed with clothes strewn on the bed.

'Dirty bastards!' he said as Foster walked towards the curtains and the open door leading to the room's balcony. He walked on to the balcony and saw only two chairs and a table. He looked over and saw the swimming pool below.

'Coffee's hot,' said Caldwell as he felt the cup that Jackie had been drinking from. 'Croissant half eaten.' he observed. 'Maybe someone was here a minute or so ago.'

Foster started looking through the clothing and suitcase contents while Caldwell said that he would ask the cleaning lady about the occupants. He left the room and found the same cleaning lady about to open another door.

He smiled at her and was rewarded with the same cold look as before. 'Excuse me,' he said brightly, 'do you speak English?'

He produced his wallet and was opening it as he walked up to her. She saw the wallet and understood. She did speak English.

Jackie ran to the exercise area and saw Sheen half-hidden behind a pillar. He didn't say anything, just grabbed the holdall in one hand and took hers in the other. He turned and ran towards the swimming pool, turning to the towel collection and disposal hut. He held her hand firmly as he wheeled her behind the hut to the gate that led to the promenade. He pushed his room key in and heard the electronic buzz as the gate clipped open. He dragged her through and, keeping to the side of the hotel's wall and hedge, steadied to a fast walk towards the castle and main beaches of Fuengirola.

'She's only just left, She's got a large bag with her. She ran to the lifts,' said Caldwell as he turned back from the door and headed to the lifts. He heard Foster following him. As they approached the lifts, they decided to separate and each search different areas. Foster would again search the public area in the foyer before checking the front of the hotel and the cars parked there. Caldwell was to check the swimming-pool area, the downstairs toilet and exercise room.

Jackie and Sheen continued to walk to the side of the hotel before going on to the beach where he could change out of his gym clothes. A minute later they walked up the side of the hotel and Sheen glanced along towards the entrance some fifty yards away. Their car was parked on the other side of the entrance and Sheen looked at the possibility of using a footbridge to cross the dual carriageway close to where they were, which would enable them to walk through a campsite on the other side of the road and on to another footbridge which would bring them back to this side of the road. They would have to take the chance of driving past the hotel entrance. He was just about to tell Jackie of his plan when he saw the man from the queue standing at the top of the steps. Sheen ducked back behind the building and put a finger to his lips. He chanced a glance around the corner and saw the man walking down the steps into the car-parking area. The cars were parked either side of the small entrance way along the whole length of the hotel and the man turned left, away from them but towards their rental car. He stopped at their car and looked in. He checked the number plate again and used his mobile phone.

Sheen had seen enough and, taking Jackie's hand, he turned back, picked up the holdall and walked back to the promenade. He turned left, away from the hotel and towards the castle. They walked quickly but not so quickly as to draw attention as they passed the castle, crossed a footbridge over a river and found themselves in the popular area of Fuengirola. The street looked as if the British had taken over – given the names of the bars and restaurants and the advertising in English for all-day breakfasts and live Premiership games. There were many more people walking along the promenade and the seafront street, which afforded them cover but at the same time caused concern as any one of the persons could be an associate of the two suited men.

Jackie still hadn't said anything and appeared to be on the verge of crying, as Sheen cut from the seafront using a small street inland towards the area where the shops were. They passed the Guardia Civil building, which brought Sheen back to his thoughts about how they had been found. Sheen saw a passing taxi and hailed it. He asked for them to be taken to Malaga and when the driver asked for a particular part, Sheen asked what was going on there today.

'Football,' said the taxi driver, 'very good game. Valencia. You watch?' he asked, looking in the mirror at Sheen.

'Yes, that would be very good, please. The stadium will be good,' he answered and at the same time squeezed Jackie's hand. He tried to smile at her but she remained stony-faced, looking through the side window.

For the remaining thirty minutes of the journey the taxi driver talked about his passion, football, and how he had learned English and liked to talk English to his passengers. Sheen had answered politely and tried to make small jokes, in the hope of improving Jackie's mood, but to no avail. He understood how she felt and, though he was as worried as she, and in truth scared, he was determined not to be beaten by these men.

Near the stadium Jackie and Sheen found a bench in the shade close to various stalls selling football merchandise to the fans who were already arriving ready for the late afternoon kick-off. They were able to talk openly and Sheen attempted to soothe Jackie's nerves. Her mood, though, was dark and her comments mostly negative.

'Face the facts, we're losing this one,' she said. 'How on earth have they found us. They may not be the police but they've got official backup of some kind. How else could they find us?'

'Don't forget the car. They must have traced us that way. But, you're right, they seem to have a very sophisticated team behind them. However, would the police really go shooting people like that... It doesn't add up.'

'Well, whoever it is, we are really in trouble now, aren't we?'

Sheen nodded. 'But they still haven't got what they want, have they? And if they are prepared to act as they have been doing, they must be desperate for that box,'

Jackie was silent for a while. 'What about if I ring Harry and ask him what the two blokes looked like, and told him that you had been shot at – he might feel like talking to me.'

Sheen laughed bitterly. 'Pity he missed and wish you had been there with me, will be what he'll say.'

Jackie watched three youths playing 'keepy-uppy' near by

with a ball and thinking of Harry. Sheen was right. He was hurt of course, but maybe he would have calmed down and would talk to her. 'I think it is worth a call. Maybe he'll still be angry and hating our guts, but it could be worth a try.'

Sheen smiled and gave her a soft kiss on her lips. 'You are a lovely girl if you think Harry will forgive either of us, but if you want to give him a ring, why not? But we'll have to dump the mobile afterwards. I'm not taking any more chances – from now on we act on the presumption that these men want to kill us and will use any means to do so.'

Jackie took out her mobile phone she had bought at Gatwick Airport the previous day and dialled her old home number. The phone was answered on the third ring by an old lady's voice. She recognised it as her neighbour three doors away who used to do odd jobs for Harry and her, some cleaning or ironing for cash, which helped everyone.

'Hello, Mrs Patterson,' Jackie said cheerfully. 'Are you cleaning for Harry?'

'Is that you, Jackie?'

'Yes, it is,' Jackie said, still keeping a cheerful tone in her voice. 'How are you?'

'Look, love, I don't know why you can be so cheerful. What's happened is terrible and you've got it on your conscience...' Mrs Patterson said with an edge of harshness creeping into her voice.

'I know I acted badly; I'm really sorry, I truly am, but Harry and I just ... well, we were growing apart. ... Is he there please?'

'What?' said Mrs Patterson loudly, so much so that Jackie's reaction was to hold the mobile away from her ear.

'I was asking if Harry was there, please; I would like to talk to him,' Jackie replied, feeling guilty for upsetting Mrs Patterson who for all her gossiping was a lovely lady who always tried to help people.

'Harry here? Haven't you heard, dear?'

Jackie was puzzled. 'Heard what, Mrs Patterson. I've not spoken to Harry since, well, since we broke up.'

'I'm sorry, dear, but Harry's ... died,' Mrs Patterson said quietly and instantly regretted not having tried to soften the blow.

'Died?' Jackie repeated, looking at Sheen who had been watching the youths with his head supported by his elbows propped on his knees.

Sheen sat bolt upright and looked at Jackie with the word 'What?' on his lips.

Mrs Patterson softened her tone. She had after all liked Jackie and had spent time talking with her and drinking coffee after doing her chores.

'I'm afraid he took his own life, dear. I found him; it was horrible.'

Jackie was stunned. 'Took his own life?'

'I'm sorry, dear. He hung himself. I know he was upset about you leaving him with that Steve man.' Mrs Patterson spoke quietly though her words stung Jackie. 'The police want to speak to you,' she added quietly as if there was some conspiracy in the offing.

'I don't understand it, Mrs Patterson. Harry was upset. He was angry with us leaving, doing the dirty on him, but to take his own life, I just don't believe it!'

'Jackie dear, I'm telling you as it was I'm afraid. I saw him just the next day, after you'd left; he was in a right state I can tell you. He'd been drinking a lot, still not sober, and that was in the afternoon. Been crying and he was angry with you two. Are you still together?' she suddenly asked.

Jackie was taken aback by the sudden question: 'Yes, yes we are still together.'

'Well, he was upset all right. We had a talk and a cup of tea ...'

Mrs Patterson was talking but Jackie wasn't listening. She

335

was thinking of Harry, the man he used to be when they had first met.

Sheen made a gesture to Jackie to finish the conversation and Jackie nodded in agreement before holding up one finger. 'Mrs Patterson, do you believe he would have done that?'

'I just saw what I saw. I called the police and told them of what had happened. I'm afraid he was there like I said.' There was hesitation in her voice. 'But when he and I talked, he was, well sort of looking forward. Didn't say nice things about you and Steve, though, but he wasn't crying and saying he couldn't live without you, that sort of thing. I think he just accepted it, would let time pass and see what happened, you know, that sort of thing.'

Jackie thanked Mrs Patterson for being such a good friend to Harry and said that she would contact the police, before closing her mobile phone. Sheen gently took the phone from her, took out the SIM card and battery and walked a few yards to put the mobile in a rubbish bin. The SIM card he twisted until the plastic cracked and he threw that into the scrub beneath the tree they were sitting under. The battery followed.

Jackie was shaking her head. 'Harry hung himself, Mrs Patterson says; she found him.'

Sheen looked at Jackie. 'Harry commit suicide! I can't believe it.'

Jackie relayed what Mrs Patterson had said about Harry and Sheen added: 'So he wasn't suicidal when he was talking to her, was he?'

Jackie agreed, then said evenly. 'He was always against suicide; his uncle had committed suicide and Harry was angry about him doing that, leaving his aunt and cousins without him. He always said that, whatever the problem, given time something could be worked out.'

Sheen was thinking. 'Do you know, when we were in the Army and blokes were injured, lost a leg or arm, something terrible, he was the first to see them and give them hope for their future. Told them they might have to change their lives but they would recover and have a good life in the end. He was really strong about it. He kept in touch with some.'

Jackie said quickly: 'Yes, he was still in touch with three men like that. On the phone to all of them every week.'

They talked about Harry for some time, unaware that the football crowd was arriving. Finally they decided to leave the area and gather their thoughts. Sheen wandered through the stalls, thinking of what their next step could be, and bought a souvenir map that showed the eastern Spanish coastline from Malaga up towards Barcelona.

They walked away from the stalls and towards a large car park that was beginning to fill with dust from the arriving cars as they tore across the dried ground.

Sheen told Jackie he was going to hot-wire a car. It was still over an hour before kick-off, so it would be at least two hours more before the owner returned to find their car missing. They walked casually along the row of cars towards the edge of the car park and within a minute he had found an old-style Fiat. After twenty seconds' fiddling with the wires under the steering wheel he had the engine running. Jackie threw the holdall in the back and was in the front seat as Sheen drove against the traffic from the car park. They had agreed to drive along the coast, away from Malaga and towards Barcelona.

The dim light from the bulb was still on but there was no comfort in seeing the starkness of her environment; perhaps it just made it worse being able to see the confined space. In blackness at least she could think freely of her parents and friends, her life before, but the light always distracted her. Josephine was in pain from wanting to go to the toilet; her legs were bent against her stomach which caused her back to hurt even more. When she had been given lunch, she had again repeated that she was sorry for her behaviour and what she had said, but the bucket had not been returned. The bottle of water that she was normally given with her meals had also stopped, which she missed as she could have pee'ed into that.

Her pain was causing her to sweat as she fought against the urge to pee. After she had suffered the pain for at least an hour beyond what she thought was possible she knew she could not stand the pain any longer. She decided she would just pee on the floor but even trying to do that was so painful that she cried. It had been more painful still trying to manoeuvre into a sitting position where she could undo her jeans. The manacled wrist prevented her from standing by the bed and before she could settle herself she felt her muscles seemingly break, followed almost instantly by the feeling of pee splashing against her legs. Her crying became stronger and her resistance, her pride, her inner mind broke. She didn't care what was happening; she could just feel the beginnings of the pain lessening. She knew in the back of her mind that she had created a problem for herself – she would be in wet clothing and have to put up with the smell of her urine. She knew that her captors would be unhappy and wondered what would their response be.

Sir Roger and Mary had spent the morning talking quietly and in a subdued way, speculating as to what would happen and when. They tried to imagine how Josephine would be after her release – she could be very quiet, in shock or maybe just very pleased to be home; they just didn't know. Mary made sure that the bedroom Josephine had occupied as a child and teenager and which still had some of her belongings in was clean, tidy and ready for her arrival. They didn't discuss the reason for her being taken; the subject would only lead them to argue and fall out at a time when they needed each other.

* * *

Sheen noted that the petrol gauge in the car was showing only a quarter of a tank of fuel and after half an hour of steady driving with the sea to their right, they decided to take the next exit, signposted Valez Malaga and Torre del Mar. They had agreed that perhaps if they went to a small town away from the main tourist areas they would be able to blend in quietly. The further they got from civilisation, Sheen pointed out, the further they got from away from computers, cameras and other modern devices that gave away their location. On their little tourist map, Jackie pointed inland, where there were many small towns dotted among the hills.

'As good a place as any!' she said with a sigh.

Shortly after taking the road to Vinuela, they stopped at a large roadside restaurant. The weather was fine and the outside tables were occupied by a variety of customers, some playing cards or dominos, others eating meals and some just with a drink in front of them relaxing. The big green sign above the roof said 'El Cruce'. They walked into the restaurant and found a table against a wall. They had brought the holdall with them as they couldn't lock the car, and, though they felt eyes upon them, they just smiled.

They ordered a starter and main course, together with a small beer each, and began to enjoy the ambience. After a second beer and feeling full from their meal Sheen paid the bill. On her way back from the toilet Jackie spotted a large relief map on the wall and called Sheen over. They looked at their map, which wasn't as detailed, and comparing them she made notes on her map as they considered their options for routes and places. They walked from the bar and towards their recently acquired Fiat car when Jackie saw a car on the other side of the road, with a sign 'Se vende' displayed.

'For sale,' Jackie said, indicating the grey and dust-covered car that Sheen couldn't identify the make or model of. They walked over to it and around the car, peering into the interior.

Sheen lowered himself into a push-up position using his arms so that he could see under the car without his clothes touching the ground. While he was there he was aware of a man talking near by. He didn't understand a word spoken but then Jackie seemed to be responding to him. He got up and, brushing the dust from his hands, joined Jackie and the Spanish man at the front of the car. They ignored him until they had finished their conversation.

'This gentleman is selling the car. He says it is a good car, his from new and only 2,000 euros. I've said that it doesn't look that good and offered him 1,250. He said fifteen hundred – the lowest he'll go to,' Jackie said, smiling and indicating the Spanish man standing next to her, who was not hiding his admiration of her body.

While Sheen took the car for a short drive, the Spaniard tried to get Jackie to join him and his friends for a game of dominos, but having been leered at by this one man she didn't fancy another five sets of eyes devouring her.

Sheen came back satisfied with the car's performance and after a little further haggling he handed over 1,500 euros. The paperwork would be the problem, Sheen knew, so he found another 500 euros and handed that to the man while Jackie explained that they didn't want the authorities to know they owned the car. She pointed to the ring on her finger and explained that she had left her husband who was a nasty and violent man and, well, would he just make up a name for the buyer? The man was looking at the 2,000 euros he held in his hand; it was 800 more than he had expected, so he agreed. He'd make up a name and send the papers away in the next week or two, when he had time.

Following Sheen, Jackie drove the Fiat back the way they had come towards the motorway. Sheen remembered having spotted a garage where they could leave the Fiat in the car park. He drove the Fiat into a covered parking space near the garage, hoping that it would be thought of as a staff member's car, before he joined Jackie in the new car. She drove to fill up with petrol at the pump then manoeuvred to the car-wash area where they washed the car using the pressure hose. With the car looking clean they left the car park with Sheen driving and retraced their route towards the restaurant.

Jackie looked at her notes on the map and directed Sheen to take a road that led up into the hills, where a town of white-painted buildings could be seen on one of the crests. The road wound its way through avocado and olive trees, through fields and vineyards, up towards the little town that dazzled in the sunlight. They drove through two small towns and further into countryside before seeing a road to the left signposted Comares. For the next seven kilometres the road went steadily uphill, causing Sheen to stay in second gear; several times the road switched back on itself and from time to time they could see long views into the distance either side of the road. Finally they reached the tiled sign for Comares adjacent to the road. Sheen continued into the village square and found the only available parking space in front of the bandstand. Sheen and Jackie left the car to admire the view, which took in several villages, a number of farms and houses and, in the distance, the sea. They smiled at each other, relieved to have found a place that they felt confident the men at the hotel wouldn't be able to find.

They had passed a small hotel just as they entered the village and saw another in the square where they parked, and although they needed somewhere to stay Sheen was concerned about the registration process, was that how they had been found at the hotel? He mentioned his fear to Jackie before suggesting that they have a drink at the café in the square while they considered their options. Jackie went in the café to visit the toilet and order two beers while Sheen listened to some English people at another table who seemed to live either in the village or its environ.

The barman brought their beers and Sheen had taken two gulps before Jackie appeared talking with another woman. They stood several feet from Sheen and he was unable to hear what they were saying, but the lady was English and using her arm appeared to be giving Jackie directions. They moved apart and Sheen heard the lady say: 'See you in ten minutes.' Jackie waved at the lady, then joined Sheen at the table.

Seeing Sheen's quizzical look, Jackie explained that she had been examining a notice board in the bar when the lady had appeared at her side.

'Unlike you men, we ladies actually talk to each other,' she smiled. 'Ruth – that's her name – asked me if I was staying here. I told her we were looking for somewhere to stay, somewhere quiet. I told her we would prefer a bed and breakfast rather than a hotel and she asked how long we would be here. I just blurted out two weeks – I had to say something – and she asked if we would consider renting a house. She looks after one and anyway some people cancelled so it's free now until next spring and we could have it cheaply. Well, I sort of said we would be very interested.' She looked at Sheen questioningly.

'It could be perfect, so what's happening?'

Jackie drank some more of her beer. 'Ruth has gone home to get the keys. She'll back in ten minutes then we can look at it. She says it's really nice and quiet, just outside the village, town, whatever it is.'

Sheen kissed Jackie to show his approval.

It was less than ten minutes before Ruth returned, driving a car with local registration plates. Sheen drove following Ruth and Jackie, who had jumped into Ruth's car for the drive.

They retraced their route out of the town and for half a mile followed the road downhill until Ruth indicated a turn to the right that at first Sheen hadn't noticed. It was a small track-like road that had been tarred over and after a hundred yards Ruth again indicated right and braked before turning into a narrow concrete driveway. Ruth pulled into a covered parking area and Jackie waved her arm to indicate where Sheen should park. The night had closed in quickly and it was now quite dark, though the shadowed hills could be seen in the distance. Ruth produced keys and unlocked the front door, switching on the interior lights as she showed them around the rooms. The whole house had what Ruth described as 'personality' with quirky small sets of steps between the rooms. Several times Jackie and Sheen exchanged smiles as each knew that the house was perfect for their needs.

Ruth asked them if they wished to see the outside and they eagerly followed her outside. They were in a courtyard in the centre of which was a large olive tree, beyond which was another area with a swimming pool. Ruth explained that it was likely to be too cold to swim in at that time of year, unless they were particularly hardy. This made both Jackie and Sheen laugh.

As they went through the formalities of the rental agreement and Sheen handed over the two-week rental charge, Ruth chatted away about her life. She had arrived in the small town nearly twenty years ago and had stayed on, even when her Spanish husband, who was in the Guardia Civil, had left her two years previously. Finally, Ruth turned to go:

'I hope you have a lovely stay. Let me know if you need anything.'

As she went back to car she suddenly asked:

'Well, this must be the ideal place for you to do some writing, don't you think?'

Sheen was glad it was dark as he was totally thrown but he recovered enough to answer: 'Yes, perfect. Perhaps my book could end here.' He didn't think he sounded very convincing.

As Ruth manoeuvred her car and drove up the steep driveway towards the track, Sheen looked at Jackie bewildered.

'What on earth did you tell her?'

'Didn't you say back in Brighton that we needed to act normally and should always have a reason for being somewhere or doing something. At the bus stop, I had to have the shopping to look natural, didn't I? So I was just trying to give a reason for us being here.'

He could feel her smiling but more than that: it showed to him that she was alert and thinking – both would be vital if they were going to complete the deal with Sir Roger.

Foster had spoken with Peter King several times during the day but nothing further had been learned regarding Jackie and Sheen's whereabouts. Peter King had made contact with a local Guardia Civil officer whose brother was shown on his computer system as being very helpful in the past in investigating British criminals in the south of Spain. The Guardia Civil officer readily agreed to do what he could and followed suggestions by Peter King checking various systems and making telephone calls, but without success.

As night fell Caldwell and Foster decided that it was time for them to do something positive, as there hadn't been any sighting of either Jackie or Sheen. They agreed that Caldwell would go to Jackie's room and search it thoroughly for anything that might be useful while Foster would see the receptionist and see what he could learn there. They met half an hour later in the bar area of the lounge where the coffee tables were now covered in glasses of wine, spirits and beers. Caldwell had found nothing and Foster could only report what bar bill Jackie and Sheen had the last evening besides the credit card details that Sheen had left with reception. Peter King had reported that the card had not been used apart from being registered at the hotel. Tired from their long day they booked themselves rooms for the night and after dinner were glad of an early night.

Sir Roger and Mary, meanwhile, had reached a position where

they had called an unofficial truce in questions relating to how the troubles had started in the first place which had led to Josephine's abduction. Though Mary had been pleased with the pictures Caldwell had shown her, she was still anxious. They were in a much better place than had been the case and they both wanted it to continue so their lives could return to what they had been before the robbery. The day had passed quietly and after all the tension both were ready for a good night's sleep.

30

Monday morning was darker than usual and both Jackie and Sheen slept until nearly ten o'clock, realising that with the wooden window shutters closed it made the room very dark. They had made love the previous night but in a tired and somewhat strained fashion almost as if neither had fully committed themselves to it or each had other matters on their minds. Sheen was the first to rise and took in the view from the patio, amazed at how lovely and extensive it was. He felt safe and that time was now on his side as he prepared their next move. He was pleased at how Jackie had recovered from the shock and scare of the two men arriving at the hotel; her renewed confidence had once again bolstered his own.

Sheen heard mugs being moved in the kitchen and a minute later Jackie arrived wearing the same clothes as she had worn the day before.

'I don't have any more clothes,' she explained in a subdued voice before sipping her black coffee.' These men are going to kill us, aren't they? What is in that box doesn't matter to us. Harry's dead and neither of us believe that he committed suicide... I've had enough.'

Sheen had thought her doubts had gone and that they were going to move on together, so he didn't expect Jackie's dark words. Slowly and speaking softly he reminded Jackie about how they had eluded their pursuers so far and that they would continue to do so. They were one step ahead and smarter, too.

'Look,' said Sheen, 'why don't we do the shopping then come back here and sit down to think about our options.

We don't have to rush anything; we can work out our plan, as we did in Brighton, and when we are happy, *totally* happy, then we go ahead. Until then, let's just bide our time. I think we are safe here; they won't find us here.'

Jackie agreed though with some reluctance. In her heart of hearts she felt so angry with the men that she determined to beat them; she just didn't want to die ... like poor Harry.

They drove to town and found the supermarket, which was on the other side of the town to the square where they had parked the previous evening. They bought supplies of food and drink, a local map, and some cheap clothes before returning to the house to relax on the patio.

Sometimes a small vehicle would travel down the tarred track that ran at the front of the house. As they watched it descending down into the valley, it would disappear and reappear as it turned each bend. It was the same on the other side of the valley where a Quad bike travelled from the west to the east, disappearing into a valley only to return for a while before disappearing again into another.

By late morning they had talked through every point and from every angle – practical, moral, financial, emotional. Sheen felt elated as Jackie finally though not wholeheartedly agreed that they should make a large last demand of Sir Roger – they would either become rich or they would just dump the box and walk away. It would be all or nothing.

On Monday morning the Beatriz Hotel was busy – conference delegates arrived even before eight o'clock, queuing at the reception desk or forming knots of small groups, while some were placing boards around the foyer to indicate which room was for what delegates and at what time. Caldwell and Carter had checked Jackie and Sheen's room at three o'clock that morning and had just done so again at eight thirty. It was obvious that neither Jackie nor Sheen had returned to the room and the presumption had to be that they had flown.

Foster had contacted Peter King who had examined all and every camera system in the area and while they had been seen on the seafront in Fuengirola for about fifty yards, they had somehow managed to avoid any cameras thereafter. Of course, there weren't as many cameras in Fuengirola as there would be in an English town, but even so Peter King was frustrated at his lack of success. He had also examined the police crime list for the area – no cars had been reported stolen from Fuengirola or its environs. There were no car rental companies in the area open on a Sunday and checks with the bus company showed that it was highly unlikely that they had caught a bus. There was no train station. They had simply vanished.

Foster and Caldwell decided to walk around the area separately, looking into restaurants and bars, in shops and on the beach. It would be hot and very boring but at least they would be doing something, and anything was better than nothing.

Early afternoon Jackie had made sandwiches from a long loaf they had bought, filling the sandwiches with salami and cheese, lettuce leaves and cucumber. They drank iced tea with their sandwiches while sitting in the shade, and between mouthfuls Sheen began to outline the type of plan he thought would work. Jackie listened attentively, making the occasional sound to indicate her agreement. As Sheen finished, they both sat thinking of the pitfalls that could be in store for them, not the least of which were the two men who had found them so easily at the hotel. She shuddered as she thought of what would happen if they were found, but tried to put the negative thoughts behind her, instead concentrating on developing Sheen's plan.

The afternoon was very warm and sunny as Sheen drove with Jackie down the winding road through the local village and on to the main north-south road on which the El Cruce restaurant sat. They drove south to the outskirts of Valez Malaga and past the Eroski supermarket where they had left their stolen car. As they drove past, Jackie strained her head and saw that the car was still in place surrounded by other cars. Sheen negotiated the one-way system and followed the signs to the beach, passing through the town centre where all the shops were closed for the afternoon. Sheen had been surprised at the shops closing but Jackie had explained that this was a very Spanish town where the old customs were still maintained; a siesta in the afternoon was a must, she laughed.

They parked under a tree in a large unsurfaced car park at the end of the promenade and Sheen got his mobile phone out. He had Sir Roger's mobile phone number and also his home telephone number; it was the latter that he chose to ring. It was answered by Sir Roger.

'Mr Smith here, Sir Roger,' Sheen said by way of introduction. 'A not very happy Mr Smith moreover, Sir Roger; in fact a very angry Mr Smith. I don't like people shooting guns at me...'

'What?' interrupted Sir Roger. 'Who's been shooting at you?' he said loudly.

'Oh come on, Sir Roger, don't play with me. Yes, six rounds or thereabouts, in Hove. Don't pretend you don't know; he's one of yours,' said Sheen, showing some signs of anger in his voice.

'Honestly, I knew he had a gun, but I swear I didn't know he was going to use it,' said Sir Roger, his voice suddenly scared.

'Sir Roger, I'm not going to argue with you. This is the final demand I will make. The price is two hundred and fifty thousand pounds. We will either do the exchange, or I will deliver the box and contents to someone to publish ... and be damned.'

'Yes, I agree,' said Sir Roger quickly.

'If those men of yours are around, then it is all off immediately – no second chances.'

'They're not around. One has been sent on holiday and the other has been told to leave. I will be alone and will do the exchange; just tell me where and when.'

'So why is the man who shot at me in Spain, Sir Roger?' asked Sheen, putting hardness into his voice.

'What? Caldwell's in Spain? I don't understand, what is going on?' There was genuine bewilderment in his voice that Sheen picked up. 'Are you in Spain as well?'

'Well, how else would I know that … Caldwell, was it? – was in Spain?'

'Look, I was there when he went. He was, well sort of sacked; he was told his services were no longer needed. He went. Honestly, I was there, saw it and heard it.'

Sheen was puzzled. '*Who* sacked him?'

There was hesitation before Sir Roger answered: 'A man from the Government. He told my security man to go on holiday and Caldwell to go. The plan is for just me to do the exchange without anyone else involved. I swear that is the truth; I just want to get it done.' His voice faltered as he fought to keep control of his emotions. 'Our daughter has been kidnapped, Mr Smith, and she will be kept until I get that box and contents back. This is killing us, my wife and me. Please, can we just do it? I'm not arguing about the money.'

Sheen was confused. He looked at Jackie who was leaning towards the mobile listening to both sides of the conversation. He frowned, then quickly said, 'Ring you back on your mobile two minutes,' and cut the call. He switched his mobile off then looked around the car park. No vehicles had arrived or left and no people were hanging around taking any interest in him or Jackie.

'Did you hear that?'

'Yes,' Jackie replied. 'Is he telling the truth. He can't be!' she said, answering her own question. 'He can't be! He's lying, or else why were those two men at the hotel. His daughter's been kidnapped – is that true? Why kidnap her for God's sake, and who would kidnap her?'

Sheen's mind, too, was overflowing with questions. The involvement of the Government explained one thing – how they had been able to find Jackie and him with such apparent ease. There was a dawn of something clicking at the back of his mind as he tried to work out what was happening.

'Jackie, let's put this together later. I'm going to ring him back on his mobile. If a Government man is involved, then his phone will be tapped, guaranteed. Maybe they can tap a mobile call, I don't know, but we'll make the call, dump the mobile, then get out of here.' Sheen dialled Sir Roger's mobile number.

'Mr Smith,' Sir Roger said, 'please, my wife is here. We are really only worried about our daughter – she is our concern. Other stuff, I really don't care any more about it. I just need it to get my daughter back, that's all, and that is the truth. Money is not the issue. So please, I promise I will be alone, please tell me where and when.'

Sheen listened to Sir Roger and found himself believing him. After all, why make up that your daughter had been kidnapped? The whole thing just didn't make sense to him but he said, 'Sir Roger the price is two hundred and fifty thousand pounds and I will let you know where and when. If those men from the hotel turn up, or anyone else, you know what will happen. If you are genuine, then make sure no one knows where you are going and it will be fine for both of us. I'll be in touch.' Sheen immediately pressed the red button, took out the SIM card and battery before starting the car engine. He took a quick look around the car park and concentrating on every car, van or scooter around him he drove slowly back to the house.

Jackie was aware of Sheen looking at everything moving on the road so she did the same, but after a five-minute spell when no vehicles were seen behind them they felt comfortable that they weren't being followed. Jackie had thrown the mobile phone, battery and SIM card from the car as they drove, checking first that no one would see her do it.

They parked at the El Cruce restaurant where the same men from the day before were playing dominos again, including the man whom they had bought the car from. He gave them a wave and went up to them speaking in Spanish as he pointed towards their car. Jackie smiled and replied, 'Si, bueno, gracias Señor.' The man pointed at another car that was parked in the space previously occupied by the car they had bought and smiled as he spoke again in Spanish. Jackie didn't fully understand what he was saying but guessing that he was asking whether they wanted to buy this car, she replied 'no gracias', which brought a roar of laughter from the man, who rejoined his domino-playing friends who laughed along with him. Sheen was amused but at the same time he was looking around the area and thinking. His plan was moving further ahead in his mind.

Mary had heard everything that was said by both men. Directly the call ended, she kissed her husband and told him: 'I love you, I really do.'

Sir Roger had put his arms around his wife's waist while she moved her arms around his neck as they kissed and held each other tightly. It was giving them both strength that they knew they needed and Mary was happy that her husband would do anything to get their daughter back.

'I am supposed to tell that man Foster about any contact I have from Mr Smith,' Sir Roger said into Mary's ear, not wanting to end the embrace.

'Are you going to?'

Sir Roger gave a sigh. 'Don't know, that is the truth. You heard Mr Smith. What happened before has meant there are no more chances for us. If I tell Foster, what will he do?'

'I don't think he'll just say thank you and keep in touch, do you?' Mary answered.

'No, but what would he do? Caldwell has gone; he's in Spain, according to Mr Smith, who is also there, so Caldwell is doing something, isn't he? And Carter is on holiday. Would Foster bring in someone else?'

'But what if you give the money and he doesn't keep his side of the bargain?' Mary asked quietly.

'That is my worry. Somehow I felt from what he said, though, that he just wants this to end as much as we do. I think it will be OK, and I really would prefer it if I could just go without anyone else knowing about it. Foster would have to do something if he knew. Why else would he want to know? No, he would get other people to be there and I can't risk it; I can't risk Josephine's safety against Foster's word. We won't tell anybody – just you and I know; that will be safer.'

Peter King had been telephoned from the department charged with listening to Sir Roger's device and they had played their recording over the telephone for him to hear. At the same time a transcript of what they could make out was appearing on Peter King's computer screen and he had heard enough of the call to know a second call, to Sir Roger's mobile phone, was expected shortly. After twenty minutes he knew there hadn't been a second call, or at least not within the hearing of the device, but nevertheless he checked with the listening department which confirmed his fears.

He telephoned Foster and gave him the news before they discussed other avenues of enquiry they could make to trace Sheen and Jackie Johns. They discussed what measures Peter King could take to ensure that, if Sheen and Jackie returned to England, he would know immediately. A full stop order could be issued, but that would entail them being stopped at their point of entry therefore alerting them, so instead a trace order would be issued where any booking by either of them would immediately be notified by the booking or travel company to the trace order maker, Peter King. Caldwell had feared that Sheen and Jackie Johns had gone to Malaga merely to lead him and Foster to Spain on a diversion so they could double-back to England and make another arrangement with Sir Roger. The fact that they were traced so quickly had heightened his fears; had they deliberately laid a trail that they knew could be found? Foster had confidently said that that wasn't the case; it was due to very solid good work by one of his men.

Jackie and Sheen had arrived back at their house and for the next two hours Sheen had studied the map and the view, paying particular interest to the village of Cutar, which he could see from their house situated on the other side of the deep valley.

Foster had told Caldwell about the call by Sheen to Sir Roger, but that a subsequent call was either not made or they didn't know what was said. Caldwell wondered how the Security Service had known so much; it was obvious that either someone was talking to them, detailing everything, or there was a listening device in the house. He thought of the second and wondered where it was and what the full extent of their knowledge was. He and Foster decided that Caldwell would hire a vehicle for himself and carry on with their searches that evening on the basis that luck could just reward their efforts, so each would again concentrate on their own areas. This allowed Caldwell to make a further call from his mobile phone which followed up his previous calls and a meeting was arranged for seven that evening.

Sir Roger didn't want to alert Mary or worry her any more than she was already, so when he was sure that she was busy he had systematically searched the living room. For Foster to have known so much of the events meant that he had overheard what was said in that room. In three separate searches he had found nothing. During the evening he had moved his search to the hallway, examining inch by inch the walls, flooring, carpet and furniture, but to no avail. He would search his study the next day but in the meantime he went into the garden to telephone his bank manager, who was at home.

As previously, the money would be ready for Sir Roger to collect the next day at anytime convenient to Sir Roger.

Josephine had cried for much of the day, after wetting herself. She calculated that she had missed two meals. She was hungry and her throat was sore from thirst. She had called out, saying that she was sorry and wouldn't do it again, but there hadn't been any response and she hadn't heard any movement from her captors. Fear was creeping into her mind that maybe she was alone, that they had just abandoned her in this room or cellar, left to die in agony. Her manacled arm caused her arm muscles to ache and the pain, no matter what position she adopted, would not lessen, let alone go away. She had tried to think clearly about the man whom she had seen upstairs but her memory was hazy and she couldn't reconstruct his face in her mind.

31

At eight o'clock Tuesday morning it was bright and sunny as Sheen left the house and began his run from the front of the house. His route was to turn right on to the tarred track and follow that track to the back of the house, down the hill towards the farm and to continue along that track into the valley where he hoped to find the dirt track that ran along the side of the hills opposite their house. That dirt track appeared to enter the village of Cutar and he wanted to confirm that was the case and to measure the route in real time without relying on the map. He set off at a steady run downhill, noting that the houses below theirs were generally spaced several hundred yards apart, though now and again two or three appeared to be in a small collection. He twice started down unmade tracks that initially appeared to be taking him in the right direction but then veered away, causing him to retrace his steps. None of the tracks were marked on his map, which maybe, he thought, could be to his advantage – they wouldn't be marked on any map. Should Sir Roger be lying and he did have some security or backup, they wouldn't be able to use a map either to locate a track.

He kept a steady pace as he realised that he was now running along the side of the hill on which his and Jackie's house was on, and parallel to the one he wanted on the other side of the valley. Another five minutes and the two tracks were suddenly getting closer, seemingly meeting at the head of the valley which would be to the west of his house. The two tracks did meet at the head of the valley where a further track branched away heading westwards into the next valley. He continued running along his track and was soon running on the south side of the hill eastwards, in the direction of Cutar.. This was confirmed when he scanned the hillside opposite and could just make out his and Jackie's house where no doubt Jackie would still be asleep. The house itself was set back but the railings could just be made out. He found the going harder as hills that he had thought were small from his viewpoint at the house were in fact steeper and longer. His track took him round a corner and into a valley where the track descended steeply while the field of vines to his right rose even steeper away from the track. He was enjoying the views and the sight of the avocado and olive trees laden with their fruit, waiting to be harvested. He ran past two ruined houses, with birds flying through gaps in the walls where presumably windows had once been. Only two occupied houses, it seemed, were accessed from the track on that side of the valley and they were upwards of fifty yards away, up their own drives. Houses on the other side of the valley, under the house he and Jackie were staying in, looked directly over the track, but at night he didn't think they would see him at all.

He kept looking up towards his house, noting in his mind where he was and what the view from their house was to where he was. He was surprised at the number of houses dotted on the side of the hill opposite; some were obviously villas with their large swimming pools while others appeared to be small farms or smallholdings. Dogs could be heard and he guessed that most of the houses kept dogs as pets or guard animals, but there were also likely to be a few wild ones, whose presence near a house would set the owned dogs barking.

He went into another valley and lost sight of the house as he again descended a hill before turning at the head of that valley and returning to a place where he could again see the house. He continued uphill on a steady climb and saw that he was approaching some older properties on the outskirts of Cutar. From a distance the village looked pretty but as he ran past some old and half-finished buildings he started to change his mind. In the village – he remembered from the map – there were two roads that basically ran parallel the whole length of the village, both starting at a car park at the other end. He looked about him and knew he was on one of the roads, the lower of the two; only it wasn't a road, more of a paved pedestrian walkway through which a car could manoeuvre only with difficulty. He walked along, noting the walls covered with varieties of bougainvillea, small tiled courtyards and narrow sets of steps leading he assumed to the top road or other houses below him. The village was small – the walk from end to end was no more than five minutes before he found himself in a large car park that also contained a bus stop and recycling bins. He stopped for a minute, stretching his leg muscles as he looked around taking note of the area, its access points and where the top road started. He took the top road back through the village and noted the steps that led down to the lower road where a car was parked which completely blocked the road except to pedestrians.

He started running as he reached the end of the road when he saw that the first road he had taken and the dirt track all came together. Two sets of dogs kept in wire-fenced yards barked as he approached and continued long after he had gone by.

He waited ten minutes again, stretching and looking over the valley, working out where he was and looking at his house trying to imagine what could be seen from there. He decided to rewalk the village again but in reverse, the top road to the car park and the lower road back, to ensure that he could pick out landmarks and particular houses that he would recognise at night.

He saw only one bar, situated off the lower road, which he didn't think would be too busy provided there wasn't any event happening in the town. He made a mental note for Jackie to check on the Internet for any events.

He spent the next ten minutes rewalking the village before returning to the dirt track and beginning the run home. Running westwards he could again see the house at different times and in just over an hour he arrived, sweating and out of breath, back at the house. Three minutes later, as he drank glass after glass of water given to him by Jackie – now freshly showered and dressed – he started to lay out his plan. Jackie had asked if he was hot enough to have a swim but after testing the water he had laughed and said that he didn't want to have a heart attack and leave her to sort out Sir Roger by herself.

Peter King was alert to the fact that Sir Roger had not notified Andy about contact from Sheen and Jackie and had continued to monitor Sir Roger's CCTV system and ensure that the listening device was receiving full attention. In his desperation, he had begun checking with the local Spanish taxi companies and was rewarded with the forty-fourth enquiry – a Manuel Ortiva who had just arrived at work recalled collecting two people matching the descriptions of Sheen and Jackie Johns. He particularly remembered the female, not just because of her looks but also because she had been in a bad mood the whole journey, not wanting to talk either to the man she was with or to him. He could say exactly where he had dropped them off and the amount of the tip that the man had given him.

Peter King immediately phoned through to Andy and told him about Sheen and Jackie Johns being dropped off at the Malaga football ground on Sunday afternoon. It was good news in so far that it indicated that Sheen and Jackie Johns could still be in the area – after all they hadn't been dropped off at the railway station or airport – but apart from that it really didn't help Foster or Caldwell in finding them.

* * *

Foster and Caldwell had moved to a hotel in the town and after hiring a car for Caldwell they concentrated their searching in the Malaga area, keeping in touch via their mobile phones.

Caldwell made another call on his mobile phone and told the man on the other end: 'Really pleased with it, but the range isn't great – can it be improved?'

The man had replied that the range of radio transmitting depended on the size and quality of the transmitter and the same with the receiving unit. In this case, provided there weren't any obstructions, the range would be about fifty metres. It would be possible to extend that range, though, by either having a more powerful transmitter which would be larger and heavier, or by having a relay between the transmitter and receiver. Caldwell considered this and the two men discussed possibilities, arranging to meet again at seven that evening.

32

At eleven thirty on a sunny morning in Brighton, Sir Roger walked into his bank with a briefcase and after approaching the customer service desk was immediately recognised by the bank employee who had been briefed to expect Sir Roger. The employee had offered to carry the briefcase, which was declined, so he took Sir Roger through the security doors and then showed him into the manager's office. The men shook hands and Sir Roger accepted a cup of coffee while the formalities were completed. Of course, there was no need to check the money; it would all be there, already counted and bundled, all one hundred and fifty thousand pounds. The manager's desk was clear of everything except the cash and some typed sheets of paper.

'Sir Roger,' said the bank manager hesitating, 'I have wrestled with myself as to whether I should ask you something or not. Please be free to tell me not to be so impertinent and to mind my own business. I ... err ... I was just considering the amount of cash that you have taken out recently and wondered if there was another way we could help you. There are electronic transfers these days...' His voice trailed away. 'I am sorry, Sir Roger, none of my business, and of course I am happy to be of help in any way I can.'

Sir Roger's mind suddenly shifted a gear and waving a hand lazily in the air he said, 'No, Charles, of course it isn't impertinent of you to ask. You and I have done a lot of business over the years and certainly the past three withdrawals have been unusual, so of course an explanation perhaps is due.'

It was the turn of the bank manager to hold up his arms and at the same time he shook his head from side to side. 'No, honestly, Sir Roger, I wasn't asking for any explanation; I was just enquiring if there weren't another way of moving the money without it being in cash – you know for security.'

Sir Roger answered carefully, hoping that Charles could read between the lines.

'There are some transactions that have to be made using the old-fashioned way. Unfortunately, I have such an occasion, but this will be the final instalment.'

Seeing the pained look on Charles' face, Sir Roger forced a smile and tried to be light-hearted. 'These things happen. That's why we save – for emergencies.'

Charles was relaxed about Sir Roger's response. Obviously he had got himself into some sort of trouble and had to pay to get himself out of it. Not that he would ever repeat anything that was said in the room between the two men, but Charles just couldn't imagine Sir Roger doing anything that would lead him to having to pay such large sums of cash. Sir Roger didn't elaborate.

'I can only say, Sir Roger, that if there is some way that I can help, in whatever small way then I would be pleased to do so.'

Sir Roger thought for ten seconds. 'Charles, you may be able to help. I want to travel abroad, at short notice and for a day or two, maybe three or four at the most. I really would like to do this very discreetly. I wonder, do you have any advice that could help me?'

Charles thought for a moment. 'I do have a client I know quite well, a discreet man for sure, flies for corporates, taking persons here and there without any fuss or bother and, most certainly, without publicity. I can ask him to ring you, if you wish, and leave any arrangements you may make to be just between yourselves.'

Sir Roger felt his heart beat just that fraction quicker. This could be the best news possible if he wanted to meet with Sheen and make the transaction. He asked for Charles to do that, but to give the pilot Sir Roger's mobile number, not the home number. Charles understood.

Peter King had been working hard, trawling through the various computer systems used by the Spanish police; each had been easy to access but nothing had really struck him of interest. He had been surprised by the number of British names that were held on the computer files and he looked closer at the more recent entries in case Sheen and Jackie Johns had somehow obtained new identities.

The call Sir Roger wanted came through to his mobile phone just after lunchtime as he was preparing to continue his search for a suspected listening device in his office. He answered the call and then walked quickly through the kitchen where Mary watched him, and into the garden, now followed by Mary. Sir Roger explained that he didn't know where he would need to go, possibly southern Spain and quite probably in the next few days. The pilot was happy to be called upon at short notice as at that time there was a lull in his business. The pilot said that he had a suitable aircraft, a small jet, and they could leave from either Biggin Hill, Shoreham or Lydd airports at any time. Sir Roger considered the advantages of each place and decided that Shoreham, which was only a few miles from his home, would be the best. Payment was discussed and arrangements made that Charles would guarantee all expenses.

Mary was happy with Sir Roger's strength and was confident that Josephine would be back in the next four days. She shuddered at the thought of Josephine being kept somewhere but then reminded herself of the laughing girl in Caldwell's photograph, which brought a smile.

* * *

That morning Foster had been to Malaga's marina and the neighbouring areas that took in the area where the cruise ships berthed. Would they try to hire a boat or hitch a ride from a boat? He had wondered. He was getting tired and frustrated by the lack of success, so when he saw that Peter King was ringing him he answered straight away.

'Andy, I've been trawling through and there is only one item of interest that *may* – it's a long shot – connect with Sheen and Johns. A car was stolen from a car park at the football ground on Sunday. I say it's a long shot but it appears that it wasn't very far from where Sheen and Johns were dropped by the taxi driver. Maybe not connected but in the absence of anything more concrete worth a follow-up perhaps. The car was found at lunchtime today in the car park of the large Eroski supermarket on the edge of a place further along the coast, Valez Malaga. The car park is just off the A7 motorway, just a stone's throw. Valez Malaga is a town just inland from Torre del Mar on the coast, where there are a lot of hotels, so I'll check their occupants over the past few days and see if our friends are there. It will take a couple of hours and I'll get back to you if I come up with anything.'

Foster thanked Peter for his efforts – he and Caldwell would head to Torre del Mar straight away.

Caldwell had mixed feelings about the news that Foster delivered. Pleased that they appeared to be following Johns and Sheen's trail but unhappy that he would have to make alternative arrangements for his planned meeting.

Sheen watched Jackie as she searched the laptop, identifying addresses of shops as requested by him and then finding those addresses on a street map brought up from another site. The shops would be closed during the afternoon, so they prepared to leave the house at five o'clock to be down on the coast as the shops opened. Sheen and Jackie went through what they would buy, item by item, and Jackie could feel the excitement building much as it had done in Brighton. She was confident in Sheen's plan and in her role; after all, she would be removed from the actual transaction and only watching from afar. There were no events or celebrations in Cutar listed on the Internet for the dates that Sheen had asked Jackie to check, though there was a large celebration on another date, which Sheen would have to consider.

Foster and Caldwell met on the outskirts of Malaga and decided to travel using the A7 motorway to where the stolen car had been found. Caldwell believed it must be Johns and Sheen who had stolen the car as coincidences like this didn't happen. On the other hand, it might be a deliberate ploy to move them away from another area – say Malaga or Fuengirola?

Foster had asked Peter King to try and find out when the Fiat had been left in the supermarket car park and could anything be learned from it. Were there any CCTV cameras that might have covered that area or any witnesses. He felt he didn't need to ask the questions as he had total faith in Peter King making all the necessary enquiries, but he was frustrated at the lack of news.

Foster drove quickly to Torre del Mar while Caldwell went to Valez Malaga, both arriving during the late afternoon while the shops were still closed.

Jackie and Sheen had collected their cash and list of shops and had worked out a route that should take them first into Valez Malaga, then into Torre del Mar and finally home again. The weather was bright and, though they felt safe, Sheen had argued against Jackie's idea of leaving earlier in order to visit some clothes shops.

Caldwell parked his car in the centre of Valez Malaga and after buying a local map of the town he decided to sit at a café and have a coffee to try and pick up the flavour of the town. The café he selected was on the main road at the junction where the smaller road to a town called Benamargosa was signposted. He spent some time on his mobile phone making calls while watching the people walking on the pavement and driving by in cars.

Foster, meanwhile, arrived in Torre del Mar and saw that the shops were closed, so went instead to the seafront where he parked his car in rough ground used as a car park at the end of the promenade, not knowing that he was only twenty yards away from where Sheen and Jackie had parked when they had made their call to Sir Roger. He locked his car and walked slowly along the promenade, enjoying the late-afternoon sun, casually walking and watching people.

Sheen drove steadily down the hill in the late-afternoon sunshine with Jackie asking questions about what Sheen had planned, trying to get everything straight in her own mind. She still had reservations and was scared, but her faith in Sheen was growing all the time. He appeared to have planned for everything, so she was feeling quite relaxed about the evening.

Sheen drove through Benamargosa and towards Torre del Mar before taking the turning to Valez Malaga town centre where the traffic was beginning to come to life again after the lull of the afternoon. The traffic slowed as he approached the centre and he was held at the traffic lights with the main road. Sheen looked around at people walking on the pavement and crossing the road in front of their car. He saw people sitting at a café on the pavement with beers in front of them and longed for one himself. He rebuked himself for thinking of a beer when he had told Jackie that they didn't have time for her to buy any new clothes. One table was empty, except for a cup of coffee – the customer had seconds before gone into the bar to order some food.

On the way home they talked through their evening's

purchases, many of which they had made individually so that any salesperson would not associate them as a couple. Sheen also wanted their time away from the house to be minimized to lessen their chance of being seen. He was really pleased with their purchases and laughed as Jackie recounted her purchase of the mobile phones.

When Jackie and Sheen arrived back at their house it was half past ten at night. The hills opposite were in darkness, outlined against the slightly lighter sky. A new moon shone in the distance and though there were many stars shining brightly very little light seemed to penetrate down into the valley. A slight mist had formed, but that would only alter visibility over a far greater distance than they would use.

Sheen changed into a plain black T-shirt and black trousers before putting on the new training shoes he had just bought. He went to the car and from the boot he lifted a cycle that he had to screw the front wheel on to. Then in the light from the front-door light he examined the cycle, checking the gears and brakes, tightening some screws and ensuring that the right pressure brought the correct braking response. The cycle was for all terrain use rather than road, the tyres wider and with a deep tread.

Jackie didn't change her clothing, though the T-shirt she was wearing was sticking to her in the still warm air. She poured herself a beer, then positioned a chair at the rail from where she would be able to see much of the valley and most of the path that Sheen would use to cycle to Cutar.

In the Army, Sheen had often used night-vision goggles. He had found them uncomfortable and disliked the feeling that his own night vision was ruined by the equipment; however, they were perfect for his present needs, and they allowed his hands to be free. He fixed the goggles then adjusted the distance and focus to give him a clear view for about one hundred yards. He struggled into the rucksack he had just bought and spent the next minute adjusting the straps so that the rucksack was secure and high on his back towards his shoulders. He put a one-to-one radio and two mobile phones in the side pockets before Jackie put six two-litre bottles of water into the rucksack. On top she put some further pieces of equipment wrapped in a towel. Sheen could feel the weight but it was comfortable for him; the water, he thought, would give him some idea of the weight of the money he would be riding back with.

From her position at the rail Jackie looked through the new ATN Night Scout binoculars that Sheen had bought and, though there hadn't been much time for her to become used to them, as Sheen rode past her downhill on the tarred track she was able to follow him until he turned a corner. She refocused further along his route and saw him again briefly, and a short while further she picked him out as he approached the farm. Sheen went from view again and Jackie knew that she wouldn't see him again until he was on the other side of the valley, heading towards Cutar on the dirt track.

Twice Sheen had scared himself on the downward part into the valley, both times he had been travelling too fast, the first time the bend had seemed to go on forever and he had been forced to use his brakes on the bend nearly making the back wheel skid. The second time was when he went on to the dirt track and had a slight skid as he braked on the approach to a bend. He had anticipated that riding a bike he was unfamiliar with in the dark on loose gravel track would be problematical and the thought of falling off with deep valley just feet away, didn't bear thinking about. Even the rucksack needed to be broken in, the straps dug in his skin over the shoulders while the goggles rubber strap had to be loosened. At least the new trainers were fine while he was cycling.

The comfort of the new equipment would improve with use and by making minor adjustment, but the goggles gave him a good view and he soon became accustomed to moving his head slightly slower than usual giving the goggles time to readjust and remain in focus. He rode steadily along the track, able to see the glow from the lights of Cutar, though the village itself was still two valleys away from him.

As he was reaching the bend at the end of the second valley before the long hill up to Cutar, he stopped and looked at the valley trying to find the suitable place for him and Sir Roger to meet. He selected a spot where the track was narrower and noted a black-looking canister hanging from a branch of a tree near by. Easy to remember and identify, he thought. He continued slowly into Cutar, seeming to set every dog in the neighbourhood into a frantic fit of barking, but even so there appeared to be no reaction from any person. He propped his cycle against a wall, then removed the goggles and rucksack and placed them on the ground in shadow. He felt the sweat on his back and also the ridged marks on his face where the rubber from the mask edging had been too tight. He rubbed his face trying to remove the ridges and took off the T-shirt, trying to give it a chance to dry out a little before he went into the village.

The spot he had chosen meant he was hidden from any window or light, with a high wall to a house on his right side and olive trees to his left. There was an abandoned house behind him and initially he was going to use that for his bike and equipment. However, having seen three wild dogs in the area, he decided that a site closer to the village would be preferable – at that time of night he thought it safer from discovery.

He put on his still-damp T-shirt and walked at a steady pace through the village using the lower road. He didn't try not to make any sound but at the same time hoped that he wouldn't be seen. As it was, there wasn't a sound apart from the occasional babble of television sets coming from inside the small terraced houses. Some voices were raised somewhere in the village but he couldn't tell where; he guessed from the clarity and volume that many locals didn't close their windows on warm autumnal evenings such as this was.

He arrived at the car park and stood in the shadows at the edge, listening to the night sounds and looking around the area. He moved his position several times until he settled on a doorway to a workshop just set back from a house on the edge of the parking area. From his vantage point he could see the whole of the area; the small road that led into the car park from the main road from Benamargosa was straight in front of him. A row of cars were parked against a high wall to the right of the car park while the left side was clear of any vehicles. Sheen knew this was because that was the bus parking area. He stood there for twenty minutes during which time only one vehicle went along the main road, continuing past the small road that led to Cutar. There was no movement in the car park, none at all, not even an animal. Sheen was thinking of his plan, running it through his mind as he gauged distances in the car park and thinking of the route through the village.

He made a further check to ensure that no one was around, then walked out of the shadows to the parked cars and walked along them. The lighting in the car park was bright from streetlights and shadows were few. He knew that he would be seen if any one was in the area so tried to look as casual as he could. At the end of the cars, he turned and walked towards where he had been, his eyes swivelling from side to side. He was aware that his heart was pumping fast and that he was breathing heavily.

He saw a Quad bike parked in shadow between the lower road where he had stood and the upper road that he intended to use to walk back through the village.

Suddenly a thought occurred to him and he whispered to himself: 'Flexibility, Steve, flexibility.' He looked around again then made his way to the quad. He had seen many in the area being driven along the dirt tracks at speeds that ranged from slow to very fast. They would be good in any weather, he thought. He looked into the basket attached to the front and saw a key lying there. He looked about himself again, then picked up the key and tried it in the ignition. It fitted. He gave it a short careful half-turn. It moved. He quickly removed the key and replaced it.

He walked to the top road and began walking back through the village. He saw a row of steps linking the upper and lower roads and he silently tiptoed down them until the halfway point. From here he could see part of the lower road at the bottom of the steps but also part of the road towards the parking area. He retraced his steps to the top road and using the balls of his feet ran through the rest of the village to where he had left his cycle.

Now he was in a hurry, watching the time on his watch as he put the rucksack on followed by the goggles, then mounted his cycle. Twenty-six seconds. Could be a bit quicker, he thought as he cycled back on to the dirt track, again setting the dogs barking.

He cycled quickly along the track until he saw the black canister in the tree and slid to a halt, tearing his rucksack from his back as he did so. He opened the rucksack and rolled the towel out across the ground, exposing the other items of equipment. He switched on the one-to-one radio.

'Hello, can you see me?'

There was a second of static before he heard Jackie's voice. 'Very clearly, see and hear.'

'Watch,' was Sheen's response and broke off. They needed to use the radio as little as possible to minimise the chances of detection. He used various pieces of equipment, simulating possible actions that he might, in a worse-case scenario, have to use. He took two minutes and then used the radio again. 'Out' was all he said and a second later the reply of 'Out' came back to him.

He repacked everything then remounted his cycle and rode

as fast as he could. He was pleased that the uphill part of the ride went better than he had anticipated, although twice dogs ran into the road barking at him. The first time was such a shock that he nearly lost his balance, the dog appearing at his side a fraction of a second before it barked.

'Bloody wild dogs!' he said under his breath.

He arrived back at the house, freewheeling down the drive bathed in sweat, his breath rasping. If only he were fitter!

Jackie had seen him approaching and in fact could hear his panting so was in the driveway outside the front door as he arrived. She laughed at his appearance, the sweat pouring from his face, dripping from his nose, chin and the bottom of the goggles. He fought to recover his breath as he removed the rucksack and goggles, lay the cycle down and walked with Jackie through the house and out on to the patio. He walked down the steps into the cold water of the pool without taking any of his clothes off, just slipping off his trainers as he walked. The water was cold and he let out a shout to let Jackie know just how cold it was. Jackie was still laughing at the state of him – sweating, clothed and freezing at the same time – and after a short time she joined him.

Josephine had struggled to remove her boots and jeans that were still wet and smelt so strongly of urine that she had put them at the bottom of her bed in the hope that they would at least dry. Her morale had sunk as she realised how hopeless her position was – the urine incident, the lack of food and drink and the uncertainty of whether she had just been abandoned, left in the cold cellar to die alone, cold and wet. She thought of her parents – they would be frantic with worry; they must know by now that she had been kidnapped surely; they would be doing things, the police would be looking for her, her friends would be looking for her. She considered so many scenarios that she was going around in circles, and whenever she allowed an occasional positive thought to enter her mind she looked around her and the terror of her real situation returned.

Several times she had called out timidly, in the hope that the person or persons were still somewhere close enough to hear her, but there hadn't been any response. She had lain still, holding her breath and forcing herself to listen as intently as she could for any sound, anything at all, whether from inside the house, nearby or even outside. The sound of an aeroplane would have at least been something, but there was nothing. She cried and tried to sleep but the pain from her empty stomach and dried mouth prevented her from falling into the comfort of sleep.

33

Jackie and Sheen were up at eight o'clock and by nine they were driving down the winding road again, towards the coast. They intended to go to a different car park to telephone Sir Roger his instructions than the one they had used previously. They had to use one of the two mobile phones which they had managed to buy without showing any identification. Jackie had told the assistant that she had lost her handbag and had only the cash that a friend had loaned her. The young sales assistant didn't believe her story but didn't care; he even asked her whether she wanted to have a drink with him later that evening when he finished work. When she answered that she would really like that, he decided that he could complete her details later. He would have been disappointed at her non-appearance.

They found a parking space at the opposite end of the promenade close to the port entrance. Sheen rang Sir Roger's mobile.

Sir Roger had been sitting in the kitchen when he heard the call and quickly he took the mobile into the hallway. He had thoroughly searched the area and was sure that no listening device was in that area.

'Hello,' he said.

'Sir Roger, Mr Smith here,' Sheen said.

'Hello, Mr Smith.'

'Sir Roger, here are your instructions. Listen carefully and make sure that you are alone. Go to Malaga Airport tomorrow morning, departure level, and ask at the information desk for a message for you. Follow those instructions.'

'Malaga Airport, morning, information desk message. Got it, Mr Smith.'

'Goodbye, Sir Roger. I do hope that we can do business tomorrow and then you can be home on Friday,' said Sheen, who immediately bit his tongue and shut down the phone without waiting for Sir Roger's response.

'Damn!' he shouted, startling Jackie.

'What?' she asked worried, as she hadn't been able to hear what Sir Roger had said.

'I said do the business tomorrow and home on Friday; it's given him a timeframe when he can be more alert, especially if he has support.'

'That's OK. The timeframe is fine and I'm not convinced that he will have anyone with him, not after what he said before. Anyway, he or they won't know where, and even if they did, they wouldn't know the route and all that sort of thing. It's fine,' Jackie concluded in a soothing tone.

Sheen nodded. What Jackie said made sense; it was just that he felt he had made a mistake, a small one maybe, but he didn't want to lose even one per cent of the advantage they had at that time.

Mary and Sir Roger walked into the garden, which even for the time of year looked in good condition. The trees were now golden, their leaves dropping to form a golden circle underneath, and the various shrubs were losing their leaves revealing the bare, sometimes brightly coloured, stalks beneath. Sir Roger repeated what he had been told by Mr Smith and Mary was relieved that the whole mess would be shortly cleared up and Josephine would be back with them.

She waited while Sir Roger spoke with the pilot and they agreed to meet at Shoreham Airport at eight-thirty in the morning for a planned departure at nine for the three-hour flight. As Sir Roger had been told that their business could be concluded by Friday, the pilot was happy to spend the time in Malaga waiting for Sir Roger.

Jackie used a mobile phone to ring the information desk at Malaga Airport where she left a message for Sir Roger, who, she said, was expected the next day, flight unknown.

Peter King had received a transcript of what was heard from the study and smiled when he saw it. 'Thank you, Sir Roger,' he said to himself. 'Thanks very much.'

Five minutes later he spoke with Foster and relayed what he had learned. Peter King assured Andy Foster that he would find out what the message was the following morning; he was loath to ask yet in case it was revealed that someone had already asked for it. Andy Foster agreed and said that he and Caldwell would be at Malaga Airport from six the following morning.

Sheen pulled into the car park at the El Cruce but remained in the car as Jackie went into the bar and handed over a letter addressed to Sir Roger. There was now no point in worrying over leaving their fingerprints or DNA; their identities were already known to the police – of that he was sure – though whether in an official or unofficial capacity he thought still uncertain.

As soon as Jackie returned Sheen drove into Benamargosa but instead of taking their usual route he turned left over the bridge of a dried riverbed and towards Cutar, advertised as seven kilometres away.

The road was not as winding as the road to Comares, or as steep, but it was still a road whose bends needed care, especially when approaching cars were using the centre of the road. Sheen parked in the parking area he had visited previously and together with Jackie walked to a wall decorated with Moorish-style brickwork. In front stood the same Quad bike that in daylight looked old and dirty but Sheen recognised it as the one that he had seen on the dirt track the previous night. The key wasn't in the ignition but he found it again in the small basket attached to the front of the vehicle. Looking around, he didn't see anyone, He inserted the key into the ignition, gave it a half turn and flicked a small plastic switch. He checked and saw that the headlight shone. Sheen was satisfied and spoke to Jackie detailing what his plan was when Sir Roger arrived there the following night.

34

Foster and Caldwell had settled their hotel bills the previous evening, leaving them free to start in convoy towards Malaga Airport at five o'clock, although the first plane from anywhere in England wasn't due until ten past eight. They wanted to be in position early. On their arrival, they parked in different car parks so that they would have at least one car available should a car park have a queue, and then met by the information desk on the first floor. A coffee shop was already open near by but it was too exposed for them to sit at so they decided to take it in turns sitting in another coffee shop where they could be largely hidden from view. The other would wait at the VIP coffee shop in the arrivals lounge on the ground floor where they could sit on a stool and view people arriving through the channel.

Foster had told Peter King that they were at the airport and they had discussed the flights Sir Roger was likely to be on. Peter King had already checked the passenger lists without finding Sir Roger's name and had contacted several of the operators to check on last-minute booking-in procedures. He had been assured that, should Sir Roger arrive, then Peter King would be notified straight away.

Mary had got up early to make a light breakfast of scrambled egg on toast for Sir Roger and was in the kitchen when he appeared with a suitcase and an old brown leather holdall. He was dressed in casual clothing with a shirt and light pullover under a sports jacket and light-coloured trousers. He wore his old brown brogues – not only were they sturdy but comfortable should he be made to walk any distance by Mr Smith. His biggest problem, if that were to happen, would be in carrying the suitcase containing the cash – it weighed more than he was comfortable with.

At just after eight o'clock Mary drove Sir Roger through their gates and into Dyke Road for the trip to Shoreham, which, they estimated, would take about twenty minutes. Their departure was picked up by Peter King who was still monitoring their CCTV system through a separate screen sat at the edge of his desk. After seeing the car pass through the gates and head away, he wasn't able to determine their route, though he would soon be able to by using the ANPR and traffic-flow cameras.

Foster telephoned Sir Peter Webb and brought him up to date with the unfolding events, which gave them both hope that the matter could be successfully completed that day. Sir Peter would inform the DG, though he doubted he would appreciate being told of developments as it would make it that much harder for him to deny any knowledge of what was afoot should it become necessary at a later date. Still, Sir Peter thought, while waiting to be put through to the DG by his personal assistant: 'a problem shared is a problem halved.' He chuckled to himself.

Jackie awoke and looked at Sheen, who was still snoring gently, his bare chest moving up and down in a steady rhythm. It was warm and through the open shutter she could see a plain blue sky promising another bright day. The previous night as they went to bed they had both agreed that in the few days they had been in the house they had felt relaxed and comfortable, which, given what was happening in their lives, was quite remarkable. They had talked about leaving the house straight away after the exchange, heading northwards further into the hills and away from Cutar, towards Cordoba about one hundred miles' distance. The argument against staying was strong: what if those henchmen were there, whoever they were working for? Jackie worried that they would be in the area for days looking for them and inevitably they would find them, holed up in the house. Sheen had conceded the threat could be there and as a contingency they would have their bags packed and ready to leave. The other side was that any search would be concentrated away from the area – only an idiot would stay within the vicinity.

Peter King was still working through various indices when he decided to ring the information desk at Malaga Airport. He introduced himself as a friend of Sir Roger's and asked whether a message had been left for him as there had been a clerical mix-up and he was concerned that the wrong one had ben left. The assistant found the message that was written by the other assistant the previous evening and read it out to Peter King. He thanked her and confirmed that luckily it was the correct message that Sir Roger needed.

Peter King's research took only minutes before he found the El Cruce restaurant in an area known as Trapiche, north of Valez Malaga and at a junction where the turn-off led to a town named Benamargosa as well as other small towns. Of one of these, Vinuela, he had heard from a friend who had stayed in the area and who had described the views from their house as spectacular and wild. Peter King's hopes rose when he looked at the map on his screen and saw the large hills, areas of woodland and the scarcity of roads – exactly the type of terrain that Sheen would pick for this, he thought.

He telephoned Foster who rushed to a bookshop and bought two maps before ringing Peter King back. On examining his map, he could see exactly what Peter King was speculating. The countryside did look ideal, he thought, with some very isolated areas in which to hide. He looked at his watch – neither he nor Caldwell had suitable clothing or any equipment for that terrain.

Caldwell looked up from his map and agreed with Peter

King's assessment of the countryside and also Foster's concern regarding their equipment and clothing. Caldwell suggested that, as he was the most vulnerable to being recognised by both Sheen and Jackie Johns, he should drive into Malaga straight away to buy an assortment of clothing for them both and whatever suitable equipment he could find. Foster readily agreed – it was better for them to be lighter in numbers at the airport – where, as far as they knew, Sir Roger wasn't due to land any time soon – than be caught wanting later that day.

Caldwell was relieved to get away from the airport where he had been thinking of excuses to find time for himself and his own plans. He made two calls arranging to meet a man in Malaga in an hour's time, then headed into the city centre.

The man Caldwell arranged to meet was at the café early. He put the shopping bag on the seat next to him. He was used to testing whether he was under surveillance and was happy that he wasn't that day – all the twists, doubling-back and 'reflection in glass' tricks showed that he was not being followed.

He had half drunk his coffee when Caldwell approached the table and introduced himself.

'James Caldwell.' he said brightly, offering his hand.

'Juan Migos' came the reply as the two men shook hands.

After ordering a coffee for Caldwell and a further cup for himself, Juan indicated the shopping bag on the chair. 'I have purchased a toy helicopter for you,' he said, smiling. 'It is unbreakable and folds up to just two inches wide and five inches long with the rotor blades folded along the fuselage. The controls are small but simple: one lever to fly up and down, the other forward, left and right. Speed is controlled by how hard you push the levers. It is battery-powered and therefore silent. There is a small relay device built inside the helicopter making it a fraction heavier and slightly more difficult to control, but only a few minutes' practice and you will master it. The relay is set to match the other item I supplied to you extending the range from the controls to about 120 metres – not far, but I hope sufficient for your purposes.'

'Thank you, Juan. I think that distance should be fine. I'll practise as soon as I can. I'll be a qualified pilot in under an hour.' He smiled.

Juan smiled and bowed his head slightly to acknowledge the humour and said with a straight face. 'The other item you requested is also in the bag fully loaded and wrapped in a cloth. There are twelve spare rounds in the tub plus a spare spring for the magazine and a short screwdriver, should you wish to make any modifications.'

Caldwell smiled again. 'Thank you, Juan. You have been excellent and have proved what we had heard of your abilities.'

'At the conclusion, if you wish me to collect any unused items and dispose of them personally, then fine. Neither of them is traceable in any way to me.'

Caldwell didn't want to risk a meeting with Juan again and said that he would be happy to dispose of anything himself.

Caldwell completed his shopping and returned to the airport where Foster was just finishing talking on his mobile phone to Peter King, who had been able to discover that Sir Roger had taken a flight on a private jet that was due to land in a quarter of an hour. Peter King had arranged that the VIP arrival suite would not be available for use, which would mean Sir Roger having to use the same arrivals exit as everybody else. Caldwell told Foster what he had purchased, leaving out the items he had obtained from Juan, one of which was tucked in a small holster in the back of his trouser belt. It was an uncomfortable position but almost impossible to detect.

Sir Roger continued to look out of the window as the Gulfstream jet flew towards Malaga, over the dried plains and hills of central and southern Spain. He had remained with his seat belt buckled and declined an offer from the pilot to join him in the cockpit, preferring instead to stay with his thoughts. He thought about his life, of his childhood before the war in Switzerland, when everything had seemed so peaceful and easy. Ever since then his life had been a mad dash after success and security, made sweet by the presence of his wife and later his daughter. Everything had gone so well, so perfectly well, until that robbery. If only – he knew regrets were pointless – if only he had not kept mementos! What had been the point of keeping them anyway – this was a question he had asked himself a thousand times ever since that robbery.

He saw the port and city of Malaga below as they headed out to sea in preparation for landing. Today would be the end-game, one way or another. Josephine was going to be safe; that is all that mattered – he just didn't care about himself. He resolved to do exactly what he was told – pay the money, follow instructions and end this affair. Neither Mary nor he could take any more.

Twenty minutes later Sir Roger walked through the Arrivals and stood on the pavement getting his bearings. He didn't look around him at the people milling about waiting to greet arrivals, but seeing the escalator inside the building he re-entered the building by a different door. Caldwell had watched Sir Roger without moving from his seat and reported to Foster that Sir Roger was making his way up to the departure floor. Foster was standing, stretching his legs, fifty yards from the information desk, trying to identify Sheen or Jackie Johns among the crowd, even if they were in disguise. No persons had remained in the area for any length of time as they made their way from the check-in desks to security. He saw Sir Roger walk to the information desk and after twenty seconds was handed a sheet of paper. This he read while standing there. He spoke to the assistant, who leaned over the counter and pointed with his arm, giving Sir Roger directions.

Good, thought Foster. The first instruction to Sir Roger had been to hire himself a car and this, it seemed, he was doing.

Caldwell had retrieved his car and driven along the A7 dual carriageway before turning into a service area, knowing that Foster was following Sir Roger. Caldwell had parked away from the main parking area and chosen a parking shed that had good deep shade from the metal roof and the tall thick trees behind. He parked the car and walked to the side of the service car park from where he could look back along the motorway towards Malaga and in the direction Sir Roger and Foster would arrive from. He telephoned Foster and gave his position, and was satisfied when Foster said that he was four cars behind Sir Roger, heading Caldwell's way, and expected to be with him in a quarter of an hour.

Caldwell returned to his car and removed from his briefcase what appeared to be a bundle of twenty-pound notes. He flipped through the first notes, revealing a small detonator held by a clip at the centre. The detonator was attached at the other end by a thin wire only an inch long that was soldered on to a small circuit board and another thin piece of wire some six inches long. This aerial, of very fine wire, was capable of picking up the signal from the radio device in the helicopter. He checked that the cover on the control panel attached to this helicopter operating device was in place and clipped it closed to prevent any accidental pressing of the button. The hand-held control device was only two inches long by half an inch thick and also had a fine wire that Caldwell had wrapped around it. He placed the fake bundle of notes into his back pocket and pulled his jacket over. The control device he put in his jacket pocket. He sat in his car to wait for Foster and Sir Roger to arrive.

* * *

Sir Roger had queued to obtain his rental car; a small bright-blue Citroën, and having finished the paperwork had again read the instructions he had collected from the information desk – this time slowly and taking care to understand it.

Sir Roger, I am afraid I have to ask you to hire a car for yourself. Please then drive to the El Cruce restaurant at Trapiche to arrive between eleven and eleven thirty this evening. Please do not be early or late; it may ruin the surprise. Directions to the restaurant: Take A7 Autovia towards Almeria. Approx. 40km exit at Valez Malaga, to roundabout, 3rd exit to Alhama de Granada and Vinuela, on the 355. Approx. 6km on left at junction with the road to Benamargosa is El Cruce, advertised in large green lettering on its roof. Please ask the bar staff for your letter. Look forward to seeing you. Regards, Mr S.

Sir Roger had decided to drive to within a short distance of the restaurant where he could wait until the correct time, and after consulting the cheap tourist map that was in the car he had driven nervously on to the main road. He disliked driving on European roads, thinking that everyone had some sort of death wish, or, at the very least, a crash wish.

He concentrated so hard on the traffic ahead of him which was building up that he didn't look in his mirror; not that he would have seen Foster some one hundred yards behind him. He had left Malaga behind and then he started to relax, noting that the built-up areas were becoming fewer and the hills to his left looked larger and more attractive. To his right, he could from time to time see the blue of the Mediterranean Sea.

He kept his speed at a steady ninety kilometres an hour,

which he estimated to be at about fifty-five miles an hour, and, unlike in England where on motorways he drove in the middle lane, here he kept to the safety of the inside lane. There was a sign for a *servicio* ahead, one kilometre the sign said, and he thought about having a break as he had so much time to kill. A car appeared alongside him but didn't overtake, so instinctively Sir Roger glanced to his left and nearly swerved out of his lane as he saw Foster driving the car. Aware that Sir Roger had noticed that he was driving, Foster pulled in front of Sir Roger and indicated right. Sir Roger was fuming – he was supposed to be alone, he was going to comply with any instructions from Mr Smith, and it was already all going wrong, he thought. He followed up the slip road then through the car park and towards the far end where a single car was parked under shade; Sir Roger was unable to see anyone in the car but Foster drove straight into the shade and pointed out of his window, indicating that Sir Roger was to park between his and the other car.

Sir Roger pulled up and was aware that Foster was already out of his car and waiting to walk around the back to Sir Roger's driver's side. There was movement from the other car and Sir Roger gasped when he saw Caldwell stand up from the driver's door. Seeing the shock his appearance had caused, Caldwell smiled at Sir Roger and gave him a mock salute. Foster watched the entrance to the car park to see whether any other car had followed them in, but none had.

Foster invited Sir Roger into the service station café where Sir Roger sat against the window with Caldwell occupying the aisle seat and Foster across the table from him. Each had a drink in front of them. There were few people in the café and those that were sitting deep inside away from the bright heat that poured through the windows.

Sir Roger hadn't spoken a word so angry was he. He wondered how on earth Caldwell and Foster had known his travel arrangements, even to the point that Caldwell was already at the *servicio*. His mind was so confused for a few fleeting seconds that he wondered whether they were in fact in league with Mr Smith, or worse still, acting independently of everyone!

Foster leaned forward to Sir Roger. 'You just cannot be trusted, can you? We didn't think so, which is why we are here.'

Sir Roger couldn't reply, his mind was turning over the possibilities of how they had come to be here, how they knew everything.

Foster continued: 'You were told quite explicitly that all and any communication from Mr Smith was to be reported, and yet we find out that you have done no such thing. You seem to forget that your daughter's freedom is at stake here – maybe her life.'

Sir Roger shot back. 'You don't' – he raised his arm towards Foster, only for it to be suddenly forced down to the table by Caldwell – 'threaten Josephine.'

'Shut up!' hissed Caldwell in Sir Roger's ear. 'Shut up and listen.' His voice was threatening.

Foster looked coldly at Sir Roger. 'On one side is the liberty and life of Josephine; on the other there is the reputation of whole organisations, even governments – which do you think is more important in the bigger scheme of things? You got your position and wealth thanks to government contracts and, well, let's call it an investment from Señor Mayer and his predecessors, so you have to continue to play the game. So shut up and bloody well listen.'

Sir Roger stared, a feeling of pure hatred towards Foster flooding through his body.

Caldwell leant towards Sir Roger. 'Señor Mayer has left Josephine's wellbeing up to me. The photographs I showed you and Mary were faked.' He watched Sir Roger's reaction and quickly Sir Roger's already florid complexion turn redder as he turned towards Caldwell.

'Faked?' he asked, his voice barely audible even a foot away from Caldwell.

Caldwell smiled. '*Faked*, as in tricked into smiling; *faked* as in being drugged so her make-up could be applied; *faked* as in her hands being free but her ankles were tied together; *faked* in that she had been carried into the room from the cellar where she lives, manacled to a wall, pissing in her trousers. *Faked*, Sir Roger, and neither you nor anyone else will stop her suffering unless you do exactly what you are told to do by us. No more chances, believe me, Sir Roger. We could do a deal with Sheen without you. Your presence is not the most important thing here, and he will deal with us as long as he gets the money. Now listen to what Andy's going to tell you.'

Sir Roger stared at Caldwell then moved his stare to Foster. 'You are the lowest of the low. What do you want?'

Foster finished his drink with an exaggerated slowness and stood. Caldwell followed suit but Sir Roger left his drink; he thought he might be sick if he drank it.

The three men walked back to their cars that were now in deeper shade as the sun had moved further behind the large trees. Foster opened his car boot and leant in. He opened his briefcase taking out a small microphone with a wire that led to a pack.

'Undo you shirt,' he told Sir Roger.

'Before that, let me have your car keys,' said Caldwell.

Sir Roger got his car keys and threw them at Caldwell, who caught them one-handed and headed for the boot of Sir Roger's car.

Foster attached the microphone with a small clip underneath Sir Roger's shirt then trailed the wire around his middle and affixed the pack to the back of Sir Roger's trousers.

'This is an open microphone; it cannot be turned on or off. It will enable us to hear your every movement and word. You will leave it attached where it is and you will talk to us when you receive instructions or when you see either Sheen or the girl. Understood?'

Sir Roger was beginning to button up his shirt and mumbled, 'Yes,' as Foster reached into his briefcase and turned on a small device that looked like a mobile phone.

'Walk over there a bit and keep talking,' instructed Foster. Caldwell opened the suitcase and switched on the tracker control device, which beeped straight away. 'Good,' he said to himself; it meant that the tracker originally obtained by Carter was still in the money and working.

Caldwell slipped his hand under the top layer of bundles of notes that were all stacked together and extracted one bundle. Chancing another quick glance to ensure that Sir Roger's and Foster's attention wasn't directed towards him, he reached into his back pocket and retrieved the bundle of notes that he had been checking earlier. He put that bundle in the space he had created in the suitcase while the bundle of notes he had removed from the suitcase he put into his back pocket. He closed the lid of the suitcase and slammed the boot lid closed.

Andy turned to him and Caldwell gave the thumbs-up sign that all was in order.

Sheen and Jackie had eaten a lazy breakfast in the courtyard, enjoying the quiet and seclusion. Now Sheen sat alone on the patio looking over the valley to where later that night the turning point of his life was to be reached. He had an apprehension that, because the stakes were so high, something would go wrong, but at the same time he was confident that his plan would work – it was so easy and straightforward.

Jackie came out carrying a box. This she opened and took out the two small radios from their polystyrene protection, together with two polythene bags each containing an earpiece, and an elasticated strap and holder in which the radio could be carried. Sheen watched her put the two pieces of kit together, then helped her select a channel to make them compatible. He put his earpiece in and walked to the other side of the patio where he could hear Jackie talking quietly. He smiled, expecting her to end with a 'testing one, two, three', but instead she said 'I love you,' to which he replied the same.

They had to finish their packing and once again check all their equipment before trying to get some sleep so that they would be alert and fresh by the time early evening came. They needed to think of nothing but what they were about to do.

Josephine's mind had been drifting into a downward spiral of despair. She had decided she was going to die, but she wanted it to be quick, not a slow and lingering painful one such as she was experiencing.

She had tried to scream in the hope that a higher-pitched noise would carry further than a normal shout, but her mouth and vocal chords were too dry to make even a squeak. She was cold and the lack of food was having an effect on her. 'Bugger this!' she said aloud, though anyone over ten feet away from her would have been unable to hear her. 'I'm not going to die, you bastards.' She reached for her jeans, determined that as they were at least only damp now she would put them on for warmth. She made the effort to place the jeans at her feet and was starting to pull them up her legs when she looked at the zip, and stopped. She looked at the screws in the wall that held the bracket to which the manacled handcuff was attached. Something suddenly sparked in her and she moved with more speed than she would have thought possible, removing the jeans and bringing them up towards her. They smelt but she disregarded that.

She looked at the zip again. The zip toggle was made of metal. She held the jeans next to the bracket and put the toggle into the head of a screw. It fitted. She adjusted her position so her left hand could hold the jeans, allowing her right hand to work the toggle. She used her forefinger and thumb, squeezed hard and at the same time tried to move them anticlockwise. The toggle slipped out of the screw head, but it had moved, she thought. She repeated the process with the same result, and again, and again, until after many attempts she knew that the screw had moved, almost half a turn. Her fingers ached, then they hurt, then they became very painful. She tried to use her thumb and second finger, which wasn't so good but still there was some movement. 'Yes,' she said through gritted teeth.

Foster telephoned Sir Peter Webb and told him of the day's events to which Sir Peter had responded with a 'Well done!' It was clear that Sir Peter was unhappy with Sir Roger flouting their instructions and was glad that the situation had been recovered by a combination of good work by Peter King and Andy. Sir Peter asked that Andy keep him informed of any developments, then he would look forward to a full debrief in his office tomorrow afternoon.

Sir Roger had sat in the restaurant for two hours over three cups of coffee idly watching people enter and leave, listening to the Spanish words being spoken loudly and with gusto. He heard the laughing from a group of older men sitting in the corner and all the while he had kept an eye on his car parked outside. He was aware of the microphone hidden beneath his shirt, knowing that Foster and Caldwell could hear every breath he took. He was especially aware when he went to the toilet and the urinal flushed. He had smiled wryly at that – serves them right, he thought.

He was about two miles north of the El Cruce restaurant and checked his watch for the umpteenth time – nearly half past ten.

* * *

391

Wendy Baxter and Michael had finished their dinner and cleared away, leaving only a plastic plate with a piece of cold chicken and cold vegetables sitting on the kitchen table. A tray was near by on which there was a setting of plastic fork, plastic knife and a plastic spoon next to a small bottle of mineral water. Wendy Baxter watched as Michael donned his white suit, his gloves and facemask, then added the plate of food to the tray.

Michael took the tray. 'You are too soft, Wendy. Another day wouldn't hurt.'

'I know, just all heart,' she laughed and pointing to the bucket she added. 'Don't forget that.'

Michael walked towards the door to the cellar then stopped to allow Wendy to move forward to open the door for him and at that moment the bucket banged into Wendy's leg and rebounded into the wall.

Josephine's spirits were higher than they had been for days as the first screw had started to turn easier and was now half an inch out of the mounting. She heard the bucket clatter. Her heart jumped as she stared at the screw but at the same time she could hear from behind her the bolt being slid back. She looked towards the door then back at the screw, it looked so obvious sitting half an inch above the rest of the screws, above the mounting.

She threw her jeans to the bottom of the bed and at the same time twisted her body to face the person who was now coming down the steps and into view. She had no time to check that her body hid the screw – she could only hope.

Through the mask Michael could smell Josephine's urine and seeing the jeans at the foot of the bed knew what had happened. He smirked. He walked up to her keeping his head lowered, taking no chances of her seeing his face as he put the bucket down. He laid the tray at the top of the bed where a pillow would have been if she had had one. He took one step backwards. Josephine stared at him, not moving a muscle. He looked up a little. Josephine just stared. Behind the mask Michael saw Josephine staring, which he didn't expect. Why didn't she say 'Thank you' if she was broken or swear at him if she still had fight in her? Just staring – why?

Josephine's natural instincts took over. 'Thank you,' she said. Michael was satisfied, turned and walked away.

A minute later Josephine was alone again, sipping the water and swirling it around her mouth. She tried to drink slowly – she knew that would be the best. The vegetables were easier to eat than the chicken, but she chewed slowly, adding some water to help, and finished the meal within a few minutes. A minute after that she picked up her jeans again and returned to the half-released screw.

Sheen and Jackie had a passionate kiss before Sheen hauled the rucksack on to his back and fitted the goggles on to his head. Jackie was standing next to him as he mounted his bike and managed to give him a quick kiss on his cheek as he started to ride up the drive.

It was dark and he was swallowed by the darkness before he had ridden ten seconds from her, but Jackie remained listening for him as he crossed the loose gravel at the top of the drive where it met the tarred road. She heard it, then quickly turned and ran back into the house, closing the front door and running through the house to the patio. She managed to reach the rail and give a wave as Sheen rode past, though she couldn't see him or see the wave he returned to her. She put her harness on, adjusted the radio volume switch, and inserted the earpiece. She sat in her chair and, using the night-sights, watched the small road until she was able to fleetingly see Sheen as he sped downhill. His progress could have been followed also by the sound of dogs barking, which worried her. She sat and waited for him to appear on the dust track the other side of the valley.

Sheen had made good speed without using much energy

going downhill and, though the occasional dog appeared in front of him barking, he found by steering straight at them they jumped out of his way. He reached the dirt track and knew that he would be in Jackie's view, just as his earpiece crackled. 'See you,' she said.

Sheen grinned. She had been ready and waiting – that was good as he could end up relying on her to spot any persons trailing Sir Roger. Sheen pressed his radio switch twice in acknowledgement of her message and continued riding at a steady pace, noting that many of the houses on the hillside opposite were in darkness – which was good for him.

Sheen approached the olive tree with the dark canister, gently slowed to a stop and got off his cycle. He undid his rucksack and carefully opened it, then laying out the pieces of equipment he needed on the towel. These he individually checked and laid in place so that he knew exactly where each item was. The knife was on the right side; the catapult and twelve ball bearings on the left. In the centre was the small electronic metal detector wand that he hoped would tell him if the money had been doctored to include a tracking device. Also laid out in line were a twenty-metre length of wire, a torch that had either a red or white light beam, a box of matches and three fireworks. He checked that the towel would roll up quickly and that none of the items would fall out. He hoped that he wouldn't need most of the items but he had planned for the worst, and the worst would be that the two men were with Sir Roger.

It was about half a mile to the village from where he was, and as he pushed the knife into the side of his belt he started jogging gently. The night was just right for him, he thought, dark and inky, the moon hidden but enough stars to allow the night-vision equipment to work well.

He reached the edge of the village and looked at his watch – five minutes before eleven o'clock. He removed the goggles in case he met someone, then ran silently through the village on the lower road, noting a parked car that restricted the width of the road in one place. The whole village appeared to be sleeping. The one bar in the village was quiet and the lights were off.

At the end of the road, as he approached the car park, he slowed to a walk and peered forward into the brightly lit parking area. It was quiet with nobody moving. He reached the doorway that he had used before to gain the maximum view of the parking area and knew that, provided he kept still, he couldn't be seen.

Sheen had considered asking Jackie to cover the El Cruce restaurant so as to ensure that Sir Roger was alone but he'd decided it wasn't a risk worth taking. He saw the Quad bike in place and walked to it. The key was in the front basket. He put the key in the ignition and turned it one stop. The fuel indicator jumped towards the halfway mark; he turned the ignition off but left the key in it. He looked quickly about the area. It was silent except for the sound of crickets chirping and some far-off dog howling like a wolf. He removed the bungee ropes from the back basket and placed the basket and bungee ropes on the ground. He returned to his doorway, leaned slightly against the door, fitted the goggles to the top of his head above his eyes and tried to relax.

Sir Roger had been briefed by Foster and threatened by Caldwell, both of whom he despised but was in fear of. He drove into the car parking area of the El Cruce restaurant. There were three other cars parked out the front of the restaurant and only one outside table was occupied, though voices could be heard from inside. He was tempted to look around. He knew both Foster and Caldwell were near by; he had been told that he would always be in their sight.

Sir Roger walked into the restaurant aware of faces turning to see who the new customer was at this time of night. He went to the bar where a barmaid greeted him – '*Hola!*'

'Er, *hola!*' Sir Roger replied. He pointed to himself and gave his name: 'Roger Knight'. He looked at the barmaid who smiled and reached under the counter, lifting a small package on to the marbled top. She pointed at the name on the package, which he saw was his and he pointed to himself. The barmaid handed him the package which he held as he thanked her and returned to his car.

He sat in the driver's seat and as instructed talked, trying not to move his lips.

'I have a package addressed to me. I am opening it now,' he said as he ripped the paper. There is a note, it says: "Drive along this road to the village of Benamargosa about ten kilometres, then in the centre of the village turn left to Cutar. After seven kilometres turn right into the village and park in the parking area, opposite the recycling bins." That's it. I'm now waiting for five minutes before I leave.'

Sir Roger sat there aware that the occupants of the table were looking at him so he unfolded the map and looked at that. In fact, he saw that the two places were both shown on the map and appeared to be further towards the hills he had seen earlier.

After three of the five minutes he saw Foster drive on the main road in the direction that he would take. No other vehicles were using the road and he didn't see anyone walking either.

He checked his watch for the fourth time and on the second that the five minutes were reached he started his car engine and moved towards Benamargosa.

He constantly checked his rear mirror but didn't see any sign of a car following him; no headlights showed at all, either in front or behind. There weren't even cars travelling towards him. Now and again, he gave his location but otherwise he concentrated on his driving.

He entered the village of Benamargosa and as he reached the centre where the now-closed bars were, the road swung to the left before bending back to the right. As he took the next left bend, he caught sight of the sign to Cutar and took the turning, saying so out loud. He drove over a bridge that spanned a dried riverbed then followed the winding road generally uphill. Again, he checked his mirror but didn't see any car following him and ahead he couldn't see any car lights. Caldwell, who had obviously improved his surveillance techniques, since Hove was impressing him. He reflected just for a few seconds and wondered if Carter was the weak link that day.

As the note had said, after seven kilometres there was a sign to the right to the village of Cutar. He drove slowly down the tree-lined road, past the tiled Cutar town sign and saw the parking area. His headlights illuminated the row of recycling bins, which he parked opposite and switched off the engine. He spoke into the microphone.

Sheen had seen only one car during the time he had been in the doorway; it had driven by on the main road travelling uphill at a steady speed and he didn't pay it further attention. He watched Sir Roger sitting in the driver's seat. His vision was excellent and he could clearly see his lips moving – so he was being shadowed again! Sheen was considering the options open to him when he heard a faint scratch of a piece of stone or gravel being stood on; it came from his right and was near by. He looked at the small road that led from the main road Sir Roger had used and saw a slow-moving car pulling into the side of the main road, about one hundred yards from him. The car had no lights on. He wanted to swear out loud, but he held his breath, waiting for whatever or whoever had made the gravel crunch to show itself. He saw Sir Roger open his car door and begin to stand.

Sheen placed the goggles over his eyes and waited for them to adjust. He had to keep them away from direct lighting or he would be blinded by the light, even if only temporarily.

Again he looked at the main road. The driver, a single person, had got out of the car. He was bent over and moving slowly towards the small road that led to the parking area. Once in the road, he would be able to use the trees as cover and Sheen wouldn't be able to see him. He knew it was a trap – there was someone in the road next to him watching the area and another one coming from the main road, and for all he knew there could be another person in the back seat of Sir Roger's car, or further back in the village along the lower road, waiting for him.

He had to do something and quickly.

He saw Sir Roger go to the boot lid and unlock it without fully opening it. Sir Roger's lips moved again but he couldn't hear what he was saying. He was obviously talking into an open microphone, which meant that his backup was very well prepared this time. He mentally cursed that he hadn't thought through the plan better; he had allowed himself to believe that Sir Roger would be alone, that he wouldn't play any tricks, and now he was confronted with the real possibility that he would be caught, or worse. He looked again at the man stealthily moving from one tree to another, now seventy yards away. He had something in his right hand. Sheen knew it was a gun and he knew it was the man from Hove.

Sheen very slowly moved his head towards the edge of the doorway and looked in both directions – all clear. He moved half a step forward, balancing on the side of his shoes to minimise the amount of contact between his shoe and the ground. He slowly allowed his weight to move on to that foot and leaned forward to the edge of the building. He held his breath as his eye gradually took in more of the scene. He could see a man kneeling behind a bush, using it as cover from the parking area, ensuring that he couldn't be seen from that direction. The man's attention was directed to the parking area where Sir Roger was lifting the lid of the car boot, extending it fully.

Sheen suddenly darted towards the kneeling man, knowing that once he had broken cover the man with the gun would see him. The kneeling man didn't have time to move except to half turn towards the sudden noise from his left. He felt a violent blow to the side of his neck as Sheen's foot connected. Without breaking his pace, Sheen turned and shouted at Sir Roger: 'Grab the money.'

Sheen reached the Quad bike and turned the key. The engine broke the still night air, and even the crickets stopped their chirping. Before they started again, after recovering from the sudden engine noise, there was the distinct sound of metal being struck by metal. Sheen knew what it was and grabbed Sir Roger who was in the process of lifting the suitcase from the boot. He pushed Sir Roger on to the back of the Quad bike and forced him to sit, facing backwards. Sheen rammed the suitcase between Sir Roger and the front seat and then jumped into the front seat, twisted the grip and slammed his right foot on to the pedal. The roar of the engine was instant as the machine jumped forward. Sheen didn't look backwards or worry about what was happening around him – he focused entirely on where he was heading.

Sheen drove down the lower road of the village, the noise of the Quad reverberating from the walls of the houses. He didn't use the headlights as his green view through the night-vision goggles was sharp from the ambient light reflecting from the walls of houses. The lack of headlights meant any person on the street in front of him wouldn't see him approaching but they would hear the noise; he would have to take his chances if that situation arose. Sheen kept the speed going, only slowing to negotiate parked cars before accelerating towards the end of the village.

He was sure that the noise of the Quad bike must have woken the entire village, as the sound intensified every time the houses closed upon him. Dogs barked madly as he approached the edge of the village and bumped on to the dirt track. Sheen slowed the Quad as the valley started to appear on his right side, the drop becoming deeper and darker. The goggles enabled him to see clearly and after he rounded the first bend he chanced to turn his head to look behind. He had to hold the look for a couple of seconds for the goggles to fully focus – there was nothing behind him except the lights and outline of buildings of the village. The suitcase was pushing against his back so he was forced to lean forward as he kept his concentration on the track ahead. He knew the bends as he approached each of them but he still reduced his speed on the track, which he knew it would be all too easy to skid on. He realised as he finished another bend that he would be within Jackie's sight temporarily, until he went into the side valley, before reappearing in less than a minute.

Caldwell had seen his shot hit Sir Roger's car no more than six inches from Sheen as he grabbed the suitcase and Sir Roger. He had fired a further two shots as Sheen had started moving the Quad bike, not caring if he hit Sir Roger or not. Those shots had also been close – one went slightly high, the other to one side by inches. Had the weapon been of his choice, calibrated and practised with, he knew all three shots would have hit their target.

Foster got to his feet and could hear the roaring in his head, a combination of Sheen on the Quad bike and the kick he had received in his neck. Caldwell ran up to him, and without either saying a word they sprinted after Sheen and Sir Roger. Caldwell's earpiece was bringing only the sound of the Quad engine, but he ignored it and concentrated on running after the noise. He sprinted hard, using his arms to pump extra strength and speed into his body, having confidence in his fitness to run at that speed for several minutes before he would be forced into a long-distance style of running. He was capable of running a marathon every day and, if necessary, he would settle for the long chase. He would not be giving up. Lights went on and windows opened as Foster and Caldwell pursued the engine noise running at a sprint. Voices were raised behind them, but neither man hesitated.

Sheen looked ahead and saw the canister hanging in the tree – his rucksack, towel and cycle just as he had left them. He pulled to a stop and turned the Quad back to face the way he had travelled, and switched off the engine. The silence was deafening, his ears still ringing with the noise from the Quad engine.

His earpiece crackled: 'See you!' said an excited Jackie

Sheen gave a wave in her direction then walked to the rucksack, opened it and pulled out the grey box file. From the towel he grabbed a small hand torch. He strode quickly to the front of the Quad bike and as Sir Roger dismounted from his perch on the back Sheen said, 'Come here.' He shone a small torch to the ground, illuminating the box but keeping his eyes diverted from the sudden light.

Sir Roger was still shaking from the exertion of holding on as Sheen had driven through the roads and along the track and had been at the point of exhaustion when Sheen had stopped. He was unsteady on his feet as he made his way to join Sheen.

'Examine it, Sir Roger. Everything is there.'

Sir Roger took the torch and pointed it at the box, almost scared of opening it and examining the contents.

Sheen rushed to the Quad and grabbed the suitcase, carrying it a few feet before opening the lid and turning the suitcase over. Bundles of cash fell on to the dirt. Sheen put the suitcase on to the back of the Quad and quickly picked up the small metal detecting wand from the towel. He placed the rucksack next to him, bent down and picked up a bundle of notes. He waved the wand over the bundle and a small metallic bleep sounded. He threw the bundle into the rucksack – this was the noise he expected and wanted to hear, given when only the metal strip in the banknotes was found. He repeated the process at a steady pace, discarding two bundles that he put to one side.

'Two men running towards you from the village,' screamed Jackie into Sheen's earpiece.

As Sheen looked up he could just see the two shapes as they headed towards the side valley.

'Are there any copies?' asked Sir Roger.

Not hearing properly and with his attention on the two figures, Sheen said: 'What?'

'Are there any copies?' asked Sir Roger again

'No, no copies. I keep my word, Sir Roger. Not like you, you old bastard,' retorted Sheen, his anger evident in his voice.

He picked up the two bundles of notes he had rejected and threw them back into the suitcase, putting it on the back of the Quad.

'Get on now,' he ordered.

He grabbed the grey box file from Sir Roger and threw it into the suitcase, closed the lid and secured it with a bungee rope from the front basket.

He stood next to the Quad and turned the ignition key. He grabbed Sir Roger and pushed him into the driver's seat and shouted instructions for him to drive. He switched on the twin headlights illuminating the road, quickly turning his head away from the light to avoid losing his night vision through the goggles.

Sir Roger slowly moved off as Sheen rushed to wrap up the towel and stuff it on top of the notes in his rucksack. He heaved the rucksack on to his back and adjusted the straps, mounted his cycle, just as he heard Jackie in his ear: 'They're still running. One is some way ahead now, approaching the end of the valley; he'll see you in a minute.'

Sheen jumped on to his cycle and heard Jackie's panicky voice. 'He's at the bend. The Quad's stopping; he's going to get on the Quad. Come on, Steve.'

Caldwell had heard Sir Roger's question and Sheen's answer

but he wanted to finish everything cleanly. He stood next to the Quad bike and managed to make out that Sheen was no more than a hundred yards away across the valley. He reached into his jacket, pulled out the model helicopter, unfurled the rotary blades and placed it on the ground. He brought out the control panel and switched on the power. He used the levers and saw the helicopter take to the air where, although he lost clear sight of it, he knew its approximate direction and position. He used the levers to take the helicopter towards where he thought Sheen was, then pulled out the other small control device. He flipped the cover up and smiled as he pushed the button.

The explosion rocked the ground, shards of slate from the vineyard erupted into the dark night sky, the flash of flame briefly illuminating the dust and the chaos that immediately followed.

From her position Jackie had been watching through her night-sight binoculars. She had watched as the Quad bike had sped along the track, had seen the dust thrown by its speed. She had held her breath when the Quad stopped and could make out the figure of Sir Roger and a hand-held torch shining through the settling dust. She had seen Sheen moving quickly at the back of the Quad. He was in darkness but she made out his movements and knew what he was doing.

She had swung the sights back along the track and had seen the man running. She had felt her hands tremble as she watched. She had swung back to Sir Roger and Sheen and had seen Sir Roger being helped into the driver's seat. Sir Roger had moved off, travelling towards the running man. Sheen had moved towards the cycle in the opposite direction. She had swung back to the man, still running. Back to Sir Roger, still driving towards the running man. Then she had tried to find Sheen.

She had warned Sheen. The man had met Sir Roger and she knew that the speed of the Quad would be greater than even Sheen on the cycle up the hill. She had watched Sheen, seeing the effort he was putting into his legs to inch the cycle further away from the man. She had willed him forward.

Then she saw the flash at the edge of her sight vision, the green turning brilliant white and the whole picture before her becoming as snow. Then came an explosion so abrupt and fierce that her heart jumped. The noise stopped all sound of the animal nightlife as the explosive noise reverberated around the hills and deep into the valleys for more than ten seconds, the rumble rising and lowering as it reached into then out of the valleys. There was absolute silence until a dog barked and the crickets nervously resumed their chirping.

No lights appeared in houses and there were no raised voices of alarm.

Jackie was shaking when Sheen got back to the house; she had been unable to find him on the track after the explosion. She had underestimated the speed at which he cycled and had trained her binoculars on areas through which he had already passed. When she heard the cycle skid to a halt on the driveway she had hurried to him, scared in case it somehow wasn't him. She had reached him before he could dismount fully and held him as she sobbed with relief and the release of her pent-up fear. He had been patient, holding her and talking gently in her ear, reassuring her that all was well and that he was unhurt, and when eventually she had seen his grin she knew it for herself.

They had a beer each as they sat at the edge of the patio looking over the black hills illuminated from time to time by headlights and torches in the area where Sir Roger and Caldwell had been standing.

Sheen told Jackie what had happened and how, fearing there were two tracking devices among the cash, he had put them back into Sir Roger's suitcase.

They decided to unpack their clothes and stay in the house for the remainder of the week.

34

Foster was sitting in the armchair in Sir Peter's office.

'So, when I heard the explosion, I ran as quickly as I could. There was a real mess. Caldwell and Sir Roger were on the track. There were limbs missing and blood was everywhere; without knowing what they were wearing, I couldn't have said who was who. There was no sign of the Quad bike; it had been blown into the valley below, I assume. There wasn't any sign of the grey box with Sir Roger's secrets – a few burnt scraps of paper, nothing else. I phoned the number in Malaga and an hour later our friends arrived and between us we cleaned the mess up as best we could. Caldwell, his remains anyway, are by now at the bottom of the Mediterranean Sea. The local police will investigate the stolen Quad bike and one day find it in the valley; vandals will get the blame, I'm sure. Sir Roger will be on his way home by now, being flown through the usual repatriation route – again, thanks to our friends. Heart attack we've put the cause down to. At his age it seemed more, well, appropriate somehow. Mary has been informed.'

'Sheen and Johns?' said Sir Peter

'No idea,' said Foster. 'Probably enjoying their money, but they will spend the rest of their lives looking over their shoulders, that's for sure.'

'Oh well, that just leaves Josephine, doesn't it?' said Sir Peter.

'Will you make the call, Sir Peter?'

Sir Peter picked up his desk telephone and, referring to a piece of paper, dialled a number.

'Señor Mayer, good morning. Please excuse me for not identifying myself. The issue regarding Sir Roger, all has been resolved, though unfortunately afterwards Sir Roger suffered a fatal heart attack. I'm afraid you friend James has gone missing. Can't say where exactly but the secret is safe. Can we expect Josephine home today, please?'

Foster listened to Sir Peter. It was almost as if he were chatting to an old friend about some past acquaintances who had suffered a slightly distressing time.

'Thank you, Señor Mayer. I'll get someone to meet her there then, goodbye.' He replaced the receiver. 'There, she'll be home this evening. Arrange for someone to meet her please, Andy – West Beach near Bridport in Dorset, six o'clock. Don't take any notice of her friends who drop her off. I'll pop down and see Mary, give her my condolences etcetera and remind her that the whole matter is just best forgotten. What with Josephine being safe I'm sure she'll understand and we can all carry on with what we were doing.'

Josephine's fingers and her thumb were numb from the pain and exertion of trying to remove the screws, to the point where she felt like stopping. She was driven on by looking at the two screws now lying on the bed and knowing that another was just about to be pulled out. She was already planning on what she would do after removing the last screw. She would wait at the bottom of the stairs with the manacled hand held behind her, ready to be swung around at the person's head. At the same time she would lunge forward, holding two of the screws in her right hand aiming for their neck. She had it all planned, the speed and the aggression she would deploy towards whoever it was in the white suit, and then straight up the stairs and attack whoever else was there.

The bolt was slid back. Josephine froze, looked at the plate. One screw left. The plate was loose. She pulled and the plate moved, a little but not enough. She looked at the stairs. The person descending was wearing ordinary clothes. It was a woman and as she reached the bottom step she looked at Josephine and smiled.

'Josephine, your time is up. Ready to go home?'

Before Josephine could reply the woman laughed and pointed towards the wall behind Josephine. 'Well done! A good attempt but there isn't a need – you are going home.'

Josephine wasn't sure whether to laugh or cry at the news. The tension poured out of her and she started to sob, holding her hands to her face.

Wendy Baxter pulled a small gun from her pocket and from a distance of six feet she took aim just as Josephine looked up and saw her. The gun gave a soft 'phut' sound as the dart was released and hit Josephine in the thigh. Josephine felt the sharp prick and looked at the dart as she quickly tried to grab it, but the effect of the drug was too quick for her.

Michael joined Wendy Baxter in lifting Josephine into their car and after a final check through the house to ensure their fingerprints wouldn't be found and everywhere was clean and tidy, they drove towards Bridport.

The following week was a quiet time – Jackie and Sheen hardly ventured from the house at all, except to buy provisions and further cheap clothing from the local supermarket. They didn't see anything out of the ordinary, nor when they were in the town did they see any strangers. Jackie had made a daily check of the newspapers and searched the Internet for news of that evening but found only an obituary for Sir Roger Knight who had died of a heart attack, though no mention was made of where he suffered the attack. Time passed quickly as they made plans for their future together and all too soon Sheen was loading their car in preparation for their departure.

Ruth walked down the driveway towards him and Jackie. Shielding the sun from her eyes, she said, 'All ready to leave?'

'Yes, thank you. A lovely place that we will always remember,' said Sheen.

'Did you finish your book?' Ruth enquired.

'Yes, thank you,' replied Sheen.

'Fiction or non-fiction?' Ruth asked.

Sheen looked at Jackie and smiled.